Sam moved briskly acr
to her knees in front
to towel-dry the long length of his legs, taking
care to gentle her movements on his injured leg,
avoiding the several healing scars running the
length of it.

'Liar,' he drawled.

Sam looked up at him sharply. 'I think you have
an overinflated opinion of your sexual prowess,
Mr Sterne.'

'Not recently, I don't,' he admitted.

The perfect opening… 'I should have mentioned
this to you before.' Sam kept her head bent as
she concentrated on drying his feet. 'I don't
think… I would prefer it if, for the duration of
our stay here, you didn't…' She began again. 'I
realise this is an imposition, but I'd prefer it if
you refrained from bringing any women to your
apartment while I'm here,' she muttered.

He arched one blond and arrogant brow. 'Are you
going to make it worth my while?'

Sam blinked. 'Sorry?'

He placed his hands on the bed behind him
and leant back, emphasising the muscles
of his shoulders and arms as he looked up at
her challengingly. 'What are you offering in
exchange?' he asked, and a smug grin spread
across his face.

THE TWIN TYCOONS

*Twin billionaire brothers—one dark and brooding,
one blond and charming—which would you choose?*

Billionaire brothers Darius and Xander Sterne have it all—
power, wealth, and the world at their beck and call. Never
challenged, always triumphant—*nothing* is unattainable
when you own the world, and they've enjoyed
every indulgence their affluent status affords.

Until now.

Because these twin tycoons are about to learn that there are
some things money and power can't buy… And that the
greatest challenges net the most satisfying rewards.

Find out what happens in:

THE REDEMPTION OF DARIUS STERNE
February 2015

THE TAMING OF XANDER STERNE
March 2015

THE TAMING OF
XANDER STERNE

BY
CAROLE MORTIMER

Published in Great Britain 2015
by Mills & Boon, an imprint of Harlequin (UK) Limited,
Eton House, 18-24 Paradise Road, Richmond, Surrey, TW9 1SR

© 2015 Carole Mortimer

ISBN: 978-0-263-25052-7

Harlequin (UK) Limited's policy is to use papers that are natural,
renewable and recyclable products and made from wood grown in
sustainable forests. The logging and manufacturing processes conform
to the legal environmental regulations of the country of origin.

Printed and bound in Spain
by CPI, Barcelona

Carole Mortimer was born and lives in the UK. She is married to Peter and they have six sons. She has written almost two hundred books since she started writing for Mills & Boon in 1978. She writes for the Mills & Boon® Modern™ and Historical romance lines. Carole is a *USA TODAY* Bestselling Author, and in 2012 was recognised by Queen Elizabeth II for her 'outstanding contribution to literature'.

Books by Carole Mortimer

The Twin Tycoons

The Redemption of Darius Sterne

The Devilish D'Angelos

A D'Angelo Like No Other
A Prize Beyond Jewels
A Bargain with the Enemy

Buenos Aires Nights

Rumours on the Red Carpet
A Taste of the Forbidden

The Lyonedes Legacy

His Reputation Precedes Him
Defying Drakon

The Scandalous St Claires

Taming the Last St Claire
The Reluctant Duke
Jordan St Claire: Dark and Dangerous

A Touch of Notoriety
The Talk of Hollywood
Surrender to the Past

**Visit the author profile page at
www.millsandboon.co.uk for more titles**

Our son Peter.
We are so proud of you!

CHAPTER ONE

'I APPRECIATE THAT you leave for your honeymoon at the end of the week, Darius, but I seriously do not need you to arrange for a live-in babysitter for me for the two weeks you're away!' Xander scowled at his twin brother across the sitting room of his London penthouse apartment.

'It's not a babysitter, just someone to help you with things you can't do yet, like getting in and out of the shower, drying off and dressing, driving.'

'We have a company driver who can do that.'

'But there's no one to help you with the rest of those things,' his brother reasoned. 'Or to cook for you.'

'For goodness' sake, Darius, it's been six weeks since I broke my leg.'

'In three places, requiring two operations to fix. You can't even stand for longer than ten minutes at a time yet.' Darius was obviously refusing to back down on this.

Xander eyed him moodily, knowing that everything his brother said was true. 'This isn't really about what I can or can't do, is it?' He finally sighed resignedly.

Darius stilled. 'What do you mean?'

'What I *mean* is that I don't have a death wish. Yes, I drove my car when I shouldn't have, and yes, I ended up crashing into a lamppost and wrecking my car, but thankfully no one else was injured. But I didn't do it deliberately, Darius. I told you at the time I was just so angry I couldn't see straight. I was *angry*, Darius,' he repeated harshly.

'Everyone gets angry, Xander,' Darius said softly.

'My anger had been building for months.'

'I know.'

Xander blinked. 'You do?'

His twin nodded. 'You were working and playing way too hard. It was as if you were trying to avoid something or someone.'

'Lot of good that did me.' If Xander had been capable of pacing the room at that moment, then he would have.

Six weeks ago, for the first time in his life, Xander had realised that he had a temper. Not the slow-burning temper of his brother, but a fiery hot volcano that had exploded out of control, resulting in Xander wanting to beat another man to within an inch of his life.

Admittedly that man had been loudly verbally abusing the woman who had arrived with him that night at the exclusive London nightclub owned by the Sterne brothers. It was a situation reminiscent of Xander's childhood memories of the way in which his father had treated his mother.

But the desire to hit someone had shaken Xander to his core, to the point that he no longer trusted himself or his responses to situations; he had never wanted to hit anyone in his life before that night. Not even the father who had beaten him when he was a child.

Lomax Sterne had been dead for over twenty years now, after a fall down the stairs of the family's London home whilst in a drunken stupor. A death that neither his wife nor his twin sons had mourned.

Lomax Sterne had been a brute of a man and a bully, with a temper to match.

And six weeks ago Xander had terrified the life out of himself by discovering that, at the age of thirty-three, he had the same temper.

'What made you so tense in the first place, do you think?' Darius looked at him curiously.

Xander grimaced. 'I don't know. Yes, I do.' His brow cleared. 'Do you remember when we were in Toronto four months ago? Remember the chairman of Bank's Corporation? We went out to dinner with him and his wife.'

'And he talked down to her all evening,' Darius realised ruefully. 'Which was the reason we both decided we didn't want to do business with him. And the reason for your pent-up anger these past few months, I'm guessing?'

'I think it is, yes,' Xander agreed.

'You controlled it then, Xander, and you controlled it six weeks ago,' Darius insisted impatiently. 'Just let it go. It's over.'

Xander wished he could dismiss it as easily.

'I really do appreciate your moving in here the past four weeks, Darius, but I just don't think I'm up to having someone else, a stranger, living with me right now.' In truth, Xander had been looking forward to having his apartment all to himself again.

He grimaced. 'It's not that I'm ungrateful, Darius. I just didn't envisage the next two weeks of having to sit across the breakfast table every morning from the no doubt muscle-bound man, Sam Smith, who you've employed to act as both my nursemaid and watchdog while you're away.'

Darius gave a chuckle. 'It would certainly make the neighbours sit up and take notice, if they thought you were living with a man who isn't your brother.'

As one of the billionaire Sterne twins, Xander had a playboy reputation with women that had long been catalogued, and speculated about, by the media. So yes, they would no doubt have a field day with the fact that he was sharing his apartment with a man.

'Fortunately, for you, none of that is going to happen. Sam*antha* Smith is a woman,' Darius assured him dryly.

Xander sat forward. 'Sam Smith is a *woman*!'

'Nice to know that your hearing wasn't affected in the accident,' his twin taunted.

Darius had taken his own sweet time sharing that little nugget of information with him!

Xander scowled. 'You don't have to look so happy about leaving me completely at this woman's mercy for the next two weeks!'

'I'll ask her to be gentle with you,' Darius teased.

'Very funny,' Xander muttered distractedly; just the thought of having some strange woman staying here with him filled Xander with a sense of unease. 'So how is it that you know this woman?'

Darius smiled. 'She's a friend of Miranda's. She really likes her, so much so that she's asked Sam to work at the dance studio with her part-time once we're back from our honeymoon. Oh, and her little girl attends one of Miranda's dance classes.'

'Stop right there!' Xander held up a silencing hand, breathing hard in his agitation. 'You didn't mention she had a child. What does she plan to do with her daughter while she's staying here with me?'

'She's going to bring her with her, of course,' his brother dismissed as if there had never been the possibility of anything else.

'Are you completely insane?' Xander exploded as he finally struggled up onto his feet with the help of his crutches. 'Darius, I *told* you what happened to me at the nightclub six weeks ago. I told you how I lost control of myself, and now you want to bring some child to live with me? How old is Ms Smith's daughter?' He knew that Miranda's ballet school was for pupils from five to sixteen years old.

'Five, I think.'

'You plan on allowing this woman to bring a five-year-old child to stay in my apartment with me?' Xander breathed in deeply in an effort to calm himself. 'This was Andy's idea, wasn't it?' It was a statement, rather than a question. 'You told her what happened to me and—'

'You didn't say I couldn't.' Darius's eyes had narrowed in warning.

'I don't care whether or not you told Andy what happened to me that night,' Xander dismissed impatiently. 'After all, she's going to be your wife and my sister-in-law. What I *do* care about is that Ms Smith and her daughter coming to stay here is most likely Andy's way of trying to show me I'm not turning into the monster I think I am. A naive attempt on her part to make me feel better about myself.'

'Careful, Xander,' Darius warned softly.

Xander was too annoyed to heed that warning. 'Life

isn't a fairy tale, Darius. Or, if it is, then I'm the monster in the story and not the prince!'

His brother gave Xander a considering look before speaking softly. 'You know, Xander, as Miranda once told me, quite succinctly as I recall,' Darius mused affectionately, 'the whole of life isn't about what you do or don't want.' He sobered. 'Putting my mind at rest apart, has it even occurred to you that Samantha Smith is a single parent? And that, as such, she might need the money I'm paying her to come here and act as your babysitter and watchdog while I'm away?'

But what if the woman did something to set off the temper he had only just discovered? What if her daughter did? Darius wouldn't find anything to laugh about then, would he? And Xander would never forgive himself if he lost his temper with either of them. That truly would make him the monster his father had been.

Darius scowled his displeasure. 'Look, as far as I'm concerned Miranda vouches for her, and the woman needs the money I'm paying her to come and live here with you while we're away. End of story.'

Xander didn't agree.

Yes, this penthouse apartment was big enough for a dozen other people to share it with him without them falling over each other; besides the six *en suite* guest bedrooms there was a full gym, a home cinema, as well as two other reception rooms, a wood-panelled study, a large formal dining room and an even bigger kitchen.

But that really wasn't the point, was it?

The *point* was that Xander didn't want to share any of that space with a woman he didn't even know, let alone her five-year-old daughter.

But what choice did he really have but to at least

try? Darius had gone above and beyond brotherly love by moving into this apartment with him and taking care of him since Xander had come out of hospital four weeks ago.

Was it fair of him to now cause his brother any further worry while Darius and Miranda were away on their honeymoon?

Unfortunately, Xander already knew the answer to that question.

CHAPTER TWO

'Is Mr Sterne a nice man, Mummy?' Daisy asked quietly as the two of them sat in the back of the limousine sent by Darius Sterne to collect them.

Was Xander Sterne a nice man?

Sam had only met the man once, during the interview she'd had with both Sterne brothers two days ago, while Daisy was at school.

Consequently, the question was a little difficult for Sam to answer, when Xander had left most of the talking that day to his brother. He'd only contributed to the conversation towards the end, when he had barked half a dozen questions at her about her daughter's schooling, and the amount of time Daisy would actually be spending at his apartment.

Making it clear to Sam that, while her new employer might be willing to tolerate her own presence in his home for the next two weeks, he wasn't in the least keen on having her daughter in residence as well.

An attitude that Sam wasn't particularly happy about.

But beggars couldn't be choosers.

She hadn't always been in such dire financial straits; her ex-husband, Malcolm, wasn't anywhere near as wealthy as the Sterne brothers, but he was nevertheless a successful businessman who owned a mansion in London, plus a villa in the South of France and another in the Caribbean.

Sam had been twenty to Malcolm's thirty-five, when the two of them had first met, she a lowly junior assistant and he the owner of the company. She had been instantly smitten with the suave and sophisticated, dark-haired and wealthy businessman, and apparently Malcolm had felt the same about her, so much so that within two months of meeting each other they had been married.

Sam had been starry-eyed and, to begin with, so much in love with her handsome and successful husband. Her parents had both died years ago, and she had been brought up in a series of foster homes. Her extended family was practically non-existent, with only a couple of distant maiden aunts whom she never saw.

However, Sam's pregnancy had changed her marriage irrevocably.

She and Malcolm had never discussed having children—or rather, *not* having them in Malcolm's case. It turned out that Malcolm didn't want children cluttering up his life as she discovered only when she'd excitedly told him she was two months pregnant.

At the time Sam had convinced herself that it was just a knee-jerk response to the thought of becoming a father for the first time at the age of thirty-six. Malcolm couldn't really have meant it when he suggested she terminate the pregnancy.

She had been wrong.

Their marriage had changed overnight, with Malcolm moving out of their bedroom, seemingly repulsed by the idea of Sam's body undergoing a transformation as the pregnancy continued. Even then, however, Sam had naively hoped for the best, sure that her marriage couldn't really be over after only a year, and that Malcolm would come around to the idea of fatherhood, either before or after the baby was born.

Again, she had been wrong.

Malcolm had remained in the spare bedroom, ignored her pregnancy totally, and he hadn't so much as visited her once in the clinic after Daisy was born. He had even been absent from the house when she came home carrying Daisy proudly in her arms and took her up to the nursery she had spent so many hours lovingly decorating and preparing for her beautiful baby.

Sam had struggled on for another two years trying to make her marriage work, sure that Malcolm couldn't continue to ignore his daughter's existence for ever. How could he not fall in love with his adorable baby daughter?

Except he hadn't.

At the end of that two years of struggle Sam had admitted defeat. Not only did she no longer love Malcolm, she wasn't sure she even *liked* him. How could she like a man who refused to acknowledge his own wife and daughter?

The past three years certainly hadn't been easy ones. Emotionally or financially.

Her emotions and how she dealt with them were Sam's own problem, of course. But how could a billionaire like Xander Sterne possibly understand how she had to scrape the money together, basically by going without lunches all week herself, just to be able to pay for something so trivial as Daisy's ballet lesson once a week? Something her daughter had talked of almost since she could walk and talk, and which Sam refused to disappoint her over.

Of course Malcolm, when Sam asked, had refused to contribute in the slightest to Daisy's happiness, over and above the minimum childcare payment paid into Sam's bank account once a month. An account set up in the name of Samantha Smith rather than her married name of Samantha Howard.

Her married name, along with the gifts and jewellery Malcolm had given her during their marriage, and any settlement she might have expected as Malcolm's ex-wife, either in a lump sum or monthly payment, were all things Sam had been asked to give up in exchange for Malcolm agreeing to give her full custody of her beloved daughter. A price Sam had willingly paid. And would willingly pay again, if she had to.

Xander, a man who owned and ran successful businesses globally with his twin brother, couldn't possibly understand how difficult it was for a single mother to even find a job, let alone one that necessarily fitted in with the hours Daisy spent at school. Waitressing at lunchtimes had been one of Sam's only options since Daisy started school the previous September, and even that became a nightmare when the school holidays came around. As they invariably did.

That last problem was going to be solved in two weeks' time, though, by her new job at Andy's ballet studio. In the meantime, this two weeks of looking after Mr Sterne would allow her to pay her electricity and gas bills.

Even so, it was mainly out of gratitude to Andy that Sam was now on her way to spend two weeks in the home of a man she had only met once, and whom she wasn't in the least comfortable being around. He hadn't exactly been outright rude to her, but he hadn't exactly been polite either.

So, was her new employer a *nice* man?

Quite honestly, she had no idea.

Oh, there was no doubting that he was fiercely masculine, with his wide and muscled shoulders, narrow waist and hips, and long legs. His hair was a tousled and overlong gold, and his eyes were a dark and piercing brown in his tanned and chiselled face; nose long and straight between sharply etched cheekbones, his mouth full and sensual, with the top lip fuller than the bottom above a square and determined jaw. As an indication of a sensual nature?

Well, probably not the latter for the past six weeks, since his car accident had resulted in a badly broken leg and basically kept him as being almost a recluse in his own apartment.

Although that obviously wouldn't have prevented women from visiting him at home!

It was something Sam hadn't thought of until now, but the bedroom exploits of billionaire Xander Sterne had been making the headlines in the newspapers and glossy magazines for more years than Sam cared to contemplate.

And the women photographed draped on his arm, at film festivals and other celebrity events, were always beautiful, always single, and always long-legged and oozing sex appeal.

'Mummy?' Daisy's curious tone reminded Sam that she hadn't yet answered her daughter.

She turned to give her daughter a beaming smile. 'Mr Sterne is a very nice man, darling.' She avoided so much as glancing in the direction of the chauffeur sitting in the front of the car—just in case she should happen to catch his sceptical gaze in the rear-view mirror as confirmation of her misgivings.

Because nice was hardly a word anyone would use to describe Xander. Dynamic. Arrogant. Lethally attractive. But nice? Not so much.

'Will he like me, do you think?' Daisy added anxiously.

It was her daughter's anxiety that made Sam's mouth tighten. It was a legacy of all these years of Malcolm's total lack of interest in his young child and an uncertainty that had resulted in Daisy being nervous around all men.

'Of course he'll like you, poppet.' Sam would rip the arrogant Xander Sterne to shreds if he did or said anything to hurt her already vulnerable daughter. 'Now, did you remember to pack teddy in your bag?' She deliberately changed the subject; there was really no reason to worry Daisy when she, herself, was already nervous enough for the both of them.

Xander didn't exactly pace the hallways of his apartment so much as clomp inelegantly up and down them on his crutches, as he waited impatiently for the arrival of Samantha Smith and her young daughter.

Xander had to admit to being a little surprised by Sam's appearance when she'd arrived at his apartment on Wednesday morning, so much so that he hadn't been able to so much as speak for most of the interview, but had instead left Darius to do all the talking.

For one thing, she must have been a child bride, because she didn't look as if she could be any older than her early twenties, certainly not old enough to be the mother of a five-year-old.

For another, she was very tiny, maybe a dot over five feet tall, and almost as slender as his future sister-in-law. Although the weary shadows about her arresting amethyst-coloured eyes, and the hollows in her pale cheeks, looked as if she owed her slenderness more to a lack of eating rather than the hours of dance practice that Miranda enjoyed.

Those unusual amethyst-coloured eyes weren't the only arresting thing about Ms Smith's face; she also had high cheekbones, with a smattering of freckles over those hollow cheeks and bridge of her pert little nose, and a full and sensual mouth. Her hair, brushed back from her face and secured at her crown but still long enough to fall silkily to mid-way down her back, was a deep and vivid red colour. And surely indicative of a fiery nature?

If it was, then Xander had seen little of that fire during that half-hour interview two days ago. Instead, the woman had spoken quietly in answer to first Darius's questions, and then his own, her long dark lashes lowered as she barely glanced at him long enough for him to enjoy those unusual amethyst eyes.

Maybe she was shy, or maybe she just didn't approve of or like playboy billionaires, but was willing to put up with him for the sake of the large amount of money Darius was paying her? His brother had preferred to attribute her quietness to nervousness at being the focus of the attention of both Sterne brothers.

Which was highly possible, Xander accepted ruefully; Darius on his own or Xander on his own could be intimidating enough, but put the two of them together…

Whatever the reason for her introspection on Wednesday, Xander was only willing to put up with her mouse-like company long enough for Darius and Miranda to enjoy their wedding and honeymoon, and not a moment longer.

So where the hell was she? Paul had left to collect the woman and her daughter over an hour ago. It was not an auspicious start to her employment here, if she hadn't even been ready to leave at the agreed time.

Xander needed to talk to Ms Smith as soon as she arrived, and make it very clear from the onset what he would or would not tolerate from her young daughter. He already had a mental list of rules prepared.

No running up and down the hallways of his apartment.

No shouting or screaming.

No loud television programmes, especially in the mornings.

No going anywhere near his bedroom suite.

And absolutely no touching any of his artwork or personal things.

In fact, Xander would prefer it if he wasn't even made aware of the child's presence in his apartment. Was that even possible with a five-year-old?

It would have to be. Ms Smith and her daughter weren't his guests but employees, and Xander expected her, and her daughter, to behave accordingly.

'Oh, look, Mummy, have you ever seen such a big television?'

Xander barely had a chance to register the presence of the woman and her young daughter, after the doors opened to his private lift, before a small red-haired whirlwind rushed past him down the hallway in the direction of the open door to the home cinema. She clipped his elbow as she passed, which knocked him off balance. Enough so that Xander felt himself falling.

Sam's stricken gaze followed her daughter's headlong flight down the carpeted hallway with all the horrified fascination of someone watching an unstoppable train wreck.

She closed her eyes with a wince as Daisy rushed past an open-mouthed Xander Sterne, opening them again just in time to see him swaying unsteadily on his feet.

Yep, definitely a train wreck!

Sam quickly dropped her shoulder bag onto the floor in order to run down the hallway, reaching Xander Sterne's side just in time to put a supportive shoulder underneath his arm to prevent him from toppling over completely.

Or, at least, that was the plan.

Unfortunately, Xander weighed probably twice as much as she did. So that when he overbalanced completely he took Sam down with him, both of them ending up on the floor, the fall slightly cushioned by the thick carpet but still eliciting a grunt from Xander Sterne as he landed on his back, Sam sprawled inelegantly across him, her denim-clad legs entangled with his much longer ones.

This wasn't just a train wreck, it was a disaster!

'Well, that's rule number one already null and void!' he muttered through gritted teeth.

'Sorry?' Sam raised her head to look down at him.

'Why are you and Mr Sterne lying on the floor, Mummy?' a bewildered Daisy enquired curiously as she wandered back down the hallway to look down at them.

'Will you tell her or shall I?' Xander Sterne's chest —his very muscled chest beneath another fitted black

T-shirt—moved beneath Sam's breasts as he bit the words out.

Sam felt the colour warming her cheeks as she realised her eyes were just inches away from the censorious brown ones now glaring up at her, and that her boss's chiselled features were twisted in displeasure.

Or perhaps it was pain he was exhibiting rather than censure?

Daisy had just succeeded in knocking this man over when he was still recovering from a broken leg, the very reason that she and Daisy were in his apartment in the first place.

'I'm so sorry,' Sam mumbled as she moved carefully, to avoid hurting Xander further, lifting herself up and away from him before standing up. She wondered whether she ought to answer her daughter first or help him back up onto his feet.

She decided to do both as she noted that his face had paled in the last few minutes.

'We fell over, darling,' she answered Daisy distractedly as she went back down onto her knees beside Xander. 'Should I call your doctor before you attempt to get up, do you think?' she prompted worriedly as he began to roll onto his right side—the side with the leg that wasn't broken—with the obvious intention of attempting to get back up onto his feet.

Xander turned to give her a cold stare, knowing it was his dignity that was injured more than his leg. Four weeks of hobbling around on crutches hadn't exactly been good for his ego, and now he had to deal with the fact that he had been knocked off his feet by a child.

Although it hadn't been all bad, Xander acknowledged grudgingly as he reached for his crutches to help him to his feet; Ms Smith might be a tiny little thing, and her build a bit too much on the slender side for his normal taste, but what little of her there was was completely feminine. A fact his body had definitely responded to as she lay sprawled on top of him. Her body had felt incredibly soft, and she'd smelt of flowers.

It was good to know, after six weeks without sex, that at least that part of him was still in working order, even if the rest of him was still shot to hell.

Even if it was an entirely inappropriate response to the woman being paid to share his apartment for the next two weeks.

'I don't need a doctor to know that the only part of me that's bruised is my ego!' Xander answered her more harshly than he had intended. Slightly regretting that harshness as she appeared to recoil and withdraw into herself.

What had she expected? That he was just going to laugh it off as childish exuberance?

Damn it, she and her daughter had only just arrived; he hadn't even had chance as yet for the talk about rules regarding her daughter's behaviour.

'Ah, just in the nick of time,' Xander muttered as the lift doors opened a second time and Paul stepped out carrying several bags, obviously the mother and daughter's luggage. 'Paul can help me get up, if you would like to take your daughter with you into the kitchen and make a pot of tea,' he bit out.

Sam knew it was an order rather than a request, and a means of getting she and Daisy out of the way.

And who could blame the man? He had already suffered the indignity of being knocked off his feet; he didn't need the further embarrassment of having to be helped back up in front of an audience.

Xander Sterne didn't give the impression he was a man who liked to show any sort of weakness. Ever. Which didn't bode well for the next two weeks, Sam acknowledged with a wince, when she was supposed to be helping him, as well as cooking for him.

She gave Paul a grateful smile before leaving him to help Xander back onto his feet, while she and Daisy went down the hallway in search of what turned out to be a beautiful red and black high-gloss kitchen, its numerous and expensive appliances all in gleaming chrome.

The sort of kitchen that she would have loved to explore further, if she weren't feeling quite so much trepidation about whether or not she and Daisy would be here long enough for her to see any more of this apartment than the kitchen. And the inside of the lift again, as they left!

She lifted Daisy up onto one of the bar stools before finding a carton of orange juice in the huge American-style fridge, and pouring some into a glass for her.

'I thought we had a rule about running in the house?' she chided Daisy gently as she moved to put the kettle on before looking for the tea, aware of the murmur of male voices out in the hallway as she did so.

'Sorry, Mummy.' Her daughter gave a guilty grimace. 'I just saw the huge television and I wanted to—Sorry,' she muttered again contritely.

Sam's expression immediately softened. 'I think you owe Mr Sterne an apology for running in his home, don't you?'

'Yes, Mummy. Do you think he'll let us stay now?' Daisy added anxiously.

It didn't help that Sam was wondering the same thing.

She raised her brows. 'Do you want to stay?'

'Oh, yes,' Daisy enthused.

Sam had no doubts that the huge TV was the reason for her daughter's enthusiasm. It certainly couldn't be because Daisy liked Xander Sterne, when all he had done so far was growl at them.

Xander had just been about to enter the kitchen, with the intention of giving the woman a blistering piece of his mind before then ordering her to leave, when he overheard the conversation between mother and daughter.

At which point his chest gave a tight and unexpected squeeze at how subdued the previously exuberant Daisy now sounded.

Because he had reacted like a bad-tempered idiot. To a five-year-old.

Damn it, he was *not* turning into his father.

He was not!

It wasn't as if the little red-haired tornado had *meant* to knock him off his feet. It had been a complete accident that she had managed to clip his elbow as she passed.

But why was he making excuses for her, when he had just been presented with the perfect opportunity— the perfect excuse—to dismiss Ms Smith? Before she'd even had chance to unpack the few belongings in the bags he had instructed Paul to leave out in the hallway before he left.

And what happened if Xander did dismiss her? He

did still need her help and he would mess up Darius and Miranda's honeymoon plans if he dismissed her now.

The fact that Sam might be counting on the money she would earn by working for him for the next two weeks was also a consideration.

Despite his reservations, even Xander wasn't selfish enough to want to be responsible for causing Ms Smith, or her daughter, unnecessary hardship.

CHAPTER THREE

SAM HAD HER back turned towards Xander when he finally entered the kitchen, allowing him to enjoy the sight of that gloriously curling red hair as it flowed loosely down the narrow length of her spine, the pertness of her shapely bottom clearly outlined by her skinny jeans.

Xander veered his scowling gaze sharply up and away from all that femininity, to instead look at the little girl seated at the breakfast bar, and currently watching him with huge and anxious amethyst-coloured eyes over the top of the glass of orange juice she was drinking.

It was an anxiety Xander remembered from his own childhood.

An anxiety *he* was now responsible for causing, as his father once had for him.

Xander's knowledge and experience of children was limited, to say the least, but even he could see that the child was a beauty, with her riot of long, red curls. Her features were more rounded than her mother's, although the promise of the same beauty was definitely there. It was a cherubic face at the moment, dominated by large and serious eyes, and she had a similar endearing smattering of freckles across her cheeks and the bridge of her tiny nose.

She now struggled down from the tall bar stool to look up at him from beneath long dark lashes. 'I'm very sorry for knocking you over, Mr Sterne.'

Oh, hell, she even had an endearing lisp when she talked, caused no doubt by that noticeably missing front tooth.

'I didn't mean to,' she continued to lisp. 'It's just that I've never seen such a big television before.' Her eyes filled with unshed tears. 'But Mummy has told me re—re—'

'Repeatedly,' Samantha supplied helpfully as she placed a cup of steaming-hot tea and the sugar bowl down on the breakfast bar in front of where Xander stood.

'Re— Lots of times,' the little girl substituted endearingly, 'not to run in the house.'

'I've labelled it "the whipped puppy look",' Sam confided softly even as she ruffled her daughter's red curls affectionately.

'What?' Xander had to drag his gaze away from the contrite-looking child in order to look at her mother.

'The tears welling up in the big eyes, the trembling bottom lip; "whipped puppy" look,' the mother supplied ruefully. 'It's a look my daughter, most young children in fact, have mastered to perfection by the time they're three!'

'Oh.' How to feel foolish in one easy lesson; he was being played, and by a five-year-old, at that!

Sam gave a rueful smile as she obviously saw the confusion in his expression. 'I assure you, the contrition is perfectly genuine, and you really shouldn't feel bad about responding to "the look"; it usually works on me too.'

Xander had the distinct impression he was fast losing control of this situation. If he'd ever had control of it in the first place!

But it was well past time that he did.

Xander looked coldly down the length of his nose at the two Smith females. 'Paul left your bags out in the vestibule, which for obvious reasons you will have to carry to your rooms yourself. You have the two adjoining bedrooms on the right at the end of the hallway. My own suite of rooms is behind the doors on the left. An area that, under no circumstances, will either of you enter without permission. For any reason,' he stated decisively.

For a heartbeat or two she looked taken aback by the harshness of his tone after their earlier conversation, before she straightened her slender shoulders, seemingly unaware of how the movement thrust forward her tiny but perfectly rounded breasts.

Something Xander was completely aware of, in spite of himself.

'Of course, Mr Sterne,' she now answered him smoothly. 'Come along, Daisy, Mr Sterne wants to be alone now.' She held out her hand to her daughter, which Daisy took before turning to bestow another shy smile on Xander as they left the kitchen together.

Leaving Xander feeling like a complete boor for having spoken to the two of them so harshly.

He instantly dismissed the feeling; if Daisy Smith had that 'whipped puppy' look down to perfection, then she had almost certainly acquired it from her mother.

* * *

'Is there anything else I can get for you, Mr Sterne?'

Sam kept her expression deliberately bland as she waited beside the formal dining table where she had just served him the first course of his dinner: perfectly cooked asparagus and Béarnaise sauce.

Her long hair was secured tidily at her nape, and she was wearing the same plain white shirt and tailored black trousers she had worn to her interview earlier in the week; it was her idea of her evening 'uniform' for the next two weeks.

Sam had brought all the ingredients with her for the meals she would be serving over the weekend, knowing that she wouldn't have the time, with Darius and Andy's wedding tomorrow, to go shopping for food until Monday.

She had decided to prepare something simple for Xander's evening meal today: the asparagus, followed by steak and a fluffy stuffed potato and buttered carrots, and for dessert she had made a pineapple upside-down cake with ice cream; easy to make, but it looked and tasted good. And there was no denying that the kitchen was a dream to work in.

Sam had always liked preparing and cooking food, and it was something she knew she was good at too. Which was why she had been deeply disappointed when Malcolm had refused to allow her to cook for him, insisting that it was what he employed his chef for. The most Sam had been allowed to do in that area was to approve the menus for the week.

Unfortunately, since the separation and divorce Sam's meagre budget had been a huge deciding factor in the meals she had been able to prepare for Daisy and herself.

Happily, there would be no such limitations in Xander's household. Sam very much doubted he had ever eaten a bowl of home-made stew in the whole of his privileged life!

'What did you have in mind?' He leant back in his chair to look up at her with those dark unfathomable eyes, his only concession to changing for dinner being to replace the black T-shirt of earlier with a white one. But then, he was in his own home, and so perfectly at liberty to wear whatever he chose, whenever he chose. Or not…

It had been a couple of hours since he had dismissed Sam and Daisy from the kitchen, and Sam had made good use of that time, by unpacking their few belongings and putting them away in the empty drawers in their bedrooms. She had also put the food she had brought with her away in the fridge and kitchen cabinets, before preparing dinner.

Sam's cheeks warmed now as she heard the unmistakeable challenge in his tone. A challenge she chose to ignore. She had been married to a man whose wealth, and the power that wealth gave him, had rendered him both arrogant and selfish, to the point that Malcolm had ridden roughshod over everybody. Including Sam and her romantic dreams of their happy future together.

She had no intentions of so much as acknowledging that Xander Sterne had that bad-boy look off to perfection, in the fitted white T-shirt that stretched tautly over his wide shoulders and chest, and revealing his tanned and muscled arms. Or that she was guilty of having noticed the tautness of his bottom earlier, in those hip-and-thigh-hugging black jeans.

Enough so that it now made Sam's heart beat faster

just to look at all that blatant maleness, her palms feeling slightly damp, a tingling warmth in her breasts and between her thighs.

None of which she wanted to feel for the arrogant man. 'You made a comment earlier,' she said coolly. 'Something about rule number one being null and void?'

'So I did.'

'What did you mean by it?'

'Where's Daisy?' He asked a question of his own rather than answer hers. 'It seems very quiet in the apartment this evening.' He raised questioning blond brows.

Sam's hackles were already up in regard to her daughter, but she stiffened defensively now; no matter what this man might think to the contrary, Daisy was not a noisy or a rowdy child. The opposite, in fact. Daisy was introspective rather than outgoing; no doubt a legacy of those early years of her childhood spent with a father who ignored her very existence, and had his own set of rules for ensuring he did so.

A guilt Sam still lived with on a daily basis.

For having ever held out even the fragile hope her marriage would one day return to their first year together, when she and Malcolm had seemed so happy together. For hoping, praying, that Malcolm would one day come to love his beautiful daughter.

She had wasted almost three years hoping and praying for those things, not just of her own life but of Daisy's too, and on a man Sam had belatedly realised she wasn't sure she had ever really known, let alone loved. A rich and arrogant man who had seen his much younger wife only as an asset, to be paraded on his arm, and to fill his bed at night. A man who was too selfish, too self-absorbed, to love the beautiful daughter they had made together.

Xander Sterne was even richer and more powerful than Malcolm could ever hope to be, and Sam didn't even want to acknowledge that he was also far more disturbingly attractive too. That he possessed a sensual magnetism she responded to, however unwillingly.

Her days of allowing herself to be attracted to rich and powerful men were long gone!

Having been forced to live by a set of rules once, Sam wasn't sure she could now adhere to another set, laid down by Xander Sterne for the time she and Daisy would be staying with him in his apartment.

'Samantha?'

She blinked before focusing on the man now studying her with piercing eyes beneath long lashes.

'Sam,' she invited automatically.

'I prefer Samantha,' he dismissed arrogantly—as if that settled the matter.

Which in Xander Sterne's self-assured eyes, it probably did. And really, what did it matter whether this man called her Sam or Samantha, when in two weeks' time they would never set eyes on each other again?

'Whatever you're comfortable with,' she allowed disinterestedly. 'And to answer your question, Daisy has already been fed, bathed, and is now fast asleep in bed.'

Xander had no idea where Samantha's thoughts had been for the past few moments, but he was pretty sure they couldn't have been pleasant ones. Her eyes had taken on a haunted look, the hollows of her cheeks paler than ever against the fullness of her rose-coloured lips.

'It's only eight o'clock.'

Samantha nodded. 'Daisy always goes to bed at seven o'clock on schooldays.'

Something else Xander didn't know about children.

'Fine.' He shrugged. 'Then perhaps you and I can talk about those rules after dinner?'

Her back stiffened. 'Of course, Mr Sterne.'

'Xander.'

'I would prefer that we keep things formal between the two of us.'

'Does that mean you would really prefer that I call you Mrs Smith?'

'No, because I'm not Mrs Smith,' she answered with a humourless twist of her lips.

Xander studied her through narrowed lids. 'I seem to remember my brother telling me you're divorced?'

'I am.' She nodded tersely. 'I reverted to my maiden name after the divorce.'

He frowned. 'Is Daisy's surname Smith too?'

'Yes.' Her mouth tightened defensively.

'I don't understand.'

Not many people *would* understand a situation like hers. One where a father insisted upon, rather than objected to, his child's surname being changed to her mother's maiden name after the divorce. Malcolm hadn't even wanted Daisy to possess his surname.

'Your food is getting cold, Mr Sterne.' She pointed out the obvious as she once again avoided meeting his gaze. 'And I have several things that need my attention in the kitchen,' she added before he could object. 'But I'll be more than happy to have that chat after I've served your coffee.'

Xander frowned as he began to eat his cooling asparagus, his attention really on watching her as she left the dining room. He was totally aware of the defensive stiffness of her very straight spine and shoulders, and the vulnerable length of her neck as she tilted her head back just as defensively.

Obviously he had said something to upset her—something *else* to upset her!

But wasn't it a little unusual to also change a child's surname after a divorce?

Not that he was acquainted with divorce on a personal level. His own parents had been unhappily married and probably *should* have divorced each other, but they hadn't, so that when Lomax Sterne died, Catherine and her two sons had continued to keep the surname Sterne. His mother had only changed her name to Latimer when she married Charles, Xander's stepfather.

Xander knew he would object strongly to any woman wanting to change *his* child's surname to her own, divorce or no divorce.

Xander gave a shake of his head; he was taking far too much of an interest in the life of his temporary employee.

'Dinner was excellent, thank you.'

Sam gave a nod of her head in acceptance of the praise as she placed the tray of coffee things down on the dining table.

'Sit,' Xander invited tersely as she began to clear the dessert bowl from the table.

'I'd rather stand, if you don't mind,' she said, trying not to bristle at being ordered about so impolitely.

His gaze was cool as he looked up from stirring sugar into his black coffee. 'I do mind.'

Sam gave a perplexed frown. 'I really don't think it's

appropriate for maintaining our employer/employee relationship for me to join you at the dinner table.'

'I think the appropriateness or otherwise of our situation will be dispensed with the moment you have to help me prepare for bed later tonight!'

Sam instantly felt the heat of embarrassment burning in her cheeks—a blush she knew would clash horribly with the red of her hair—at this reminder that this was one of the duties she had agreed to when she took this job. A totally ridiculous embarrassment, when she had been a married woman for over three years.

Except she hadn't been married to Xander Sterne.

Xander Sterne was in a whole different category from Malcolm when it came to physical prowess. Despite the inconvenience of having had a broken leg for six weeks, which had seriously affected his mobility, he was still all lean muscle and barely leashed power.

The thought of having to help him prepare for bed later tonight, including being available in case he needed help with his shower, was enough to make Sam feel hot all over, and she had to clasp her hands tightly together behind her back so that he wouldn't see they were trembling.

'All the more reason for us to maintain the formalities between us,' she countered coolly.

Xander rarely used this formal dining room, and he hadn't enjoyed eating dinner on his own in here this evening either. So much so that he was going to instruct Samantha to serve his meals in the kitchen in future. But he couldn't help notice her discomfort at his mention of needing her help later tonight.

He wasn't exactly looking forward to the awkwardness of that experience himself, but for a few seconds

Samantha had looked positively horrified at the reminder of it, before she quickly masked the emotion. An emotion that was still evident in the flush in her cheeks, and the trembling hands she had attempted to hide from him by thrusting them quickly behind her back.

Proving she wasn't quite as cool and composed as she wished to appear...

'I'm starting to get a crick in my neck from looking up at you,' he bit out impatiently.

'I'm not tall enough for you to get a crick in your neck.' She eyed him sceptically.

She had a point; even with Xander seated at the table their eyes were almost on the same level.

'Look, Samantha, I really am trying to refrain from actually ordering you to sit down,' he rasped testily.

'Why?'

'Because you obviously took exception to it a few minutes ago,' he bit out irritably.

Once again Xander watched the emotions flickering across Samantha's delicately thin face, seeing reluctance, and then irritation, as good sense obviously won out, and she pulled out the chair opposite him before lowering herself down to perch uncomfortably on its edge.

She raised her chin. 'I believe you wanted to discuss the rules for the time Daisy and I are staying here?'

That *had* been what Xander wanted to discuss with her, but now it came to it he felt like a complete and utter heel for having even mentioned the subject. It had seemed to upset Samantha earlier, and even more so now, although he had no idea why.

Admittedly, he hadn't been in the best of moods after

falling over earlier but he had accepted Daisy's apology, hadn't he?

He hadn't heard so much as a peep out of the little girl for the last three hours or so. In fact, it had been so quiet he wouldn't even have known there was a child staying in his apartment.

Which was exactly what he had wished for earlier this evening, wasn't it?

His mouth thinned. 'I'm sure you'll agree there have to be some rules for the three of us living here together?'

'Which we should perhaps have discussed in more detail before I accepted the job,' she said with a grimace.

'No doubt,' he conceded impatiently.

Samantha nodded stiffly. 'The first one of those rules is no running in the hallways, I believe?'

Xander searched that pale face for either sarcasm or humour, but she gazed back at him without emotion. As if Samantha had heard all of this before, in another time and another place.

'My requests are really only a matter of common sense,' he snapped his irritation. 'For your own and Daisy's sake, as much as for my own.'

'Oh?' Samantha raised one auburn brow.

'Yes, I— Look, I'm not used to having children around me, okay?' Xander ran an exasperated hand through his hair. 'I wouldn't want to—I wouldn't want—' He wouldn't want to what? Explode in temper at that timid little girl?

Would he do that to her? Could he do that? Was that monster he had discovered inside him capable of doing something so horrible to a five-year-old girl?

Xander no longer *knew* the answer to that question; that was the problem!

His mouth firmed. 'No running in the hallways, no screaming or shouting, no loud television programmes—especially in the mornings. And, as I've already said, no entering my bedroom suite, and definitely no touching any of the artwork.'

None of which applied to her, Sam acknowledged wearily, but was all aimed specifically at her daughter.

She certainly wasn't prone to screaming and shouting, or watching loud television programmes at any time of the day or night. Nor did she have any intention of entering Xander's bedroom suite, other than those occasions when she had to help him in or out of the shower, or to dress. Nor was there any reason for her to touch any of his no doubt priceless artwork. Why would she need to? He had a cleaning service that came in twice a week to vacuum and dust and do the laundry.

All of his rules were for the benefit of her daughter.

They were very similar to the rules that Malcolm had laid down for Daisy's behaviour. Except he had gone even further once Daisy began to walk and talk, and stated that he didn't so much as want to see or hear her. At least Xander hadn't gone that far.

Sam stood up and began to walk towards the kitchen. 'That all seems perfectly clear.'

'Samantha!'

She halted abruptly but didn't turn, swallowing as she realised her throat felt clogged with emotion. With tears. For having brought her daughter into yet another household where Daisy could perhaps be seen this time, but was certainly never to be heard.

Somehow she had expected more of Xander Sterne.

Oh, she had known before she met him, from reading newspaper articles about him over the years, that he was an arrogant playboy, who played as hard as he worked. She had also been aware, when she'd met him on Wednesday, that he obviously resented needing her help while his brother was away and she had been prepared to deal with that.

But she wasn't sure she could deal with having to subdue her daughter's enthusiasm for life just to make him happy.

She was no longer interested in making any man happy. Which was the main reason Sam hadn't so much as dated once these past three years; she had vowed never to put her daughter in a situation like the one she had suffered with Malcolm for the first two years of her life.

Once again Sam reminded herself that beggars couldn't be choosers.

Perhaps not, but she didn't have to let another arrogant man dictate his terms to her, either.

She wanted this job—the money was too good for her not to want it—but there was only so much she was willing to put up with in order to keep it.

Sam turned sharply on her heel, an angry flush in her cheeks as she glared across the dining room at Xander Sterne. 'I heard what you said, Mr Sterne, and I'll do my best to see that you aren't unnecessarily inconvenienced by having Daisy here. But I won't go any further than that.' She met his gaze challengingly now. 'If you aren't happy with that, then perhaps you should say so now and Daisy and I can leave tomorrow morning so that other arrangements can be made for you?'

Samantha was magnificent when she was angry. Her

red hair, even though it was confined in a band at her crown, seemed to bristle and shimmer with electricity, her eyes glowed a deep amethyst, and her cheeks were flushed.

Her nipples were also tight against the fitted white shirt she was wearing.

Not that Xander was stupid enough to say any of that out loud; in his experience, and contrary to what a lot of other men believed, most women did not appreciate being told they looked magnificent when they were angry. Not surprising, when it sounded so damned patronising.

'I'm fine with the present arrangement,' he rasped dismissively, knowing his love for Darius and Andy gave him no real choice in the matter. But that didn't mean he had to like it!

Samantha blinked, her expression uncertain now. 'You are?'

'Do you consider any of my requests to be unreasonable? And they are requests, Samantha, not rules. If there is a problem, then tell me so now, so that we can discuss it.'

'I— Well— No.' She looked disconcerted. 'But obviously Daisy is a child and—'

'It will be fine,' Xander bit out impatiently as he stood up from the table, his hand resting on the back of his chair for balance. 'Have you been divorced long?' he asked, the sharp shift in conversation catching Samantha off guard.

'Three years,' Samantha answered woodenly, her gaze no longer meeting his.

'Bad divorce?'

'Is there such a thing as a good one?'

'Probably not.' Nevertheless, Xander couldn't help but feel dissatisfied with her answer. Again.

All of the answers Samantha had given him so far, concerning her marriage and divorce, had been ambiguous, to say the least.

Darius had been right when he accused Xander of having become too self-centred in the weeks since his accident, deliberately so, after what had preceded that accident.

No matter how much Xander might wish it were otherwise, the arrival of Samantha and Daisy in his apartment now seemed to have made it impossible for him to continue to maintain that aloofness.

In fact, since their arrival earlier this evening Xander had felt a burning and increasing curiosity to learn all and everything there was to know about the woman who was to share his apartment for the next two weeks.

As much, it seemed, as Samantha was determined not to tell him.

Just what was she hiding?

'Have you and Miranda known each other long?' Xander decided to try a different approach to find out what he really wanted to know.

Samantha frowned slightly before answering him cautiously.

'Andy and I met six months ago, when Daisy started taking ballet lessons.'

He nodded. 'When I talked to Andy earlier in the week she spoke very highly of you.' He wasn't about to admit how protective his almost sister-in-law had been about Samantha and her young daughter. To the point where Andy had warned him to keep his hands to himself where her friend was concerned!

Xander had found the warning amusing at the time; after all, he couldn't even stand on his own two feet without the assistance of his crutches at the moment, so he was hardly likely to be making a move on the woman.

After spending just a few hours in Samantha's company, however, he found himself definitely regretting that lack of mobility.

'That's very kind of her.' Samantha smiled. 'Andy's very easy to get along with.'

Xander nodded. 'I bet Daisy is good at ballet too?'

Her smile became openly affectionate. 'She loves it.'

'And does Daisy spend much time with her father?'

Sam drew in a sharp breath as she realised that Xander had been lulling her into a false sense of security these past few minutes, and that he had now decided to pounce. No wonder he and his brother were so successful in business; most people would know, from a single meeting, to be cautious where the brooding Darius was concerned, but they would feel less of a need with the supposedly easy-going Xander.

But perhaps she was being unfair, and Xander hadn't had this hard edge to him before his car accident six weeks ago?

No, he'd still have had the edge, Sam decided ruefully, he just chose to hide it behind that easy-going charm. A charm he was making no effort to maintain in front of her. And why should he? She was here to work, not be charmed into his bed as so many other women had been.

Her eyes narrowed. 'Daisy will be spending all of her time here with me for the next two weeks when she isn't at school.'

'That didn't exactly answer my question.'

Sam maintained that steady eye contact. 'I thought it did.'

His mouth firmed. 'Is your husband away?'

'Ex-husband,' Sam corrected. 'And I have no idea whether he's away or not. Now if you will excuse me?' she added briskly as she gathered up the used dessert bowl. 'I still have to tidy up in the kitchen.'

'It can wait.'

'I'm tired, Mr Sterne, and would like to relax for a while before bedtime,' she stated firmly.

Xander only just managed to bite back his frustration with the way Samantha continued to avoid or refused to answer any of his questions about her marriage or her ex-husband. Deepening the mystery she was fast becoming to him.

Because there was something very intriguing about the way she clammed up every time Xander so much as mentioned her ex. And the fact that she had no idea whether or not he was even in the country, let alone when he would be seeing his daughter again, was decidedly odd.

When *did* the man see his daughter?

More importantly, what had the other man done to Samantha to cause those shadows in her eyes every time the subject of him was so much as mentioned?

CHAPTER FOUR

'ARE YOU GOING to stand in the doorway all night or do
you actually intend to come into the room, where you
might actually be of some use in helping me?' Xander
Sterne rasped impatiently from where he sat on the side
of the huge four-poster bed that dominated his bedroom.

Sam had taken one look at Xander and frozen where
she stood, her heart pounding in her chest and her pulse
racing.

But she wasn't drooling.

At least, she hoped she wasn't.

Surely any woman could be forgiven for finding herself momentarily unable to move or speak after being
confronted with an almost naked Xander Sterne?

Almost, because he had a small towel secured about
his waist that only just covered his—well, it just about
covered his modesty.

Not that he had any reason to feel in the least modest from where Sam was standing.

And looking.

She was captivated by the sight of his completely
bare, tanned chest and wide, muscled shoulders. His
chest was covered in a fine dusting of golden hair, a six-
pack rippling at his abdomen.

Sam's fascinated gaze shifted lower as he stood up, drawn to the long lean length of his bare and muscled legs, the temporary cast he wore in the day having been removed in preparation for his shower, and revealing the reddened scars from his operations six weeks ago.

Even his feet were attractive: long and elegant. Very long and elegant, Sam acknowledged slightly breathlessly, her gaze moving higher as she recalled reading somewhere that the length and size of a man's foot was in direct proportion to his—

'Samantha!'

She gave a guilty start as she reluctantly dragged her gaze away from the concealing towel to look up into Xander Sterne's handsome but obviously impatiently irritated face.

'Sorry.' She moved briskly into the bedroom and approached where he now stood beside the bed, her cheeks feeling warm with embarrassment as she realised she was behaving like a starstruck teenager.

Come to think of it, Xander wouldn't look out of place in any action movie, his perfect form blazoned across the big screen.

'Samantha…!' Xander now sounded exasperated rather than just annoyed by her obvious distraction.

'I can't continue standing unaided for too much longer, Samantha,' he reminded harshly.

No, of course he couldn't.

Just because Xander was the most glorious male specimen she had ever seen, on or off the big screen, that was no reason to keep ogling him as if he had the starring role in her favourite sexual fantasy.

'I'll go and turn on the shower,' Sam told him as she put an instant stop to *those* thoughts, her gaze shifting sharply away from continuing to look at all that breath-taking manhood as she walked towards the bathroom, needing a few minutes alone in order to pull herself together.

Which didn't mean her thoughts didn't continue to churn as she distractedly opened the smoked-glass door to the shower that ran the length of one wall of the bathroom, her gaze becoming unfocused as she drifted off into thought again after she had turned on the water and stood waiting for the temperature to adjust.

Responding so viscerally to her boss's nakedness was something Sam hadn't expected! Especially with a man who was even more wealthy and powerful than her ex-husband. She hadn't so much as *looked* at another man since leaving Malcolm, let alone reacted so physically to one! Her breasts felt uncomfortably tingly, her nipples highly sensitive.

Sexual arousal.

For Xander Sterne, of all people.

And because she had never in her life been this close to such a gorgeous—and very naked—man before tonight; Malcolm had *never* looked so blatantly, predatorily male, not even when the two of them had first met. Malcolm never *could* have the physique and looks of Xander, not in a million years of working out at the gym three times a week.

No doubt Xander had been using his gym here in the apartment these past few weeks in order to maintain that upper-body physique.

As for his lower body…

No doubt he usually maintained that by carousing all evening and having sex all night! Although he certainly wouldn't have been able to indulge in the sex part of that since his accident.

At least, Sam presumed that he hadn't?

Which reminded her that she had one rule of her own, regarding his own behaviour, while she and Daisy were staying here, that she still needed to discuss with him.

'Samantha?'

Sam gave a sharp intake of breath, having been so lost in thought that she hadn't even noticed that Xander had entered the bathroom behind her.

She was so startled by his presence she spun quickly round to face him, not having realised he was standing quite so close to her, and succeeded in doing exactly as Daisy had earlier, accidentally knocking his elbow with the hand she had raised defensively.

Unfortunately, with the same result!

'Not again,' Xander had time to mutter disbelievingly as he felt himself falling sideways towards the hard marble floor of the bathroom.

Oh, yes, a concussion was definitely just what he needed to finish off this already disastrous day.

Except it didn't happen.

Somehow—and Xander had no idea how she managed it—Samantha moved quickly enough to lodge her shoulder underneath his armpit. At least arresting his fall, even if they did both still stagger as his weight once again proved too much for her, before they were able to drop down onto the marble ledge running along the length of the bathroom wall opposite the shower.

'You know,' Xander snapped as he righted himself on the marble seat, 'I'm not sure if you and Daisy aren't determined to break my other leg—or worse!'

It certainly must look as if they were, Sam acknowledged with a guilty wince, shifting uncomfortably as she realised she was still tucked cosily beneath Xander's arm. Her hand, having fallen onto the firmness of his abdomen, was lying dangerously close to the top of the towel, her cheek resting against the warmth of his bared chest.

A chest that felt wonderfully solid, his skin smelling of the cologne he must have put on that morning, and a heat that spoke purely of earthy male.

It was a delicious and arousing combination.

And Sam didn't want to be aroused by this man any more than she already was. Wouldn't allow herself to be attracted to another man who believed his wealth and power gave him the right to ride roughshod over everyone else.

She jerked into a sitting position before scrambling inelegantly to her feet and moving sharply away from him. 'You startled me, creeping up on me like that!'

He eyed her exasperatedly. 'I should have guessed it was somehow going to be my fault. I'll try announcing my presence next time, shall I?'

'That might be best,' Sam replied tersely.

It was totally unfair that he looked so blatantly *male*; his overlong blond hair was tousled, and the towel, having slipped slightly during the fall, shockingly revealing more of the lean length of his thighs. Or that he so obviously felt absolutely no awkwardness at being almost naked in her presence.

But then, why should he, when he had the face and body of a Greek god? Or, more accurately, a blond Norse god.

She was absolutely not going there!

Not just because an attraction to him would be a mistake on her part, but she had Daisy to think of too.

Sam turned away abruptly. 'You should get in the shower now; it's starting to steam up in there.' She opened the glass door in readiness.

'I believe that's what I was trying to do earlier,' he bit out.

Sam kept her gaze averted as she heard Xander limping across to where she stood, her cheeks feeling warm as she heard the rustle of the towel before he held it out for her to take.

'Oh, for—!' Xander sighed his impatience as he saw that Samantha couldn't even look at him directly. 'Go and wait in the bedroom if my nakedness offends you so much.'

'It doesn't!' she snapped defensively, the colour that suffused her cheeks giving lie to that claim.

'No?' Xander challenged.

'No!'

'It certainly looks to me as if it does,' he mocked.

'Then there must be something wrong with your eyesight.' Samantha grabbed the towel from him before fleeing the bathroom.

As if the hounds of hell were chasing her, Xander noted.

Because it certainly wasn't him!

He couldn't catch a snail at the moment, let alone a fit and healthy woman determined to avoid being alone with him.

A fact his arousal seemed totally unappreciative of. 'Not going to happen tonight, I'm afraid,' he murmured to himself. 'Or for some nights to come,' he added grimly. Samantha had made it obvious she was completely unavailable.

It would have been far better for his peace of mind—
and his aching body—if his carer had been that muscle-
bound tattooed man.

Tattoos…

Now that was a tantalising thought. *If* Samantha did
have a tattoo what would it be and *where* would it be?
A flower or a butterfly, perhaps? On her shoulder? Her
breast? Or maybe her lower back, at the top of the curve
of that deliciously rounded bottom?

Not helping, Sterne.

And yet the image—the fantasy—lingered as he
washed his hair and rinsed his aching body.

'You can turn around now. I'm perfectly decent!'

Then Xander's definition of decent must be vastly
different from her own, Sam decided as she turned to
watch him as he limped awkwardly into the bedroom,
another towel, only slightly larger than the previous one,
secured about his naked hips. Making the decision she
had made, while he was showering, not to show any
reaction to his nakedness, completely null and void.

Because he was definitely perfect. But decent? Absolutely not!

He looked like a pagan god who had risen from the
sea, his chest still gleaming with droplets of water from
where he had obviously washed his hair in the shower,
that tousled blondness appearing darker when damp,
the long length of his legs obviously also still wet and
dripping water onto the carpet.

'I can't bend down that far,' he drawled as he saw
the direction of her gaze.

'You should have called me,' Sam said briskly.

'I didn't want to embarrass you again.'

'I wasn't—'

'Yes, you were,' he rasped harshly. 'Are.' He moved to sit on the side of the bed as he looked up at her through narrowed eyes. 'The question is why are you, when you've been married and have a daughter to prove it?'

'I told you, I'm not embarrassed.' Sam moved briskly across the room to drop down onto her knees in front of him as she began to towel dry the long length of his legs, taking care to gentle her movements on his injured leg, avoiding the several healing scars running the length of it.

'Liar,' he drawled.

Sam looked up at him sharply. 'I think you have an overinflated opinion of your own sexual prowess, Mr Sterne.'

'Not recently I don't,' he admitted.

The perfect opening… 'I should have mentioned this to you before.' Sam kept her head bent as she concentrated on drying his feet. 'I don't think—I would prefer, for the duration of our stay here, that you didn't—I realise this is an imposition,' she began again, 'but Daisy is only five, and I really don't—'

'Do you seriously think there's a danger of any woman being interested in going to bed with me the way I am at the moment?' Xander bit out harshly as he obviously guessed where her fumbling conversation was going.

What Sam *thought* was that there was a distinct possibility that women would still want to go to bed with this devastatingly handsome and sensual man, even if he were on his deathbed!

There was an innate sensuality to Xander Sterne that

would no doubt still be with him when he was ninety. And the bone structure of his face was such that he would always have that chiselled handsomeness that so many women—including Sam, unfortunately—found so devastatingly attractive.

'Or that I'm even capable of making love to a woman at the moment?' he demanded.

Sam raised her brows. 'I'm sure if you were to experiment that you would find a position that was comfortable— Forget I said that,' she dismissed as she stood up quickly from drying his feet, her cheeks once again blazing with embarrassed colour.

What had she been thinking?

Too much about being in bed with Xander, that was what she had been thinking about!

'I'm intrigued, Samantha.' He now regarded her teasingly. 'Exactly what position did you have in mind?' He looked thoughtful. 'The woman on the top would probably be the most comfortable for me, I suppose.'

'Look, all I was trying to say a few minutes ago was that I know this is an imposition, but I really would prefer it if you refrained from bringing any women to your apartment for the next two weeks while Daisy and I are staying here,' she muttered exasperatedly.

He arched one blond and arrogant brow. 'Are you going to make it worth my while?'

Sam blinked. 'Sorry?'

He placed his hands on the bed behind him as he leant back on his arms, emphasising the muscles of his shoulders and arms as he looked up at her challengingly. 'What are you offering if I agree not to bring any women to the apartment while you and Daisy are staying here?'

Sam's mouth firmed at what she had been sure was a deliberate and blatant display of his masculinity, followed by what sounded like a proposition. 'I'm not offering anything in exchange for what I consider to be a reasonable and polite request.'

'That's one answer, I suppose.'

'It's the only answer you're going to get from me,' Sam assured him stiffly. 'At the risk of receiving yet another one of your less than subtle replies—do you need anything else from me tonight?'

Xander couldn't help but grin as he saw the challenge sparkling in the boldness of Samantha's gaze, and realised that he was starting to like her. Not just in a sexual way—after his physical response to her earlier, that was a given!—but he definitely approved of her spirited conversation, and her sense of humour too.

Possibly a first for him where a woman was concerned.

Over the years Xander had fallen into the habit of dating models and actresses, visually beautiful and physically desirable women. But he hadn't necessarily got to know them well enough to discover their personalities too. Mainly, because he hadn't been particularly interested in knowing them that well, as long as they were beautiful to look at and satisfied him in bed. Which really wasn't as selfishly one-sided as it sounded, because the same was true in reverse; as long as those women could be seen out and about and be photographed on the arm of the billionaire Xander Sterne, they seemed more than happy with the arrangement.

A little—a lot!—shallow of them, and him, perhaps,

but the sort of wealth and power he possessed seemed to attract that type of woman.

Samantha was totally different from any of the women he had known before.

And not just because she was a divorced woman with a young daughter.

Samantha interested him in ways Xander had never even considered with any other woman. He wanted to know about *her*: her marriage, her husband, and her divorce. More importantly perhaps, what she had done and how she had lived in the years since that divorce.

And none of that had anything to do with the fact that he'd also like to take Samantha to bed.

Well, perhaps it had a little to do with it!

He certainly wouldn't say no, for instance, if she were to offer to go to bed with him without first telling him any of those things. In any position she wanted.

Although, from the look of disgust she was shooting him now, he didn't think that was even a possibility!

'I'm good, thanks,' Xander drawled.

Sam didn't think this man was good at all. Impossible. Temperamental. Sexy. Wickedly outrageous. But he definitely wasn't good.

She straightened. 'I'll see you in the morning, then, Mr Sterne.'

'Oh, you can count on it, Samantha,' he murmured as he watched her cross the room to the door before speaking again. 'I meant to ask, do you have any tattoos?'

Sam froze halfway across the bedroom before turning slowly back to face him, her eyes wide. 'What?'

'Do you have any tattoos?' he repeated as if this were a perfectly normal conversation.

Which it certainly wasn't. 'What does that have to do with anything?'

'Ah ha, that means you do,' he murmured with satisfaction. 'If you didn't you would have said no,' he explained at her perplexed frown.

Sam grimaced. 'Maybe I'm just too surprised by the question to have instantly denied it?'

'Still not saying no, Samantha,' he mocked, a wicked glint in his eyes as he looked her over from her head to her toes. 'Now where would you choose to have a tattoo, I wonder?'

Sam could feel the colour once again warming her cheeks under the frankness of that gaze. 'This really isn't a suitable conversation, Mr Sterne.'

'Oh, come on, Samantha, I've been stuck in hospital and this apartment for the past six weeks; surely you aren't mean enough to deny me a little entertainment?'

'The puppy-dog look doesn't look so good on you,' Sam assured him cuttingly.

'Then answer the question! Sorry.' He scowled darkly. 'I'm just—' He ran a frustrated hand through the thickness of his blond hair. 'You aren't seeing me at my best.'

'No?' Sam wasn't sure she could cope with seeing this man at his best.

'No,' he confirmed heavily. 'I was just— What's wrong with telling me where you have your tattoo?'

'Goodnight, Mr Sterne.' Sam turned towards the door.

'Is it on your breast?'

Sam faltered slightly but managed to keep on walking.

'Your shoulder?'

Why did the door suddenly seem so far away?

'Maybe your deliciously rounded bottom?'

Sam's hand shook slightly as she was finally close enough to reach out to take hold of the door handle.

'Or maybe it's at the top of your thigh where only a lover would see it?'

Sam quickly pulled the handle down and opened the door.

'Now the thought of *that* is definitely going to keep me awake long into the night!' Xander murmured.

'Goodnight, Mr Sterne,' she repeated firmly before stepping out into the hallway, closing the door behind her before leaning weakly back against it, able to hear Xander's soft laughter echo from behind it.

The man was impossible. Worse than impossible!

And the tiny tattoo on the top slope of her left breast seemed to throb as much at the moment as it had on the day she'd had it done five years ago.

'How do you like your toast, Daisy?' Xander frowned across the kitchen at the little girl as she sat at the breakfast bar in her pyjamas, her hair a glorious tangle of red curls about her slender shoulders. 'I can do lightly golden or burnt?'

'Burnt, please,' she answered politely.

Xander had been the only one up when he'd come to the kitchen a short time ago, but that hadn't lasted for long. Daisy had appeared shyly in the doorway just a few minutes later, obviously having heard someone moving about in the kitchen, and no doubt assuming it was her mother.

Xander's first reaction was to panic. To wonder if he was up to dealing with her, or if he should just go and get Samantha.

What if Daisy spilt some juice and he lost it? What if she dropped cereal or jam on the breakfast bar, and his violent temper made another unwanted appearance?

The rage he had felt that night in the Midas night-club had been frightening enough, but Xander knew he would never forgive himself if he verbally or physically hurt a child. As he had been hurt by his father.

After staring blankly at Daisy for several minutes Xander had forced down the panic, decided not to go and wake Samantha, but to instead test himself and offer Daisy the same breakfast he was having.

So far it was going reasonably well. He had tried to smile as he poured Daisy some juice, and his voice had remained reasonably calm when he offered to make her some toast along with his own.

He usually didn't eat breakfast at all, preferring to grab a quick cup of coffee, but he was making an ex-ception by eating a slice of toast this morning, unsure of when he would be able to eat again.

Darius and Miranda's wedding was at one o'clock today, but the meal wasn't being served until four o'clock, to allow time for the taking of photographs after the service, and the greeting of guests at the Midas Hotel later.

As Darius's best man, Xander had his own wedding duties to take care of.

'Oh, no!' A breathless Samantha suddenly appeared in the kitchen doorway, looking almost as dishevelled as her young daughter, in a robe belted tightly about her slender waist, her red hair a wild tangle about her shoul-ders, her legs bare. 'I am so sorry!' She rushed into the room. 'I should have been up and getting your break-fast long before this. I must have overslept.'

'Calm down, Samantha,' Xander advised abruptly. 'Daisy and I have been managing just fine on our own, haven't we?' He placed Daisy's plate of buttered—and burnt—toast in front of her on the breakfast bar, once again congratulating himself on having got through the past ten minutes without having a single urge to lose the temper he now feared.

Although he couldn't say he was sorry that Samantha had put in an appearance.

Sam had never felt so disorientated in her life as when she woke up in a strange bed a few minutes ago, before the reality that she was currently staying in Xander Sterne's apartment came crashing down on her. A glance at the bedside clock had shown her it was already eight o'clock, way past the time Daisy usually woke her in the morning.

She had leapt out of bed, quickly pulling on and tying her robe over the vest and shorts she wore to sleep in as she hurried next door to Daisy's bedroom, only to find her daughter's bed had obviously been slept in but was now empty.

The last thing Sam had expected, after hurrying down the hallway to the kitchen, was to find her daughter sitting at the breakfast bar while Xander made and served her breakfast.

Especially when Sam was being paid—very generously—to make and serve *his* breakfast!

It didn't help that his face looked a little pale this morning, and his limp was much more pronounced too as he hobbled about the kitchen.

Because he shouldn't be standing on his leg for any length of time yet. Because *she* was being paid to ensure that he didn't.

She had also promised him that he wouldn't even know Daisy was in his apartment, and yet here he was, the morning after their arrival, preparing her breakfast!

'I really am sorry,' Sam mumbled awkwardly as Xander poured some coffee into a mug before handing it to her.

Today he wore a fitted brown T-shirt and faded blue jeans, his feet bare on the tiled floor.

The latter no doubt because he couldn't bend down far enough to put on his own socks and shoes and she hadn't been around to do it for him.

How *could* she have been so stupid as to oversleep on her very first morning here?

Probably because she had tossed and turned in her bed for most of the night before, unable to sleep because she was so totally aware of that last conversation with Xander. Of the fact that he was lying naked in his own bed just down the hallway!

How did Sam know he was naked?

Because while he was in the shower she had searched through the drawers in his dressing table and the wardrobes for pyjamas, in readiness for when he came out of the shower. Pyjamas that simply weren't there.

A knowledge that wasn't in the least conducive to Sam being able to fall asleep once she had climbed into her own bed.

Consequently, it had been the early hours of the morning before she had managed to drift off to sleep, resulting in her oversleeping this morning.

Sam was more than a little surprised by how relaxed Daisy seemed to be in Xander's company; usually her daughter was extremely shy around men. Big men like him especially.

No doubt yet another result of Malcolm's complete indifference to his daughter. Malcolm wasn't as big as Xander, but no doubt he would appear so to a small child. A small child who knew to leave a room if Malcolm came into it.

And yet Daisy seemed perfectly happy in Xander's company.

'I have to be at Darius's apartment by ten-thirty this morning, if you could drive me over there? I'll shower there before I dress for the wedding.'

'Of course.' Sam breathed an inward sigh of relief that he seemed to have tired—for the moment!—of teasing her. And that she didn't have the ordeal of accompanying him to the shower to get through either this morning.

'Although quite how helpful I'm going to be as best man is anyone's guess,' he added bitterly.

'I'm sure that, if nothing else, Darius will welcome your moral support today.' Sam still found Darius a little intimidating, but Andy loved him very much, and surely even a man that arrogantly self-confident must be feeling a little nervous on his wedding day?

'I won't be back until late this evening,' Xander continued dismissively, 'so it's up to you what you and Daisy do with the rest of your day.'

Sam gave him a startled look. 'Er—'

'As long as you're back here in time this evening to help me shower—'

'Mr Sterne.'

'It shouldn't be a problem—'

'Xander!'

'Sorry?' He gave an irritated frown.

Sam gave an uncomfortable grimace. 'Daisy and I are invited to the wedding.'

Well, of course they were, Xander realised.

If Samantha was a good enough friend for Miranda to recommend her for this job, then she was obviously going to invite her to the wedding too…

CHAPTER FIVE

'LEAVING ALREADY?'

Sam turned from where she was helping Daisy into her coat, looking across to where Xander stood watching her, the three of them in the gold and black marble entrance hall of the fabulously exclusive London Midas Hotel, where Andy and Darius's wedding reception was still taking place. 'It's almost nine o'clock, and Daisy's tired.' She gave a rueful smile as her daughter gave a yawn.

It had been a beautiful wedding; Andy had made a beautiful bride, Darius a handsome and distinguished bridegroom. Xander's best-man speech at the reception had caused much hilarity as he'd related—as was the custom—some of Darius's more embarrassing teenage adventures. He had wisely refrained from mentioning any of his twin's more risqué adult exploits; both the Sterne brothers had been making headlines in the newspapers for the past twelve years regarding those!

After the delicious wedding breakfast there had been dancing, and Andy and Darius had made an absolutely stunning couple as they danced that first dance alone, one so dark and handsome the other very fair and beautiful. The two of them had eyes only for each other as they moved gracefully about the dance floor.

They were joined by Darius's mother and stepfather for the second dance of the evening, a time when Xander should have also stood up with the chief bridesmaid, but obviously couldn't. Instead Andy's sister Kim had danced with her husband, Colin.

Sam had noted that Xander remained at the top table talking to one of the other two bridesmaids.

As a friend of the bride rather than a relative, Sam and Daisy had been seated at a table towards the back of the huge ballroom, but close enough to be able to watch and enjoy all of the wedding party. She had even been asked to dance by a couple of the single male guests. Invitations she had refused, using the excuse of not wanting to leave Daisy sitting on her own.

Yes, it had been a beautiful wedding, but it had made for a long day, and at nine o'clock in the evening it really was time for her to take her sleepy daughter back to Xander's apartment.

Sam had thought she had said her goodbyes to Andy and Darius without anyone noticing, before slipping quietly out of the ballroom. Obviously she had been wrong.

She straightened. 'Darius assured me it would be no problem for you to take a taxi home later.'

'Did he?' Xander enquired mildly.

'Yes.' Sam frowned at that mildness. 'Please don't let me keep you any longer from enjoying the rest of the wedding reception. I think the bridesmaid might be missing you,' she dismissed teasingly.

In all honesty Xander was more than a little tired of the company of the bridesmaid, a young woman who

seemed bound and determined on achieving the tradition of one of the bridesmaids going to bed with the
best man the night of the wedding. A tradition Xander
would normally have been only too happy to satisfy!
But not tonight. And the excuse that his broken leg was
still healing didn't seem to have deterred the woman in
the slightest from succeeding in her mission!

Oh, she was attractive enough with her blonde hair,
limpid blue eyes and curvaceous figure, and usually
Xander wouldn't have hesitated in taking her up on the
obviously blatant offer.

But instead of responding to that overt flirtation,
he had found himself constantly seeking out a head of
fiery red curls, both during the wedding ceremony at
the church, and later during the reception.

Samantha was wearing a figure-hugging red gown
that should have clashed with those red curls, but somehow only deepened the colour of her hair to a vibrant
copper, adding a creamy glow to her cheeks and the
tops of her breasts visible above the scooped neckline
of the gown.

Something Xander had noted several other men ad-
miring during the wedding reception, a couple of them
having approached her table and asked her to dance.
Invitations she had refused with a smiling shake of her
head.

Refusals that had caused Xander to smile in satisfaction.

And warning him that he was taking altogether too
close an interest in the woman temporarily employed to
drive and take care of him, and currently staying at his
apartment.

A warning he had taken absolutely no notice of,

when he saw Samantha quietly making her excuses to Miranda and Darius, before slipping from the ballroom with the obvious intention of leaving.

'You aren't,' he clipped abruptly in answer to her comment regarding the persistent bridesmaid. 'I've actually had enough for one day too, so if you wouldn't mind waiting a few minutes, while I make my own goodbyes, I'm ready to come home with you and Daisy now.'

Sam felt a little uncomfortable hearing Xander describe his apartment as home for all of them. Because they all knew, as far as she and Daisy were concerned, it was only a very temporary accommodation.

Looking at Xander a little more closely, though, she could see that he did indeed look a little pale under his tan, and there were also dark bruises of tiredness and strain beneath his eyes. He was leaning rather heavily on the walking stick he had insisted was going to be his only walking aid at his brother's wedding.

Was it so surprising, when Xander had barely been out of his apartment for weeks, but had now spent the whole day and part of the evening socialising with his brother and Andy's wedding guests, that he was now feeling the effects of such a busy day?

'Of course.' Sam nodded. 'We'll wait out here for you.'

'Thanks.' He gave a rueful grimace as he turned awkwardly and limped back to the ballroom, leaning heavily on the walking stick as he did so.

'Xander looks tired too, Mummy,' Daisy observed softly.

'Mr Sterne, darling,' Sam corrected distractedly, more than a little concerned for him herself.

Daisy frowned. 'He told me this morning that I should call him Xander.'

Sam looked down at her daughter in surprise. 'He did?'

'Yes.' Daisy gave a gap-toothed smile; she looked adorable in the amethyst-coloured knee-length party gown that had been bought especially for the occasion. Sam had happily missed out on lunches to see her daughter looking so happy.

She regarded her daughter quizzically. 'You like him, don't you?'

Daisy nodded. 'He's nice.'

After spending the last twenty-four hours with him, that was even less the word Sam would have used to describe Xander Sterne than it had been when Daisy had asked about him yesterday afternoon!

He was impossible. Infuriating. Arrogant. Most certainly outrageous on occasion; Sam still hadn't forgotten that intimate conversation the previous evening regarding whether or not she had any tattoos, and where she might have them if she did. A tattoo that the scooped neckline of her gown barely managed to cover...

But *nice*? Xander was much too immediately male to be described with such an insipid word.

And yet Daisy, who was so often shy in the company of men, seemed totally relaxed in Xander's company.

Obviously Daisy saw something in him that Sam didn't.

Or, more likely, not...

Being only five, Daisy wouldn't be aware of Xander's immediacy, of how disturbingly *male* he was. Or recognise that the man possessed a lethal and sensual magnetism. And the naked body of a Norse god—

'Ready?'

And the stealth of a predator!

Sam had been so lost in her own thoughts that she hadn't even been aware of Xander's return, despite the sound the rubber end of his walking stick must surely have made on the marble floor.

She straightened her shoulders determinedly. 'Ready.' She nodded briskly. 'If you and Daisy would like to sit here and wait, I'll go down in the lift to the car park and bring your car round to the front of the building?' She looked down questioningly at Daisy.

'Good idea.' Xander nodded. 'We'll be okay here together, won't we, Daisy?' He hadn't missed Samantha's deference to her young daughter over the suggested arrangements.

Did Samantha somehow sense that inner rage Xander was at such pains to try and keep under his control?

He and Darius had found plenty of time to chat this morning, once Samantha had dropped him off at his brother's apartment. Darius had once again been at pains to reassure Xander that the reason for his rage six weeks ago was perfectly understandable, that *he* would have reacted to that situation in the same way, and that Xander had only responded so strongly to that situation because of their own family history of having an abusive father. That it didn't mean Xander would ever feel that angry again.

But what if Darius was wrong? And what if Samantha had sensed that rage inside him?

Xander gave a jolt of surprise as Daisy smiled up at him shyly as she slipped her warm little hand into his much larger one. 'I'll stay here and look after Xander for you, Mummy.'

Xander was so bemused by having that little hand resting so trustingly in his that it took him a second or two to register exactly what Daisy had said. Causing him to grimace, when he looked up to find himself the focus of the laughing eyes of Daisy's mother.

Great; not only was his blasted leg aching like the devil, because he had been on it for most of the day and had stubbornly refused to use his crutches, but now he was the focus of Daisy's sympathy and the butt of Samantha's amusement.

Still, there was some compensation to remaining here with Daisy, Xander decided as the two of them sat down in two of the armchairs in the marble reception area, and so allowing him to watch the sexy sway of Samantha's hips and bottom as she walked over to the lift that would take her down to the car parked in the underground car park, which he had insisted she use to drive herself and Daisy to the wedding earlier.

For all that she was only a little over five feet tall, Samantha's slender legs looked long and silky above the three-inch-heeled shoes she was wearing today.

Causing Xander to muse as to how it would feel to have those silky legs wrapped about his waist…

What the…?

While Xander had been sitting there imagining how he would make love to Samantha, another man had approached her and was now holding tightly to her arm as he talked to her.

A man, Xander noted grimly as Samantha turned briefly to shoot a worried glance in his own and Daisy's direction, who had caused her face to pale.

Xander instantly felt that rising tide of anger he had

hoped never to feel again. And for the same reason: the sight of a man roughly manhandling a woman.

The man's fingers painfully gripped the top of one of Samantha's arms as he talked to her in a lowered and intense tone.

'Take your hand off me, Malcolm!' Sam snapped agitatedly as she stared up into the face of the man she had once been married to but had hoped never to set eyes on again after the divorce.

It was a handsome face still, dominated by glittering blue eyes, the darkness of Malcolm's hair, at the age of forty-one, showing only a distinguished sprinkling of grey at his temples, his perfectly tailored suit emphasising the width of his shoulders, and narrow waist and hips.

What were the chances, the probability, that Malcolm would be at the London Midas Hotel on the very same evening that Sam happened to be here for Andy and Darius's wedding reception?

What were the chances, with Sam's change in circumstances after their separation and divorce, that she would ever have been inside the exclusive Midas hotel at all, let alone on the same evening as her ex?

Unless…

Was it possible that Malcolm could be one of the evening guests invited to Andy and Darius's wedding?

Sam had mentioned her brief marriage and divorce to Andy, of course, but only in passing, and in relation to how that might affect Daisy. She certainly hadn't told her friend the name of the man she had once been briefly married to.

Sam knew the newly married couple had invited fifty

or so guests for the evening part of the wedding reception, most of them parents of the children to whom Andy taught ballet, or business acquaintances of Darius's.

Was it possible that Malcolm was one of the latter?

It was more than possible, Sam acknowledged with an inward groan, wondering why it had never occurred to her before that Malcolm and Darius might know each other. Malcolm was a successful businessman, just as Darius and Xander were, and—

Did that mean that Xander knew Malcolm too?

'I asked what you're doing here, Sam,' Malcolm rasped harshly, her request that he release her obviously having had absolutely no effect, as his fingers continued to bite painfully into the top of her arm.

Her eyes flashed. 'And *I* told *you* that it's absolutely none of your business what I do any more.' She glanced behind him to where a beautiful blonde stood waiting for him.

'And aren't you being a little rude just leaving your date standing over there alone while you verbally abuse your ex-wife?'

'I don't give a damn whether it's rude or not.'

'Well, I do!' Sam snapped, her days of being intimidated by this man—visibly, at least—long over. Inwardly it was a different matter. Inwardly Malcolm still made her quake, but mainly with revulsion, she now realised with a frown. 'Take your hand off me, Malcolm, or I'll call someone over from hotel security and have them make you do it,' she warned coldly.

His face twisted viciously. 'Why, you little—'

'Now, Malcolm!' She met his furious gaze unflinchingly.

She wondered how she could ever have been married to this man. How she could ever have tried so hard to make that marriage work after Daisy was born. How she could ever have thought she *loved* him.

Oh, there was no doubting that Malcolm was still an attractive man, but Sam could now see and recognise the edge of cruelty to his mouth, and the cold calculation of those blue eyes that looked down at her so possessively.

'I think I like you like this, Sam.' Malcolm's gaze swept over her in blatant insolence. 'You look absolutely amazing in that red dress. Even better out of it, if my memory serves me correctly!'

Sam gave a shudder of revulsion as she recognised the flash of desire as Malcolm blatantly undressed her with his eyes.

'Lucky for me that I haven't forgotten a single thing about you!' she dismissed scornfully. 'Most especially how much I despise you!'

Malcolm's face flushed with fury. 'What have you done with your precious daughter this evening while you're out enjoying yourself?'

It took every effort of will on Sam's part not to glance across the hotel reception to where Daisy sat beside Xander. The last thing she wanted was for Malcolm to realise that Daisy was here too, and possibly make even more of a scene in one of Xander's prestigious hotels.

Daisy hadn't so much as asked about her father once since the separation and divorce, and Sam doubted her daughter would even recognise him if she did see him. She *hoped and prayed* Daisy wouldn't recognise him.

She raised her chin. 'Again, Malcolm, that's absolutely none of your business.'

'She's my daughter too.'

'Daisy was never your daughter!' Sam hissed, her eyes flashing darkly as she felt absolutely incensed by Malcolm's claim. How dared he, after the way he had treated Daisy? How *dared* he? 'Get your hands off me now or I *will* call security.'

Malcolm regarded her through narrowed lids, that gleam of sexual admiration still glittering in his eyes as he slowly released her. 'How about I ditch my date for the evening and the two of us take a room here for the night instead?'

Sam drew in a harsh breath even as she gave another shiver of revulsion, wanting nothing more at that moment than to slap the man she had once been married to. 'Goodbye, Malcolm,' she said coldly instead, having just dared a glance across the reception area and seen that Xander was getting awkwardly to his feet, his tiredness making that more laborious than it might otherwise have been, while the darkness of his gaze was fixed steadily on where she and Malcolm stood in obviously heated conversation.

The last thing Sam wanted was for Xander to come over here and realise that she was talking to her ex-husband. An ex-husband he might possibly know too.

Bad enough that Sam and Malcolm had met again at all, but she knew Xander well enough to know he was the sort of man who would demand answers from her regarding the man who had spoken to her. That he would want details of the acquaintance. All of them.

They were details Sam didn't want to give him.

Mainly because she was too ashamed. Of how much, and for how long she had tried to make her marriage to Malcolm work, and the sacrifices she had made trying to achieve that.

Looking at Malcolm now, she was able to see beyond that surface charm and handsomeness that had once dazzled her into believing she was in love with him, as much as he claimed to be in love with her, and could now clearly recognise Malcolm's coldness, as well as his cruelty.

'Malcolm?' His date for the evening had obviously tired of waiting as she looked over at him in puzzled enquiry.

Malcolm turned to smile charmingly at the other woman. 'I'll be right there, Sonya.' His eyes hardened as he turned back to Sam. 'This conversation isn't over,' he warned her softly.

'Oh, it's most definitely over,' Sam assured him.

He smiled tauntingly. 'No, Sam, it really isn't. I'm sure I'm going to find you so much more fun now that you're all grown up.'

Sam's eyes widened in alarm. 'We're divorced.'

'So?' he taunted. 'Never heard the phrase one more for the road?'

Surely that applied to a drink, and not—not—

'We have a deal,' she reminded shakily. 'Daisy and I will stay out of your life and you will stay out of ours.'

Malcolm gave an unconcerned shrug. 'And I'm willing to continue doing just that. For a price.'

'I already paid your price.'

'And now I'm going to collect the interest.' His eyes had narrowed darkly. 'Give my daughter a hug for me when you see her,' he added softly. Threateningly.

'You—'

'Enjoy the rest of your evening, Sam,' Malcolm

taunted before turning on his heel to join his date for the evening, his hand beneath the other woman's elbow as the two of them then proceeded, as Sam had suspected that they might, towards the ballroom where Andy and Darius's wedding reception was being held.

Oh, why hadn't she left sooner? Why had she come here at all?

'Everything okay, Samantha?'

Sam was shaking so badly, her knees knocking so much, she wasn't sure she was going to be able to remain standing for much longer, let alone be capable of finding a suitable answer to Xander's puzzled query.

Was everything okay?

It couldn't have been less so.

Not only had Sam seen Malcolm again when she had been least expecting it, tonight or any other night, but he had definitely threatened her, and used a tacit threat against Daisy as leverage to cash in on it.

And the intelligent and astute Xander had been a witness to that meeting. Even if he could have no idea about the content of their conversation.

As for Daisy?

Sam looked down anxiously at her young daughter. She'd walked over with Xander, her hand still resting trustingly in his. Had Daisy recognised Malcolm as her father?

There was nothing in Daisy's face to indicate that she had. Her expression was one of tiredness rather than any sign of recognition for the man Sam had been talking to; Daisy's eyelids were drooping and her cheeks were slightly pale.

And really, why should Daisy recognise Malcolm?

Her daughter hadn't even seen Malcolm since she was two years old, and only rarely before then.

'Who was that man, Samantha?'

She swallowed before answering. 'Just someone who obviously mistook me for someone else.' She shrugged dismissively.

Xander frowned. 'The conversation seemed rather protracted just for you to tell him he'd made a mistake in identity?'

Her mouth firmed stubbornly. 'Nevertheless, that's what I was doing. We might as well all go down in the lift to the car park together now that the two of you are right here?' she prompted lightly as the lift doors opened and she stepped inside to look at him enquiringly.

Xander had absolutely no doubt that Samantha was lying to him.

The intensity of the conversation he had witnessed, the expressions on Samantha's face as she spoke to the other man, certainly hadn't looked as if she was politely assuring a stranger that he had mistaken her for someone else. The opposite, in fact. Samantha had initially looked distressed, and then her expression had become coldly impenetrable, followed by one of fear. Xander had also recognised an almost proprietary gleam of ownership in the other man's eyes at one stage of that intense conversation.

Because the man felt proprietary in regard to Samantha? Perhaps because he was an ex-lover?

It was certainly a more plausible explanation for the heated encounter than the one Samantha had just given him.

That flare of temper Xander had felt—and so feared feeling again—when he first saw the guy manhandling Samantha had now settled into a deep-down coldness.

He still wanted to strangle the man, for daring to put his hand on Samantha, but it was in a cold and measured way, rather than down to a heated lack of control.

Whether or not that control would last was anyone's guess!

'Fine,' he agreed tersely to Samantha's suggestion as he and Daisy stepped into the lift beside her, deciding to let the conversation go. For now.

But he had every intention of making Samantha tell him the truth about the man who had accosted her.

And sooner rather than later.

'Daisy okay?' Xander enquired as Samantha hovered in the doorway of the sitting room after bathing her daughter and putting her to bed.

'Already fast asleep.' Samantha nodded. She'd changed into a thin blue sweater and faded jeans, her feet were bare, and her hair once again secured at her crown.

'Join me for a nightcap.' Xander held up a decanter of brandy, having removed his morning jacket and cravat, and unfastening the top button of his wing-collared white shirt. 'And before you even think about saying no thank you, in your oh-so-polite manner—' his voice hardened as he poured the brandy into two crystal glasses '—it wasn't a request.' He looked across at her challengingly.

Sam felt an uneasy lurch of her stomach as she recognised Xander's uncompromising expression. 'I'm tired.'

'It's only a little after ten o'clock.'

'And it's been a long and exciting day.'

'Then a brandy will help relax you before you go to bed.' He left his walking stick beside the fireplace as he limped slowly across the room to place the two glasses of brandy down on the coffee table before sinking down onto the cream leather sofa.

'I'm already relaxed.'

'Liar.' Xander could literally *feel* Samantha's tension, and he could see it too, in the way she held herself so stiffly.

She frowned. 'I don't think I care for the way you keep calling me that.'

His eyes flashed darkly. 'And I don't think *I* care for being lied to.'

Her mouth set in a stubborn line. 'Then maybe you should stop asking questions I obviously don't want to answer.'

Xander felt some of his rising tension leave him as he smiled ruefully. 'Now *that* was honest.'

She frowned. 'I am invariably honest. You just keep asking me questions that are none of your business, and then won't accept it when I refuse to answer them.'

'Would you please sit down and enjoy your brandy?' he invited huskily as he patted the leather seat cushion beside him.

Samantha walked further into the room, but she made no effort to sit beside him as she instead picked up one of the glasses of brandy from the coffee table and took a large swallow, only to then draw her breath in sharply as the fiery liquid caught the back of her throat. 'Whoa,' she gasped breathlessly, her cheeks becoming flushed, tears blurring her vision.

Xander chuckled softly. 'You're supposed to sip a fine brandy, Samantha, not glug it back like cheap wine.'

'And what would you know about cheap wine?' she scorned as she moved to sit in one of the armchairs, bending her legs at the knees before tucking her bare feet beneath her, the glass of brandy cradled in both her hands.

'Absolutely nothing,' he acknowledged dryly. 'So who was he, Samantha?'

'Who was who?' She tensed guardedly.

A very revealing guardedness and tension.

'The man at the hotel. Was he a past lover?' Xander pressed. 'Or maybe a current one, that you discovered was out on the town with another woman behind your back?'

'Don't be ridiculous!' she snapped crossly.

'Which part of what I said was ridiculous?' Xander raised his brows. 'The old lover or the new lover?'

'Both,' she dismissed. 'I don't have any old lovers, and I'm too busy working and being a mother to Daisy to have the time for any new ones either.'

Interesting...

Did that mean that Daisy's father had been the only man ever to share her bed? To touch every naked inch of her?

That seemed a little hard to believe when he knew that Samantha had been divorced for the past three years. Was she saying she also hadn't had sex with anyone for the past three years?

Xander didn't think he'd ever gone three months without a woman in his bed, let alone three years.

He looked across at her now through narrowed lids. 'How old are you?'

'I— What?' She looked nonplussed by the question.

'How old are you?' Xander repeated with a shrug. 'It's a simple enough question, I would have thought.'

Simple maybe, but Sam didn't see what her age had to do with anything, let alone their present—and deeply personal—conversation. 'How old are you?' she countered challengingly.

'Thirty-three,' he answered without hesitation.

That put Sam in the position of looking petty if she didn't reciprocate.

She sighed. 'I'm twenty-six.'

His brows rose. 'You must have been very young when you married?'

She grimaced. 'What does age have to do with anything when you fall in love?' Or *believe* you've fallen in love.

'I can't answer that, as I've never fallen in love.' Xander shrugged. 'That means you could only have been twenty-one when Daisy was born.'

'Yes.'

'And just twenty-three when you and your husband separated and then divorced?'

Sam felt her tension deepen as she wondered exactly where this conversation was going. 'Yes.'

'And you're saying that you haven't had sex even once since then? Not even with your ex-husband, for old times' sake?' Xander seemed to remember reading that a high percentage of separated couples did that.

Samantha's face paled, her hands shaking as she tightly gripped the glass of brandy. 'Don't be disgusting,' she finally managed to gasp.

Xander's eyes were narrowed as he gave a slow shake of his head. 'I don't buy the story you gave me earlier,

Samantha. I believe you did know the man who spoke to you at the hotel. That you know him very well.'

'Did *you* know him?'

'Me?' Xander frowned as he brought an image of the man back into his head. 'I couldn't see his face properly, because he was turned away from me, but I didn't know him, that I'm aware of.' Although it was interesting that Sam had asked. 'I still think that you did, or still do, know him very well indeed.'

She sat forward to slam the bulbous brandy glass down onto the table beside her with such vehemence that some of the alcohol spilt over the rim of the crystal glass. 'How did we progress from me telling you I'm tired, to you accusing me of having once been intimate with some stranger I met in a hotel who mistook me for someone else?'

Considering Xander's misgivings these past months, in regard to his own temper, and his doubts in his ability to control it, Samantha really *did* look amazing when she was angry.

Everything about her seemed to spark with life: her hair, her eyes, that flush in her cheeks, a puffy fullness to her slightly parted lips, her nipples aroused and pressing against her bra and the thin jersey of her jumper.

'I don't know—how did we come to that?' Xander asked softly. 'Maybe if you were to stop ly— Maybe if you told me the truth,' he amended as Samantha looked ready to explode if he called her a liar one more time tonight, 'I wouldn't have to keep asking the same question but in a different format.'

'The question being who was the man at the hotel earlier?' she snapped impatiently.

'Yes.'

'I've told you, I don't—' Sam broke off her protest as the sound of a piercing scream filled the apartment.

'Daisy!' She sprang quickly to her feet, not sparing Xander a second glance as she fled from the room and down the hallway to her daughter's bedroom.

CHAPTER SIX

SAM HAD LEFT Daisy's door slightly ajar and a night light on, as she always did, and she quickly pushed the door fully open now before running across the room to where her daughter was sitting up in bed. Daisy's eyes were wide, the tears streaming down her feverishly flushed face as she continued to scream.

'I'm here, Daisy.' Sam sat on the side of the bed to take her daughter into her arms. 'It's okay, darling,' she soothed as her daughter struggled to be set free. 'It's Mummy, darling. It's Mummy, Daisy,' she repeated firmly as she stroked her daughter's hair back from her flushed face.

Daisy stopped struggling but still trembled as she now looked up uncertainly. 'Mummy?'

Sam smiled at her reassuringly. 'You had a bad dream, darling. Just a dream,' she soothed as Daisy, calmer now, snuggled against her for comfort.

At the same time Sam's thoughts were inwardly racing. Had Daisy recognised Malcolm at the hotel earlier, after all? Either consciously, or subconsciously? And was that the reason for her daughter's nightmare?

It was like one of those night terrors that Daisy had suffered from as a very young child, but she hadn't had a single one in the past three years. Not since they'd left Malcolm.

'Is she okay?'

Sam turned sharply to look at Xander as he quietly entered the bedroom, an anxious frown on her face as she wondered how Daisy would react to the presence of a man in her bedroom so soon after her nightmare.

'Xander!' Daisy pulled out of Sam's arms before launching herself off the bed towards him.

Giving Sam a very definitive answer to that question.

Xander only just managed to open his arms in time to the little girl. As it was, he had to drop his walking stick on the floor, swaying precariously for several seconds as his injured leg threatened to collapse beneath him. Daisy might only be a lightweight, but her sudden weightfirm grasp on his leg caused a jolt of pain from Xander's thigh down to his knee.

Xander glanced at Samantha, noting the pallor of her cheeks, and the tears glistening in her shadowed eyes, her expression dazed, lost, as she sat on Daisy's bed looking at them both. Had there been something more sinister to Daisy's nightmare than that the little girl had simply had an over-stimulating day?

Daisy gave a yawn as she nestled against him and he slowly led her back to the bed.

Within seconds of her lying down, it seemed, the little girl had fallen back to sleep, as if the nightmare had never occurred or woken her up screaming. Chances were—Xander hoped—that Daisy wouldn't even remember she'd had the nightmare in the morning.

Her mother looked far less composed, Xander noted. Samantha's expression was still one of devastation, her face drawn and pale, shadows having deepened in those beautiful eyes.

'Let's go and finish our brandy,' Xander encouraged, wincing slightly as he straightened from picking his cane up from the bedroom floor.

'Maybe I should stay here for a while, just in case?' Samantha looked worriedly at her sleeping daughter.

'We'll hear her if she calls out again.' Xander held his hand out to Samantha as encouragement for her to stand up and leave the bedroom with him. It was the most he could manage, his leg now a painful and throbbing ache. 'Come on, Samantha,' he encouraged gruffly, knowing he badly needed to sit down.

Sam looked up at him blankly, too disturbed still by Daisy's nightmare to be able to respond.

Nightmares had been a regular occurrence when Daisy was much younger, and at the time Sam hadn't equated them with the tension of living with Malcolm. She had only realised that significance when they had abruptly stopped once she and Daisy had moved out of Malcolm's house and begun living on their own.

Until tonight.

It was too much of a coincidence, surely, that this should have happened after seeing Malcolm at the hotel earlier?

Admittedly Daisy had given no indication at the time that she had recognised her father, but maybe it hadn't been a conscious recognition but a subliminal one? The mind often played strange tricks on people, so maybe Daisy *had* recognised Malcolm without even being aware that she had?

'Samantha?' Xander asked again gently.

She blinked, focusing on him with effort. 'Sorry.'

She grimaced, giving herself a mental shake as she stood up. 'That was…unexpected,' she murmured as she followed him from the bedroom, leaving the door wide open this time, the better to be able to hear Daisy if she should call out again.

'Just over-excitement, do you think?' Xander wondered, replenishing their brandy glasses once they had returned to the sitting room, before handing one to Samantha. 'You'll feel better if you drink some more of that,' he encouraged gruffly. 'Slowly this time.'

Sam obediently took the glass from him, still worried about Daisy's nightmare, and not in the mood to argue with Xander over a glass of brandy. 'It was a different sort of day for her, with lots of unusual, if exciting, stimuli,' she answered him woodenly.

'But?' Xander observed her closely as he moved to sink down onto the sofa.

Because he really did think he was now in danger of falling down.

And wouldn't that look just wonderful, very manly, if he were to keel over and collapse at Samantha's bare feet?

His leg was giving him hell, after he had been on it for so many hours already today, and it hadn't helped when Daisy had launched herself at him just now when he hadn't been expecting it.

Although physically painful, having Daisy turn to him in that way for reassurance and comfort had surprisingly felt quite nice.

To know that Daisy liked him enough, trusted him enough, to want to turn to him for comfort was a good feeling after Xander's weeks of uncertainty about himself.

It made him even more determined to be worthy of Daisy's trust.

Samantha looked as if she was in need of a little comfort too right now.

'Come and sit beside me,' he instructed in a voice that brooked no argument. 'Don't make me have to stand up again and come get you, Samantha,' he added with a pained wince.

She looked at him blankly again for several long seconds, almost as if she had forgotten he was there, before moving stiffly across the room to sit down beside him.

Maybe she really had forgotten he was there?

Surely children of all ages had nightmares? A result of a too-active imagination at that age? Xander seemed to remember having them as a child himself. Of course, his had been due to living with his bastard of a father, but—

His gaze sharpened on Samantha as he once again took in the pallor of her cheeks, and those dark shadows in her unusual amethyst-coloured eyes.

He recalled the sense he'd had earlier that she was lying to him...

'The man at the hotel...' he spoke softly now '...he was your ex-husband, wasn't he?' It was a statement rather than a question. Because Xander didn't need to ask the question when he already knew, instinctively, that he had guessed correctly.

The man who had accosted Samantha at the hotel, and taken such a painful grip of her arm, causing her face to pale as he spoke to her so intensely, was Samantha's ex-husband, and Daisy's father.

Sam turned on the sofa to look at Xander, intending to deny the statement, only to think better of it as she saw the implacability of his expression, and the challenge in the darkness of his eyes. As if he expected her to deny it, and was silently warning her against even trying.

She drew in a deep and ragged breath before answering him.

'Yes,' she sighed. 'Yes, he was,' she repeated, her shoulders slumping as she sank back against the sofa, head resting back as she closed her eyes. 'It was— I— It was such a shock because I haven't set eyes on him for almost three years.'

'Until tonight.'

'Until tonight.' She nodded.

'It didn't look as if it was a joyful reunion?'

Sam didn't open her eyes. 'Not exactly the highlight of my day, no.'

'Well of course not—that was coming into the church earlier and seeing how handsome I looked in my morning suit!'

Sam opened one eye as she turned her head to look at Xander seated beside her, receiving a cheeky smile for her effort. 'Your modesty is just overwhelming!' she drawled as she closed her eye again.

It didn't help that Xander *had* looked gorgeous in his morning suit. Or that Sam's heart *had* given a lurch as she had gazed down the aisle on her arrival at the church, and seen him sitting at the front, looking as handsome and golden as that Norse god he so resembled.

The Sterne twins had made such a contrast as they'd stood up together at the sound of the Wedding March playing to announce Andy's arrival outside the church, Darius so dark and compelling, Xander all mesmerising light.

'Isn't it?' Xander teased lightly, relieved to see the smile now curving the fullness of Samantha's lips, even if it was being forced for his benefit.

Full and delectable lips that Xander had wanted to kiss since the moment he saw her in that red dress as she walked into the church earlier today.

His thoughts drifted back to the hotel earlier, and what he had been able to see of the man he now knew to be Samantha's ex-husband. He had been tall in an expensively tailored dark suit, his face strong in profile, dark hair peppered with silver at the temples. He must have been some years older than Samantha.

But what did it matter what he looked like or how old he was, when Samantha claimed the man had been out of the picture, out of her life, for the past three years?

And out of Daisy's, too?

Xander turned on the sofa, his thigh now gently touching the length of hers. 'How does Daisy visit her father if you haven't seen your ex-husband for three years?'

Her mouth twisted. 'She doesn't.'

Xander frowned. 'But—'

'I don't want to talk about this any more tonight, Xander, okay?' Samantha snapped as she sat forward with the obvious intention of standing up.

'No, it's not okay.' Xander put his hand on her shoulder to prevent her from standing up. 'I want to understand, Samantha. I need to understand.'

'Why?'

'Because for some unknown reason I care!'

She gave a shake of her head. 'You don't even know me.'

'But I'm trying to.'

Samantha looked at him for several long seconds before giving a shake of her head. 'No. I—I can't do this.' Once again she attempted to stand up.

Unacceptable.

Totally unacceptable.

Samantha might not want to answer his questions right now, but that didn't change the desire Xander had felt all day to take this woman in his arms and kiss her. And now he wanted to keep on kissing her, until Samantha could think of nothing and no one else but him.

Was that even wise on his part, when the two of them were going to be living here together for the next two weeks?

After all the upsets Samantha had already been through today?

Oh, to hell with what was wise!

Xander *needed* to kiss Samantha, more than he wanted to breathe, and as much as he wanted to eliminate the sadness from her lips and those deep shadows from her eyes. 'Let me in, Samantha,' he groaned achingly as he moved closer to her.

Sam's eyes widened as Xander's face began to lower towards hers, the arm draped across the back of the sofa now dropping lightly down onto her shoulders, as she realised he was about to kiss her.

'Xander—' Her weak protest was cut short as Xander's lips claimed hers in a gentle exploratory kiss.

Her heart leapt in her chest at the first touch of those sensually sculpted lips against her own, her hand seeming to move up of its own volition to cup Xander's slightly bristly cheek as he deepened the kiss, caressing and tasting, his arms moving about her waist as he pulled her body in close against him.

Sam had no resistance to those heated kisses, each more passionate than the last, the desire thrumming hotly through her body as she pressed her breasts against Xander's chest in an effort to try and ease some of the ache in her sensitive nipples.

Her breath caught in her throat as Xander's tongue now swept inside the heat of her mouth, with all the assurance of a Viking invader laying claim to his prize.

Xander gave a groan as he pressed Samantha gently back, until she lay beneath him on the sofa, her breasts warm and soft against the hardness of his chest, his legs becoming entangled with hers as they lay together, the evidence of his arousal a throbbing ache between them.

He murmured his pleasure as he felt Samantha's fingers in his hair as his lips now trailed across the warmth of her cheek and down the column of her throat, teeth nipping lightly on the lobe of her ear, causing her to moan huskily.

His lips moved lower, exploring the shadowed hollows at the base of her silky throat, one of his hands moving beneath her sweater against the heat of her skin. Samantha groaned low in her throat as one of his hands cupped her breast, its fullness filling his palm.

It was Xander's turn to groan as he felt the turgid heat of her nipple pressing against the material of her bra. He pushed her sweater up and out of the way as his lips trailed down to kiss the bared slopes of her breasts before unfastening her bra. He raised his head so that he could look down at her deliciously bared breasts.

Completely bared breasts that revealed the tattoo of an eagle soaring on the upper slope of her left breast.

'I knew it,' Xander groaned achingly even as he lowered his head and his tongue traced the outline of that utterly sexy tattoo.

He immediately realised his mistake in having spoken, as he felt Samantha tense and still beneath him, her fingers tightening briefly in his hair before moving down to his chest as she began to push him away.

'Please, Xander,' she groaned when he didn't move. 'You have to stop now!'

'Why do I?' he murmured distractedly as he continued to gaze down at those perfect breasts, tipped by swollen and aroused nipples. He was too turned on, too lost to the pleasure that was Samantha, to want to stop this just yet.

'Xander, please!' Her tone was more urgent now. 'I don't— We can't do this.' A sob caught in her throat as she pushed against his chest in earnest.

The haze of desire was slow to lift inside Xander's head, and it took him several seconds to realise that Samantha was pushing against him.

His head lifted slowly as he looked at her, those perfect rounded breasts quickly rising and falling as she breathed heavily, her cheeks pale, her kiss-swollen lips parted, and her eyes wide pools of anguish.

Anguish?

Because Xander had kissed and caressed her?

Kisses and caresses she had seemed to enjoy?

Seemed...

Could Xander be wrong about Samantha's response? Could he have wanted to kiss and touch her so much that he had mistaken her initial lack of protest as encouragement?

Was it possible that it had been so long since he last spent any time with a woman, held a woman in his arms, that he had misread the signals? That he was so physically frustrated he was guilty of kissing the first woman who had seemed willing?

Well, that last bit wasn't true, at least; the bridesmaid at the wedding had been more than willing to share his bed tonight. Hell, she had been more than willing for them to book into a room at the hotel for the night!

She just hadn't been the woman that Xander wanted.

Because the woman now lying beneath him was the woman he wanted. Samantha Smith. Mother to Daisy Smith.

And the ex-wife of the man who had upset her earlier at the hotel...

Damn it, *of course* he had misread the signals!

Samantha hadn't been inviting him to kiss her just now. He had seen it himself; she had been in need of comfort after being so suddenly, so unexpectedly, confronted by her ex-husband. And then her daughter had woken screaming from a nightmare. A nightmare that had caused Daisy to turn to him for that same comfort.

Xander lifted himself up and away from Samantha before standing up, instantly wincing as the aching pain intensified in his leg. 'I'm sorry.' He ran an agitated hand through the heavy thickness of his hair.

The same hair that Samantha had tugged and pulled on a short time ago as she'd returned—when he had *thought* she'd returned—the heat of his kisses. Hell, maybe she had been trying to push him away even then!

Xander turned away from the guilt he felt just looking at Samantha as she refastened her bra and straightened her sweater before sitting upright on the sofa, her eyes dark and bruised-looking, her lips puffy from their kisses. 'I'm sorry,' he repeated abruptly. '*That* really was inappropriate of me.'

Sam knew it had been.

But oh, how she wished she hadn't needed to stop their kisses but could instead have taken what Xander had so obviously been offering: a night of uncomplicated and passionate sex.

Except it wouldn't be uncomplicated, not when Xander was the man she wanted to make love with, rather than her ex-husband who was demanding she go to bed with him again. Just thinking about Malcolm's threats earlier was enough to give *her* nightmares!

But her problems had nothing to do with Xander. The only reason she was staying in his apartment at all was to take care of him.

This was a *job,* for goodness' sake.

A job that certainly didn't come with the fringe benefit of sleeping with the boss.

Thank goodness Xander had spoken to her and broken the sensual spell she had fallen under, reminding her of where she was. Who she was with!

She was just so aware of his lethal attraction. The desire he had aroused in her that she had thought long dead.

But it wasn't only that. She was just as drawn to knowing the reasons behind those dark shadows that she occasionally saw lurking in the depths of his eyes. As if he had his own painful memories he had to deal with on a daily basis. Memories Sam wanted to know, and possibly share with him.

Which was utterly ridiculous.

Why on earth would Xander Sterne, billionaire playboy, have any painful memories, let alone want to share them with someone like her?

Admittedly his father had died when Xander was still quite young, which must have been difficult for him, but other than that he had led a charmed life. He was rich as Croesus, was obviously loved by his twin and his mother and stepfather. And, if the bridesmaid from earlier was any example, then women were obviously falling over themselves just to be with him.

So why on earth would he ever feel anything more than a fleeting attraction towards her, let alone a need to share any of his private life with the woman hired to take care of him while his brother was away on his honeymoon?

He wouldn't, came the unequivocal answer.

Even if there was something to share. Which there so obviously wasn't.

'I *am* sorry, Samantha.'

She didn't look at Xander as she nodded abruptly. 'So am I.'

'What do you have to be sorry about?'

A desire that had shocked her to her core.

Acknowledging Xander's lethal attraction and acting upon it were two distinctly different things, when Sam hadn't so much as looked at a man with interest since the end of her marriage to Malcolm. Even without Malcolm's threats earlier this evening, her ex-husband's unreasonable behaviour during their marriage should have been a stark lesson to her never to be fooled again by a good-looking face and a charming manner.

Tonight she had definitely returned the hunger of Xander's kisses. And allowed Xander to touch her more intimately than any other man had but her husband. She'd also been aroused in a way she could never remember being aroused before. Not even at the start of her marriage to Malcolm, the man she had believed herself to be in love with...

And that knowledge now terrified her!

She didn't want to feel anything for Xander Sterne beyond the necessary concern of a carer for her charge. She didn't want to like him. Or desire him. She certainly didn't want to ever be stupid enough to fall in love with him!

'Go to bed, Samantha,' Xander bit out harshly as he saw the way her face had now paled. 'I'll manage to undress myself this evening and you can help me shower in the morning,' he assured her dryly as she looked at him questioningly.

Her expression was noticeably one of relief. 'Are you sure?'

'Very,' Xander confirmed as Samantha rushed from the room.

Or a lustful Xander Sterne...

CHAPTER SEVEN

'GET IN THE CAR, Sam!'

It was such a pleasant sunny Monday morning that Sam had decided to walk Daisy to school, before leaving her daughter safely in her classroom.

Despite Malcolm's threats on Saturday night—threats Sam had been trying to forget all weekend—she was completely unprepared, as she left the school grounds, to see Malcolm sitting behind the wheel of the sleek black saloon car, the passenger-seat window lowered so that he could speak to her.

Sam desperately tried to gather her scattered wits together as she glared into the open window at him. She didn't fool herself for a moment that this was going to be any more pleasant a meeting than the one on Saturday evening had been.

Malcolm's eyes narrowed to blue chips of ice as she made no move to do as he instructed. 'Get in the damned car, Sam,' he repeated harshly. 'Unless you would prefer I get out of the car and we talk right there on the pavement?' he added challengingly, as several of the other mothers leaving the school gave them obviously curious looks as they walked past them.

Unsurprisingly, when for the last eight months Sam

had always been alone when she delivered and collected Daisy from school.

'What are you even doing here, Malcolm?' she demanded as she wrenched the car door open and slid into the passenger seat beside him, knowing she had no other choice if she didn't want to cause a scene. And for Daisy's sake, she really didn't.

Her one defiant gesture was to deliberately slam the car door shut. She knew how it would irritate Malcolm; unlike his behaviour towards his wife and daughter, Malcolm had always been obsessive about the care and treatment of his cars.

Shut in the confines of the vehicle with him, Sam instantly became aware of the spicy—and expensive—aftershave Malcolm had always worn, and which she had only ever associated with him. To a degree that if she had happened to smell it randomly these past three years, on some other man, it had always made her feel slightly nauseous. As it now caused her to swallow down the bile rising in her throat.

Goodness knew the rest of her weekend had been awkward enough, without this.

There had been Malcolm's horrible threats for her to deal with, and on top of that Sam had been dreading seeing Xander again on Sunday morning after the intimacies of the previous evening.

But she needn't have worried about the latter, because Xander obviously regretted that lapse as much as she did. The two of them had barely exchanged half a dozen words as she'd helped him in and then out of the shower yesterday morning. Later he had refused her polite invitation for him to join her and Daisy when they went swimming an hour or so after lunch. And he had been secluded in his study working when the two of them returned to the apartment, assuring Sam he would get himself a snack to eat later in the evening if he felt hungry.

If he had done so then Sam had been fast asleep in her bed when it happened.

The only positive thing about yesterday had been that Daisy had seemed completely unaware that she'd had a nightmare the previous night. Nor had there been a repeat of it last night, thank goodness.

Sam looked at Malcolm warily. 'I wasn't even aware you knew where Daisy went to school.'

He gave her a satisfied smile. 'You might be surprised at what I've been able to find out about you and Daisy in the past twenty-four hours.'

She gasped. 'Have you had someone spying on me?'

That smile faded as he now looked at her with icy eyes through narrowed lids. 'I had no idea I needed to until I saw you at the Midas Hotel on Saturday evening,' he dismissed harshly.

Sam's heart sank at the mention of that meeting and Malcolm's threats to her.

Malcolm's mouth thinned. 'I hired a private investigator, and guess what he's already found out? My ex-wife and my daughter are currently living with Xander Sterne in his apartment.' His eyes glittered darkly.

Colour warmed Sam's previously pale cheeks. 'It's none of your business where we live, Malcolm.'

'I'm making it my business, Sam!' Malcolm reached out to take a painful grip of her wrist. 'Xander Sterne!' He gave a disbelieving shake of his head.

She struggled to free herself. 'Let go of me!' she ordered when Malcolm's fingers tightened more painfully.

He gritted his teeth. 'You obviously have a thing about rich and powerful men,' he taunted.

'If you mean that I despise them, then yes I do.'

'The fact you're living with Sterne would seem to contradict that statement.'

Sam gave an inward shiver at the cold fury she could now see in Malcolm's eyes. 'I am not romantically involved with Mr Sterne.'

'My information says you are,' Malcolm rasped. 'And you've dragged my daughter into your little affair,' he continued purposefully. 'I think that might be grounds for bringing your fitness as a mother into question.'

'How dare you?' Sam rounded on him furiously, breathing hard in her agitation. 'How dare you even say that to me after— *You're* the one who has always refused to acknowledge her existence! The one who *sold* his daughter in exchange for my not asking for a divorce settlement, which would have enabled me to stay at home and be a full-time mother to Daisy. How dare you now accuse me of being an unfit mother, when you have never been a father to Daisy, even for a minute?' She glowered at him.

He shrugged broad shoulders. 'Maybe I've changed? Maybe I realise it's time I got to know my daughter better? I'm sure the courts would lend a sympathetic ear if I were to—'

'No!' Sam protested fiercely at the threat. 'I won't allow it. I won't allow *you* anywhere near— We had a deal!' she accused heatedly. 'No divorce settlement for me in exchange for full custody of Daisy.'

'And as I said to you on Saturday evening, there's absolutely no reason why that can't continue,' he came back softly. 'Once you've ditched Sterne and become my mistress, of course.'

Sam stared at him in complete horror, feeling as if her feet had been knocked from underneath her. 'I won't—I can't!'

'But you will,' Malcolm insisted. 'For Daisy's sake, you know you will.'

Sam looked at him searchingly, once again able to see that cruelty in Malcolm's eyes and in the harsh slashes beside his nose and mouth. She wanted Daisy to have nothing to do with this man. Being her daughter's biological father didn't make Malcolm any less the cruel and controlling man he had always been beneath that outward layer of social charm. There was no telling what damage Malcolm might do to Daisy emotionally if he were to obtain weekly visiting rights with her.

'Why are you doing this, Malcolm?' she prompted emotionally, knowing she was on the verge of tears. And she really didn't want to give Malcolm the satisfaction of reducing her to tears, when he must already be aware, by the hold he had of her wrist, how badly she was shaking. '*Why?*'

'Obviously because I've decided that I want you back in my bed.' He shrugged.

Sam stared at him dazedly. 'I don't love you, Malcolm. I don't even like you!'

'What has that got to do with anything?' He looked at her pityingly. 'The thing is, Sam, I really don't like the idea of you belonging to any other man but me. I realised when I saw you again the other night that what's mine should stay mine.'

'I don't *belong* to anyone, Malcolm.'

'Not for the past three years you haven't, no.' Malcolm confirmed that he really had had her investigated. 'And you aren't going to belong to anyone else now, either. So I suggest that you and Daisy move out of Sterne's apartment as soon as you've told him your little affair is over. Preferably before the end of the week,' Malcolm bit out.

Sam frowned. 'I can't do that.'

'That's a pity.' His tone was deceptively mild.

And Sam wasn't deceived for a moment. 'You don't understand,' she came back agitatedly. 'I don't *live* with Xander Sterne, I work for him. As his carer,' she added impatiently as Malcolm eyed her sceptically. 'He was involved in a car accident, and now needs help to— to—' Somehow Sam didn't think it was a good idea to tell Malcolm that one of the things she did for Xander was to help him in and out of the shower! 'I cook for him and help him when necessary,' she substituted.

Talking of which, it was almost time for her to drive Xander to his physiotherapy session as Paul had the day off.

'And those *duties* include you sleeping with him too?'

'You're wrong!' Embarrassed colour heated her cheeks as she recalled how close she had come to doing exactly that on Saturday night.

A guilty blush which caused Malcolm's eyes to narrow dangerously. 'Even if what you say is true, you aren't seriously expecting me to believe that Xander Sterne has a beautiful woman living in his apartment with him, but that he hasn't slept with her yet?'

'That's exactly what I'm telling you,' Sam maintained stubbornly.

'And there's no yet about it,' she added firmly. 'I'm

only staying at his apartment for a couple of weeks,' she insisted. 'Just until his brother returns from his honeymoon. You were at the wedding on Saturday, too, so you know I'm telling the truth.'

'About Darius being away on his honeymoon, at least, yes.' He nodded. '*If* what you say is true—'

'It is.'

'Then it won't be difficult to find someone else to take care of him while his brother is away so that you can move out in the next few days.'

Not difficult at all, which was why Sam was so grateful to have this job at all; the Sterne family could have employed anyone to care for Xander, but they had chosen her, Andy had chosen her.

'I can't do that,' she insisted, knowing she couldn't let Andy down, or forget the fact that the money she earned these two weeks would pay her bills.

Malcolm now eyed her thoughtfully. 'You've changed, Sam; once upon a time you wouldn't have dreamt of answering me back.'

'Once upon a time I was stupid enough to think myself in love with you, too!' she replied heatedly, knowing she shouldn't antagonise Malcolm in the circumstances, but totally unable to stop herself from retaliating to that last jibe.

His mouth twisted into the semblance of a smile. 'But not any longer.'

'That's one of the reasons we're divorced, remember?' Sam eyed him warily.

'I remember only too well.' Malcolm's mouth thinned. 'I have never liked failure, Sam. And I definitely consider my marriage to you to be in that category.'

She gave a pained frown. 'And whose fault was that?

If you had told me you didn't want children then I would never have married you in the first place.' Having long been an orphan, Sam had always wanted children of her own. She hadn't just wanted children, she had *ached* for a family of her own, to love and care for, and to be loved and cared for in return. Instead she had got Malcolm.

And Daisy...

Daisy made up for all the pain, all the disillusionment of those unhappy years of being married to a man as cold and controlling as her ex-husband.

She would do anything to protect Daisy.

Anything at all.

'I want you back in my bed, Sam, and I think you know me well enough to know that I'll use any means at my disposal to achieve that,' Malcolm informed her confidently.

Almost as if he had been able to read her thoughts.

And maybe he had. Malcolm already knew that Daisy was Sam's weak spot, her Achilles heel. And now he was once again using that weakness to his advantage, in an effort to force her into resuming a relationship with him. A relationship that horrified Sam so much she felt physically ill.

'No,' she answered him woodenly.

He arched mocking brows. 'No?'

'No,' she repeated firmly.

She had thought about this all weekend, finally accepting that she couldn't allow herself to be browbeaten by Malcolm again, to be forced into becoming his mistress. She just couldn't!

There had to be some other way. Some way to stop his blackmail once and for all. There just had to be.

'And if I insist?'

Sam was breathing hard, her emotions in turmoil. But she couldn't, she wouldn't, give in to Malcolm's blackmail. Because she knew that once it started it would never stop. Until one day she would wake up and find herself once again imprisoned, totally entrapped.

She drew herself up determinedly. 'You can insist all you like, Malcolm, but my answer will still be no.'

He shrugged, his fingers once again tightening painfully about her wrist. 'Obviously you would rather the two of us talked through our lawyers.'

'I would *rather*—' She broke off, her eyes stinging with unshed tears, knowing she had to get away, before she gave Malcolm the satisfaction of seeing those tears fall. 'I have nothing more to say to you, Malcolm. And I have to go now,' she added before he could speak again. 'I have to drive Mr Sterne to his physio appointment.'

'Have dinner with me this evening, Sam, and we can discuss this further then.'

Sam repressed a shiver of fear. 'I'm not going to do this, Malcolm,' she told him shakily. 'Not dinner this evening, not any of it.'

He chuckled softly. 'Give it time, Sam, and you'll do exactly as I want,' he drawled confidently. 'You have until the end of the week,' he added coldly. 'After which I'm calling my lawyer.'

Sam wrenched her wrist painfully from his grasp before opening the car door and climbing quickly out onto the pavement, slamming the door closed behind her, before turning on her heel and walking off in the direction of Xander's apartment.

All the time aware that her wrist ached abominably, her knees were knocking together, and her body was shaking in complete awareness of the fact that Malcolm had just demanded that she become his mistress by threatening Daisy.

A demand, despite her defiance of him, that placed her as the fly to Malcolm's spider...

Xander had been aware that there was something seriously wrong with Samantha from the moment she'd returned from walking Daisy to school earlier that morning. Her face was pale, her eyes almost feverish, and she was totally distracted as she went off to change into a red long-sleeved shirt before silently driving him to his physio appointment. The return journey had been made just as quietly.

Xander was thoroughly worried by her uncharacteristic silence by the time they arrived back at his apartment just before one o'clock, and he now sat at the breakfast bar watching her as she moved about the kitchen preparing lunch. 'Are you still angry with me for what happened on Saturday evening?' he finally prompted gruffly.

Events that had resulted in him spending two sleepless nights unable to banish thoughts of Samantha, who was lying in her own bed just a short distance down the hallway. He had wondered if she was also awake and thinking of him.

Somehow Xander doubted that very much.

Samantha had been so cool towards him on Sunday, so businesslike in her dealings with him today, even when helping him in and out of the shower this morning. An occasion when he had been unable to hide the arousal her touch incited in him. He might as well have been a block of wood for all the notice Samantha had taken of that!

And that rankled.

This whole indifference thing Samantha now had going towards him rankled!

Okay, so he had read the signs wrong on Saturday evening, had realised almost immediately that he should have offered her comfort, with his arms and words, rather than kissing her. He was also aware he wasn't feeling his best right now. His leg was still aching badly from all the extra activity on Saturday; the wedding, Daisy throwing herself at him, *kissing Samantha*. But he had never had a woman react towards him with such indifference as Samantha had been doing these past two days and nights.

Maybe he was losing his touch?

And maybe Samantha would just rather forget those kisses had ever happened?

Wouldn't that be a dent to his already bruised ego?

'What?' She turned to look at him blankly now, almost as if she had forgotten he was there for a moment, colour suffusing her cheeks as his words penetrated her thoughts. 'Not in the least,' she dismissed, her head now buried in the refrigerator. 'I'd forgotten about it.'

Her sudden blush seemed to indicate that it really had been the last thing on her mind.

Oh, she hadn't forgotten about it yesterday, had been very skittish towards him over breakfast, so much so that Xander had decided it would be better if the two of them avoided each other's company for the rest of the day, especially in front of Daisy.

But here and now? Yes, Xander could well believe that this Samantha had completely forgotten about the two of them kissing on Saturday night. The question was, what had happened since yesterday—since breakfast this morning, in fact—to cause Samantha to be so distracted that she wasn't even defending herself? It was very unlike her.

'Do you want ham or cheese for your sandwich?' she asked distractedly now.

'Both,' Xander answered her just as dismissively. 'Samantha?'

'In that case, your lunch is ready,' she announced briskly.

Xander glanced down at the breakfast bar, his eyes narrowing as he saw that only one place had been laid. 'Aren't you eating too?'

'I'm not hungry.'

'You only had coffee for breakfast.'

'Are you spying on me, too?' She glared at him accusingly. 'Because if you are, I advise you to stop. Right now!' She was trembling with anger.

'Whoa, Samantha.' Xander reached out with both arms to grasp her about the waist as she would have turned and marched angrily from the room, his leg giving a protesting jolt of pain as he did so. Xander ignored that pain as he instead looked down searchingly into Samantha's face; her eyes still sparkled with that earlier temper, her cheeks were flushed with anger, her mouth—her mouth…!

Xander was breathing hard as he gazed down at that perfect, tempting bow, the bottom lip fuller than the top. These were the lips that had haunted him day and night these past two days. And right now those delicious lips were as red and plump as ripe berries, no doubt caused by that same flush of anger.

Why was Samantha so angry? It seemed completely out of context to their conversation.

'What did you mean when you said *too*?' Xander asked, his eyes narrowing suspiciously. 'Who else has been spying on you, Samantha?' he prompted.

Sam's anger left her as quickly as it had arisen as she realised her mistake. Xander was just too intelligent, too astute, not to have noted and questioned her earlier comment. Or to add two and two together and not to come up with the right answer. If not now, then at some later time.

Xander hadn't recognised Malcolm on Saturday, and a part of Sam didn't want Xander to know that she had once been married to a man like Malcolm Howard, let alone that he was now threatening her.

She trembled every time she thought of her earlier conversation with Malcolm—which had been often in the past few hours! She knew she couldn't allow Malcolm to come even close to demanding visiting rights with Daisy.

Which meant what?

That she would have to telephone Malcolm and agree to have dinner with him this evening, at least?

Sam hated the thought of even doing that, let alone agreeing to Malcolm's other demands.

But she knew Malcolm too well, knew how clever he was at pretence, how charming he could be, and how easily he would be able to fool a judge into believing he was totally contrite regarding his previous attitude towards his daughter, and that he now wanted the chance to become a father to her.

Daisy would be totally bewildered by suddenly having a father she had never known thrust into her life. Her daughter would be hurt and confused. Miserable. And Sam would be just as miserable, but also worried out of her mind on those occasions when Malcolm was allowed to take Daisy out. It simply couldn't be allowed to happen.

She looked up at Xander. 'Would you please release me?'

Xander looked down at her searchingly, totally unsettled by the look of pained resolve in her eyes. As if she had come to a decision she didn't like. A decision she hated, if the grey tinge to her cheeks was any indication.

His mouth thinned. 'Answer my question, Samantha.'

'Release me now, Xander.' She challenged him as she pulled out of his arms.

Leaving Xander with no choice but to reach out and grasp hold of the breakfast bar in an effort to stop himself from overbalancing and toppling over, at the same time as he reached out with the other hand to fold the length of his fingers about Samantha's wrist to prevent her from moving any further away from him.

Samantha's gasp of pain was the last reaction Xander was expecting to so light a physical touch. 'What's wrong?' He scowled darkly as he lifted her arm and saw the bandage wrapped about her wrist, previously concealed beneath the long-sleeved red shirt she had changed into after taking Daisy to school. 'What happened to your wrist?' he demanded. 'Did you cut yourself? Sprain your wrist? Tell me how you did this, Samantha.'

'Or what? Will you *make* me tell you, Xander?' she added scornfully. 'Refuse to release me until I do?'

All of the above, as far as Xander was concerned, because he was not allowing Samantha to leave this kitchen until he knew exactly what was going on with her. Because something most certainly was!

Except…

He could see by Samantha's almost resigned expression that she was expecting him to bully her into giving him an answer.

Xander might be guilty of a lot of things—might now be living in fear of his temper allowing him to do even worse things—but bullying a woman, in any way, certainly wasn't one of them.

He maintained a light hold on Samantha's arm as his thoughts drifted back to this morning. She had seemed quiet but cheerful enough when she'd made them all breakfast. Her mood had only changed to one of complete introspection after she'd returned from taking Daisy to school. The same time that she had changed into the long-sleeved shirt.

Xander's eyes narrowed purposefully as he lifted that wrist before folding back some of the elasticated bandage to reveal the multicoloured bruising beneath.

Samantha immediately attempted to snatch her wrist out of his grasp. 'Don't!'

'Who did this?' Xander demanded with icy intensity, a red tide of anger washing over him as he recognised the bruises about the delicacy of Samantha's wrist as being in the pattern of fingerprints. A man's larger fingerprints, if he wasn't mistaken. 'Who did this to you, Samantha?' he demanded harshly.

Tears glistened in her eyes, her lashes blinking, and her bottom lip trembling as she attempted to prevent those tears from falling. 'I caught it on—'

'Don't even attempt to lie to me about this,' he advised softly. 'I assure you that you won't like me when

I'm angry,' he added as he felt that red tide threatening to overwhelm and control him.

Samantha's eyes were wide, her throat moving convulsively as she swallowed. As clear evidence that she also saw and recognised that anger? That it frightened her?

Well, damn it, it frightened Xander too!

It was exactly what he had been running away from facing these past few weeks. The reason he had begun to avoid other people. The reason he had distanced himself from his family. And hadn't taken a woman to his bed. The very reason he had been so against Samantha and Daisy coming to live here with him in the first place.

Xander released Samantha abruptly before stepping away from her. 'Who hurt you, Samantha?' His gaze sharpened as a thought suddenly occurred to him. 'It was him, wasn't it? Your ex-husband,' he stated flatly. 'You saw him again this morning when you took Daisy to school. Did you *arrange* to meet him?'

'No! Absolutely not. Never,' Sam instantly denied the accusation, giving a shudder of distaste at the mere suggestion she would deliberately spend time with Malcolm ever again.

Except it was what she was thinking of doing now, wasn't it? By giving in to Malcolm's demands?

She dropped down onto one of the stools at the breakfast bar. Before her knees buckled beneath her and she fell down.

'Samantha?'

'Just give me a minute or two.' She waved a hand dismissively in front of her face, head bent as she breathed in deeply.

'Do you still love him?'

Sam's gaze flew incredulously to the grimness of Xander's face. 'I absolutely do not!'

'Obviously.' Xander winced as he both heard and saw her obvious vehemence to the idea. 'So why would you—?' He paused, breathing softly. 'You were obviously upset after seeing him again on Saturday evening. He physically hurt you this morning, as well as upset you again. You're almost in tears now just talking about him.' He studied Sam intently. 'What hold does he have over you that you don't just tell him to go to—? Daisy.' Xander's brow cleared as realisation dawned. 'The bastard is threatening Daisy in some way.'

That red tide of anger rose even further at the thought of Samantha's ex-husband daring to threaten Daisey's happiness. In any way.

Bad enough that Samantha's ex-husband had physically hurt her today, the man deserved to be horse-whipped for that alone, but the thought that he might also have threatened Daisy in some way was totally unacceptable.

Xander came to a decision.

'Samantha.'

'Yes?' She raised her head to look up at him uncertainly.

'Samantha, I—' Xander drew in a deep breath, knowing he was about to take a huge leap of faith, but also knowing that he had no choice if he was to persuade Samantha into trusting him again.

He never talked about his abusive childhood to anyone, but if he wanted Samantha to talk to him now then he knew he had to tell her what had happened to him. That *he* now had to trust her, to confide in her, if he wanted her to trust and confide in him.

And he did want that. He wanted more than anything for Samantha to trust him.

He drew in a deep and ragged breath. 'Samantha, until I was twelve years old I lived with a father who enjoyed beating the hell out of me.'

She blinked, and then blinked again, as if she were having difficulty taking in what Xander had just told her. As no doubt she was. His childhood hardly fitted in with that charming billionaire playboy image the media were so fond of portraying.

An image that hid the vulnerability beneath.

A vulnerability Xander found himself surprisingly willing to share with Samantha.

'Darius, too?' she finally asked huskily.

A nerve pulsed in Xander's jaw. 'No, just me.'

Samantha moistened the dryness of her lips with the tip of her pink tongue. 'What happened when you were twelve?'

Xander's jaw tightened. 'My father died.'

Malcolm had been emotionally cruel, deliberately so, but he had never been physically violent, either towards herself or Daisy. Until today, Sam reminded herself with a frown. Today Malcolm had felt absolutely no compunction about hurting her. In fact, she thought he had rather enjoyed it.

She swallowed. 'How?'

'Shortly after putting me in the hospital with a broken arm and concussion, my father fell down the stairs in a drunken stupor and broke his neck.'

'I don't recall any of this ever being in the newspapers.'

'It wasn't,' he confirmed abruptly. 'No one outside of my close family has ever known about the abuse.'

Sam was absolutely horrified at the thought of this man's childhood. 'Xander.'

'Samantha, I didn't tell you this so that your compassionate heart would feel sorry for me.'

'It doesn't,' she assured swiftly, knowing that Xander's pride was such that he wouldn't want, or welcome, pity from anyone. That the self-confident man he had become, the caring man *he* was towards Daisy, the empathy he had just shown her, were clear evidence that he had risen above his abusive childhood.

'Not even a little bit?'

'Well, of course a little bit!' Sam replied exasperatedly, a large part of her wishing that Xander's father were still alive, so that she could verbally upbraid him for his treatment of his son.

As a way of slaying Xander's dragon for him in a way that she couldn't seem to slay her own?

She grimaced. 'I would have to be completely heartless to remain immune to what you've just told me about your childhood,' she assured him briskly.

If he was honest with himself, Xander was feeling a little off-kilter now that he had actually spoken to Samantha about his father. He really didn't discuss his private life with people outside his family. Ever. And yet he had just done so with Samantha.

Admittedly it had been as a way of encouraging Samantha to feel that she could confide in him about her ex-husband, that she could trust him, but even so it was something Xander had never imagined sharing with any woman.

And yet...

He had confided in Samantha as a way of letting her know she could trust him with her own secrets, he

had never imagined that by doing so he would somehow feel…free. As if a heavy weight had been lifted
from his shoulders.

And his heart.

CHAPTER EIGHT

XANDER GAVE A humourless smile. 'Maybe you would feel differently about all that and about me, if I were to tell you that for the past few months I've been inwardly fighting the possibility that I might actually be like him?'

'That's utterly ridiculous,' Samantha dismissed without hesitation.

Xander's eyes widened at the absolute certainty in her voice. 'What makes you say that?'

She smiled confidently. 'I may not have known you for very long, Xander, but I do know you well enough to be able to see you are totally incapable of hurting a woman or a child. You obviously didn't want Daisy and I here, and yet you have been incredibly kind to both of us. So much so that Daisy adores you,' she added firmly even as she stepped forward to place the palm of her hand on Xander's chest. 'There's a good heart in there, Xander Sterne. A kind heart. One that wants to protect, not destroy.'

Xander looked down at her searchingly, breathing shallowly beneath the warm touch of her hand on his chest. 'Do you really believe that?' he finally asked.

'I know it.' Sam nodded.

Even after only a few days in his company Sam knew that initial fear she'd had, that he might be selfish and controlling like Malcolm, because he was even richer and more powerful than her ex-husband, wasn't even a possibility. Xander was arrogant and self-confident, and grumpy—no surprise given his present situation and the pain he was suffering.

But ultimately he had a good heart, a kind heart; his care and consideration of Daisy these past three days had proved that. As did his concern for her now. Sam had absolutely no doubt that Xander was a man who protected, that he was totally incapable of lashing out physically at a woman or child in temper.

'We may have our parents' genes, Xander,' she said quietly. 'You have your father's, as Daisy has her father's, but I have yet to see any of Malcolm in Daisy. Or any of the father that you have just described to me in you.' Her eyed narrowed. 'You had your car accident six weeks ago?'

'Sorry?' Xander frowned at her sudden change of subject.

'You said that you've been questioning yourself for the past few months as to whether or not you might be like your father,' Sam reminded him as she stepped back and allowed her hand to fall back to her side. 'Did your accident have anything to do with that?'

Xander gave a rueful grimace at her astuteness. 'Something had been building inside me for weeks before that night, but that night I witnessed a man in the Midas nightclub verbally berating and humiliating the woman he was with. And I wanted to pulverise him into the ground,' he acknowledged grimly.

'A perfectly understandable reaction; *I* would have

wanted to pulverise him too,' Samantha assured vehemently. 'Did you do it?'

'No.' A nerve pulsed in Xander's tightly clenched jaw. 'I wanted to, but somehow managed to keep control long enough to pass the problem off to security.'

'Doesn't that restraint prove to you that you're nothing like your father?' Samantha gave him an encouraging smile. 'That you never could be?'

Xander continued to look down at her for several long minutes, before drawing in a deep breath. 'Thank you for that. I appreciate it, after all I've just told you.'

He did appreciate Samantha's confidence, belief, in him. More than he could possibly say. More than he *dared* think about, when Samantha seemed so determined to keep him at arm's length, physically, at least. For the moment he would settle for her opening up to him emotionally.

'I want to help you, if I can, Samantha,' he encouraged gruffly. 'You aren't without powerful friends of your own now,' he pointed out softly. 'Andy and Darius. And now me.'

Was Xander her friend?

Sure, he had become fond of Daisy these past four days, but things had been so strained between the two of them since Saturday evening, that Sam had been sure Xander must be counting the days until she left his apartment.

His concern now and the confidences he had shared with her regarding his own childhood, while not exactly making them friends, had certainly broken down the barriers they had both been keeping about their emotions since Saturday evening.

'What did your ex-husband say to you this morning, Samantha?' he prompted gently.

She drew in a deep breath. 'Well, for one thing, he apparently isn't happy that Daisy and I are staying here in your apartment, even temporarily.'

'Tough.' Xander scowled. 'What else?'

'He wanted me to have dinner with him this evening.'

Xander stilled as he looked at Samantha.

'And are you going to accept the invitation?'

'I already turned him down.' She gave a humourless smile. 'And it was more of a threat than an invitation.'

'What does he want besides dinner?' Xander rasped harshly. As if he couldn't guess. As if he didn't already *know* what the man wanted!

Samantha was an incredibly beautiful woman, a woman with a warm and loving heart; any man would have to be completely stupid to have ever let her go in the first place.

'He wants me to become his mistress,' Samantha confirmed, her gaze no longer able to meet his.

Xander drew in a deep controlling breath, continuing to breathe deeply until he felt capable of talking again. 'And how does he intend to retaliate if you don't agree to that?'

The colour drained from Sam's cheeks. 'He said he'll apply to the court for visiting rights with Daisy. Which I can't allow to happen,' she continued emotionally. 'Malcolm never wanted Daisy in the first place. He ignored her very existence when we lived with him, by imposing all sorts of ridiculous rules regarding her behaviour. And he's had absolutely no interest in seeing her since the two of us parted and divorced.'

A nerve pulsed in Xander's tightly clenched jaw at the thought of any man—any father!—ignoring his own daughter in that way.

Although it certainly explained why it was Daisy never visited her father and why Samantha didn't want her to now.

It also explained the way Samantha had bristled with reaction to that list of rules Xander had come out with the evening she and Daisy arrived here.

No way, absolutely no way, was Xander going to allow Samantha's ex-husband to bully and blackmail her into doing what he wanted. Into forcing her to share his bed.

'Exactly who is he, Samantha?' he grated. 'Well you've already told me his name isn't Smith,' he rasped as Samantha looked up at him questioningly.

'Howard.' She swallowed, her gaze now avoiding meeting his. 'His name is Malcolm Howard.'

Xander's eyes narrowed. 'Of Howard Electronics? *That* Malcolm Howard?' He only knew the other man by reputation, mostly to do with business, although he seemed to recall hearing Howard had been married briefly a few years ago. He didn't remember ever hearing mention of a child from that marriage, though. Obviously that was because Howard had chosen never to tell anyone about the daughter he had no interest in.

Samantha drew in a deep breath. 'You know him?'

Xander shook his head. 'Not personally. I seem to recall he has a membership to the Midas nightclub.' A privilege Xander was now going to look into cancelling at the earliest opportunity! 'Darius knows him far better than I do. Of course, that's what Howard was doing at the hotel on Saturday; he was one of the evening guests invited to Darius and Miranda's wedding.'

'Yes.'

'I'm pretty sure Darius has no idea what sort of man he is.' Xander scowled. 'Did you know he—? No,' he answered his own question impatiently. 'You had absolutely no idea your ex-husband was going to be at the wedding too. If you had you would have made sure to leave before he arrived. Or possibly you would not have gone to the wedding at all.'

'No.'

'What did he do to you when you were married to him, Samantha?' Xander pressed softly.

She looked up at him wordlessly for several long seconds, a frown creasing her creamy brow. And then that frown cleared as she glanced down at her bandaged wrist. 'Emotional cruelty can be just as unpleasant as physical violence.'

He knew that, had watched his father torment and control his mother and brother for years, by physically threatening Xander. Just as Malcolm Howard's threats now, regarding Daisy, were designed to deliberately torment Samantha, to control her.

To a point that she was actually thinking of giving in to Howard's demands?

Over Xander's dead body was that going to happen.

He gave a shake of his head.

'Malcolm Howard is a very wealthy man, and yet you and Daisy—' He hesitated, wincing his discomfort as he realised what he had been about to say.

'And yet Daisy and I live in a one-bedroomed flat and I work at jobs like this one, and the one at Andy's studio, to make ends meet.' Samantha obviously felt no such reticence.

'Yes.' He frowned darkly.

She gave a rueful grimace. 'You already know so much, so why shouldn't you know the rest? Malcolm offered me a deal when I divorced him, a small monthly maintenance payment for Daisy, no alimony or settlement for me, the return of all the jewellery and gifts he had given me during our marriage, and in exchange he would give me full custody of Daisy.'

'Full custody of the child he didn't want in the first place?' Xander said softly.

'Yes.' She smiled shakily.

Xander had never heard of anything so diabolical in his life. It was utterly disgusting. Malcolm Howard was worth millions, and yet he had begrudged his ex-wife even the small amount of money she needed to be able to take care of her daughter?

A diabolical deal he was now threatening to renege on unless Samantha gave in to his demand that she become his mistress.

What sort of man did that to the woman he had once been married to, the same woman who was the mother of his child?

'Do you trust me, Samantha?' Xander asked huskily.

'To do what?' She eyed him warily.

'To help you and Daisy?'

To make sure that Howard suffered, in the way he had made Samantha and Daisy suffer, in the past, and now!

Did Sam trust Xander? It had been so long since she had relied on anyone. Since she had *trusted* anyone enough to rely on them; she had thought she could trust and rely on Malcolm once, and look how well that had turned out!

'Don't think about the past for now, Samantha,' Xander encouraged as he obviously saw, and guessed, the reason for her frown. 'Just concentrate on whether or not you trust me to find a way that will free you, and Daisy, of your ex-husband's hold on you once and for all.'

Did she want Xander to do that? Was this the answer, the miracle, she had been praying for earlier?

Did Sam really have any choice but to trust Xander, when her own and Daisy's future hung so precariously in the balance, once again because of Malcolm's threats?

She moistened the dryness of her lips before speaking. 'Why would you even want to help us? It isn't your problem.'

'I'm making it so,' he insisted grimly.

Sam looked at him wonderingly. 'You really are a sheep in wolf's clothing, aren't you?'

His mouth twisted wryly at that description. 'I'm actually a wolf in a wolf's clothing. But even wolves have a heart, Samantha. And, for obvious reasons, I utterly despise bullies,' he added harshly. 'So...' he straightened '...will you let me help you?'

Sam looked at him for several long seconds before she slowly nodded her head. 'He gave me until the end of the week to make my decision.'

'Big of him.'

'He seemed to think so, yes.'

'I'll have something in place by then,' Xander assured her grimly.

'Then, yes,' she accepted huskily. 'Yes, I'll gladly let you help me, if you really want to.'

'I want to.' He nodded tersely.

* * *

Sam lived in a state of trepidation for the next four days. Malcolm had given her until the end of the week to make her decision, but she knew him too well to believe anything he said, and lived in fear of him waiting for her at Daisy's school again one morning or evening.

And she worried even more when the days passed and she heard nothing further from him.

Xander had assured her he had the situation under control, when Sam had voiced her concerns a couple of days before, adding that he would have some positive news for her by the end of the week.

But he must also have been concerned Malcolm might turn up again at Daisy's school because he had insisted on accompanying them in the car to and from school these past four mornings. Much to Daisy's delight.

And so giving Sam another worry—that her daughter was becoming altogether too attached to Xander. They all ate their meals together now, and had done since Sunday morning when Xander had insisted he would be eating all of his meals in the kitchen in future. And it was Xander who Daisy was eager to see when she came out of school every day. Xander that Daisy asked to read her a story every night before she went to sleep.

Which was exactly what he was doing on Friday evening while Sam cleared away in the kitchen after dinner.

It was all a bit too cosy for comfort.

Sam's comfort, at least; Xander and Daisy seemed perfectly happy with the arrangement.

So, along with worrying about Malcolm, she also had the extra worry of how Daisy was going to react when the two of them had to move out of Xander's apartment in just over a week's time.

Not that Sam didn't completely understand Daisy's infatuation; she was afraid she had one of those going herself where Xander was concerned.

As if by tacit agreement, the two of them hadn't spoken again of the things Xander had told her of his childhood. But the knowledge of those shared confidences was there between them, nonetheless, creating a subtle but discernible shift in their relationship. There was an unspoken companionship between them now, coupled with that underlying physical awareness. The latter on Sam's part, at least.

Xander had made no attempt to step over the line with Sam again, and that was despite the fact that his desire was more than obvious every time she helped him in and out of the shower!

And was that disappointment she was feeling?

Because Xander hadn't made a single attempt to kiss her again?

Was she actually feeling a little *jealous* of the closeness that existed between Xander and Daisy?

No, not jealous exactly; how could Sam possibly resent any kindness and affection Xander might show towards Daisy? It was just that she ached to be closer to him herself.

'Everything okay?'

She almost dropped the plate she was placing in the dishwasher at Xander's unexpected reappearance in the kitchen. Usually she was able to hear his progress down the hallway on his crutches, but the daily physio sessions were going so well that the physiotherapist had advised just yesterday that he need only use the walking stick now. After which Sam had been caught out more than once when Xander appeared unexpectedly in a room.

She placed the plate in the dishwasher before straightening, her gaze focused somewhere over Xander's left shoulder as he stood in the doorway; she was far too physically aware of him after her recent thoughts. 'I was just wondering what Daisy and I should do over the weekend.'

Xander stepped fully into the room, immediately dwarfing what had previously seemed a spacious room. 'Strange, the two of us were just discussing that too. Daisy would like us to take her to the cinema tomorrow and then she suggested we all go swimming.'

Sam's heart sank at the thought of a Xander-filled weekend; hours and hours when she would have to hide the growing feelings she had for him. 'I really appreciate all the time and effort you've taken with Daisy this past week—' she began.

'But?' He quirked one blond brow.

Sam still couldn't look at him directly, that disturbing awareness of him thrumming beneath her skin. 'But perhaps you shouldn't spend quite as much time with her as you do? Daisy shouldn't come to rely on your attention so much,' she added regretfully. 'We're going to be leaving here at the end of next week, and—'

'And you think I'm then just going to forget all about her, is that it?' Xander barked harshly, more than a little insulted by that assumption. 'You said you trusted me, Samantha,' he said gruffly.

'I *do* trust you.' Samantha chewed on her bottom lip. 'It's just—I appreciate the time you've spent with Daisy, I really do. It's simply that I know you're still incapacitated, at the moment, and can't do the things you usually do,' she hurried on as Xander scowled. 'That it must be boring for you being stuck in this apartment all the time, as well as frustrating. But you're improving rapidly, and once you're completely fit again, you'll obviously want to return to your own life, and—'

'And then I'll no longer have time for Daisy, is that what you're saying?' Xander realised that he and Samantha had deliberately not discussed personal subjects again since revealing so much about themselves to each other on Monday. Possibly because neither of them were used to doing that? But Samantha's implication now, that he was just going to cast Daisy aside like a pair of old shoes once he was fit again, was hardly fair.

He had grown genuinely fond of Daisy. For herself. But also, Xander knew, because she was a miniature version of her mother.

He had grown more than a little fond of Samantha too. In fact, the desire he felt to make love to her was now a physical ache that he lived with on a daily basis. A desire he was determinedly denying himself from even attempting to satisfy, because he knew he shouldn't take advantage of this situation.

Maybe it was selfish of him, but he had been putting off discussing Howard with Samantha again, had enjoyed this past week too much, having Samantha relax in his company, having her trust him, to want to ruin that peace and harmony. He had even taken to having cold showers every morning, in an effort not to ruin that trust by attempting to kiss her again!

That Samantha should now more or less accuse him of using Daisy as a diversion for his *boredom,* and that he would forget about her, and Samantha, once he was fit enough to resume his own life, just added salt to the wound.

Did those confidences he had shared with her about his father mean nothing to her? And what of the trust she had placed in him by agreeing to let him help her?

'Well, thanks for that, Samantha,' he grated. 'Nice to know you think me insensitive as well as shallow!' He turned abruptly, leaving the kitchen to walk down the hallway, and shut himself in his study before sitting down heavily behind his desk.

Before he said anything he might regret.

Such as, that he hadn't been bored for a single moment these last few days.

That, despite the initial doubts he had voiced to Darius on the subject he *liked* having Samantha and Daisy living with him, and genuinely enjoyed their company.

That he woke up every morning with a smile on his face, in anticipation of spending the day with them.

That he had the feeling his apartment was going to have all the warmth of a morgue after they left next weekend.

That it was testament to how *much* he liked Samantha that he had shared those confidences of his childhood, a subject he had never discussed with anyone outside his immediate family.

Damn it, Xander valued all of those things so highly that he had deliberately chosen to keep his desire for Samantha to himself, for fear that it might damage the peaceful existence they now had.

Maybe he did need to get out of his apartment for a while, away from both Samantha and Daisy, and try to get some perspective back into his life?

His assistant had been arriving promptly at the apartment at nine-thirty every morning this week so that the two of them could spend an hour or so going through what needed to be dealt with urgently, and what could wait until Darius either came back from his honeymoon or Xander was fit enough to spend the day in his office.

But he hadn't been out of his apartment for weeks on a social basis, apart from to attend the wedding last weekend.

Security was downstairs, so Samantha would be safe enough from her ex-husband in his apartment, and a couple of hours checking out the Midas nightclub might be just what Xander needed to put himself, and this situation, back into perspective.

'Xander?'

He had been so lost in deep and brooding thought that he hadn't even heard Samantha open the study door. She hovered in the doorway looking across at him uncertainly.

She looked so very beautiful, with her flame-coloured hair loose and curling about her shoulders and down her back, her face slightly flushed from cooking and clearing away after dinner. Her small and perfectly rounded breasts were pert against the white fitted shirt she wore, her tailored black trousers clinging lovingly to the sweet curve of her hips and bottom.

Xander's body reacted sharply to the sight of her.

So much so that the need he now felt, to stand up and move restlessly about his study, became an impossibility. 'What is it, Samantha?' he enquired softly.

'I wanted to apologise. I didn't mean to imply—I know that you genuinely care for Daisy—I just don't want—I would never deliberately insult you,' she finished lamely.

'Just indirectly,' Xander drawled. 'Let's just forget it,' he dismissed. 'You were probably right to be concerned.' He shrugged. 'I am basically shallow and insensitive.'

'I didn't say that.'

'No, I did.' He sighed. 'What do I know about five-year-olds anyway?'

'Well, you were once one yourself.'

Yes, he had been, and he knew exactly how it had felt to be so young and so totally bewildered by his own father's dislike of him. As Malcolm Howard's years of lack of interest in his own daughter seemed to imply the other man also disliked Daisy.

So yes, on that level Xander could relate totally to Daisy.

It was the increasing desire he felt to make love to her mother that had become the biggest danger.

'Let's not argue, Xander.' Tears glistened in her eyes as Samantha looked across at him imploringly. 'This business with Malcolm has unsettled me. I certainly didn't mean to insult you by anything I said earlier.'

Xander knew that. Knew that Samantha wasn't the type of woman to ever deliberately insult or hurt anyone. She was sweet and kind, and had been infinitely patient and understanding from the onset, despite his bad-temperedness. She was also a wonderful mother to Daisy.

Nor did he have a single regret about telling her about his own childhood; he knew that it had been necessary at the time. It had also, in some strange inexplicable way, continued to act as a balm to his own feelings about the past.

He drew in a deep and ragged breath. 'You're obviously tense and worried about your ex, and I should probably have talked to you about this sooner.' He sighed heavily. 'I didn't because...' He paused, knowing it had been selfish of him to want to keep the status quo for as long as possible. 'After making extensive enquiries about Malcolm Howard, I've decided to make my strike against him through his business,' he revealed grimly. 'In fact, I've already set those plans in motion. Don't look so worried.' He gave Samantha a reassuring smile. 'By the time I've finished with him Howard will wish he had never so much as spoken to you again, let alone threatened you by using Daisy.'

She gave a worried frown. 'What are you going to do?'

'What *am* I doing?' Xander corrected grimly as he stood up, his erection having finally subsided. 'Howard Electronics is shortly going to experience a severe problem with the loan they're currently requesting from their bank, putting in jeopardy the plans Howard currently has for expansion into the Japanese market,' he added with satisfaction.

Xander had also cancelled Howard's membership to the Midas nightclub the day after he and Samantha had spoken, a move guaranteed to ensure the other man knew exactly where his troubles were coming from. It shouldn't take too long, once Howard discovered his membership to Midas had been discontinued, for the other man to make enquiries and realise Xander was also behind the difficulty with his bank loan. A deliberate move on Xander's part, to ensure that he became Howard's target, rather than Samantha or Daisy.

'You can do that?' Samantha eyed him doubtfully.

Xander gave a grim smile of satisfaction. 'I can when it turns out I have a financial interest in the bank Howard uses. At the moment he is running around like a headless chicken trying to secure a loan from another bank.'

'And what happens when he stops running around in circles?' She frowned.

Xander grimaced. 'My lawyer will have contacted him before then, strongly suggesting Howard comes to his office for a meeting. A meeting at which, in exchange for a guaranteed loan from me, with a low interest rate, he will sign a contract agreeing never to come near you or Daisy ever again. This needs to be settled once and for all, Samantha,' he insisted huskily as he saw she still looked worried.

'What if he still doesn't agree?'

'He will.' Because if he didn't Xander would feel no compunction whatsoever in breaking the other man completely.

She gave a shake of her head. 'I can't let you do that.'

'It's already done, Samantha.'

Sam could only stare at him. This was insane. Unbelievable. She had known Xander was extremely rich, but it seemed he was even more powerful than she could ever have imagined. And she had never dreamt that he would go to such lengths on her own and Daisy's behalf.

Xander took a step forward to look down at her searchingly. 'I won't let him hurt you, or Daisy, again, Samantha.'

That was laudable, it really was, except that Sam had realised these past few days that it was Xander himself who was now capable of hurting her, far more than Malcolm ever had, but in a completely different way.

She had been fighting her attraction to him all week,

avoiding being alone with him whenever possible, as well as keeping their conversations light and impersonal. It hadn't always been possible to remain completely immune, of course; shower time with Xander had become both Sam's daily torture and pleasure. Especially given his blatant desire.

But Sam had put his arousal down to the weeks he had been denied a sex life, rather than a direct response to her. Xander was probably so sexually frustrated, after almost two months of drought, that he would have responded physically to any woman, rather than specifically to her.

Nevertheless, that hadn't prevented Sam's own reaction to all that taut, tanned, and naked flesh: wide and muscled shoulders she ached to touch, a sleek and lean chest, his waist and hips narrow, his legs long and muscled.

His hair had also grown longer this past week, falling in shaggy blond waves onto the back of the rounded neckline of his T-shirts, and falling silkily over his forehead.

He looked even more like a sleek and muscled Viking about to plunder and pillage and—

'Samantha?' Xander queried huskily as he took in the slightly fevered glow to her eyes and the delicate flush that had appeared in her cheeks, the tenseness of silence between them now such that he could hear the clock ticking out in the hallway.

Her gaze was focused on his mouth as she moistened the plumpness of her own recently chewed lips with a sweep of her tongue. 'I should get back to the kitchen.'

'I thought you had finished in there for the night?'

She looked flustered. 'I— Not quite. I—I'll leave

you to—to get on with whatever it was you were doing when I interrupted you.'

He shrugged. 'I was just sitting here thinking of going out.'

She raised startled eyes. 'You were?'

'To the club.' Xander nodded. 'But I'd really rather stay here. With you.'

Dark lashes fanned against Samantha's cheeks as she lowered her lids. 'You would?'

'Look at me, Samantha.'

She gave a slow shake of her head. 'I'd really rather not.'

'Why not?'

Her gaze flickered up to his and then quickly away again.

Clearly she had seen and correctly read the desire he was no longer making any effort to hide.

The same desire he had been fighting for the past week. A desire he wasn't sure he was capable of fighting any longer. He wanted Samantha so much right now he could no longer think straight. And her scent was driving him insane; insidiously warm and desirable woman combined with an underlying floral smell, possibly lavender soap?

'This really is a bad idea, Xander.'

'The most enjoyable ones usually are.' He stepped forward to take her in his arms, the softness of her curves instantly accommodating his much harder ones.

She placed her hands on his shoulders in an effort to hold her body away from him. 'We really shouldn't do this, Xander.' Her voice was pleading, asking for a level-headedness he simply couldn't give her right now.

'Do you really want me to stop?' Xander murmured throatily.

Of course Sam didn't want him to stop, not when his lips and tongue were tasting the dips and hollows of her throat, his teeth gently biting her earlobe, his breath warm against her skin.

'We could always look on it as research,' he murmured throatily, his hands roaming the length of her spine as his lips now plundered the sensitive hollows at the base of her throat, the five o'clock shadow on his chin a pleasurable rasp against her sensitive flesh. 'A way of settling once and for all which position is most comfortable for me to make love?' he teasingly reminded her of that previous conversation.

Sam knew that she really shouldn't let this go any further than it already had. But it had been so long since a man had touched her in this way. Since any man had touched her with such gentle appreciation. As it had the week before, her long-denied body betrayed her, reacting instinctively to just the thought of that pleasure, her breasts swelling, nipples hardening to sensitive pebbles, and heat building between her thighs.

Xander smelled so good too, a light and spicy cologne, and the lemon shampoo she knew he used to wash his hair. There was an underlying smell that was all Xander; a healthy male in his sexual prime.

Sam *wanted* this.

Wanted Xander.

Surely any regrets could come later?

And she had no doubt there would be regrets. The main one being that she could never mean anything more to Xander than a single night—or possibly two, if she was lucky!—of pleasure.

But other women went to bed with men all the time just for the pleasure of it, so why not her?

Yes, why the hell not her?

Xander didn't need to profess undying love for her to be a caring and considerate lover. A lover she already knew was capable of giving her pleasure. Any more than she needed to be in love with him in order to give him that same pleasure.

Live a little, Sam, she mentally encouraged herself. *Take what he is offering and think of the consequences later.*

She looked up at him sharply. 'I'm not on any sort of contraception.' She couldn't think of *those* consequences later.

His eyes darkened at the realisation her comment signalled her capitulation. 'I'll take care of it,' he assured her gruffly.

Of course he would; no doubt Xander had a bedside drawer full of condoms. After all, who knew when he was going to get lucky?

Could she really do this? Indulge in hot and meaningless sex with a man—with Xander—just for the pleasure of it?

Oh, yes!

CHAPTER NINE

She looked up at Xander shyly. 'Your bedroom or mine?'

Xander gave her an approving smile as he released her before taking her hand firmly in his much larger one. 'My bedroom is where the condoms are,' he reminded teasingly as they walked out of the study together and down the silence of the hallway.

Sam felt her cheeks warm at the intimacy of their conversation. Which was pretty silly of her, when she intended getting naked with this man in just a few minutes' time.

Xander turned on a softly glowing bedside lamp as they entered the masculine bedroom, dominated by the opulence of the four-poster bed. That beautiful mahogany bed was covered with an abundance of gold and cream silk pillows and bedcover, and had matching drapes tied back at the four sides and the two windows.

Decadence personified.

As was the beautiful Viking god at her side.

'Stop over-thinking, Samantha,' Xander encouraged gruffly as he saw the uncertainty in Samantha's expression as she looked at the bed, and easily guessed the reason for it; she had already revealed that he would be her first lover since her husband. 'It's going to be fine, trust me,' he encouraged softly even as he ran the soft pad of his thumb over the enticing pout of her bottom lip.

'I just—I don't want to disappoint you.'

'I don't want to disappoint you either.'

'You couldn't!'

'Lovemaking is all about learning what pleases the other person, giving as well as receiving,' Xander reassured her gruffly. 'And I do want to give to you, Samantha,' he added huskily. 'Feel how much I want you.' He placed one of her hands over his jeans, against his arousal.

Xander watched in fevered fascination as Samantha moistened the fullness of her lips with the tip of her tongue.

In anticipation of running that moist tongue over the throbbing fullness she cupped in her hand?

Xander certainly hoped so.

He held her gaze as he took her with him and moved back slightly until he was able to sit on the side of the bed and stand her in between his parted thighs. His gaze continued to hold the shyness of hers captive as he began to unfasten the buttons of the fitted white shirt she was wearing.

His breath caught in his throat as he slid the unfastened shirt down her arms to reveal the white satin and lace bra she wore beneath, the paleness of her skin a pearly white. 'You're so beautiful,' he groaned in appreciation as his fingers caressed lightly across the swell of her breasts and down the length of her slender waist. 'So, so beautiful, Samantha,' he murmured, his arms about her waist as he nuzzled his face against the heated softness of her breasts encased in satin and lace.

Sam could barely breathe as she rested her hands on Xander's shoulders for balance, the intimacy of this situation so beautiful. Utterly, utterly beautiful.

As was the man now kissing the tops of her breasts, his lips a heated caress as his hands roamed restlessly along the slender length of her back.

His hair felt soft beneath the fingers she entwined in its silky length, his T-shirt an arousing abrasion against her bared flesh as he continued to nuzzle and kiss her breasts.

Xander moved back slightly. 'This has to come off,' he murmured achingly even as his fingers dealt deftly with the fastening at the back of her bra and he slipped the straps down and off her arms before dropping it onto the carpet with her shirt. His eyes darkened to black as he drank in the sight of her naked breasts. 'I absolutely love this.' His fingers stroked lightly across the soaring eagle tattoo. 'It's almost as beautiful as you are.'

Sam *felt* beautiful under Xander's appreciative ministrations, her breath catching in her throat as she felt the first touch of his lips against a bared nipple. Gently kissing first one, and then the other, over and over again, his tongue a slow and velvety rasp against her engorged flesh.

She made a husky groan of need in her throat, wanting, needing.

'Yes!' she hissed weakly, her fingers tightening in Xander's hair and holding him to her as he finally suckled one ripe and aching berry deep into the heat of his mouth, his tongue no longer velvety as it rasped over and against that arousal at the same time as his hand cupped her other breast, rolling her nipple between finger and thumb.

Sam's back arched into those caresses as the pleasure gathered between the heat of her thighs as she moved restlessly against him.

Xander fell back against the silk pillows covering the bed, taking Samantha with him, so that she now lay above him, her parted legs straddling his thighs.

He lay his head back on the pillows, lids narrowed as he cupped her beautiful and responsive breasts. Petite and firm, they were perfectly rounded, with deep rose-coloured nipples that were just begging for more attention from his hands and mouth.

Xander pushed the aching in his left thigh to the back of his mind as he raised his head slightly, his gaze deliberately holding hers as he slowly laved one ripe and juicy nipple with his tongue before suckling her deeply into the heat of his mouth, groaning low in his throat, his own arousal pulsing against her heat. He saw Samantha close her eyes in pleasure, an aroused flush to her cheeks as she leant into him, allowing him to suckle her deeper as she rested her hands on the pillows beside his head.

Sam looked down at Xander as she told herself over and over again in her head that she could do this, that she could just enjoy the moment. Enjoy Xander.

She gasped as his mouth on her breasts took her to a level of pleasure she had never experienced before, her position above him allowing her to arch herself slowly and rhythmically against him, the hardness of his arousal pressing against the heat between her thighs, the two layers of denim between them acting as an extra abrasion, until her breath came in short pleasurable gasps and she knew herself to be teetering on the edge of climax.

As if aware of that, Xander bit down onto her aching nipple at the same time as the finger and thumb of his other hand squeezed its twin, sending Sam over the edge of that pleasure and into the most intense and pleasurably prolonged orgasm of her life.

Sam gasped again as she rode out the pleasure of that orgasm, until her arms gave way and she collapsed against Xander's rapidly rising and falling chest, his breath a harsh rasp against her as his arms wrapped around her.

She lay weakly against him, her own breathing ragged as her body pulsed in the aftershocks of that pleasure.

'Are you okay, Samantha?' Xander finally asked.

Was she okay? Sam had never felt so okay before in her life.

She felt liberated. She had experienced a freedom she had never known before.

Before Xander.

Her gaze was sultry as she sat up and looked down at him, feeling a triumphant thrill as she saw his eyes were dark with his own arousal; there was a flush to his cheeks, the gold of his hair tousled from the caress of her fingers.

'I think we found the comfortable position, don't you?' Sam teased huskily as she continued to hold his gaze as she slid slowly down the length of his body, kneeling between his parted thighs as her fingers moved to the fastening at the front of his jeans.

She felt emboldened as Xander looked at her between narrowed lids, as she slipped the three buttons loose, revealing that he wore black body-hugging boxers beneath, his desire long and thick. Sam scooted back to pull his jeans down the long length of his muscled legs before discarding them completely.

She unfastened and pushed off her own trousers and panties before running her hands along the length of his long and muscled legs, from ankle to thigh, pausing to caress the slightly reddened scar on his left thigh, before her hands moved higher still, lightly caressing the length of his arousal through the thin material of his briefs.

'Take them off, Samantha!' Xander groaned as he moved restlessly against her, hands clenched into fists at his sides. 'I want to feel your hands against me.'

He was just so gorgeous, Sam groaned inwardly as she slowly lowered the boxers, hardly aware of discarding them as her heated gaze remained fixed on the long and throbbing length of his arousal.

'Touch me, Samantha,' Xander encouraged gruffly. 'Yes, just like that!' He groaned achingly, his eyes closing as she curled the fingers of her hand about him and lowered her head to take him into the heat of her mouth.

Xander felt his control slipping within minutes as he watched Samantha's head slowly bob up and down, the fullness of her lips wide about him, her wicked tongue rasping the length of him, the tingling at the base of his spine telling him he was very close to release.

His hands were gentle on her shoulders as he pulled her up and away from him, knowing he had to stop the torment before he did just that. 'Not like that, Samantha,' he groaned as he saw the disappointment of her expression. 'I want to be inside you,' he explained as he reached over and opened the top drawer of the bedside cabinet before taking out a condom.

'Let me,' Samantha offered huskily as she took the packet from him, tearing off the top before taking it out.

Xander felt that renewed tingling at the base of his spine as Samantha's caressing fingers slowly rolled it over and then down the length of him, fearing that he wasn't going to last long once he was buried to the hilt inside her heat. Not sure he was even going to last that long if he didn't get inside her right now.

'On top of me,' he grated. 'I need to be inside you now,' he encouraged gruffly, his hands on her hips as he entered her, trying to take it slowly.

Knowing he had lost the battle the moment he was fully buried inside Samantha. 'I can't! Forgive me, Samantha, but I just can't take this slowly. Next time. I promise next time,' he groaned achingly as he held onto her hips as he began to thrust into her.

Sam tightly gripped his shoulders as she rode the fierceness of his lengthy thrusts, her body flooding with desire as she revelled in the intensity of need she could see in Xander's almost pained expression, his fingers digging into her hips as he pushed hard and deep.

Her eyes widened in shock as she felt a second climax building rapidly inside her. 'Xander!' she had time to cry before that climax crested, and then broke with an intensity of pleasure even stronger than the first.

As if that was all he had been waiting for, Xander cried out at his own release thrusting hard and deep as he pulsed hotly inside her.

What a fool she had been, Sam acknowledged regretfully the following morning as she looked down at the beautiful man sleeping in the bed beside her, knowing there could be no next time for the two of them.

Because no matter what she might have told herself last night when the two of them made love, the reassurance she had given herself to believe she could have casual sex with a man, with Xander, before just as happily walking away, was all nonsense. A lie she had told herself because she had wanted, desired, Xander so very much.

Now she realised not only had she lied to herself about the casual sex, but also about her feelings for Xander.

And those regrets that could come later?

Well, they had come crashing down about her head the moment Sam had been woken at five o'clock this morning, the sun streaming in through the window of his bedroom, because they had forgotten to draw the curtains the evening before.

Sam had felt totally disorientated when she'd first woken up, taking several seconds to get her bearings, before remembering exactly where she was, and then turning sharply to look down at the man sleeping in the bed beside her.

One look at Xander's beautifully chiselled face relaxed in sleep, and that gloriously tousled blond hair fanned out on the pillow behind him, with only a thin sheet covering the nakedness of his hips and thighs, leaving his muscled chest bare, and Sam had realised she was in love with him.

That somewhere, somehow, during this past week of sharing an apartment with him—of sharing her past with him; of him sharing the horrors of his childhood with her, and the battle he had suffered these past few weeks, fearing he might be like his father; of just *being* with Xander constantly; of feeling moved by his protectiveness towards her and his kindness to Daisy—Sam had fallen deeply in love with him.

Which was why she was now going to climb quietly and carefully out of his bed, taking care not to disturb or wake him, and go back to her own bedroom.

To consider how she was ever going to face Xander again.

At least she didn't have to make the walk of shame, and could simply gather up her scattered clothes from the bedroom floor and walk the short way down the hallway in order to reach the relative sanctuary of her bedroom.

No doubt there had been dozens of women between Xander's bed sheets over the years. Beautiful women. Sophisticated women. Those same beautiful and sophisticated women who could enjoy casual sex with as accomplished a lover as Xander Sterne, before dressing the following morning and walking away without any regrets.

Unfortunately, Sam now knew she wasn't *any* of those things.

She wasn't beautiful, or sophisticated, but worst of all she certainly wasn't capable of walking away from Xander without regrets.

Any more than she had wanted to see Xander's disappointment if he should wake up and feel regret at finding her there beside him in his bed.

Xander felt wonderfully relaxed when he woke up, the warmth of the morning sun shining across his face and closed lids.

Thoroughly relaxed. And wonderfully satiated in a way he could never remember feeling before. Almost as if he— Not almost. He *had* made love with Samantha.

Xander's eyes opened wide and he turned sharply to look at the bed beside him, the events of the previous night washing over him in bright and glorious colour.

He sat up abruptly as he saw the bed beside him was empty. As was his bedroom, Samantha's clothes gone from the carpeted floor. Nor could he hear any sounds coming from the adjoining bathroom, as evidence that Samantha was taking a shower.

The clock on the bedside table read only six o'clock, so where was she?

Gone, came his immediate answer.

Just to her own bedroom, or from his apartment completely?

Even if Samantha regretted what had happened between the two of them—and her disappearing act seemed to imply she did—surely she wouldn't have woken Daisy up in the middle of the night and just left without saying a word to him? Especially with her ex-husband on the prowl and ready to pounce.

No, Xander was sure Samantha wouldn't have done that.

But there was no denying she *had* left his bedroom. Why?

She'd seemed happy enough the night before, as she had snuggled comfortably in his arms before they both fell into an exhausted sleep.

Damn it. He had been so thoroughly satiated the previous night, so exhausted by their lovemaking after suffering weeks of physical limitations, that he hadn't even woken when Samantha crept from his bed!

He now ran an agitated hand through his already tousled hair, the tenderness of his scalp reminding him of the way she had tightly gripped his hair when she climaxed a second time as he'd fiercely thrust and pulsed inside her.

Now she had gone, crept from his bed like a thief in the night. As if last night had meant nothing to her. As if *he* meant nothing to her.

And perhaps he didn't, Xander realised with a frown, as he recalled their conversation just before they had made love. Their discussion of the problem of her ex-husband, and the way in which he intended dealing with that problem, for both her own and Daisy's sakes.

Could Samantha have gone to bed with him, made love, out of *gratitude* for just the thought of that help reaching fruition?

Because he had made it obvious he wanted her, and she hadn't liked to say no?

'Cereal, pancakes, or eggs and bacon?' Sam prompted briskly as Xander made an appearance in the kitchen doorway just after eight o'clock, her daughter already seated at the breakfast bar eating the last of her pancakes.

It was a grim-faced Xander who looked at her with dark and wary eyes, nothing like the wild and satisfying lover of the night before. Or the relaxed and satiated man Sam had left asleep in bed earlier this morning.

Any more than she looked—or felt—like the uninhibited woman of the night before.

Her cheeks felt warm just thinking of the intimacies the two of them had shared the previous night. 'Or maybe just your usual coffee?' she carried on hurriedly as Xander made no reply but just continued to look at her searchingly with those dark and enigmatic eyes.

But searching for what?

Regrets?

Sam had plenty of those!

Rebuke?

She had absolutely nothing to rebuke Xander for, had been a more than willing participant to their love-making.

So what was Xander looking for as he gazed at her so intently?

Whatever it was, he didn't seem to have found it, the expression in his dark eyes becoming even more guarded as he stepped further into the kitchen. 'Just coffee is fine, thanks,' he answered as he moved to sit opposite Daisy. 'How are you this morning, Daisy-flower?' His voice noticeably softened as he spoke to the little girl.

Sam efficiently poured coffee into a mug and placed it in front of him before collecting up Daisy's empty plate and returning to tidy up the stove top, her back turned towards the room as tears blurred her vision.

This was awful. Worse than she had even imagined it might be.

In her imaginings there had at least been a stilted conversation between herself and Xander, in which he would say something like *you were right, last night was a bad idea*, and Sam would urge him to forget about it, as she already had.

The fact that Daisy was present this morning, and would be all weekend, was going to make even that brief conversation difficult, if not impossible.

And Sam wasn't sure her already frayed nerves could

take the added tension, especially if Xander decided to spend time with them this weekend.

Because they weren't a normal family. And they never could be.

Xander's past record, of having been involved with a legion of women, clearly spoke for itself, and he certainly hadn't made any rash declarations of love to Sam the evening before. He hadn't needed to, she reminded herself, after she had made it more than obvious she'd wanted him as much as he'd wanted her.

She had been a willing scratch to Xander's itch, at best. And the fact that he meant so much more to her than that wasn't his problem.

That was something Sam definitely intended keeping to herself.

Xander would run a mile if he thought for one moment that she had feelings for him. Worse, that she had been stupid enough to fall in love with him.

Just the thought of leaving Xander at the end of next week, of never seeing him again, was enough to break her heart.

'Daisy, how about I put a cartoon on for you?' Xander suggested lightly as he stood up, very aware of the fact that Samantha was keeping her back turned towards the two of them for a reason; the slight shaking of her shoulders, and the occasional soft sniff he could hear, clearly indicating that she was crying.

Could he feel any more of a heel than he already did? Xander wondered heavily as he accompanied Daisy into the television room and put a film on for her.

He had taken advantage of Samantha last night. Had used her emotions against her—fear of her ex-husband? Her gratitude for Xander's help? The compassion she felt for his past? Take your pick! And then he'd forgotten all of those things in order to take what he wanted.

The fact that Samantha had left his bed before he had woken up, that she was crying this morning, had to mean that she regretted what had happened between the two of them last night.

And Xander had no idea how to put things right between them.

Did he apologise and tell her that he knew and accepted that last night had been a mistake?

Even if it hadn't been?

Did he promise her it would never happen again?

A promise, desiring her as much as he still did, that Xander knew he couldn't keep.

Or did he put her through the even worse embarrassment of being the one to speak first about last night?

No, that last definitely wasn't going to happen; it would totally humiliate Samantha, and that was the last thing Xander ever wanted her to feel in regards to him or their lovemaking.

What he had *wanted* to happen was for the two of them to wake up in each other's arms this morning, to make mind-blowing love again, before they discussed exactly where they were going to go with their relationship.

Except Samantha had already left when he'd woken up this morning.

Consequently there had been no opportunity for a repeat of the night before.

Both of those things telling him that, as far as she was concerned, at least, there was also no relationship for the two of them to discuss.

At the same time as Xander knew they couldn't continue to live together for the next week without one or both of them saying at least *something* about last night. Acknowledging that it had happened, at least. Not to do so would be juvenile. And their actions last night had been anything but that.

'I'm just going back to the kitchen to have a chat with Mummy, okay, Daisy?' he told the little girl lightly as he raised the volume on the television.

'Okay.' Daisy nodded distractedly, her attention already focused on the animated film on the screen.

Xander closed the door softly behind him as he stepped out into the hallway, drawing in a deep breath once he was outside; he wasn't in the least looking forward to the next few minutes' conversation with Samantha. Or what the outcome of that conversation would mean for the two of them.

Any thoughts of that conversation fled his head the moment he walked back into the kitchen and saw how deathly pale Samantha's face was as she stood as still as a statue, the telephone receiver about to fall from her limp fingers.

'Samantha?' Xander quickly crossed to where she stood to look down searchingly into that pale face as he took that receiver from her and placed it back on the wall, frowning darkly as he saw the pain in those dark amethyst eyes as Samantha stared off into the distance. 'Samantha?'

The way she now looked up at him so blankly, as if she not only didn't see him, but was having trouble even remembering who he was, wasn't in the least reassuring.

Xander lightly clasped the tops of her arms as a way of gaining her attention. 'Samantha!'

'Security just called from Reception downstairs.'

She spoke flatly, not an ounce of emotion in her voice as she continued to look up at him blankly.

'And?' he prompted tensely as Samantha didn't add anything to that statement.

She blinked, seeming to come out of her stupor slightly as she finally focused on him. 'Malcolm is downstairs.'

'He is?'

She nodded. 'And apparently he told Security that he has no intention of leaving until he's spoken to one or both of us.'

Xander had known this confrontation was inevitable, had deliberately designed this situation so that Howard would make him the target rather than Samantha and Daisy.

He just hadn't expected it to be this morning, and before he'd even had a chance to talk to Samantha about last night.

CHAPTER TEN

Maybe if he hadn't been so caught up, so blinded by his desire for Samantha and the need he felt to protect her, he would have realised that the bombastic Malcolm Howard was arrogant enough to come to his apartment. Everything Xander had learnt about the other man this past week had indicated he was someone who didn't care about anyone else's feelings, least of all Samantha's.

'I thought you said that your lawyer would contact Malcolm and arrange for him to visit his offices?'

Xander winced at the complete lack of accusation in Samantha's tone. At the lack of any emotion in her voice at all. 'He was going to do that on Monday morning.' He grimaced. 'Obviously I underestimated the speed of Howard's powers of deduction.'

She smiled without humour. 'Don't feel bad about that; a lot of people have underestimated Malcolm's intelligence,' she said flatly.

'I'm so sorry, Samantha.' Xander looked down at her, frowning as he saw her expression was just as unreadable. As if the shock, the possibility of seeing Howard again, had robbed her of all feeling. 'You don't have to do this, Samantha,' he reassured her gently. 'I can go downstairs and tell Howard that my lawyer will contact him on Monday morning as planned.'

Sam knew that would be the safest thing to do. But it was also the coward's thing to do. And she no longer wanted to be that person. 'No,' she said firmly, determinedly rousing herself from the stupor of the shock of knowing that Malcolm was actually downstairs refusing to leave until he had spoken to her. And Xander...

It was her worst nightmare realised.

Well, no, that wasn't strictly true any more; her *worst* nightmare was knowing she had fallen in love with Xander, while understanding that that love wasn't, and never could be, returned.

So, did she want to talk to Malcolm?

Absolutely not.

Did she want this situation between the two of them settled once and for all?

Absolutely yes.

'Is Daisy fully occupied with the TV, do you think?' She chewed worriedly on her bottom lip at thoughts of her young daughter so much as realising that the man who was her father was actually here, in Xander's apartment.

Xander's mouth twisted. 'She's watching one of her favourite animated movies. Very loudly,' he added dryly, as the volume was audible all the way down the hallway.

Sam nodded. 'Then I would rather the two of us talked to Malcolm now, if that's okay with you?' She looked up at Xander expectantly.

'Are you sure?' He frowned darkly, obviously not happy with her decision.

'Just say if *you* aren't comfortable with this.' Sam

frowned, noting Xander's pallor, the tightness of his jaw, the nerve pulsing at the base of his throat, and the grimness of his expression. 'You've done so much for us already.'

'The fact that Howard is here at all would seem to imply I didn't do it quickly enough!' He scowled darkly.

'I'm really grateful for all the help you've given me.' Sam frowned as he gave a pained wince. 'I am grateful, Xander, but I can deal with the rest of this on my own if you would rather not be involved any further.'

'That's the last thing I want! Sorry,' he muttered as Samantha flinched at the fierceness of his tone. 'I apologise for raising my voice.'

She grimaced as she placed her hand lightly on Xander's arm. 'Your reaction is perfectly normal, Xander,' she reassured him. 'Believe me, Malcolm has this effect on most people.' She gave his arm a reassuring squeeze before stepping away from him. 'Let's just get this over with, shall we—before I lose my nerve?' she added shakily.

Once this conversation with Malcolm was over, and the matter was hopefully settled, Sam knew then would be the time for her and Xander to talk. If last night had made it awkward for them to continue living together for the next week, this added fiasco with Malcolm could make it impossible!

'I should have been able to protect you from this confrontation,' Xander said.

'Because your instinct is naturally to protect rather than to destroy.'

Xander drew in a sharp breath at the total trust in Samantha's voice. 'We'll talk to Howard in my study,' he stated decisively before picking up the receiver and calling down to Reception, instructing them to send Howard up before ending the call and turning back to Samantha. 'Would you like to go and wait for us in my study, and I'll go and meet Howard at the lift?'

'You really don't have to do this, Xander.'

'Yes, I most certainly do,' he bit out tensely. 'I'm responsible for him being here, and I have absolutely no intention of leaving you to speak with him alone.'

'But—'

'Please go to my study,' he repeated gently before turning to make his way out into the hallway, deliberately leaving his stick propped against the breakfast bar. The last thing he wanted was to appear physically weak in front of Malcolm Howard.

To that end Xander was leaning casually against the wall outside the lift when the doors opened to reveal his unexpected, and equally unwanted, guest.

His eyes glittered with challenge as Howard stepped out into the corridor. Xander disliked him on sight.

For so many reasons.

For having once mattered to Samantha.

For having been married to her and not appreciating her as the jewel that she was.

For being Daisy's father.

Most of all, for having made both of their lives a misery.

The feeling of dislike was obviously mutual as the older man's face flushed with anger as he looked at Xander. 'Are you aware of the humiliation you caused me last night when I arrived at the club with my date, only to be told that the almighty Xander Sterne had personally cancelled my membership?'

Xander's top lip curled back with distaste. Howard

believed his ex-wife and daughter were currently living with Xander in his apartment, and yet all that was bothering the guy at this moment was his cancelled membership to one of his clubs?

Xander's hands clenched into fists at his sides. Only Samantha's continued faith in him, her complete belief that he wasn't a violent man like his father, held him in check.

'You no longer met the criteria of membership to the Midas nightclub,' he dismissed harshly, at the same time cursing himself for having acted so impulsively by cancelling the other man's membership when he did, prematurely alerting Howard to his plans.

It had been a stupid reaction on Xander's part, even petty, and was the reason for Howard's unwanted presence this morning.

But just the thought of going to Midas one evening, of seeing this man enjoying himself in *his* club, a man capable of blackmailing his ex-wife into going to bed with him, had just been too much for Xander to contemplate. He wasn't sure even Samantha's faith in him would have been enough to prevent him from reacting under those circumstances.

'And what criteria would that be?' the other man challenged. 'No man is allowed to be a member of the Midas nightclub if you are currently sleeping with his ex-wife? If so, then I'm surprised there are any men left in London to fill your club!'

Xander counted to ten in his head. And then counted another ten. And another. And another.

He was determined, he would *not* let Samantha down, and let his temper get the better of him.

'Nothing to say?' Howard challenged.

'I resent even having to breathe the same air as you,' Xander said icily.

Howard's face twisted into an ugly sneer. 'I'm guessing you conveniently forget that aversion when it comes to you sleeping with my ex-wife?'

'Don't say another word,' Xander warned harshly. 'Not. Another. Word.' A nerve pulsed rapidly in his tightly clenched jaw.

How he would like to knock this man unconscious and put an end to this conversation. Just one little punch to that sneering face, that was all it would take for him to silence Howard and his vile mouth.

But Xander knew he couldn't let himself do it, no matter what the temptation. That he couldn't betray the trust, the belief, that Samantha had in him.

He drew in a deep and controlling breath. 'I have no intention of saying anything else to you without Samantha being present. She's waiting for us in my study.' He didn't wait to see if the other man followed him as he turned and walked down the hallway, ignoring the jarring pain in his leg as he did so.

Welcoming that pain if it stopped him from giving in to the anger now consuming him.

Malcolm Howard was supposed to have loved Samantha and Daisy, protected them both, and instead he'd deliberately hurt them.

How could Samantha have ever thought she was in love with such a man, let alone married him?

But Xander knew exactly how. From their conversations he knew she had been very young and completely alone in the world when she and Howard had met.

No doubt she had been flattered by the attentions of this older and seemingly charming and sophisticated man. The man she had trusted to love and take care of her.

Xander turned to look at the other man coldly as he paused outside the closed door to his study. 'Know this, Howard—if you hurt Samantha again, then I would also advise that you keep a watchful eye over your shoulder in the future.' He showed his teeth in a feral smile.

Howard's face flushed angrily. 'Are you threatening me?'

'That wasn't a threat, it was a promise,' Xander assured him softly as he opened the study door before standing back to allow Howard to enter the room ahead of him.

Xander followed close behind him and saw that Samantha was standing by the window, the sun shining into the room behind her preventing him—and consequently Howard, too—from being able to make out her expression. But Xander could tell by the stiffness of her slender shoulders, and the way her hands were clasped tightly together in front of her, that the next few minutes were going to be an ordeal for her.

He crossed the room to stand in front of her, deliberately blocking her from Howard's view, as he took both of her icy-cold hands in his. He was able to see how white her face was now, casting those freckles across her nose and cheeks into sharp relief, and her eyes were dark with unspoken pain as she looked up at him trustingly.

Xander vowed there and then that he would never, could never, let down or betray this warm and vulnerable woman's trust in him.

'Ready?' he asked softly.

Sam wasn't sure she would ever be ready for what she knew was going to be a very unpleasant confrontation with her ex-husband. And she still felt guilty, as well as grateful, that Xander had become so deeply involved in her personal problems. Admittedly, he had asked to be involved, but she doubted that when he had he'd realised just how unpleasant this situation was going to get. She had known from his expression earlier that he certainly hadn't imagined her ex-husband would turn up at his apartment this morning.

'Touching as this scene undoubtedly is,' Malcolm bit out scornfully behind them, 'perhaps you could take your hands off my ex-wife long enough for the three of us to actually *have* this conversation!'

Sam had taken advantage of Xander's short absence to steel herself against showing any reaction to seeing Malcolm again, but there was no way she could stop the nausea that now roiled in her stomach as she listened to his sarcastic taunt. She should have remembered that words had always been Malcolm's weapon of choice.

'Ignore him and look at me,' Xander urged softly, his hands tightening about hers as she did as he asked and looked up into his warm and compassionate eyes. 'Whatever happens, know that I'm here to protect you and Daisy,' he encouraged gruffly. 'That I won't let him hurt either of you.'

Grateful tears now blurred Sam's vision even as she straightened her spine determinedly. 'Let's do this.' She nodded.

'Well done,' Xander murmured, giving her hands a last squeeze before releasing them. 'When I move away, go and sit behind the desk,' he told her softly. 'It will give you a degree of power,' he explained as she eyed him quizzically.

Sam smiled, sure that Xander had used that degree of power a few times himself. 'Thank you,' she mouthed before stepping to the side and then past him, noting Malcolm sprawled comfortably in the chair on the opposite side of the desk even as she seated herself in the high-back leather chair behind it.

She was aware of Xander moving to stand with his back leaning against the wall behind her so he could look directly at Malcolm.

Her gaze was icy as she looked across the desk at her ex-husband. 'This conversation should have been left to our lawyers.'

Malcolm's top lip curled back in a sneer. 'My, my, how brave you've become since you began sharing the bed of a billionaire.'

'Stop this right now, Malcolm.' Sam glared across the width of the desk at him as she heard Xander pushing fiercely away from the wall behind her.

'So defensive on your lover's behalf,' Malcolm continued as he eyed the younger man speculatively. 'Nothing to say for yourself, Sterne?' His voice hardened challengingly.

Xander had hoped, with the help of his warning out in the hallway, that this conversation might have at least given a semblance of civility. The older man's continued and insulting aggression told him that wasn't going to happen.

'I don't feel the need to defend myself to men like you,' Xander scorned. 'Weak men, who take pleasure in hurting women and children.'

The older man snorted. 'I don't remember hearing Sam complaining at the time.'

'Maybe you just weren't listening?'

Howard's expression darkened. 'You—'

'Let's just get to the point of this meeting, shall we?' Xander sighed wearily, not sure how much longer he was willing to put up with this man's insulting behaviour.

'I haven't finished.'

'Oh, you're finished,' Xander assured the other man coldly. 'You just aren't smart enough to know when you're down, let alone out!'

Howard's face twisted into fury as he sat forward tensely. 'You arrogant bast—'

'Not quite, I believe my parents had been married for almost seven months when my twin and I were born,' Xander interrupted dismissively.

'I meant figuratively not literally.'

'Okay, I'll start this conversation, if you won't.' Xander stared at the other man coldly. 'For the past week you have been experiencing difficulties, in obtaining a business loan from a certain bank, I believe.'

The older man surged angrily to his feet. 'Are you saying you're responsible for that too?'

Xander gave Samantha a rueful glance. 'I thought you said he was intelligent?'

She shrugged. 'I believed he was.'

'Obviously you were wrong.' Xander smiled. 'So, let's just cut to the chase, shall we, Howard? My lawyer has already drawn up a contract, which you *will* go to his office and sign on Monday morning, which declares that you agree to give Samantha the divorce settlement of one million pounds that you should have given her three years ago, as well as giving up all and any claim to Daisy, with the added agreement that you will make no attempt to see either one of them ever again.'

'Are you completely insane?' Howard laughed incredulously.

It was everything Sam wanted, of course—except the million pounds. She didn't want anything for herself, least of all Malcolm's money. All she wanted was the freedom to know that she need never again fear Malcolm making any sort of claim on Daisy.

But she wasn't stupid enough to turn the money down either if it was given, knew that with a million pounds she would be able to put most of the money into trust for Daisy, and that the rest would allow her to raise her daughter without worrying where every penny came from.

Was Xander really capable of intimidating Malcolm into agreeing to sign such a one-sided contract? One look at the cold determination in his face was enough to answer that.

'I really should listen to Xander if I were you, Malcolm.'

'Do you think I give a damn about the opinion of a little nonentity like *you*?' Malcolm turned on Sam sneeringly. 'You might be feeling all brave and fearless right now, but let's just wait and see how brave you're feeling once Sterne gets bored with you and kicks you out of his bed.' Malcolm seemed to flinch then as Xander stepped forward threateningly.

Control it, Xander told himself as he came to a halt just inches away from the other man. *Keep it together. Don't do this. Don't let this man bait you into doing something you'll regret.*

Especially don't lose it in front of Samantha.

That would surely be unforgivable when she continued to look at him so trustingly.

His eyes glittered down at the other man in warning. 'Maybe you should consider putting some respect in your tone when you talk to Samantha?'

The older man gave a snort. 'Why should it matter to you how I talk to her?'

'All you need to know is that it does,' Xander stated coldly.

'And maybe *you* should stop giving her the false hope that you actually care?' Howard scoffed. 'Okay, so you're enjoying playing the part of the White Knight right now, but we both know she's just an amusement to you, a pretty toy to warm your bed for a while. But only until you get bored with her and move on to the next conquest.'

The scornful taunt was so close to what Sam already knew was going to happen between herself and Xander, and sooner rather than later, that she couldn't help but feel the pain of it twisting deep inside her.

Which was exactly the reaction Malcolm had hoped for.

She was made of stronger stuff than that. Was bigger than Malcolm. Was certainly a far better person than he could ever be.

And so was Xander.

'Xander,' Sam cut in determinedly, 'you do realise that if you give in to the impulse you feel to hit him, that you'll have to disinfect your hand afterwards?' Somehow Sam managed to keep her voice light and mocking as she remained seated behind the desk—the latter because she doubted her legs would support her if she attempted to stand!

It was possible to visibly see the tension leave Xander's shoulders as she taunted Malcolm, those dark brown eyes glowing with admiration, an approving smile slowly curving those sculpted lips.

Sam shakily returned that smile, dearly hoping she looked more confident than she felt.

Xander's warmth faded as he turned back to face the other man. 'Which of us is the more powerful, do you think, Howard?' he mused dryly. 'How long do you think you'll be able to continue to be in business if I don't come through with that loan? And how long would you continue to be invited to the fashionable parties you so enjoy, if I should decide to make my aversion to you public? How many restaurants would suddenly find they have no tables available? How many of London's elite would begin to question *why* it is I find you so obnoxious?'

'Because you're obviously having an affair with my ex-wife!' the other man blustered.

'I work for him,' Sam corrected firmly, decisively, her gaze hardening as she realised from Malcolm's bluster just how weak he really was. 'You *will* go to Xander's lawyer, Malcolm. You will sign the contract. And then you will never show your face anywhere that I might ever see it again. Because if you don't,' she continued coldly as Malcolm would have spoken, 'I will let Xander ruin you.'

Xander had never admired Samantha more than he did at that moment. She looked magnificent. All fiery eyed, and with her hair like a living flame about her shoulders.

Howard breathed hard. 'And if I do sign this contract what guarantee do I have that you'll keep your side of the bargain?'

'You have my own and Samantha's word on it,' Xander answered the other man harshly. 'And, unlike you, Samantha's integrity is unimpeachable. My own word, again unlike your own, is completely dependable as well as deeply respected.'

The older man's face twisted into an ugly mask. 'Why the hell should I give you that power?'

'Because I *will* take delight in ruining you if you don't sign the contract?' Xander retorted mildly.

Howard snorted. 'I would be living with the sword of Damocles hanging over my head for the rest of my life!'

'Better than having it thrust into your cold dead heart,' Xander countered unsympathetically.

Howard eyed him for several long moments, obviously fighting an inner battle with himself; arrogance as opposed to good sense. 'Okay, I'll sign your blasted contract!' he finally burst out fiercely as the latter obviously won. 'But you had better make sure you keep to your side of the bargain.'

'I just said I would,' Xander rasped, wishing this man would just go now. He so badly needed to hold Samantha, to comfort her, to take away that lost look he could see in her eyes.

Malcolm eyed them both scornfully. 'The two of you are welcome to each other.'

'Is that really the best you can do?' Sam asked, wondering why she had ever been frightened of this man. Certainly wondering how she could ever have thought she was in love with him!

'Oh, and, Malcolm,' she added as he turned to where

Xander now pointedly held the door open for him to leave, waiting until she had Malcolm's full attention before continuing, 'for the record, you were too damned selfish to ever know what I liked in bed!'

His face darkened as he took a threatening step back towards her.

'I ought to just—'

A little red-haired whirlwind dashed past an obviously surprised Xander to enter the study and begin kicking Malcolm's shins. 'Don't you dare hurt my mummy!'

Malcolm looked stunned for several seconds and then he reached down to grasp his daughter's shoulders in an attempt to hold her away from him. 'It's Daddy, Daisy.'

'You're not my daddy! Daddies are nice, and you're mean,' Daisy stormed. 'I hate you!' Tears streamed down Daisy's face as she continued to kick him.

Sam had been so stunned when Daisy rushed so unexpectedly into the room that for a few seconds she had been completely unable to react. But she now rose quickly to her feet before rushing round the desk to pull Daisy away from Malcolm and take her into her arms. 'It's all right, darling,' she assured Daisy as hot tears coursed down both their cheeks. She held her daughter tightly in her arms. 'Everything is going to be all right. I promise.'

Daisy clung to her. 'Make him go away, Xander! Make him go away!' She sobbed into Sam's shoulder.

Sam looked appealingly at a white-faced Xander over the top of Daisy's head, giving a choked sob as she watched him grasp hold of the back of Malcolm's shirt before pulling the other man out of the room and closing the door behind them.

Leaving Sam the privacy she needed to calm and soothe her broken-hearted daughter.

'Whew, it's been quite a day.' Xander sat in an armchair in the sitting room later that evening, Samantha seated opposite. And if Xander felt emotionally exhausted by the events of the day, then Samantha still looked shell-shocked.

'Daisy and I have to leave.'

'What?' Xander sat forward, frowning darkly at Samantha's quietly spoken comment.

Sam focused on him with effort; she was so tired she just wanted to crawl into bed, pull the covers over her head, and stay there for the rest of the weekend.

It was not going to happen, of course.

Once Sam had calmed Daisy down, promising her daughter over and over again that she would never see that horrible man again, Daisy had seemed to recover, with the resilience of all small children, from her emotional outburst. Xander's suggestion, when he returned to the study a few minutes later, of them all going to the cinema to see the film that Daisy wanted to see had clinched the deal.

Whereas Sam's recovery had all been a front, for Daisy's sake, and later that day she had found the tears slipping silently down her face as she stared up unseeingly at the animated film on the big screen in front of her. The feel of Xander's comforting fingers curling about hers in the darkness had been her complete undoing, and she had found herself falling slowly towards him, her head resting on his shoulder as she continued to quietly sob.

The rest of the day had been a blur, something to be endured rather than enjoyed. Xander had taken them all for a pizza after the cinema, and then read Daisy a story and tucked her up in bed after Sam had given her daughter her evening bath.

Upsetting as Daisy's outburst to Malcolm had been, it was Xander who was now at the centre of Sam's concerns.

Sam had realised today that it wasn't just Daisy who had come to rely on him too much this past week. She was also guilty of leaning on him. Depending on him too much.

And it had to stop.

Oh, she wouldn't dream of stopping Xander from continuing to see Daisy, if he wanted to; that would just be too cruel when her daughter so obviously adored him.

But Sam's own dependence on him had to end.

Right now.

'I think, after all that's happened, that Daisy and I have to leave. I can't tell you how grateful I am for all you've done for Daisy and me, but—'

'I don't want your gratitude, Samantha!'

'Nevertheless, you have it,' Sam insisted quietly, eyes downcast so that she didn't have to look at him. So she didn't have to acknowledge how much she loved him. 'You're recovering more and more every day, and I'm pretty sure you can manage on your own now. Malcolm is too scared now, of what he knows you can do to him, to ever bother us again. You're more than welcome to continue seeing Daisy, of course.'

'How generous of you!'

Sam winced at the sarcasm in Xander's voice. 'Please don't be angry, Xander.'

'What the hell do you expect me to be?' He ran an agitated hand through the blond thickness of his hair as he surged to his feet. 'What about last night, Samantha?' He frowned darkly. 'What about *us*?'

She gave a sad shake of her head. 'There is no us. There never could be.'

'You don't know that.'

'Yes, I do!' she said vehemently. 'Last night was— Well, it was wonderful,' she acknowledged huskily. 'But it can't happen again. And my staying on here, under those circumstances, would just be—I need to leave, Xander, can't you see that?' She looked up at him imploringly, silently pleading with him not to make this any harder for her than it already was.

The last thing she wanted was to leave him. How could it not be, when she was in love with him?

But they had come together under far from perfect circumstances. And Xander had been wonderful, amazing, both with Daisy, and with helping Sam deal with Malcolm once and for all. But Sam wasn't about to take advantage of his generous nature by allowing him to feel even more responsibility towards her because of what had happened between the two of them last night.

'I need to leave,' she repeated as she stood up with determination. 'Please don't make this any harder for me than it already is,' she added firmly as she could see Xander was about to make another protest. 'Daisy and I will be leaving in the morning. But I would appreciate it if you were able to see Daisy again. She loves you so much,' she added gruffly, knowing that she loved

Xander as much as, if not more than, her daughter did. Just as she knew it was breaking her heart to leave him.

Xander had never felt so impotent in his life as he did at this moment, knowing by the expression on Samantha's face that she meant what she said. That she had also made it clear that last night hadn't meant the same to her as it had to him. That she really did intend leaving him tomorrow.

And there wasn't a thing he could do or say to stop her.

CHAPTER ELEVEN

One month later.

'WHEN ARE YOU going to stop brooding and go and claim your woman?'

Xander hadn't heard his brother open the door as he leant back in his chair staring sightlessly—broodingly—out of the window of his office at the Midas Enterprises building in London.

He turned now to glare at Darius as his brother leant casually against the doorframe. 'I'm far too busy to deal with your warped sense of humour today, Darius!' he snarled aggressively as he straightened in his chair.

Darius straightened slowly before crossing the room. 'I can see that.' A mocking smile curved his lips as he looked down at Xander's obviously empty desk. 'I thought you might like to know I've just come back from visiting Miranda at the dance studio.'

Xander tensed. 'And why should that interest me?'

Topaz eyes gleamed with amusement. ''Possibly because I saw Sam too while I was there?'

Xander felt a painful lurch in his chest; he hadn't spoken privately to Samantha for four and a half weeks. Not since the day they had routed Howard so completely, and afterwards she'd told him she was leaving him the following morning. She'd then packed her bags and done exactly that.

He had tried to talk her out of it, of course. But Samantha had been stubbornly determined. She had again thanked him very politely for all his help, and reassured him he really was well enough to take care of himself now. That he didn't need her any more.

That he didn't *need* her any more?

Xander wasn't even sure he had drawn in breath without pain since Samantha left him that Sunday morning. He knew that not a moment went by when he didn't think about her. When he didn't want to see her, to just be with her again.

And he had been absolutely correct about his apartment having all the warmth of a morgue, once Samantha and Daisy were no longer living there with him. He now avoided being there as much as possible.

Xander's mouth tightened. 'Samantha has made her lack of interest in seeing me again very obvious, Darius.' *More* than obvious.

'Strange, she always asks how you are whenever I see her at Miranda's studio,' his brother told him softly.

Xander stood up abruptly to cross the room and stand in front of the floor-to-ceiling windows, his back to the room as he looked out blindly. 'She's just being polite, because she's grateful that I helped rid her of Howard from her life once and for all.'

Howard had duly kept his appointment at the lawyer's office, and neither Xander nor Samantha had needed to be present when the other man signed the contract. Howard had also paid Samantha's belated divorce settlement, and she and Daisy were now renting a two-bedroom apartment overlooking a park. Samantha had still taken up the part-time job at Andy's dance studio, and the two women had become even firmer friends, according to his sister-in-law.

Darius joined Xander by the window. 'Sam doesn't look well today, Xander.'

He turned sharply to look at his brother. 'What do you mean? What's wrong with her?' he demanded, frowning darkly.

'How would I know?' Darius shrugged.

Xander's scowl deepened. 'Maybe because your wife is Samantha's best friend as well as her employer?'

Darius eyed him pityingly. 'And Miranda and I have far better things to do than talk about Sam when we're alone together.'

'You are so annoying.' Xander turned abruptly to stride determinedly across his office and collect his coat from the back of his chair before quickly pulling it on.

'Where are you going?'

He shot his twin an angry glare as he strode over to the door. 'Out!' He ignored Darius's chuckle as he wrenched the door open before striding impatiently out into the hallway towards the lift.

He wasn't in the least surprised to find the car, and driver, waiting for him downstairs as he stepped outside the building; Darius might be annoying, but he could read his twin like a book.

'I'll drive myself, thank you, Paul.' He managed to smile at the other man as he took the keys from him to get in behind the wheel.

Xander felt more light-hearted than he had for the past four weeks as he drove through the busy London streets towards Andy's dance studio. He knew it was because he was going to see Samantha again. Was going to talk to her again.

Whether or not Samantha would be as pleased to see him was another matter.

'Dare I hope that you're finally here to see Sam?' his sister-in-law teased as he entered her dance studio a short time later, obviously having just finished taking her last dance class of the day.

Xander narrowed his eyes. 'You and Darius should seriously think about becoming a comedy team.'

Andy gave a husky laugh. 'Sam's in the office. If you're interested, that is?'

'Oh, I'm interested,' Xander confirmed determinedly.

'Good luck!'

Xander had no doubt he was going to need it!

'Samantha?'

Sam stilled as she heard the husky sound of Xander's voice in her head.

A voice she had heard so many times, and in exactly the same husky tone, these past few weeks. When she was here at work. Or at home with Daisy in their new apartment. When she lay alone in her bed at night.

And each time she heard it Sam felt a twisting pain in her chest. As evidence of the empty hollowness inside her, that she knew only Xander could fill. But never would.

She closed her lids as her eyes suddenly filled with scalding tears, silently willing them not to fall. Wishing the pain of loving Xander would stop. But knowing it never would.

'Samantha?'

Sam almost jumped out of her chair, her heart

pounded erratically in her chest, as she felt caressing fingers against her cheek, her eyes widening with disbelief as she found herself looking up at Xander.

He was the suave and sophisticated Xander Sterne today, successful billionaire businessman. A man so unlike the casually dressed Xander she had known and grown to love four weeks ago. Today he wore a dark, sleekly tailored suit and shirt, with a meticulously knotted tie, and his hair was professionally styled rather than the overlong and shaggy look he had favoured a month ago.

But it was the changes in his face that now caused Sam to frown; his cheeks seemed thinner even than the weekend, the last time he had called and picked Daisy up for the day, with deep grooves beside his mouth and eyes, and his mouth was a grim and uncompromising line.

Her throat moved convulsively as she swallowed, still not completely sure he was really here or just a figment of her aching imagination. 'Are you real?'

He gave a rueful smile. 'Unfortunately for you, yes, I'm very much real.'

Sam's frown deepened. 'Unfortunately for me?' She had never been so pleased to see anyone in her life before as she was Xander.

Just to be alone in the same room with him. To be able to drink him in: how he looked, how he moved, how he *smelled*.

'That last evening at my apartment you made it pretty clear that you had no interest in seeing me again.'

'I did?' The whole of that last day in his apartment had become something of a hazy dream to Sam the past few weeks.

'You did,' Xander confirmed grimly as he stepped away from her before thrusting his hands into his trousers pockets. 'Are you okay, Samantha?' He could see what Darius meant now; without Daisy as her protective shield, Samantha's cheeks were pale and hollow, those beautiful amethyst-coloured eyes dark and haunted.

'Has Howard been bothering you again?'

'No, absolutely not,' she assured him hastily. 'I'm pretty sure we've all seen and heard the last of him. And Daisy loves our new apartment. She so much enjoys going to the park after school.'

'I'm so glad to hear that. But I asked how *you* were, Samantha,' he said gruffly.

Her gaze now avoided meeting his. 'I love working here at the studio with Andy, and to no longer have any money worries—'

'That isn't what I was asking, either. Sorry,' Xander apologised as he realised he had raised his voice. 'I didn't mean to shout.' He grimaced. 'I just—I've missed you, Samantha.'

'You have?' she gasped softly.

Xander nodded abruptly. 'Very much. I— Look, will you have dinner with me this evening?' A nerve pulsed in his jaw as he waited for her answer.

Sam stared up at him, not altogether sure she had heard him correctly. Why would Xander invite her out to dinner with him? 'I really am okay, Xander,' she assured him ruefully. 'Malcolm signed the contract, and paid the divorce settlement into my account. I'm happy working here, and nicely settled into the new apartment. Daisy is happy—'

'I don't give a—!' Xander broke off, breathing heavily as he ran one agitated hand through the heavy thickness of his blond hair. 'Well. Yes.' He grimaced. 'Of course I care about those things, Samantha. But I'm asking you out to dinner for *me,* not so that we talk about your new flat, or how much Daisy loves the park or how she's doing at school.'

She gave a puzzled shake of her head. 'I don't understand.'

'Obviously not,' he muttered. 'Samantha, I'm trying to ask you out on a date, and all you keep doing is talking about everything else. Do you have any idea how frustrating that is? How irritating it is to have you keep telling me how good your life is now, when my own is completely messed up?'

'It is?'

He nodded abruptly. 'I can't eat or sleep. I can't *think.*'

Sam could barely breathe as a faint glimmer of hope began to burn in her chest. A hint of light in the heaviness that had been weighing her down for so many weeks. 'Why not?'

He gave a groan. 'Why do you think?'

She gave a cautious shake of her head. 'I have no idea.'

'Because I'm in love with you, damn it!' His eyes gleamed darkly. 'I'm so in love with you that nothing and no else is important to me any more. Not my family. Not my business. Just you. I can't think of anything else *but* you. Of how much I miss you. How much I want you and Daisy back in my life. How much I love you.'

'But you let me go,' Sam breathed softly.

'Because you said you *wanted* to go!'

'That was because—' Sam drew in a deep and steadying breath, totally stunned at having Xander tell her he loved her. Xander *loved* her? 'I didn't want to

leave, Xander. I just thought— You had been so good
to me already, saving me from Malcolm, being so patient and caring with Daisy. I didn't want you to let
me stay because you felt sorry for me, or because you
were still trying to protect me. I couldn't bear that.' Her
voice broke emotionally. 'If you couldn't think of me
as your equal—'

'I don't think of you as being my equal, Samantha. I
think of you as being so much better than I could ever
be—and I *adore* you for it!' He began to pace the room.
'But I didn't want you to stay with me out of gratitude,
either. Just because I had helped you sort out the situation with Howard.'

'I don't,' Samantha assured him. 'Well, of course I'm
grateful…' she smiled ruefully '…but that's certainly
not the reason I—that I made love with you the night
before that awful confrontation with Malcolm.'

'It isn't?'

'Absolutely not.'

There was no way that Xander could doubt Samantha's sincerity. 'Then why did you?' He gave an impa-
tient shake of his head. 'Do you have any idea how much
I've missed you? How empty my apartment is without
you in it? How empty my bed is without you in it?' He
breathed raggedly. 'I'm going quietly insane here, Samantha; so please will you say *something*?'

Sam stood up slowly, that glimmer of light bursting
into full brilliance inside her as the heavy weight of un-
happiness evaporated and left as if it had never been.
'I didn't want to leave you, Xander. I thought you just
felt sorry for me, and I didn't want that from you. You
had done so much for me already, I thought the least I
could do was leave you in peace.'

'Peace? I've been in living hell without you!' he insisted fiercely.

She reached up to gently touch the side of his face. 'Xander, the only reason I left that day was because I realised I'd fallen in love with you, and I didn't want you to feel in the least pressured to—to continue the relationship because you felt sorry for me.'

'What?'

She smiled shakily. 'I'm in love with you, Xander. So much that it *hurts*. You asked how I've been? Well, I've been just awful. I can't eat. I can't sleep. I think about you all the time. I *miss* you all the time.'

'Can we both really have been that stupid?' Xander gazed down at her in wonder.

Sam gave a tremulous smile. 'It certainly looks like it.'

His expression softened as he took her into his arms in a crushing hold. 'I love you!' he groaned achingly into her hair. 'I love you, Samantha. Do you have any idea what it meant to me—how much I value that you believed in me, trusted me, when I didn't?'

'And look how right I was about that,' she said huskily. 'Your protectiveness of those weaker than yourself is a blessing, Xander, and has absolutely nothing to do with men like your father and my ex-husband.'

Xander's arms tightened. 'I've felt so empty without you in my life, Samantha.'

'Me too, without you.' Sam held onto him just as tightly.

'Does that mean you'll marry me?'

Sam opened startled eyes. 'Marry you?'

Xander's hands moved up to cradle each side of her face as he looked down with all of his love for her shining in his eyes. 'You don't have to marry me immediately if it's too soon for you. Just tell me that you'll be my wife one day very soon.' His hands trembled. 'I love you so very much, my darling Samantha, and I can't bear the thought of not being with you for ever now that I know you love me too.'

It was more, so much more than Sam had ever thought, had ever imagined might happen in her life.

Xander loved her.

As she loved him.

And she couldn't bear the thought of the two of them not being together for ever either.

'Yes, I'll marry you, Xander,' she answered him exultantly.

'You will?' He looked down at her wonderingly.

'I will.'

'When?'

'Next week? Tomorrow?' She laughed huskily as she saw the urgency in Xander's expression.

He grinned. 'I want you to have a big white wedding. In a church. Surrounded by all our friends and family. Daisy can be your bridesmaid.'

Sam was sure it wasn't accidental that Xander was describing a wedding that was the exact opposite of that hurried union to Malcolm in a register office six years ago. Or that Daisy would be a large part of that ceremony.

Xander was tacitly telling her their marriage, his love for her and Daisy, would be nothing like her previous one.

As if Sam had ever thought otherwise.

She hadn't thought it possible, but she loved Xander more than ever at that moment, and she knew she always would.

'It sounds perfect.' She beamed up at him.

'*You're* perfect,' he assured her warmly. 'I promise you we'll be so happy together, Samantha. We can buy a house, with a garden for Daisy, and—'

'And have more children?' Sam ventured cautiously. 'I always wanted a big family,' she explained shyly.

'Then we'll have a houseful of children,' Xander promised her. 'As long as I have you to love, and you to love me, then I'll be happy.'

It was all that Sam could ever have hoped or wished for…and more.

EPILOGUE

'WHAT ARE WE looking at, Daddy?' Daisy asked in a loud whisper.

'I'm not too sure,' Xander muttered, Daisy sitting on his knee as the two of them frowned at the monitor in front of them, his free hand tightly holding onto Samantha's as she lay on the bed beside them.

'It doesn't look much like a baby, Daddy,' Daisy said doubtfully as they watched the movements being projected from inside Samantha's womb onto the monitor.

Xander felt his panic rise; it didn't look like any baby he had ever seen either. Admittedly there was the thud-thud sound of a heartbeat, but even that sounded too rapid, and there were definitely too many legs visible—

'That's because it's two babies, darling,' Samantha murmured indulgently.

'What?' Xander gasped.

'Two babies,' she repeated emotionally.

'Two babies,' Xander echoed faintly, realising that must be the reason the heartbeat sounded too rapid: because it was two heartbeats, not one.

'It would seem that we're having twins, darling,' Samantha assured him lovingly.

He swallowed, his mouth dry. 'I can't— We can't—'

'Of course we can.' She smiled indulgently. 'You're a twin,' she reminded him calmly.

'Twins.' Xander put Daisy down to stand up and hug his wife. 'We're having twins!' he cried, tears of happiness shining in his eyes.

'Yes, we are.' Samantha laughed huskily as she hugged him back.

He gave a sudden groan as he slowly released her before straightening. 'You do realise Darius is never going to stop teasing me?' he explained as Samantha gave him a questioning glance.

'He won't,' she assured him.

'Of course he will.' Xander groaned again.

'He really won't.' Sam laughed softly, her heart bursting with love for the man who had been her husband for this past wonderful year. 'Andy told me yesterday that the two of them are expecting twins too!'

'Hah!' Xander gave a grin of triumph. 'My mother and Charles are going to be thrilled at the idea of more grandchildren!'

Sam couldn't have asked for nicer in-laws than Catherine and Charles, and they absolutely adored Daisy. She had no doubt there was plenty of room in those two kind hearts for a dozen more grandchildren.

'Wait.' Xander gave a teasing grimace. 'How will I cope if it's two girls and I have three little Samanthas twisting me round their little fingers?' He gazed down at Daisy, whom he absolutely adored and who adored him back.

'Look on the bright side, darling,' Sam teased. 'It could be two little Xanders to twist me round their little fingers!'

'Would you like to know the sex of your two babies?' the technician asked softly.

Sam looked at Xander and Xander looked at Sam, and then both of them shook their heads at the same time.

Sons, or more daughters, they would love all of their children.

As much as they loved and adored each other.

* * * * *

'You *lied* to me?'

'I wouldn't exactly call it a lie…' Naturally Lucas had expected surprise—incredulity, even—but at the end of the day a ski instructor had been swapped for a billionaire. He had taken it as a given that his newly discovered status would do its usual job and bring a smile of servile appreciation to her lips. It hadn't.

'Well, *I* would.' Milly was struggling to contain her anger. How *dared* he? How dared he play her for a complete fool?

'You made false assumptions,' Lucas told her with barely concealed impatience. 'I chose not to set you straight.'

She sprang to her feet and stormed over to the window, stared out for a little while, and then stormed back towards him, hands on her hips. 'Why didn't you just tell me who you were?'

Because I was enjoying the novelty of being with someone refreshingly honest… Because in a world where wariness and suspicion are bywords it was a holiday, not having to guard every syllable, watch every turn of phrase, accept instant adulation without being able to distinguish what was genuine and what was promoted by a healthy knowledge of how much I was worth…

'When you're as rich as I am, it pays to be careful.'

'In other words, I could have been just another cheap, tacky gold-digger, after your money?'

'If you want to put it like that…'

His dark eyes were cool, assessing, unflinching. She could have hit him.

But there was no denying that she still wanted to kiss him.

Cathy Williams can remember reading Mills and Boon® as a teenager, and now that she's writing them she remains an avid fan. For her, there is nothing like creating romantic stories and engaging plots, and each and every book is a new adventure. Cathy lives in London, and her three daughters, Charlotte, Olivia and Emma, have always been and continue to be the greatest inspiration in her life.

Books by Cathy Williams

Seven Sexy Sins

To Sin with the Tycoon

Protecting His Legacy

The Secret Sinclair

One Night In…

His Christmas Acquisition

The Uncompromising Italian
The Argentinian's Demand
Secrets of a Ruthless Tycoon
Enthralled by Moretti
His Temporary Mistress
A Deal with Di Capua
The Secret Casella Baby
The Notorious Gabriel Diaz
A Tempestuous Temptation
The Girl He'd Overlooked
The Truth Behind His Touch
Her Impossible Boss

**Visit the author profile page at
www.millsandboon.co.uk for more titles**

THE REAL
ROMERO

BY
CATHY WILLIAMS

Published in Great Britain 2015
by Mills & Boon, an imprint of Harlequin (UK) Limited,
Eton House, 18-24 Paradise Road, Richmond, Surrey, TW9 1SR

© 2015 Cathy Williams

ISBN: 978-0-263-25052-7

Harlequin (UK) Limited's policy is to use papers that are natural, renewable and recyclable products and made from wood grown in sustainable forests. The logging and manufacturing processes conform to the legal environmental regulations of the country of origin.

Printed and bound in Spain
by CPI, Barcelona

THE REAL ROMERO

To my fabulous and inspiring daughters.

CHAPTER ONE

'AMELIA? IS THAT Amelia Mayfield?'

Milly pressed the mobile phone against her ear, already regretting that she had been stupid enough to pick up the call. How many more instructions could Sandra King give about this job?

She was going to be a chalet girl! Two weeks of cooking and looking after a family of four! Anyone would think that she was being primed to run the country. It wasn't even as though she hadn't done this before. She had, two years ago, for three months before she'd started the hotel job in London.

'Yes.' She sighed, allowing her eyes to drift over the pure, dazzling canvas of white snow all around her. It had been a fantastic trip, just the thing to clear her head and get her mind off her miserable situation. She had travelled in style and she had enjoyed every second of it. It was almost a shame that she was now in the back seat of the chauffeur-driven SUV with her destination only half an hour away.

'You haven't been picking up your phone!' The voice down the other end was sharp and accusatory. Milly could picture the other woman clearly, sitting at her desk in Mayfair, her shiny blond hair scraped back with an

Alice band, her long perfectly manicured nails tapping impatiently on her desk.

Sandra King had interviewed her not once but three times for this job. It was almost as though she had resented having to give the job to someone small and round with red hair when there were so many other, more suitable candidates in the mix: girls with cut-glass accents, braying laughs and shiny blond hair scraped back with Alice bands.

But, as she had made clear with unnecessarily cruel satisfaction, this particular family wanted someone plain and down to earth, because the last thing the *señora* wanted was a floozy who might decide to start flirting with her rich husband.

Milly, who had looked up the family she would be working for on Google after her first interview, had only just managed not to snort with disbelief because the husband in question was definitely *not* the sort of man any girl in her right mind would choose to flirt with. He was portly, semi-balding and the wrong side of fifty, but he was filthy rich, and she supposed that that was as compelling an attraction as being a rock star. Not that she was in the market for flirting with anyone, anyway.

'Sorry, Sandra…' She grinned because she knew that Sandra didn't like being called by her first name. It was 'Ms King', or 'Skipper' to the chosen few. The other girls in the exclusive agency that dealt specifically with part-time positions to the rich and famous called her Skipper, one of those silly nicknames that Milly guessed had been concocted in whatever posh boarding school they had all attended.

'The service has been a bit iffy ever since I left London…and I can't talk for long because my phone's almost out of charge.' Not strictly true but she didn't need yet another check list of the various things the special family ate and didn't eat; or the favourite things the special little kids, aged four and six, insisted on doing before they went to bed. She didn't need to be reminded of what she could and couldn't wear, or say or couldn't say.

Milly had never known people to be as fussy with just about everything. The family for whom she had worked two years previously had been jolly, outdoorsy and amenable.

But she wasn't complaining. They might be fussy but the pay was fabulous and, more importantly, the job removed her from the vicinity of Robbie, Emily and heartbreak.

She had managed to push her ex-fiancé, her best friend and her broken engagement out of her head, but she could feel them staging another takeover, and she blinked rapidly, fighting back tears of self-pity. Time healed, she had been told repeatedly by her friends, who had never liked Robbie from the start and, now that she was no longer engaged, had felt free to let loose every single pejorative thing they had thought about him from day one.

On the one hand, their negative comments had been bolstering and supportive. On the other, they had shown up her utter lack of judgement.

'In that case,' the well-bred, disembodied voice informed her, 'I'm afraid I have to inform you that the job has been cancelled.'

It took a few seconds for that to sink in. Milly had been busy being distracted by the unfortunate turn of events that had catapulted her life from sorted and happy to humiliated and up in the air.

'Did you hear what I just said, Amelia?'

'You're kidding, aren't you? Please tell me that this is a joke.' But Sandra King was not the sort who had a sense of humour. Any joke, for her, would be foreign territory.

'I never joke,' the other woman said, on cue. 'The Ramos family has pulled out at the last minute. I only took their phone call a few hours ago and, if you had *picked up your phone* instead of *letting it ring,* you would not have wasted your time travelling.'

'Why? Why is it off?' Visions of slinking back into the flat she had shared with Emily, risking bumping into her one-time best friend clearing her stuff before she took off to America with Robbie, were so horrifying that she felt giddy.

'One of the kids has come down with chicken pox. Simple as that.'

'But I'm only half an hour away from the lodge!' Milly all but wailed.

They had left the exclusive village of Courchevel behind and the car was wending its way upwards, leaving the riff-raff of the lower slopes behind as it entered the rarefied air of the seriously rich. Hidden, private lodges with majestic views; helipads; heated indoor swimming pools; saunas and steam rooms by the bucket load...

There was an elaborate sigh from the end of the line. 'Well, you'll have to tell the driver to swing round and head back, I'm afraid. Naturally, you will be compensated for your time and trouble...'

'Surely I can spend *one night* there? It's getting dark and I'm exhausted. I have a key to the place. I can use it and make sure that I leave the lodge in pristine condition. I need to sleep, Sandra!'

She couldn't get her head round the fact that the one thing that seemed to be working in her favour, the *only* thing that had worked in her favour for the past couple of horrific, nightmarish weeks, was now collapsing around her feet like a deck of cards, kicked down by one of the odious rich kids from the family who had bailed at the last minute. A wave of hopeless self-pity threatened to engulf her.

'That would be highly irregular.'

'So is the fact that my job here has been cancelled at the last minute, when I'm *fifteen minutes* away from the lodge—having spent the past eight hours travelling!'

She could see the lodge rearing up ahead of them and for a few seconds every depressing, negative thought flew from her head in sheer, wondrous appreciation of the magnificent structure ahead of her.

It dominated the skyscape, rising up against the blindingly white snow, master of all it surveyed. It was absolutely enormous, the largest and grandest ski lodge Milly had ever seen in her life. In fact, it was almost an understatement to classify it as a 'lodge'. It was more like a mansion in the middle of its own private, snowy playground.

'I suppose there's little choice!' Sandra snapped. 'But for God's sake, Amelia, pick up when you hear your phone! And make sure you don't touch anything. No poking around. Just eat and sleep and make sure that when you leave the lodge no one knows you've been there.'

Milly grimaced as she was abruptly disconnected. She leaned forward, craning to get glimpses of the mansion as it drew closer and closer to her, until the SUV was turning left and climbing through private land to where it nestled in all its splendour.

'Er…' She cleared her throat and hoped that the driver, who had greeted her at Chambery airport in extremely broken English and had not said a word since, would get the gist of what she was going to say.

'Oui, mademoiselle?'

Milly caught his eye in the rear-view mirror. 'Yes, well, there's been a slight change of plan...'

'What is that?'

She sighed with relief. At least she wouldn't have to try and explain an impossible situation using her limited French, resisting the temptation to fill in the gaps by speaking loudly. She told him as succinctly as possible. He would have to stay overnight somewhere and return her to the airport the following day... Sorry, so sorry for the inconvenience, but he could phone...

She scrambled into her capacious rucksack and extracted her wallet and from that the agency card that she had not envisaged having to use for the next couple of weeks.

She wondered whether he might stay at the lodge, it was big enough to fit a hundred drivers, but that was something he would have to work out for himself. She suspected that she had already stretched Sandra's limited supply of the milk of human kindness by asking if she could stay overnight in the place.

It was a dog-eat-dog world, she thought. As things stood, she was rock-bottom of the pack. She had been cheated on by her fiancé, a guy she had known since childhood and, as if that wasn't bad enough, she had been cheated on by her best friend and flatmate...

To top it off, she had been told that the reason he had become engaged to her in the first place was because his parents were fed up with his twenty-four-seven lifestyle of living it large and womanising. They had given him a deadline to find himself a decent girl and settle down or else he could forget about taking over the family business that had just opened a thriving branch in Philadelphia and was going places.

Banished from the family fortune and a ready-made job, he would have been faced, she assumed, with the terrifying prospect of actually buckling down and finding himself a job without Mummy and Daddy's helping hand. And so he had plumped for the slightly less terrifying prospect of charming her into thinking that they really had a relationship, proposing marriage whilst playing the field with her much taller, much skinnier and much prettier flatmate.

His parents had approved of her. She had passed the litmus test with them. She was his passport to his inheritance. She was small, round and homely; when she thought of Robbie and the angular Emily, every insecurity she nursed about her looks rose to the surface at the speed of light.

The only thing worse than catching them in bed together would have been actually marrying the creep, only to discover once the ring was on her finger that he had zero interest in her.

She gazed mournfully at her finger where a giant diamond rock had nestled only a few weeks ago.

Her friends had all told her that it was a monumental mistake to have chucked it back at him, that she should have kept it and flogged it at the first available opportunity. After all, she deserved it, after what he had put her through.

And the money would have stood her in good stead, considering she had jacked in her hotel job so that she could play happy families with him in Philadelphia. It was galling to think that he had had the nerve to tell her that he hoped she understood and that she could count on him if she ever needed anything!

As things currently stood, she was out of a job, banished from her flat until Emily cleared out and with a shockingly small amount of money saved.

And she had no one to turn to. Her only living relative, her grandmother who lived in Scotland, would have sold her cottage had she known about her granddaughter's state of near penury, but Milly had no intention of filling her in on that. It was bad enough that she had had to pick up the pieces when she had been told fifteen days ago that the fairy-tale wedding was off the cards.

As far as her grandmother was concerned, Milly was taking time off to work as a nanny for a family in Courchevel, where she would be able to do what she loved most, namely ski... She had glossed over the trauma of her breakup as just one of those things, nothing that a couple of weeks in the snow couldn't cure.

Milly had painted a glowing picture of a cosy family, practically friends, who would be there for her on her road to recovery. It had helped her grandmother to stop fretting. Furthermore, she had embroidered the recovery theme by announcing that she had another job lined up as soon as she was back in London, far better than the one she had jettisoned.

As far as her grandmother was concerned, she was as right as rain, because the last thing Milly wanted to do was worry her.

'Shall I call...er...the agency and see if you could stay overnight at the lodge...?' Her better instincts grudgingly cranked into gear and she resigned herself to another awkward conversation with Sandra, who would probably spend a ridiculously long time telling her that being let down was all her fault because she should have just *answered her phone,* having confirmed that the driver would not, definitely *not,* be allowed to sully the mansion, no way.

But, no; Pierre, the driver, was a regular at one of the hotels in Courchevel, where one of his relatives worked, and he would be fine there.

Milly was tempted to ask whether being let down by the special family came with the job. Maybe he had a permanent room there for when he got messed around.

She didn't. Instead, she allowed him to help her with her luggage, the luggage containing the clothes that would never be worn, and he only drove off when she had unlocked the imposing front door to let herself into the lodge.

It was blessedly warm and indescribably stunning, a testimony to the marvels of modern architecture and minimalism. The entire space was open-plan, with two sitting rooms cleverly split by a wall in which a high-tech, uber-modern fire caught the eye and held it. Beyond that, she could glimpse a vast kitchen, and beyond that yet more, although she was drawn to the floor-to-ceiling windows that captured the spectacular views of the valley.

She gazed out at the untouched, pristine snow, fast fading as night descended. It had been an excellent ski season so far—good accumulation of snow, which had collected on the roofs of the lodges lower down the mountain and lay there like banks and banks of smooth, marzipan icing.

Having no idea of the layout of the lodge, she decided to take her time exploring. She wasn't going to be there long, so why not enjoy the adventure of discovery? Her flat was small and poky. More than four people in the sitting area constituted a traffic jam. Why not pretend that this place belonged to her?

She explored each room exhaustively, one at a time. She admired the sparse, expensive furnishings. She had never seen so much chrome, glass and leather under one roof in her life before. Much of the furniture was white, and she marvelled at a couple confident enough to let loose two small children in a space where there was so much potential for destruction.

The kitchen was a wonder to behold: black granite counters, a table fashioned from beaten metal and an array of gadgets that made her culinary fingers itch.

She decided that she was glad she no longer worked at the Rainbow Hotel. It boasted three stars, but everyone there reckoned palms must have been greased to get that rating because the rooms were basic, bordering on the criminally dull, the restaurant should have been updated half a century ago and the two bars were straight out of the seventies but without a cool, retro feel.

Not to mention the fact that she had never been allowed, not once in a year and a half, to do anything on her own, Chef Julian, whilst only dabbling in the actual cooking, had specialised in peering over her shoulder and picking fault with her cooking whenever he got the chance.

Here, she could have let her imagination go wild—within the constraints of the various faddy food groups they did and didn't eat, of course. She trailed her hand over the gleaming, spotless counter and brushed a few of the marvellous gadgets, none of which bore the hallmarks of anyone ever having been near them. When she checked the fridge, it was to find that it was fully stocked, as were the cupboards. A horizontal metal wine rack groaned under the weight of bottles, all of which bore expensive, fancy labels.

Absorbed in her inspection of the kitchen, daydreaming about what it might feel like actually to have enough money to own a place like this as a second home, Milly was unaware of anyone approaching.

'And you are…?'

The deep, cold voice coming from behind crashed through her pleasant, escapist fantasy with the unwelcome force of a sledgehammer and she spun round, heart pounding.

Her brain, which had been lagging behind, caught up to point out mockingly that there was a stranger in the house and she should be looking for something handy with which she could defend herself.

Because the man could be….*dangerous*…

Her mind went blank. She forgot that she should be scared—terrified, even. She was in a bloody great rolling mansion packed full of valuables and the owners weren't there. The man standing in front of her, all six foot something of him, had probably broken in. She had probably disturbed him in the middle of ransacking the place, and everyone knew what happened to innocent people when they happened to interrupt a robbery.

But, God, had she ever seen someone so beautiful?

Raven-black hair, slightly longer than was conventionally permissible, framed a face that was, simply put, a thing of perfection: a wide, sensual mouth; chiselled features; eyes as dark and as fathomless as night. He was in jeans and a T-shirt and was barefoot.

It seemed unusual for a robber to take his shoes off to make off with the silver, but then it occurred to her that he had probably removed them so that he could sneak up on her unannounced.

'I could ask you the same thing!' She tried to keep the tenor of her voice calm and controlled—a woman in charge of the situation, someone who wasn't going

to be intimidated. 'And don't even *think* of taking a
single step closer to me!' Idiot that she was, she had
left her mobile phone lying in her rucksack, which was
currently reclining on the kitchen counter. It was infuriating, but how could she possibly have anticipated
something like this?

In stark disobedience of her orders, the man took a
couple of steps closer to her and she fell back, bumped
into the counter and spun round to grab the nearest
heavy thing to hand—which happened to be the kettle,
a glass concoction that didn't look as though it could
stun a flea, never mind the muscled man who was now
only a metre away from her and had folded his arms,
cool as a cucumber.

'Or else what? Don't tell me you have plans for using
that thing on me…?'

'You'd better tell me what you're doing here or else
I'm going to…call the police. And I'm not kidding…'

This had not been the way Lucas had anticipated his
evening going. In fact, he hadn't actually banked on
being here at all. He had lent the place to his mother's
annoying friends, only for them to cancel at the last
minute, which was when he had decided to head there
himself for a few days.

He would get away from his mother, who was becoming more strident in her demands for him to settle
down and get married. She had suffered a minor stroke
three months previously, had been pronounced fit and
able, yet had decided that she had stared death in the
face, had become acquainted with her own mortality—
and now all she wanted was to hold a grandchild in her
arms before she died. Was that asking too much of her
only beloved son?

Frankly, Lucas thought that it was, but he had not

been inclined to say so. Instead, he had wheeled out consultant after consultant, but no amount of reassurances from these top consultants could convince her that her fragile grasp on life wasn't about to be snipped.

Add to that an annoying ex-girlfriend who refused to believe that she had been dumped, and a few days' skiing had suddenly seemed like a brilliant idea.

Bracing conversations with his mother could be better faced after he had vented his frustrations in a few black runs.

Peace and quiet seemed to have nosedived, however, and he was not in the best of moods to be standing here, staring down a crazy woman brandishing his kettle and threatening to call the police.

A short, crazy woman, with red hair that was all over the place, and who thought he was looting the place. Hilarious.

'You don't really think you could take me on, do you?' With lightning reflexes, he reached out and relieved her of her dangerous weapon, which he proceeded to set back down on its base. 'Now, before *I* call the police and have you forcibly removed, you're going to tell me what the hell *you're* doing here.'

Deprived of the kettle, Milly stuck her chin out at a stubborn angle and stared at him defiantly. 'You're not scaring me, if that's your intention.'

'It's never been my intention to scare a woman.'

The man oozed sex appeal through every pore. It was off-putting. How could she get her thoughts in order when he stood there, looking at her with those darker-than-night eyes that were insolent and intransigent at the same time? How was she supposed to *think*?

'I'm actually *employed* here.' Milly broke the silence. A thin film of perspiration had broken out over her body and, try as she might, she couldn't seem to peel her eyes away from him.

He raised one enquiring eyebrow, and she glared at him, because she had every right to be here which he, almost certainly, did not.

What, she wondered, could possibly go wrong next? How could one person's life get derailed in such a short space of time? She should have been here recovering, looking forward to an essential break from normality while she mentally gathered her forces and rallied her troops in preparation for returning to London. She should have been using the splendid kitchen to whip something up that was gluten-free for Mrs Ramos, meat-based for her husband and healthily braised for their children! Instead, she was having a staring match with someone who looked like Adonis but behaved like a caveman.

'Oh, yes?'

'Yes,' she snapped. '*Not* that it's any of your business! I'm the chalet girl the Ramos employed to work for them for the next two weeks. And they'll be here *any minute now...*'

'Ah...chalet girl... Now, why am I finding that hard to believe when I know for a fact that Alberto and Julia won't be here because one of their children is ill?' He strolled over to the fridge and helped himself to a bottle of mineral water, which he proceeded to drink while keeping his eye on her.

'Oh.' The annoying, arrogant man wasn't a robber but, instead of rushing to reassure her, he had prolonged her discomfort by not deigning to tell her that he knew the family who owned the lodge. Were there *any* nice guys left in the world? 'Well, if you think that I'm going to apologise for...for...'

'Coming at me with the kettle?'

'Then you're mistaken. I don't know what you're doing here, but you shouldn't sneak around, and you should have told me that you knew the owners…' A thought occurred to her. 'I suppose they've let you down, as well?'

'Come again?'

'They let *me* down,' Milly expanded glumly. Now that she was no longer in danger of imminent attack, her breathing had more or less returned to normal, but she still found that she had to put a little distance between her and Adonis, who was still standing by the fridge and yet managing to have a very weird effect on her nervous system.

His legs, she noted absently as she sat down on one of the high-tech leather-and-chrome chairs by the table, were long and muscular and he had good ankles. Not many men had good ankles but he had excellent ones—brown like the rest of him…with a sprinkling of dark hair…

She surfaced to find that he had said something and she frowned.

'Not you, as well.' She groaned, because from the tail end of his sentence she gathered he had been pointing out the obvious—which was how it was that she had managed to make the trip without being notified that the job had been cancelled. 'I've had enough lecturing from Sandra about not picking up my phone; I don't think I have the energy to sit through you telling me the same thing. Anyway, why are *you* here? Didn't your agency let you know before you made a wasted trip here?'

Lucas had the dazed feeling of someone thrown into a washing machine and the spin cycle turned to full blast. She had raked her fingers through her wild red hair, which he now appreciated was thick and very long, practically down to her waist, a tumbling riot of curls and waves.

'Agency?' Never lost for words in any given situation, he now found himself speechless.

'Sandra's the girl at the agency that employed me. In London.' She permitted herself to look at him fully and could feel hot colour racing up to her face. He was obviously foreign, beautifully and exotically foreign, but his English was perfect, with just a trace of an accent.

'My job was to cook for the Ramos family and babysit their children.' It suddenly occurred to her that he had called them by their Christian names. She had been under strict instructions to use their full titles and to remember that they weren't her friends. It just went to show how different agencies operated; just her luck to have got stuck with snooty Sandra. 'What were *you* employed to do? No, you don't have to tell me.'

'I don't?' Fascinating. Like someone from another planet. Wherever Lucas went, he generated adulation and subservience from women. They tripped over themselves to please him. They said what they imagined he wanted to hear. Born into wealth, he had known from a tender age what the meaning of power was and now, at the ripe young age of thirty-four, and with several fortunes behind him—some inherited, the rest made himself. He was accustomed to being treated like a man at the top of his game. A billionaire who could have whatever he pleased at the snap of his imperious fingers.

What did this woman think he did? He was curious to hear.

'Ski instructor.' Milly discovered that this strange turn of events was having a very beneficial effect on her levels of depression. Robbie, Emily and the horror story that had suddenly become her life had barely crossed her mind ever since Adonis had appeared on the scene.

'Ski instructor.' He was parroting everything she said. He couldn't believe it.

'You have the *look* of a ski instructor,' Milly said thoughtfully.

'Am I to take that as a compliment?'

'You can if you want.' She backtracked hastily just in case he got it into his head that she was somehow trying it on with him, which she wasn't, because aside from anything else she was far too upset even to look at another man. 'Isn't it amazing how rich people live?' She swiftly changed the topic and watched, warily, as he dumped the bottled water on the counter, making no effort even to look for the bin, and sauntered towards the kitchen table so that he could sit on one of the chairs, idly pulling another towards him with his foot and using it as a foot rest.

'Amazing,' Lucas agreed.

'I mean, have you had a chance to look around this place? It's like something from one of those house magazines! It's hard to believe that anyone actually ever uses this lodge. Everything's just so…shiny and expensive!'

'Money impresses you, does it?' Lucas thought of all the other apartments and houses he owned, scattered in cities across the world from New York to Hong Kong. He even had a villa on an exclusive Caribbean island. He hadn't been there for at least a couple of years…

Milly leaned on the table, cupped her chin in the palm of her hand and gazed at him. Amazing eyes, she thought idly, with even more amazing lashes—long, dark and thick. And there was a certain arrogance about him. She should find it a complete turn-off, especially considering that Robbie had had his fair share of arrogance, and what a creep he had turned out to be. But Adonis's arrogance was somehow *different*... Just look at the way he had stuck his feet on that chair.

'No...' she admitted. 'I mean, don't get me wrong, money is great. I wish I had more of it.' *Especially considering I have no job to return to.* 'But I was brought up to believe that there were more important things in life. My parents died in a car accident when I was eight and my grandmother raised me. Well, there wasn't an awful lot of money to go round, but that never bothered me. I think people create the lives they want to live and they do that without the help of money...'

She sighed. 'Stop me if I'm talking too much. I do that. But, now that I know you're not a burglar, it's kind of nice having someone here. I mean, I'll be gone first thing in the morning, but... Okay, enough of me... Is this the first time you've worked for the Ramos family? I mean, I couldn't help noticing that you called them by their first names...'

Lucas thought of Alberto and Julia Ramos and choked back a snort of derisive laughter at the thought of working for them. In actual fact, Alberto had worked for his father. Lucas had inherited him when his father had died and, because of the personal connection, had resisted sacking the man, who was borderline incompetent. He found them intensely annoying but his mother was godmother to one of their children.

'We go back a way,' he said, skirting round the truth.

'Thought so.'

'Why is that?'

Milly laughed and it felt as though this was the first time she had laughed, really laughed, for a long time. Well, at least two weeks, although there had been a moment or two with her friends post-traumatic break-up. Manic, desperate laughter, probably...

'Because you've got your feet on the chair and you've just dumped that empty bottle on the kitchen counter! Sandra told me that under *no circumstances* was there to be any sign that I'd stepped foot in this lodge when I left. I might even have to wipe all the surfaces just in case they find my fingerprints somewhere.'

'You have a wonderful laugh,' Lucas heard himself say with some surprise. She did. A rich, full- bodied laugh that made him want to grin.

And looking at her...

That first impression of someone small and plump with crazy hair was being rapidly dispelled. She was small, yes, barely skimming five-four, but her skin was satiny smooth and her eyes were the clearest blue he had ever seen. And when she laughed she had dimples.

Milly went bright red. In the aftermath of her horrible, *horrible* broken engagement, her self-confidence had been severely battered, and his compliment filled her with a terrific sense of wellbeing. Even if he had only complimented her on the way she laughed, which, when you analysed it, was hardly a compliment at all. But, still, coming from Adonis...

'Must be great being a ski instructor,' she said, all hot and bothered now. 'Would you like to know something? I mean, it's no big secret or anything...'

'I would love to know something...even if it's no big secret or anything...' Hell, this impromptu break was certainly proving to be a great distraction in ways he had never anticipated.

'I used to ski—I mean *really* ski. I went on a school trip when I was ten and somehow I took to it. When I was fifteen, I even thought I might try and go pro, but you know… We didn't have the money for that sort of thing. But it's why I was looking forward to this job…'

Her situation hit her like a blast of cold air: no fiancé, no job, no two weeks' chalet income with the bonus of skiing now and again. She shook away her sudden despondency, which wasn't going to get her anywhere. 'Frankly, it's why Sandra employed me in the first place when there were other better looking girls lining up for the job.' *That and my low levels of physical attractiveness.* 'I thought I might be able to sneak a little skiing in, but now… Oh, well, that's life, I guess. My luck's been crap recently so I don't know why I'm surprised this fell through.'

She smiled, digging deep to recover some of her sunny nature. 'Hey, I don't even know your name! I'm Amelia, but my friends call me Milly.' She held out her hand, and the feel of his cool fingers as he shook it sent a wave of dizzying electric charge straight through her body, from her toes to the top of her head.

'And I am…Lucas.' So she thought he was a ski instructor. How frankly refreshing to be in the company of a woman who didn't know his worth, who didn't simper, who wasn't out to try and trap him. 'And I think we might just be able to solve the matter of your lost job…'

CHAPTER TWO

IT WAS A SPUR-OF-THE-MOMENT decision for Lucas, but whoever said that he wasn't a man who could think creatively on his feet? How many times had he won deals because he had approached them from a different angle; played with a situation, found the loopholes, cracks and crevices and exploited them to his own benefit? It was the crucial difference between moderate success and soaring the heights. He had been bred with confidence and it had never once occurred to him that he might not be able to get exactly what he wanted.

Right now, he had made the snap decision that he might enjoy the woman's company on the slopes for a few days.

She obviously wasn't the type he normally went for. His diet was tall, thin, leggy brunettes from social backgrounds very similar to his own—because there was nothing worse than a tawdry gold-digger—but she had a certain something…

Just at this minute she was gaping at him as though he had taken leave of his senses.

'I beg your pardon?' Milly could scarcely believe her ears. In fact, she was on the way to convincing herself that she was trapped with a madman. He might be well in with the Ramos family if he happened to be their personal ski instructor, but how much influence did ski instructors have anyway? It wasn't as though they weren't disposable.

'But first, food.'

'Food?'

'I actually came to the kitchen to grab myself something to eat.' Originally he had toyed with the idea of just importing a chef from one of the hotels, the regular chef he was accustomed to using whenever he happened to be at the lodge, but in the end it had hardly seemed worth the effort when he hadn't planned to stay longer than a couple of nights. And when he knew for a fact that the fridge would be brimming over with food in preparation for the non-appearing Ramos family.

'You came here to grab something to eat? Are you completely *crazy?* You can't just go rummaging around in their fridge, eating their food and drinking their wine. Have you taken a look at the bottles in that wine rack? They look as though they cost the earth!'

Lucas was already heading for the fridge.

'Bread…' He opened the fridge door and turned to look at her. 'Cheese… Both in plentiful supply. And I'm pretty sure there'll be some salad stuff somewhere.'

Milly sprang to her feet. 'I can, er, cook you something if you like…if you're sure. After all, cooking *was* to be part of my duties.'

Lucas looked at her and smiled and that electric charge zipped through her again. It was like being struck by a bolt of lightning.

Had Robbie the creep ever had this effect on her? She didn't think so, but then again disillusionment might have put a different spin on her memories of their somewhat brief courtship.

She and Robbie had attended the same small school in remote Scotland until they were fourteen, at which point grander things had beckoned and he had moved with his family down to London. At fourteen, gauche and way too sporty to appeal to teenage boys whose testosterone levels were kicking in, she had had a secret crush on him.

They had kept in touch over the years, mostly via social network with the occasional visit thrown in whenever he'd happened to be in the city, but his sudden interest in her had only really kicked off six months ago and it had been whirlwind. Milly, still finding her feet in her job, had been first pleased to see a familiar face and then flattered when that familiar face had started take an interest in her. Ha! The reason for that had become patently clear after he had dumped her for leggy Emily.

Lucas had slammed shut the fridge in favour of opening a bottle of the expensive wine from the wine rack, much to Milly's consternation.

So, women cooking for him had never been part of the deal; tinkering in the kitchen smacked of just the sort of cosy domesticity he had never encouraged. On the other hand, this was a unique situation.

'I'm actually a chef by profession.' Milly grinned and joined him by the fridge, the contents of which she proceeded to inspect, although she made sure not to remove anything. She could practically feel Skipper Sandra peering down at her, about to ask her what the hell she thought she was doing.

'Would-be professional skier, chef… Is there no end to your talents?'

'You're teasing me.' Their eyes met and she blushed. 'I still don't feel entirely comfortable digging in their cupboards but I suppose we *do* have to eat. I mean, I'm sure Sandra wouldn't expect me to *starve*...'

'This Sandra character sounds like a despot.' Lucas removed himself from her way as she began extracting bits and pieces. He had no idea what she intended to do with the stuff. He himself had zero interest in cooking and had never really seen fit to do much more than toast a slice of bread or, in dire circumstances, open a can of something and put it in a saucepan.

'Like you wouldn't believe.' She began hunting down utensils whilst reminding him, just in case he reported back that she had made herself at home, that she still didn't feel 100 percent good about using stuff from their fridge. 'Want to help?' She glanced over her shoulder to where he was lounging indolently against the kitchen counter with a glass of red wine in his hand.

Talk about making himself at home!

'I'm more of a spectator when it comes to cooking,' Lucas told her. And from where he was standing, the view was second to none. She had removed her thick jumper and was down to a clingy long-sleeved T-shirt that outlined every inch of a body that had been woefully kept under wraps.

'We'll eat quicker if you help.'

'I'm in no hurry. You were about to tell me about Sandra the despot...'

'I had to have three interviews for this job. Can you believe it? Three! The Ramoses are just about the fussiest people on the planet. Oh, sorry; I forgot that you're their regular ski instructor. You probably see a different side to them.' She sighed, her throat suddenly thick as she thought of the neatly packaged life she had been looking forward to flying through the window.

And yet, in a strange way, she was sure that she should be feeling sadder than she actually was.

Mortified, yes. She was about eleven out of ten on the mortification scale, although less so here where her well-meaning friends weren't hovering around her, hankies at the ready, as though she was on the verge of a nervous breakdown.

But sad?

The presents had all been returned; the dress had been sold online because the shop had refused to have it back; the small church in Sunningdale where his parents had lived ever since they had moved from Scotland had been cancelled. But she didn't get a lump in her throat when she thought about the details.

The lump came when she thought about the fairytale future she had had planned, when she thought about being in love and then being let down...

'I doubt that.' Lucas recalled the last time he had seen the couple at his mother's house in Argentina, where Julia Ramos had spent most of the evening lording it over anyone she thought might be a lesser mortal.

Despite being wealthy beyond most people's wildest dreams, his mother had a very solid streak of normality in her and frequently hosted parties to which all and sundry were invited, regardless of their income or status. She had never forgotten that both she and his father had come from nothing and had made their fortune through hard graft.

'There aren't many complex sides to Alberto and Julia Ramos. They have money and they insist on showing the world, whether the world wants to know or not.'

'Poor you.' Milly looked at him sympathetically. 'I guess it must become a bit of a drag if you're having to deal with people you don't especially like...' She returned to her chopping and he dragged one of the bar stools over so that he could see her as she worked. By now, she had given up on being appalled at the liberties he took. Perhaps that was the relationship he had with his employers. Less of an employee and more of an equal.

'But,' she continued as she tried to focus on the onions in front of her and ignore the fact that his dark eyes roving over her were making her feel a bit dizzy, 'we all have to do stuff we don't particularly like for the sake of earning a living. What do you do when you're not instructing?'

'This and that.'

Milly didn't say anything. Maybe he was embarrassed because being a ski instructor might be glamorous but it was hardly a ladder-climbing job, and she wasn't sure why, but Lucas struck her as the kind of guy to have ambition.

'Why are you doing a two-week stint as a chalet girl when you're a professional chef? You're not drinking your wine. You should. It's an excellent vintage.'

'I hope you don't get into trouble opening that bottle...' But the cooking was now done so she wiped her hands on one of the towels by the range, took the proffered glass of wine and followed him out of the kitchen and into the sprawling sitting area, where, through the vast panes of glass, they could see the spectacular sight of night settling on the snowy mountain ranges.

'I never get into trouble,' Lucas assured her as he joined her on the sofa. The white sofa. The white sofa that she would probably have to pay for if she made the mistake of spilling her red wine on it.

She perched awkwardly on the edge and made very sure to keep a firm hand on the stem of her wine glass.

'You *never* get into trouble…ever? That's a very arrogant thing to say!' But strangely thrilling.

'I confess that I can be arrogant,' Lucas told her truthfully, eyes steady on her face as he sipped his wine.

'That's an awful trait.'

'Deplorable. Have you got any?'

'Any what?' Her glass appeared to be empty. How had that happened?

'Deplorable traits.' Not red, he decided; her hair was not red…more a deep, rich auburn with streaks of lighter auburn running through it.

'I tend to fall for creeps. In fact, you could say that I specialise in that. I went out with boyfriend number one three years ago for three months. Turned out he had a girlfriend, who happened to be doing a gap year leaving him free to play the field while she was away…'

'The world is full of creeps,' Lucas murmured. He himself always made it very clear to the women he dated that rocks on fingers were never going be part of the game. If, at any point, they got it into their heads that they could alter that situation, then they were very sharply brought up to date with his ground rules.

'You're not kidding.'

'And boyfriend number two?'

'Boyfriend number two was actually my fiancé.' She stared at her empty glass, wondering whether she dared risk another drink. She wouldn't want to face the trip back to London on a hangover. She sneaked a glance at Lucas, who was reclining on the leather sofa, utterly and completely comfortable in his surroundings.

'Fiancé?'

Milly stuck her hand out for inspection. 'What do you see?'

Lucas shifted position, leaned forward and looked.

'An extremely attractive hand.' He glanced up at her and was charmed by the dainty colour in her cheeks.

'It's a hand without an engagement ring,' she said mournfully. 'Right now, at this precise moment in time, I should actually be a married woman.'

'Ah…'

'Instead, here I am, drinking wine that doesn't belong to me—which the Ramos family will probably discover and report back to Sandra the despot—and pouring my heart out to a complete stranger.'

'Sometimes complete strangers make the best listeners.'

'You don't strike me as the sort of guy who pours his heart out to other people.'

'It's not a habit I've ever actively encouraged. Tell me about the ex-fiancé…'

Milly thought that she had spent the past two weeks offloading about the ex-fiancé. Her friends had been fertile ground for endless meandering conversations about Robert and *types* like Robert. Over boxes of wine and Chinese take-out, hours had been spent discussing every aspect of Robert and men in general. Anecdotes of various Mr Wrongs had been cited like a never-ending string of rabbits being pulled from a magician's hat.

'You're not really interested…' She couldn't see *him* ever going through the trauma of being dumped from a great height.

'You fascinate me,' Lucas murmured, reaching over to the bottle, which he had casually dumped on one of the spotless glass tables so that he could refill both their glasses. Milly noted that the bottle had left a circular stain on the table and she mentally made a note to make sure it was wiped clean before she went to bed.

'I do?' She decided that that rated slightly higher than the compliment he had paid her about her laugh.

'You do,' Lucas told her gravely. 'I have never known anyone as…open and forthcoming as you.'

'Oh.' Deflated, Milly looked at him. 'I suppose that's just a kind way of saying that I talk too much.'

'You also have amazing hair.'

Was he *flirting* with her? Milly made her mind up that there was no way that she would allow herself to be flattered, especially not by a ski instructor who probably slept with every woman he taught over the age of twenty. Weren't they notorious for that? The last time she had worked as a chalet girl, the other two girls who had also been working with her had both had flings with ski instructors. Ski instructors were usually young, cute, unnaturally tanned and extremely confident when it came to enticing women into bed.

She shot him a jaundiced look, which was not the reaction he expected on the back of a compliment. He wondered how she would react if he told her that what he would really like to do, right here, right now, was sift his fingers through that wonderful hair of hers and watch it as it rippled over them.

'So what was the ex called?'

'Robert,' Milly told him on a sigh. Determined to make this glass last as long as possible and thereby avoid any nasty early-morning consequences, she took a miniscule sip.

'And what did *Robert* do?'

'Fell into bed with my best friend. Apparently he took one look at her and realised that he couldn't resist her. It turned out that he had proposed to me because I fitted the bill. His parents wanted him to settle down and I was *settling down* material. But not in a good way.

More in an "if he could do as he pleased, he wouldn't settle down with me" sort of way. He thought his parents would approve, which they did.'

She sighed and swallowed a more robust mouthful of wine. 'He said he really *liked* me, which is the biggest insult a girl could have, because he obviously wasn't actually that attracted to me. At any rate, he must really have fallen for Emily because he braved his parents' wrath to tell them about her and now…what can I say? She'll be having the life I had planned on having.'

'Married to a bastard who will probably find another skirt to chase within two years of getting hitched? I wouldn't wallow in too much self-pity if I were you…'

Milly laughed. To the point. Where her friends would spend literally hours analysing, he had cut to the chase in a few sentences.

'And now shall we see how that food of yours is doing?' Lucas stood up and stretched and Milly tried not to let her mouth fall open at the ripple of muscle discernible under his clothes.

'Yes, the food; the stolen food.'

'And I shall make a few calls; do something about this job of yours that's disappeared under your feet.'

Milly hadn't forgotten about that but she had decided not to mention it again. People had a way of saying stuff they seriously meant at the time but five minutes later had completely forgotten. Sometimes she had been guilty of that particular crime. A wide, sweeping invitation to friends to come round for drinks only to realise afterwards that she would actually be at work on the evening in question.

'You're going to make a few calls?'

'Two, in actual fact.' He watched her cute rear as she preceded him into the kitchen. He knew more about her life after five seconds than he had about anyone he had dated in the past, but then he didn't naturally encourage outpourings, and the women he dated were all too conscious of the fact that they had to toe the line. No outpourings. No long life stories. No involved anecdotes.

Was it any wonder that he was frankly enjoying himself? He would never have imagined that being a ski instructor could be such a liberating experience. He wondered whether he shouldn't become a ski instructor for a week every year just so that he could refresh his palate with a taste of normality.

He disappeared, heading back to the sitting room so that he could make his calls as he stood absently looking down at the sprawling white vista outside his lodge.

One call to his mother, to tell her that he might be staying on slightly longer than originally thought. The other to Alberto, to tell him that his chalet girl had arrived to find herself jobless and that he would be digging into his pocket to pay her what she was due, because she would be staying on, and that he should contact whatever agency he got her from and relay the message. Lucas could easily have afforded to pay her himself but on principle he saw no reason why he should pick up the tab. The man was grossly over-paid by his company for what he did, and Lucas suspected that he had told the agency that the deal was off at the last possible minute because neither he nor his wife would really have given a damn if their chalet girl's nose was put out of joint.

He sauntered into the kitchen, snapping his phone shut just as she was dishing out two heaped bowls of pasta.

'Done.'

Alone and away from his overpowering personal-

ity, Milly had had a little while to consider the prospect of spending two weeks with a man she didn't know
in a lodge that belonged to neither of them. The plan
made no sense. Were they to deplete the contents of
the fridge? Guzzle all the alcohol? Then leave with a
cheery wave goodbye? Wouldn't a bill catch up with
her sooner or later? There was no such thing as a free
lunch, after all, not to mention two weeks' worth of free
lunches.

And, also, what if the ski instructor with the drop-
dead good looks turned out to be dodgy? He didn't
seem the violent type but who was to say he was trust-
worthy? He could be a gentleman by day and a sex maniac by night.

Bracketing Lucas and sex in the same thought
brought hectic colour to her cheeks. Even if he *was* a
closet sex maniac, there was no chance he would look
twice in her direction. Robert, who had been nice looking but definitely not in Adonis's league, hadn't found
her attractive. That, in a nutshell, said it all as far as
Milly was concerned.

But she still found herself hesitating, clearing her
throat and sitting down at the sleek kitchen table with
burning, self-conscious hesitation.

Would it be inappropriate to ask him for a CV? she
wondered. Maybe a few references from women he had
happened to be thrown together with inadvertently who
had found him to be a decent, honourable man with up-
standing moral values?

'The look of joy and satisfaction seems to be missing from your expression.' Lucas tucked into the pasta,
which was as good as anything he had had in any restaurant. He had wondered about the 'professional chef'
description of herself—had thought that maybe it was

a bit of self-congratulation when, in fact, she worked behind the scenes at the local fast food joint—but she was a seriously good cook.

'Well….' Curiosity got the better of her. 'How did you manage to do that? I mean when you say *done...*'

'You'd be surprised at the things I can accomplish when I put my mind to it. Your job here is safe, and you'll be fully paid for the duration. Even if you decide to leave after two days.'

Milly's mouth dropped open and Lucas grinned wryly.

'Admit it. You're impressed.'

'Wow. You must have an awful lot of influence with the Ramos family.' A thought struck her and she went bright red and took refuge in her pasta.

'Why do I get the feeling that there's something on your mind?' Lucas drawled drily.

'What makes you think that?'

'Maybe it's because you've suddenly turned the colour of puce. Or maybe it's because you have a face that's as transparent as a pane of glass. Pick either option. The food's delicious, by the way. Were it not for the red hair, I would be tempted to think that you have a streak of Italian running through you.'

'Auburn, not red. I don't like the word "red",' Milly automatically asserted, still staring down at her plate.

'Spit it out, Milly of the "auburn not red" hair…'

'Well, you probably wouldn't like it.'

Lucas helped himself to more pasta, poured himself another glass of wine and allowed the silence to stretch between them. Eventually, he rescued her from her agonising indecision.

'Trust me, I'm built like a brick wall when it comes to being offended.' Not that he could think, offhand, of anyone who would dare say something offensive to him. The joys of wealth and power.

'You really *are* arrogant, aren't you?' Milly said distractedly and he delivered her a slashing smile that temporarily knocked her for six. 'Well, if you must know, I just wondered whether you managed to pull strings because you're sleeping with Mrs Ramos…' She said it in one rushed sentence and then held her breath and waited for a reply.

For a few seconds, Lucas didn't actually believe what he had just heard and then, when it *had* sunk in, he wasn't sure whether to be outraged, amused or incredulous.

'Well…' She dragged that one syllable out, licking her lips nervously. 'It makes a weird kind of sense.'

'In what world does it make a weird kind of sense?'

'How else would you be able to get me my job and ensure that I get paid for it?'

'Ski instructors can have a lot of influence, as it happens.' Lucas skirted over that sweeping and vague statement because it was one thing to delicately economise on the truth and another to lie outright, especially to someone who, he suspected, had probably never told so much as a white lie in her entire life. 'I've helped Alberto out on a number of occasions and, put it this way, he was more than happy to do as I asked. Furthermore, I would never go near a married woman.'

'You wouldn't?'

'Don't tell me—all the ski instructors you've met have been more than obliging with women whether they were wearing wedding rings on their fingers or not?'

'Their reputations *can* be a little racy.' But she breathed a sigh of relief. 'Just one other small thing…'

'You *do* take testing conversations to the outer limits, don't you?'

'I wouldn't normally…er…choose to be alone in a ski lodge with someone I actually don't know.'

This time Lucas *was* outraged. He flung his hands in the air in a gesture that was mesmerising and typically foreign and leaned back into his chair. 'So, not only do you clock me for a womaniser who doesn't bother to discriminate between single and married women, but now I'm a pervert!'

'No!' Milly squeaked, on the verge of telling him to keep his voice down because, with all the food and wine they had consumed, guilt was making its presence felt in a very intrusive way. It would be just her luck to find out that he hadn't made any phone calls at all, that he was in fact a burglar who had decided to make himself at home before getting down to the serious business of nicking the silver, and to top it off somewhere lurking behind a wall was Sandra and her band of blond-haired guard dogs.

'How do I know that you've actually spoken to Mr Ramos?'

'Because I just told you that I had.' Unaccustomed to having his word doubted, Lucas was finding the conversation more and more surreal. 'I can prove it.'

'You can? How?' She cast him a dubious look. What was it about the guy? Her instinct was just to believe everything he told her, zombie-style. She was pretty sure that if he pointed to the sky and told her that there were spaceships hovering she would be more than half-inclined to wonder if they contained little green men.

Lucas dialled a number on his cell phone and, when it connected, spoke rapidly in Spanish and then placed the mobile on the table and put it on speakerphone.

Then he sat back, a picture of relaxation, and spoke. Very slowly and very clearly. Without taking his eyes off her face. Which, when inspected in-depth, as he was now doing, was really an extraordinarily attractive face. Why was that? She didn't have the sharp, high cheekbones of a model, nor did she have the haughty, self-confident air of a trust-fund chick, but there was just something soft yet stubborn about her, sympathetic yet outspoken…

She was the sort of person who would never give in without a fight and for a few seconds he felt impossibly enraged at the unseen but much discussed ex-fiancé who had dumped her. He almost lost track of the conversation he was in the middle of having with Alberto, who, naturally, had adopted the usual tone of subservience the second he knew who was on the line.

Like someone pulling off a magic trick, Lucas waved to the phone and folded his hands behind his head as he listened to Alberto do exactly what he had been told to do, which, in actual fact, was simply to tell the truth.

Yes, of course she could stay on! On full pay. *No hay problema.* Furthermore, there was no need for her to replace any of the food eaten or wine drunk, nor was there any need to run herself ragged trying to keep the lodge clean. All that would be sorted at a later date. Meanwhile, he would be transferring her pay directly into her account, if she would just text him the details of her bank account, and furthermore there would be a bonus in view of the inconvenience she had suffered.

'I feel just terrible,' was the first thing Milly said as soon as Alberto had signed off, having wished her a very pleasant stay and apologised for any inconvenience caused.

'You feel terrible. You give new meaning to the word "unpredictable". What's that supposed to mean? Why do you feel terrible? I thought you would be leaping around this kitchen with joy! Face it, you don't have to return to London and risk bumping into your charming "best friend" and the loser ex...nor do you have to worry about money for the time being because you'll be paid for your stay here. You can take the time out you wanted and oh, what joy, you won't even have to slave over a hot stove catering to the Ramos family. In other words, you won't have to sing for your supper. From where I'm standing, you couldn't have wished for a better deal...yet you look as though someone's cancelled your birthday.'

'I haven't exactly been nice to poor Mr Ramos, have I?' She flung the rhetorical question at him in a voice laden with accusation.

'Have I encouraged that?'

'I made assumptions. I just thought that—because I had a list of a hundred different things I had to pre-pare for them individually to eat, and because I had so many strict instructions on what I could wear and what I couldn't wear, and what I could say and couldn't say—they were a pretty demanding, diva family. And yet...' She dug into her rucksack, grabbed her phone and texted the relevant information to Alberto.

'He couldn't have been more decent about the whole thing.' In record time she heard the ping of her phone as he confirmed that the money had been deposited into her account. 'After Robbie, it's nice to see that there are some decent people left in the world.'

Lucas was fighting down annoyance over Alberto and his ridiculous demands. He could kiss sweet good-bye to any further freebies at the lodge, whatever the family connection.

'So is the Dance of Joy and Happiness about to take place? Oh, no, I forgot, you still think that I'm a pervert you can't trust...'

'No.' Milly sighed. And anyway, had she really been conceited enough to imagine that he would make some kind of pass at her? Which was something she would obviously reject out of hand, because she was recovering from a broken heart! Not that he would anyway. Adonis types went for Aphrodite types—known fact.

'I'm weak with relief.'

'I guess we should clean here and then turn in for the night,' she said, standing up. The rollercoaster ride loosely called 'her life' was still looping her around in a million different directions. So now, unbelievably, she was staying on at the lodge for the full duration of her contract. From jobless and heading back on the first flight to still in work, earning her fabulous wage for two weeks of having fun and skiing...

'Clean?'

'Do the dishes.' She waved at the plates, the glasses, the saucepans. 'You might not be able to cook, but you can certainly help tidy this kitchen. I'm not doing it on my own. We both contributed to the mess.'

Lucas stood back, arms folded, and realised that 'do the dishes' had never been words applied to him, but he obligingly began clearing the table while she spent a little more time expressing completely unnecessary levels of remorse for having been uncharitable towards Alberto and his family.

As consciences went, hers appeared to be extremely overactive.

'Okay!' He held up one hand, cutting short yet another take on how kind the Ramos man had turned out to be. 'I get the general picture. Not,' he added darkly, 'that you actually know the first thing about Ramos... er...Alberto... But no point going down that road.' He leaned against the kitchen counter and folded his arms.

His contribution to tidying the kitchen had consisted of moving two plates and a glass from the table to the sink.

Good-looking men were always spoiled, first by their adoring mothers, who ran around doing everything for them, then by adoring girlfriends who did the same, and finally by their adoring wives, who picked up where the girlfriends had left off.

'Let's just cut short the Ramos eulogies. Now that you're here, I'm going to be here for a couple of days. We can talk about which runs we do.' She was someone capable, by all accounts, of skiing to a high standard, as opposed to dressing to a high standard with lamentably average skiing skills, which had always been the case with his girlfriends in the past. The actual process of skiing had always been an interruption to the more engaging business of looking good in skiing outfits.

A quirky, amusing companion who didn't know him from Adam. Who knew what the outcome of their brief, unexpected meeting of ways would be?

In his highly controlled and largely predictable life, the prospect of the unknown dangled in front of him like a tantalising carrot.

He smiled and closely watched the way she blushed and lowered her eyes.

Yes, coming here had definitely been the right decision...

CHAPTER THREE

'SOMETHING'S ONLY JUST occurred to me...'

The dishes had been done, mostly by Milly, while Lucas had relaxed and fiddled with the complicated coffee-making machine, eventually succeeding in producing two small cups of espresso that she was embarrassed to tell him would probably keep her up all night. It had taken him such a long time finally to get there that it would have seemed churlish to politely refuse. She had never met anyone more clueless when it came to knowing his way around a kitchen. Or less interested, for that matter.

Now they were back on the white sofa although, with permission granted to stay in the lodge, she felt a little less uncomfortable in her surroundings.

'And I take it that this sudden thought is one you want to share with me.' This was a brave, new world. She had already berated him for not helping enough in the kitchen and had then proceeded to give him a mini-lecture on the wonders of 'the modern man'. Apparently those were men who shared all the domestic chores, cooked and cleaned with the best of them and gave foot massages to their loved ones. He had told her that, quite frankly, he could think of nothing worse.

'I should have asked you this before but with everything going on my mind was all over the place...'

Lucas grunted. The emails that he had planned to spend the evening ploughing through had quickly taken a back seat to the girl now staring off into the distance with a thoughtful frown.

'I should have asked you whether you're...er...involved with someone or not.'

'Involved with someone...'

'Are you married?' she asked bluntly. 'Not that it makes any difference, because we're both just employees who happen to be stranded in the same lodge.' *The same empty lodge.* 'But I wouldn't want your wife to be worried. You know...'

'You mean you wouldn't want her to be jealous.'

'Well, *anxious*...' So he *was* married, despite the lack of a wedding ring. Lots of men didn't wear wedding rings. She felt a stab of disappointment. Why wouldn't he be married? she thought, restlessly pushing aside that awkward, uninvited emotion that had no place in her life. He was sinfully sexy and oozed just the sort of self-assurance and lazy arrogance that women went wild for.

'Interesting concept. A jealous and anxious wife worried about her beloved husband sharing a ski lodge with a total stranger...' He tried the thought on for size and tried not to burst out laughing.

When it came to women and commitment, he was the least likely candidate. Once bitten, twice shy and he had had his brush with his one and only near-escape. It had been a decade and a half ago but as learning curves went it had been a good one. He had been a nineteen-year-old kid, already with plenty of experience but still too green to recognise when he was being played. He'd been young, cocky and arrogant enough to think that gold-diggers all came wrapped up and packaged the same way: big hair, high heels, obvious charms.

But Betina Crew, at twenty-seven nearly eight years older than him, had been just the opposite. She had been a wild flower-child who went on protest marches and waxed lyrical about saving the world. He had fallen hook, line and sinker until she'd tried to reel him in with a phoney pregnancy scare, which he had so nearly bought, and had so nearly walked down the aisle. It was pure chance that he had discovered the packet of contraceptive pills tucked away at the back of one of her drawers and, when he'd confronted her, it had all ended up turning ugly.

Since then, he had never kidded himself that there was such a thing as disinterested true love. Not when the size of his bank balance was known. His parents might have had the perfect marriage, but they had both started off broke and had worked together to make their fortune. His mother still believed in all that clap trap about true love, and he hadn't the heart to disillusion her, but he knew that when and if he ever decided to tie the knot it would be less Cupid's bow and arrow than a decent arrangement overseen by a lawyer with a watertight pre-nup.

'No.' He shook his head. 'No anxious, jealous or whatever-you-want-to-call-it wife keeping the home fires warm.'

'Girlfriend?'

'Why the interest? Are you suggesting that there might be something for a woman to be jealous about?'

'No!' Milly nearly choked on her espresso. 'In case you'd forgotten,' she added, regaining her composure, 'I came over here to try and escape. The last thing on my mind would be involvement with anyone! I just don't want to think that there's anyone out there who cares about you and who might be alarmed that we happen to be stuck here together through no fault of our own.'

'In that case, I'll set your mind at rest, shall I? No girlfriend and, even if there was a girlfriend, I'm not a jealous guy and I don't encourage jealousy in women I date.'

'How can you discourage someone from being jealous?' She hadn't been at all jealous when it came to Robbie. Why was that? she wondered. Was it because she had known him off and on for a long time, and one was never that jealous when it came to people they were familiar with? She hadn't even thought twice about Robbie and Emily being alone together. And yet there was something deep inside telling her that surely jealousy was something that attacked at random and couldn't be debated or ordered out of existence?

'I've never found a problem with that. The women I date know my parameters and they tend to respect them.'

'You're the most arrogant guy I've ever met in my entire life,' Milly said with genuine wonderment.

'I think you've already told me that.' He drained his cup and dumped it on one of the coffee tables, then he stood up and flexed his muscles, watching as she uncurled herself from the sofa and automatically reached to gather his cup along with hers.

His automatic instinct was irritably to tell her to leave it, that someone would tidy it away in the morning, then he remembered that there would be no cleaner trooping along to make sure she tidied in his wake.

'I'll show you to your room.'

'Feels odd to be here without the owner in residence.'

Lucas had the grace to flush but he refrained from saying anything, instead scooping up her holdall, which had seen better days, and heading out towards a spiral staircase that led up to a huge galleried landing that overlooked the ground floor.

There, as on the ground floor, soaring windows gave out to the same spectacular views of the open, snow-covered mountains. It was dark outside and the snow was a peculiar dull-blue white against the velvety darkness.

For a few seconds, Milly paused to admire the vista, which was truly breathtakingly beautiful. When she looked away it was to find his dark eyes speculatively pinned to her face.

She was here with a guy she didn't know and yet, far from feeling threatened in any way, she felt *safe*. There was something silent and inherently strong about him that was deeply reassuring. She felt that if the place were to be invaded by a clutch of knife wielding bandits he would be able to dispatch them single-handedly.

'I have no idea where Ramos was going to put you,' Lucas told her truthfully. 'But I expect this room will do as good as any of the others.'

He flung wide the door and she gasped. It was, simply put, the most splendid bedroom she had ever seen. She almost didn't want to disturb its perfection by going inside. He breezed in and tossed her bag on the elegant *chaise longue* by the window, yet another of those massive windows designed to remind you of the still, white, glorious silence that lay outside.

'Well?' Lucas rarely noticed his surroundings but he did now because the expression on her face was so tellingly awestruck.

Playground for the seriously rich—this was what

the lodge was. He had had zero input into its decor. He had left that to a world famous interior designer. When the job had been done, he had dispatched three of his trusted employees to give it the once over and make sure that everything had been done to the highest possible standard, no corners cut. Thereafter he had used it a handful of times when the season was at its height and only if the skiing conditions were perfect.

It was a beautiful place. He looked at the cool, white furnishings, breathed in the air of calm, noted the quality of the wood and the subtlety of the faded Persian rug on the ground. Nothing jarred. In the bowels of the lodge, there was a comprehensive spa and sauna area. He'd used that once.

Now, he had an intense urge to take her down there and show it to her just so that he could see that expression of awe again, even though, regrettably, the lodge was not his as far as she was concerned. For the first time in living memory, he had an insane desire to *brag*. Hell, where had *that* come from?

'It's amazing.' Milly hovered by the door. 'Isn't it amazing? Well, I guess you're used to this, but I'm not. My entire flat could fit into this bedroom. Is that an *en suite* bathroom?'

Amused, Lucas pushed the adjoining door and, sure enough, it opened out to a bathroom that was almost as big as the bedroom and contained its own little sitting area. He wondered what the interior designer had had in mind when she'd decided on sticking furniture in the bathroom.

'Wow.' Milly tiptoed her way to the bathroom and peered in. It was absolutely enormous. 'You could have a party in here,' she breathed in a hushed voice.

'I doubt anyone would choose to do that.'

'How can you be so blasé about all of this?' She was too busy inspecting her glorious surroundings to look at him but she was acutely aware of his masculine presence next to her. 'I mean, do you teach lots of rich people? Is that it? You're accustomed to places like this because you're in them all the time?'

'I've been to a number of places along these lines...'

Milly laughed that infectious laugh that made him want to smile. 'Must be a terrific anti-climax when the season's over and you have to return to your digs.'

'I cope.'

Suddenly exhausted after a day of travelling and the stress of finding herself out of a job, then back in one, Milly yawned behind her hand and wandered over to her holdall, which was not the quality of bag that should have adorned the *chaise longue*.

'I've talked about myself all night,' she said sleepily. 'Tomorrow you can tell me all about yourself and your exciting life working for the rich and famous.'

A minute later she closed, and after a few seconds' thought locked, the bedroom door behind him and began running the bath. The ridiculously luxurious bath that was so big and so deep that it was almost the size of a plunge pool.

She wouldn't have believed it but she was having an impossible adventure and—okay, admit it—was so transfixed by Lucas that there had been no room in her head to feel sorry for herself.

She wondered what he did when he wasn't playing ski instructor to rich adults and their kids. Did he while away his summers in the company of wealthy social-ites? He was good-looking enough to be a gigolo but she dismissed that idea as fast as it entered her head be-cause she couldn't imagine that he could be that sleazy.

He'd said didn't sleep with married women and she believed him. There had been a shadow of repugnance when that suggestion had been mooted.

But he was a man of experience, from the way he had talked about the women he dated, in the casual voice of someone who was accustomed to getting a lot of attention and to dating a lot of women.

She thought about her own circumstances. When it came to experience with the opposite sex, she was wet behind the ears. She had never really been the kind of teenager who had become swept up in boys, in make-up, in short skirts and mini bottles of vodka at house parties. Maybe if she had had a mum; maybe if she hadn't been raised by her grandmother. She adored her grandmother, but she could reflect back and see that the generation gap had not been conducive to giggly conversations and experiments with make-up.

Nana Mayfield was a brisk, no-nonsense woman with a great love of the outdoors. Widowed at the age of forty-five, she had had to survive the harsh Scottish winters in unforgiving terrain and she had thrived. That love of the great outdoors was what she had brought to the relationship with her granddaughter and Milly had grown up loving all things to do with sport. She had followed sport on TV and had played as many sports as she could possibly fit into her school timetable.

Of course, she had been to parties, but hockey, tennis, rounders, even football, and later as much skiing as she could possibly do, had always come first.

And so the stages of infatuation, the teenage angst and disappointment, the adolescent broken hearts and the comparing of notes about boys with her friends, had largely passed her by.

Was that why she had fallen for Robbie in the first

place? Because her lack of experience had allowed flattery and compliments to blind her to the reality of a relationship that was built on sand? Had a crush at fourteen predisposed her to become the vulnerable idiot she had been when he had swanned back into her life ten years later? And then, had she held on to him because she had wanted someone to call her own?

He hadn't even shown much interest in getting physical with her. How did that fit into the equation of two love birds on the brink of a happy-ever-after life? And she hadn't pushed him. That should have sounded the alarm bells, but nope, she had merrily continued sleep walking her way to the inevitable.

She had made sure to keep that to herself. She knew, from listening to her friends, that they would all have read the writing on the wall and would have known that his only half-hearted attempts at touching her, and her cheerful acceptance of that situation, did not augur a healthy relationship. They had all been born and raised in London and they were streetwise in ways she couldn't hope to be.

She fell asleep to images of a dark, swarthy, sexy face. He wasn't replacement therapy, but he was a distraction, and maybe that was exactly what she needed right now: a harmless distraction.

The following morning it was snowing when she awoke. She hadn't drawn the curtains and from the bed she could look straight across to ceiling panes of glass to the winter wonderland outside. She itched to put on her skis and get out there.

Before she did anything, she telephoned her grandmother to tell her that she arrived safe and sound but that the family in question had had a slight change of plan, after which she managed to avoid directly lying about her new circumstances, about sharing the lodge with a stranger. Then she texted her friends, brief texts telling them that she'd arrived. No more.

Once changed, she went downstairs and after prowling through the lodge finally located Lucas in a big, airy room behind a desk. She came to a halt outside the door and looked at him. There were papers spread around him and he was peering at a thin laptop computer, frowning.

'You're going to express concern that I'm sitting here without due respect for the owner, aren't you?' he said, without looking away from the computer.

He had had time to question his motives in offering her the use of his ski lodge. She was a young girl recovering from a broken relationship. In short, she was vulnerable and vulnerable, along with married, was something he didn't do.

Was he so jaded that he was prepared to try and take something simply because it made a change? And was a change as good as a rest? Yes, she was refreshing, as was the fact that she had no idea who he was or what he was worth, but was that any reason for him to amuse himself with her?

In any equation where 'vulnerable' appeared, hurt was always its companion.

He was immune but she wouldn't be. He knew what it was like to have complete control over the outcome of his emotional life, whilst she clearly didn't.

And yet…he couldn't escape the tempting notion that it would be utterly relaxing to spend a couple of days in her company. He could look without touching. It was called restraint and, whilst it was something he had never had any need to practise, it should be something that he could manage.

He needed to take time out from the combined stresses of his mother, who would not let up on reminding him that he needed to settle down, and an ex-girlfriend who was still texting him in a way that was heading dangerously into stalker land. The fact that she knew his mother, albeit remotely, had foolishly led her to believe that their fling was more significant than what he'd had in mind.

He needed to take time out from being Lucas Romero. It was an elevated position he had occupied for his entire life. He had been born and bred to manage the family fortune and to add to it. He had never known what it felt like to be a normal person, with normal concerns. Wariness, suspicion, caution: those were the bywords in a life that was as wealthy and as powerful as his was.

'How did you know?' Overnight, Milly had wondered whether exhaustion and a build-up of stress were responsible for her exaggerating Lucas's overwhelming physical impact.

Not a bit of it. He was sprawled in front of his computer in all his devastatingly good-looking glory.

His near-black hair was swept back, accentuating the hard, chiselled lines of his face, and he was wearing a pale blue short-sleeved polo shirt that exposed the rippling, muscled strength of his arms and a glimpse of bronzed collarbone that made her mouth suddenly go dry.

'Because I'm getting the impression that you have a highly developed sense of guilt.' He stood up, dark eyes fixed on her face.

She was in a pair of jogging bottoms and a black base-layer long-sleeved T-shirt that clung to every curve of her small, sexy little body. It was just as well Ramos was not around. His wife would have spent the entire time trying to peel his eyes back into their sockets. The man was a notorious womaniser.

'What are you doing?'

Lucas logged off and leaned back, hands folded behind his head. 'Work.'

'Oh.' Milly looked at him, confused.

'A man has to get by.'

'What work?' Then her face cleared and she smiled. 'Oh, I remember. This and that. You didn't specify. How long have you been up?' It wasn't yet nine and he looked bright eyed and bushy tailed.

'I'm usually up by six.'

'Wow. Are you? Why?' Fascinated, she watched as he strolled towards her, pausing to stand directly in front of her so that she had to look up to him.

'What do you mean *why*?' Lucas asked, amused and puzzled.

'Why would you get up so early if you don't have to?' She felt breathless and exposed. 'I stay in bed as long as I can,' she confessed. 'Admittedly, my hours at the Rainbow Hotel are pretty long. *Were* pretty long. I'm out of a job now.'

She followed him towards the kitchen, chewing her lip, thinking about having to apply for more jobs as soon as she returned to London. How was she going to afford the rent on the flat? Emily would have disappeared off to her shiny new life that left her without a flatmate and with a disgruntled landlord. He might give her a little bit of leeway, if she explained the circumstances to him, but he wasn't a Good Samaritan and unless she found the rent money fast she would be out on her ear with nowhere to live.

'I like to be awake for as much of the day as possible,' Lucas murmured. Lie-ins were unheard of. Even if there was a woman in bed with him, he found it impossible to waste his time next to her, unless they were making love.

Sex got him into bed and kept him there. Sleep was something essential he had to grab. But, for him, those were the two main functions of a bed.

The kitchen was as they had left it. Milly stared around her, dismayed.

'You were up at six, made yourself a cup of coffee and yet you couldn't be bothered to tidy up?'

Lucas surveyed the kitchen as though seeing it for the first time. 'What's wrong with it?'

'Everything. The dishes need putting away…the counters need wiping…the milk's been left out…'

Lucas shrugged and looked at her with his head tilted to one side. 'I fail to see the point of tidying away anything that's going to make an appearance later on in the day. Same goes for the kitchen counters. Why wipe them? Unless you're planning on having a food-free day?'

'How can you be so blasé about someone else's property? You should respect the things that don't belong to you.'

'You're cute when you're being self-righteous,' he murmured and Milly stood stock still and folded her arms.

'You might think you're the hottest guy on the planet,' she said on an indrawn breath, 'and you might be bored because your job here with the Ramos family fell through, but that doesn't give you the right to flirt with me just because I happen to be around.'

'Who's flirting?' He surveyed her lazily. 'Simple statement of fact.'

'And I won't be running around cleaning up behind you like a maid either. I realise I'm being paid by Mr Ramos, who's been more than generous, all things considered—and I know that that's thanks to you—but I'm going to use my time here to really relax and try and forget about what I've been through. I don't want to feel as though I've got to be on full alert every time you're around.'

'I'm at a loss. What do you imagine I'm going to do?'

'Well, I just think we should lay down some boundary lines.'

'Agreed.' He held up both hands with a wicked grin that seem to utterly contradict what he had just said. 'Shall we have a spot of breakfast and then put our skiing skills to the test? The weather looks perfect. We could save the boundary line conversation for a little later.' He watched her hesitate, wondering whether to carry on the argument, maybe add to the 'boundary line' suggestion, but in the end the thought of taking to the slopes proved too much of a temptation and she smiled, her good humour restored.

Inexperienced.

Vulnerable.

He should be laying down more than just a few boundaries himself. He should be the one warning her off. He had the instincts of a born predator when it came to women and, however much she amused him, the last thing he wanted was for her somehow to get it into her head that he might be a worthwhile replacement for the vanishing ex-fiancé. The guy was obviously a complete loser, and she was well rid of him, but transference was a dangerous possibility and a complication he could do without.

As are women who have romantic notions of love and marriage, a little voice added. A complication he could do without...

Milly's face was flushed with happiness when, several hours later, they returned to the lodge.

The day's skiing had been exhausting, exhilarating, wonderful. It had been over a year since she had last taken to the slopes. The *real* slopes. She had managed to keep her hand in by going as often as she could to the nearest dry slopes, but nothing could come close to the feeling of euphoria when, poised at the very top of the mountain, you looked down to the naked, white beauty of snow-covered slopes. It was the closest you could get to your mind being empty, with just you and the infinite snowy space around you, your whole body yearning for the thrill of speed.

They had raced. She was good but he'd made her look like an amateur. He knew where to go to avoid all crowds. He would, she supposed. He would know these ranges like the back of his hand.

Dressed completely in black, including a black woolly hat and dark sunglasses, he was unbearably sexy, and she'd found her gaze drifting back to him repeatedly.

He moved as though he had been born to ski. He was skilled, fast, at times disappearing to reappear like a speeding bullet far ahead of her on the slopes.

They'd broken off for lunch at a tiny café nowhere near the hubbub of the town centre. This café was in the opposite direction, and there wasn't a single designer shop in sight—unlike the town centre, which heaved with rich and famous people spending money in the expensive shops that had sprung up to cater for their exclusive clientele.

Milly had loved it. She had never felt more relaxed as she'd sipped hot coffee and told him all about her childhood, her love of sports, the football team she supported. She'd told him about being brought up by her grandmother, the way it made you feel vulnerable to being left by the people you love.

It was weird but she knew that if she had met him under more normal circumstances there was no way she would ever have approached him. But here, things were different. She was recuperating from the humiliation of a broken heart, and he was the objective listening ear who didn't know her and so was not interested in tea and sympathy. In fact, he made no mention of Robbie except, when he could sense her drifting off, to tell her that the guy was a loser and she was better off without losers in her life.

'Tough times make you stronger,' had been his bracing observation when she had mentioned the uphill struggle of having to return to London to find work so that she could pay the rent on a house she couldn't really afford unless she found another lodger pronto.

Everything about him was as sexy as hell and by the end of the day she had stopped trying to pretend that she didn't want to just keep looking at him. She had stopped trying to figure out how it was that she could be broken-hearted and yet still open to his incredible, mind-blowing, raw animal magnetism...

Their joint love of skiing had banished her nerves. When she was moving on the snow, she was no longer the small, round red-haired girl who couldn't hold a candle to the tall glamorous models men found attractive. No, when she was skiing, she was at the top of her game and bursting with self-confidence.

* * *

Lucas had planned to stay no more than two nights at the ski lodge.

It was all the time he could spare. His high-octane life did not leave room for impromptu holidays. The impulse to go to the ski lodge where the isolation and privacy would recharge his batteries had been a good one.

The unexpected presence of Milly, her freshness and openness, had turned out to be even better for recharging his batteries.

By the second day, he had already made up his mind to take a couple more days off.

What was the point in having highly paid executives in place if you needed to hold their hand every time a decision had to be made? They could all do without him for a few days. Some of them could definitely do with an injection of backbone.

The truth was that he was enjoying himself. He was even enjoying his self-imposed rule of looking but not touching. He liked the way she coloured when he occasionally flirted with her. He liked the challenge of restraint when, the more he saw of her, the more he wanted to see. He liked her openness and he liked the way she confided, her pretty face pink and open and earnest.

The joy of restraint, however, was the certain knowledge that it could be broken at any given moment in time.

She fancied him. He had picked that up with finely tuned antennae: the way she sneaked sultry, stolen glances at him; the way she stilled whenever he got within a certain radius, as though ordering her body not to betray what she was feeling.

Her attempts to keep her distance were like constant

gauntlets being thrown down. His libido, jaded after a diet of the same type of woman, was being tested to its absolute limit.

It was invigorating.

It made him think that he had not faced up to any sort of challenge for a very long time. He had flat-lined. He made money, more than he could ever hope to spend in a lifetime. He owned things and occasionally even enjoyed some of his possessions. And he had women. However many he wanted and whatever variety he chose.

He was keeping his hands to himself but his determination to keep in mind that she didn't play by his rules, that she had been hurt once and he didn't want to be responsible for adding to the tally, was beginning to fray round the edges.

Right now, she was downstairs cooking something. It would be good. She would be moving around the kitchen in clothes that showed off a body she seemed to have downgraded to the lowest possible rating, despite the fact there wasn't a red-blooded man on this earth who wouldn't have appreciated those generous breasts, that tiny waist and those womanly hips.

Wouldn't it do her good to have a man—a *real man,* not a wimp like the vanishing ex—tell her how sexy she was?

Wouldn't it do her self-confidence a power of good for her to know what it felt like to be desired? From what he had read between the lines, the ex had been a waste of space from day one. They had met, gone to the movies, gone on walks, enjoyed meals out. From where he was standing, it had been a courtship that had shrieked 'boring'—and most women with a little more about them would have picked that up and moved on after deadly date number four.

But Milly hadn't and, now that fate had seen fit to bring them together for a few days, wouldn't he be doing her a *favour* if he showed her that she was a desirable woman? If he conclusively proved to her that she was well rid of the man, that she could have any guy she wanted...?

With the logical, clear-minded and concise brain any lawyer would kill for, Lucas made a mental list of all the many reasons why he could be justified in sleeping with her.

At the very end, he tacked on *no more restless nights for me wondering...*

He got downstairs to find the kitchen empty, with a note on the counter propped up against the salt shaker.

She had popped down to the town to get some stuff.

It had been snowing sporadically for the past twenty-four hours but the snow had gathered pace overnight. Optimum skiing conditions were bright-blue skies and good accumulation of snow. Too much falling snow could end up being inconvenient and, in some cases, downright dangerous to safe skiing.

He looked outside at what appeared to be a gathering snow storm. The lifts would be running at half-empty, if that. The line between safe and treacherous was slim. But she was a damned good skier. The best skiing companion he had ever had—courageous without taking unnecessary chances. He would wait for her to return and give himself a chance to catch up on work.

But there was no internet connection. Nor, when he tried his mobile phone, could he get a signal.

He waited a further twenty minutes and then realised that he had no choice but to hunt her down.

Chances were she was fine and on her way back but there was the very slender possibility that the sudden heavy snowfall had disorientated her, as it was wont to do with skiers unaccustomed to these slopes.

A disorientated skier very quickly became a skier at high risk. There had also been three avalanches in the past eighteen months. No casualties, but it only took one…

One disorientated skier, unfamiliar with the terrain, reacting without thinking, panicking…

When that happened, experience on a pair of sticks counted for nothing.

He dropped everything: the coffee he had just made; the historic files he had been about to review on his computer; the report waiting to be concluded.

He hit the slopes at a run, strapped himself into his skis and took off.

This was more than just a bit of fun for a couple of days. This was a serious case of *wanting* a woman and he was sick of playing mind games with himself. Hell, when he thought of her disappearing without him having bedded her…

He killed every single scruple that had been holding him back, because he was a man who was accustomed to taking what he wanted, and why bother trying to break the habits of a lifetime?

CHAPTER FOUR

THE GOING WAS slower than it would normally have been. Lucas was familiar with the slope down to the town centre but the thickly falling snow meant that he had to take it more carefully, which went against the grain when it came to skiing.

What the hell had she been thinking, venturing out when she must have known that there was the possibility of getting lost? She had never been here before and so far had only seen the slopes in his speeding wake.

He did his utmost to cover as much ground as possible, cross-skiing, eyes peeled for anything that might be a figure in distress. Or even a figure moving at a snail's pace, trying to get her bearings.

Nothing.

The slopes were virtually empty. The height of the tourist season was over and the falling snow would have kept most of the skiers indoors. Good food, good wine, expensive lodges—some, like his, with saunas and gyms. Being cooped up indoors would hardly be a hardship.

After twenty minutes, he saw the town approaching in the distance, a clutch of shops and restaurants, bars and cafés.

He hadn't planned to make this trip. He had planned

to stay put in the lodge, testing the less obvious ski slopes, maintaining his privacy. It was a small town and he was its wealthiest occasional visitor.

Cursing fluently under his breath, because he had no idea what 'stuff' she could possibly have needed to buy when the house was stocked with enough food for them to survive a sudden nuclear war, he resigned himself to a door-to-door search for her.

He hadn't signed up for this.

He was recognised within minutes of entering the first shop. He was stopped as he tried to progress through the town. His dark, striking looks halted people in their tracks, even those who didn't know who he was.

Somewhere, there would be someone with a camera. The place was a magnet for the paparazzi.

Hell! It made no difference to him whether some sleazeball with a camera snapped a photo of him but he would rather have avoided it. He valued his privacy, little of it as there was.

He found her in the very last café, huddled in front of a mug of hot chocolate, watching the snow storm. He had just spent the past hour trudging to find her and here she was, cool as a cucumber, sipping her drink without a care in the world!

He burst into the smart café and was, of course, immediately recognised by the owner. He might not have been a regular visitor but he was so extraordinarily high-profile that people went out of their way to garner his attention.

Even when, as now, he patently didn't want it. Especially not when she had spotted him and was frowning as she absorbed the café owner's deference.

The man was practically bowing as he retreated.

Lucas ignored him, choosing instead to hold her gaze as he strode towards her.

'What the hell do you think you're doing?'

'Enjoying a cup of hot chocolate.'

'Are you a complete idiot?' He remained standing, his face dark with anger. 'Have you noticed what's happening with the weather outside? Or are you in a world of your own? Come on. Let's go. Now!'

'Don't you dare order me around!'

Lucas leaned down, hands flat on the table, crowding her so that she automatically flinched back.

The café was half-empty but the few people there were whispering, looking covertly in their direction.

How dare he stride into this café and order her around like a schoolteacher telling a misbehaving kid what to do? *How dare he?* And where was the laid-guy who had listened to her rattle on about her life? The guy who had offered sparse but good advice, who had actually succeeded in helping her put her nightmare broken engagement into some kind of healthy perspective? Where had *he* gone? In his place, this was a dark, avenging stranger bossing her about, embarrassing her in front of other people.

Thanks to her lying, cheating ex-fiancé, she had spent the last two weeks smiling and putting on a brave face to mask her total humiliation. She wasn't about to let any stranger drag her back to that place!

'I am *not* ordering you around. I am very politely but very firmly telling you to drain the remnants of that hot chocolate and follow me out of here. Unless you want to find yourself spending the night in whatever hotel can fit you in!'

'I didn't ask you to come flying down here to rescue me!' Milly snapped, digging her heels in as a matter of principle, even though he was right. She had barely noticed the worsening weather. She should have. She knew all about worsening weather from growing up in Scotland—but she had been lost in her thoughts. 'And, for your information, it wasn't like this when I came out this morning.'

Lucas didn't answer. He pushed himself away from the table with the unswerving assumption that she would follow him, which she did.

'I haven't paid!' she gasped, catching up with his furious stride.

'There's no need to pay...' This from behind her.

Milly looked round, startled. 'Wh-what do you mean?' she stammered.

'Mr Romero is a very special visitor.' Like nearly every person working in the shops and cafés, the owner of this café was deferential to the wealthy and politely but condescendingly accommodating to everyone else. Money talked.

'A *very special visitor*...?' Milly's mouth wobbled on the brink of laughter because she wondered what a simple ski instructor could have done to have been awarded the title of 'very special visitor'. So he might have a handful of rich clients, but since when did their prestige rub off on him? Was he a *very special visitor* because of the way he looked?

'Enough, Jacques!' Lucas forced a smile but he could feel curiosity emanating from her in waves. 'Naturally your bill will be paid.' He turned to Milly. 'Did you have anything else? No? In that case, put it on my tab, Jacques.'

'Tab? What *tab*?'

She trailed out of the café behind him. The cable car was still in operation but for how long? Another hour and she might have been stranded downhill, unable to make her way back up to the lodge. 'I apologise if you felt you had to rush down to find me,' she offered grudgingly as they began the trip back up the hill. 'Like I said, conditions were a lot better when I started out.'

'And when they worsened, you intended to stay put, drinking hot chocolate and waiting for things to blow over?' Lucas turned to her, jaw clenched. 'I don't do rescue missions, so if you want to risk life and limb do me a favour and wait until I've vacated the lodge. Then you're more than welcome to take your life in your hands.' Not a very fair remark, but damn if he was going to retract it. When you went out to ski, you had to have your wits about you. One false move and you could end up endangering not just your own life but someone else's life, as well.

'I'm not responsible for you while you're out here,' he continued coldly.

'And I never asked you to be!' Her eyes flashed but he was right. She should have known better. That said, she had apologised, and he hadn't been big enough to accept it.

She turned away and stared off into the distance. What was it about her that was so poor when it came to reading men? Lucas had shown her a funny, charming side to him and she had been instantly captivated and disarmed. She'd have thought that experience, *very recent experience,* might have toughened her up a bit, made her just a little more jaundiced when it came to believing people and their motivations, but not so.

Apparently, he was fine when it came to her cooking for him and tidying up behind him like a skivvy. And if she wanted to chatter on inanely about herself, then he was happy enough to listen, because really, what choice did he have when he happened to be in the same room as her? But woe betide if she was stupid enough to think that any of those things amounted to him actually *liking* her.

She took people at face value. She always had. Growing up in a small town in remote Scotland where everyone knew everyone else had not prepared her for a world where it paid to be on guard. How many learning curves did one person need before they realised that having a trusting nature was a sure-fire guarantee of being let down? Especially when it came to the opposite sex?

Once back in the lodge, Milly stalked off to have a shower and get changed. The relaxed atmosphere between them had changed just like that after a silent trip back. She took her time having a very long bath and then changing into a pair of jeans and a comfortable cotton jumper. Her hair had gone wild in the snow and she did her best to tame it with the blow drier in the bathroom but in the end she resorted to tying it back in a loose braid down her back. Wisps and curly tendrils escaped around her face, but too bad.

For a few seconds, she looked at the reflection staring back at her in the mirror.

She couldn't remember ever having been envious of any of her friends when she had been growing up. They had been interested in cultivating their feminine wiles and getting with boys, and she hadn't. Not really. She hadn't been interested in make-up or skimpy clothes and she had been amused at how much time and effort some of her friends had devoted to their looks and to attracting boys. It had all seemed a bit of a waste of time, because they had all been in and out of relationships, spending half their time hanging around waiting for a text to come or else putting everything on hold because they were 'going steady' with a boy and somehow that left no time for anything else.

She was pretty sure that those girls would have matured into women who would be savvy enough to spot someone like Robbie for the fraud that he was—and would certainly have spotted Lucas for the arrogant kind of guy who thought he could say what he wanted and do as he pleased with the opposite sex.

He didn't *do* jealousy and he didn't *do* rescue missions and there were probably a million other things he *didn't do*. What it came down to was that he was someone who just did whatever he wanted to do and he didn't really care if he trampled on someone's feelings in the process.

It was not yet lunch time and the snow had already picked up a pace. Lucas was in the kitchen when she finally went downstairs, sitting at the table with a pot of coffee in front of him. Cut off from the outside world thanks to the snow storm, he had given up on trying to sift through paperwork he had brought with him.

She had sat in stony silence on their trip back, head averted, back rigid as a plank of wood as the cable car had carried them back up the slopes. There had been no pleading for him to listen to her and no trying to tempt him out of his foul mood. He had been spoiled by women who tiptoed around him. Despite her open, chatty nature, she was as stubborn as a mule.

'Perhaps I should have been a little less…insistent,' Lucas drawled, pushing aside the file he had given up on and watching the way she was deliberately avoiding eye contact with him. 'But you don't know this area and you don't know how fast and how severe these snow storms can be.' This was the closest he was going to get to an apology and it was a damn sight more than he would have offered anyone else.

'Is that your idea of an apology?' Milly asked, finally turning to look at him.

He must have showered during the time she had been upstairs, taking as long as she could in the bath without shrivelling to the size of a prune. His dark hair was slicked back and still damp, curling at the nape of his neck, and he was in loose grey jogging bottoms and a sweatshirt that managed to achieve the impossible—it was baggy and yet announced the hard muscularity of the body beneath it. He hadn't shaved and his jaw was shadowed with stubble.

He looked insanely gorgeous, which made her feel even more of a fool for having been sucked into thinking that he was Mr Nice. Since when were insanely gorgeous guys *ever* nice?

'Because if it is,' she continued, folding her arms, 'Then it's pretty pathetic. I told you that I was sorry for not having paid sufficient attention to the weather, but I left very early this morning so that I could do a little skiing before I went into town and, yes, it was snowing, but nothing like it's snowing now...'

Had she just told him that his apology was pathetic?

'I'm not going to waste time discussing whether you should or shouldn't have been on the slopes in bad weather.'

'*And...*' she carried on, because she wasn't ready to pack in the conversation just yet. They were going to be spending at least another night under the same roof and she might as well clear the air or else they would be circling one another like opponents in a boxing ring, waiting to see who landed the first blow.

'There's more?'

'You had no right to storm into that café and start laying down laws as though you're my lord and master. You're not.'

'I never said I was.'

'I've been taken for a mug by my ex and I haven't come over here for a complete stranger to pick up where he left off!' Okay, so some exaggeration here but, the more Milly thought about her idiocy in actually thinking that Lucas was a nice guy, the angrier she became. She thought of the high-handed, autocratic way he had delivered his command for her to follow him or else find herself stuck trying to get into a hotel—because she wouldn't be able to make it back to the lodge, presumably because *he* would have had no qualms about leaving her to her own devices, having made sure grudgingly that she hadn't died on the slopes...

Lucas was outraged at that suggestion. She had somehow managed to swat aside the small technicality of her rashly having ventured out without due care and attention because she had wanted to have a little 'early-morning ski' before 'dashing to the shops for something and nothing and a cup of hot chocolate'. While he had been worried, imagining her skiing round and round in ever decreasing circles in a wilderness of unfamiliar white, she had been gaily sightseeing! And, when he'd run her to ground, not only had she expected an apology but she had the barefaced nerve to compare him to an ex-fiancé who had made off with her best friend!

Was there a crazier way to join dots?

'So now I'm on a par with a guy who strung you along before he got caught in bed with your best friend?'

'I'm *drawing a comparison*.' Milly pushed herself away from the counter and turned her back on him so that she could make herself a cup of coffee. She could feel his eyes boring into her back. Typical! He was charm personified when she was obeying his rules but the second she so much as expressed an opinion that didn't happen to tally with his, the second she stood up to him and refused to let him treat her like a kid, he suddenly couldn't see her point of view!

'It's a ridiculous comparison and I'm not having this conversation. The phone lines are temporarily dead, and it looks as though I'm going to be staying on here a little longer than I originally anticipated, so you might want to rethink your sulkiness—because it's going to be a little charged if you're either jumping down my throat or stalking around in surly silence.'

Had he actually considered the challenge of bedding the woman? Was there a less appropriate candidate? He shot her a glance of pure exasperation. How much more illogical could one human being be? And how much more temperamental? One minute, she was as chirpy as a cricket, pouring out her life story with gay abandon. The next minute, she was a raging inferno, behaving as though his act of kindness in putting himself out to find her had been *offensive* somehow.

'I just bet you're like that with all those women who fling themselves at your feet,' Milly snapped, turning back to face him and plonking herself at the kitchen table with her mug of coffee in front of her.

'Are we still embroiled in this pointless argument?' Lucas flung his hands in the air and then raked his fingers through his dark hair and folded his arms. 'Like *what*?' He wondered why he was being drawn into this when there was nothing to stop him getting up and walking out of the kitchen, leaving her to stew. 'What am I like with all those women who fling themselves at my feet?'

Histrionic scenes annoyed him. In fact, he could think of nothing more unacceptable than a woman having a hissy fit. Women should be obliging, soothing, a source of undemanding pleasure to interrupt the ferocity and stress of his working life.

He assumed that the only reason he was putting up with the red-faced, throbbing little ruffled angel in front of him was because she wasn't *his* woman.

More to the point, he wasn't exactly awash with choices, considering she was in his lodge, sharing his space.

But you could always walk away, a little voice in his head pointed out, and Lucas brushed it aside. This was not an occasion for walking away.

'High-handed and annoying!'

'You're telling me that you find me *annoying*?'

'You think you can do whatever you like because of the way you look.'

Lucas smiled, a slow, devastating smile that made her pulses jump. 'Is there a backhanded compliment in there somewhere?'

'No. I bet you play the field and lead women on because you *can*...'

Lucas stifled a groan. 'You're like a dog with a bone.'

'I take it there's a backhanded compliment in there somewhere?' Milly parroted tartly and his smile broadened. How was she supposed to get on with the business of being angry with him when he smiled like that? How was she supposed to remember what an arrogant jerk he could be?

Lucas tilted his head to one side, as though seriously considering her rhetorical question.

'Possibly,' he said slowly, his dark eyes roving over

her flushed face. 'I'm surprised you stuck it out in a job where you were forced to take orders.'

Milly glared. It had taken a lot of tongue biting to work in a hot, understaffed kitchen where she had never been given the opportunity actually to produce anything of her own…but she still didn't care for him pointing that out to her.

'There are always up sides to any situation,' he told her, accurately reading the expression on her face and following her thoughts as seamlessly as if they were written in big, bold letters across her forehead. 'You can waste time feeling sorry about yourself and moaning about the job you've lost…'

'I wasn't moaning!'

'Of course you were. Or, you can see it as a good thing. So you no longer have to run around taking orders from someone you don't particularly like in a job that was going nowhere anyway. And, getting back to your sweeping generalisation that I lead women on because *I can,* I think it's wise for me to dispel that myth before it has time to blossom into another full-blown argument.'

His dark eyes were cool and Milly stiffened.

'I'm not interested in—'

'Well you'd better start working up an interest because, frankly, I wasn't interested in hearing you compare me to the bum who let you down.'

Milly reddened because she knew that she had been unfair.

'You were high-handed,' she began weakly in her defence and the temperature in his eyes dropped a few notches from cool to glacial.

'I've already told you that I would never sleep with any woman who was involved with someone else. Likewise, I would never sleep with any woman if *I* was involved with someone else. The thought of that disgusts me, so I couldn't be further from the unprincipled bastard you got yourself involved with.' He didn't take his eyes off her face. 'When I go out with a woman, she is safe in the knowledge that I'm not going anywhere else and I'm not looking anywhere else either.'

Milly shivered at the rampant possessiveness in his voice. She wondered what it would be like to have that possessiveness directed on *her,* to have this big, powerful man focus all his attention on *her,* to the exclusion of anybody else.

'And yet you're not a jealous guy.' She moved on the conversation to dispel the alluring thought of him wanting her so badly that he literally didn't have eyes for any other woman. Her skin tingled, as though he had brushed it with his fingers, and her whole body shrieked into heated response.

'I've never had cause to be.'

'Because all those women who come running when you snap your fingers wouldn't dream of ever giving you anything to be jealous about?' She thought of the way everyone had looked at him in that expensive café, on the street as they'd been leaving...

Something stirred at the back of her mind but she shoved it aside because she wanted to hear what he had to say.

'Because I have yet to meet anyone I'm interested enough in,' Lucas answered bluntly. He picked up his phone, searching for the signal that might or might not appear at any given moment. The lines were down but hopefully not for long. Like anywhere else where the weather could become suddenly and wildly unpredictable, there was no telling when normality would be restored.

The endless cry of the commitment-phobe, Milly thought. Men who could have whoever they wanted never had an interest in settling for one because why opt for one type of candy when there were so many jars and bottles to choose from? He could barely be bothered to have this conversation with her. He was searching his phone for a signal. She knew that. He was desperate for an outside line and connection with the real world. He'd already gone beyond the line of duty in putting himself out to stage a rescue mission for someone he happened to be stuck with.

'Am I boring you?' she asked and Lucas looked at her.

'You're the most demanding woman I have ever met in my entire life.'

'What's that supposed to mean?' Milly bristled.

'You're still annoyed because I rescued you?' Lucas had never done so much delving into any woman's psyche in his life before. Even in his wild and mis-spent youth, when he had been gunning for the wrong woman, he had let sex do the talking.

'Don't start thinking of yourself as a knight in shining armour,' Milly jumped in to correct him and he raised his eyebrows in an expression that was lazy and amused.

'Ah. Still annoyed. Where has Little Miss Sunshine gone?'

In a flash, Milly had insight into what he thought of her. While she had been shooting her mouth off, *confiding,* losing herself in the thrill of being in the company of a guy who was actually *listening* to her...not to mention thrilling her with those dark, saturnine good looks…he had not been similarly entranced. The opposite. She had been a spot of comic relief with her 'Little Miss Sunshine' personality.

She turned away, hurt.

'I apologise if you were embarrassed,' he said gruffly. 'I realise that, along with *arrogant,* I can be prone to occasionally lapsing into caveman tactics.' When she didn't say anything, he reached forward and, finger on her chin, turned her gently to face him.

Milly's eyes widened and her body was suddenly, horrifyingly, excitingly, in meltdown. She could barely breathe. Her mouth parted. Her nipples stiffened, poking against her bra, sensitive as they scraped against the cotton. Between her legs, she was dampening.

'Hell, you should be careful when you look at a man like that,' Lucas said roughly. But he didn't remove his finger. His libido had been in retreat for a while. Dealing with his ex had left a sour taste in his mouth and he had submerged himself in work because it was, frankly, blessed relief from the whining demands of a woman who didn't want to go away.

Milly, with her disingenuous ignorance of who he really was, with her open, confiding nature and her easy laughter—despite having come through circumstances that would have knocked back anyone else—had stirred his interest.

'Forget it. Not interested.' She pulled away and stood up. 'Just out of curiosity, when were you thinking of leaving?'

Lucas felt the reassuring buzz of his mobile as the outside world was once more connected. Normality could be restored within twenty-four hours. This unusual interlude could be left where it was and he could return to his formidably controlled and predictable life.

Since when had he ever been a fan of surprises anyway? Since when had he ever been interested in exploring anything that came in an unpredictable package? Hadn't he already been there? Done that? Got burned?

'I'm considering my options.'

'That being the case, I suggest we do our own thing. If I decide to go out skiing, then I don't expect you to instigate a search party if I happen to be a couple of hours late.'

Lucas shook his head and briefly closed his eyes. 'Demanding,' he drawled. 'And bloody stubborn.'

'Would that be because I disapproved of you making an idiot out of me in a public place?' She opened her mouth to fume a little bit more but his phone beeped with a series of incoming text messages, voicemails and emails.

Exasperated, she walked off towards the window where the furious snowfall was already showing signs of abating. Blue sky was doing its best to break through. By tomorrow, if not later in the day, the skiing would be good.

And who knew? Lucas might be gone.

She told herself that that would be the best possible outcome. She needed her time out, undiluted time to mourn the passing of a significant relationship. Under normal circumstances, if the Ramos family had showed up, she would have been busy but her busyness would not have distracted her from her thoughts. Lucas distracted her from her thoughts. Robbie had barely registered on her radar! In fact, when she tried to think of him, a darker, leaner image instantly superimposed itself.

Behind her, she was aware of Lucas talking rapidly on his phone. He seemed to be very well known in these parts. A man with connections. He was probably doing all sorts of networking right now, getting things lined up now that his stint here had fallen through.

'You were asking me,' a dark, sexy drawl said from behind her, 'how long I intended staying here and I told you that I was keeping my options open...'

Milly spun around, tensing up. 'I'm fine to stay here by myself,' she told him without hesitation.

'But would that require you to curb your keen sense of adventure?' Lucas couldn't help asking. He thought of her here, on her own, deciding to explore the slopes at midnight just for the fun of it. 'Tell me what your plans are when you leave this place. Do you intend to stay here for the full fortnight? Or will you return to London and start looking for another flatmate? What happens if you don't find one? '

Milly frowned, taken aback at his change of subject. 'I'm keeping my options open,' she mimicked, and Lucas smiled.

'Come and sit down. I want to have a talk with you.'

'What about?'

Lucas didn't answer. Instead, he strolled towards the sofa, his face revealing nothing of what was going through his head.

Was there anything more annoying than an actively functioning grapevine? He had been in the town no longer than an hour and the world at large seemed to know.

His window of freedom appeared to have shut and now he had a problem on his hands.

Of course, there was no problem that did not carry a solution, but he could definitely have done without this particular thorn in his side. His mouth tightened as he thought of the series of texts he had received, texts that had been in a toxic holding bay until service resumed and he could pick them up.

'What are the chances of you finding a job the second you return to London?' he asked, relaxing back on the sofa, his face revealing nothing of what was going through his head or of the vague plan slowly beginning to cohere into shape. 'In the catering arena? I'm guessing that there are a lot of jobs to work at burger joints but I'm also guessing that those jobs won't be top of your list.'

'I honestly don't see what my future job hunting has to do with you!'

'And then there's the little technicality of paying rent when you don't have a job. Difficult. Unless you have a stash of money saved...' He steamrollered over her interruption as though she hadn't spoken. 'Have you a stash of money saved?'

'That's none of your—'

'Business. Is that what you're about to say?'

'Where are you going with this, Lucas? Okay, so I may not have much money saved, but...I'll have what I've earned for this fortnight.' She frowned and wondered how long that would last. Why did he have to throw reality in her face? Had he no heart *at all*?

'"Water through fingers" is the thought that springs to mind,' Lucas said with what she thought was a callous lack of empathy. 'The cost of living is astronomical in London.'

'How would you know?' Milly muttered and again Lucas opted to ignore her interruption.

'I guess, in all events, you could always return to your grandmother's place in Scotland. Ah. I can see from the you way you blanched just then that that option lacks appeal.'

'Why are you doing this?'

'Doing what?' Lucas asked with a show of innocence that set her teeth on edge because it was so clearly false.

'Ramming all my problems down my throat. I wish I'd never confided in you.'

'I wasn't ramming your problems down your throat.'

'I didn't come here to…to…'

'Confront that awkward little thing known as *reality*?'

'You can be really horrible.' Okay, so obviously she would have to address the pressing issue of how she was going to survive without a job and, hard on the heels of that, probably nowhere to live either. But she had been quite happy to put that on hold, at least for a few days. Once she had sorted out the emotional mess she was in which, thinking about it, she realised she seemed to be sorting out rather nicely, all things taken into account.

'There's a point to my timely reminder of the problems you're facing,.' Lucas leaned forward, resting his forearms on his thighs. He wondered where he should start. Her mouth was pursed into a sulky downturn, her eternally upbeat personality dampened by the way he had forced unpleasant reality upon her.

'And that point being…?'

'Point being that I'm about to come to your rescue. In fact, I'm about to open up your world to tantalising new possibilities, and in return all you have to do for me is one small favour.'

CHAPTER FIVE

MILLY STARED AT Lucas in confusion. For a few seconds, she wondered whether he was joking, whether he was having a laugh at her expense, somehow getting his own back for the tantrum she had pulled earlier.

She dismissed that idea as fast as it had come. His face was impassive, deadly serious. And if her gut was telling her that he wasn't the sort of guy who liked tantrums, it was also telling her that he wasn't the sort of guy who would do anything to get his own back for something as silly as her snapping at him.

Whether he had deserved it or not. Which he had. More or less.

'Tantalising new possibilities?' she laughed a little weakly. 'Are you feeling okay, Lucas? How are you going to open up my world to *tantalising new possibilities*?' She wished he would stop looking at her like that, with such deadly calm.

'You might be a little…surprised by what I'm about to tell you.'

'Then don't tell me,' she said promptly. 'I hate surprises. They're never good.'

'Well, that's one thing we have in common,' Lucas murmured, momentarily distracted. He stood up and she followed the easy, fluid movement of his long body with something close to compulsion. He walked across to the window and stared out and, even with his back to her, she could tell that he wasn't really seeing what he appeared to be staring at. She could sense his distraction and that made her nervous because, and she could see this now, there was something so intensely *focused* about him. *Distracted* was not his normal frame of mind.

He spun round, caught her staring at him and allowed himself a small smile which immediately made her glower. And *that* was why he was just so damned arrogant, she thought. Because women followed him with their eyes, irresistibly drawn to mindless gazing.

'I'm not quite the person you think I am.'

For a few seconds, Milly thought that perhaps she had misheard him. Who on earth ever said stuff like that? Her mouth fell open and she stared at him in silence, waiting for him to enlarge on that enigmatic statement.

Lucas was taking his time. He walked slowly back towards her, maintaining eye contact.

'And, before your over-active imagination starts casting me in the starring role of homicidal maniac, you can rest assured that it's nothing like that.' He sat down and continued looking at her thoughtfully, trying on the various options at his disposal for telling her who he really was and what he wanted from her. And why. Much as he loathed justifying his decisions to anyone, he would have no choice in this circumstance.

'The Ramos family,' he began. 'This house…everything in it…doesn't belong to them.'

'Oh, please…' Milly raised her eyebrows in rampant disbelief. 'I don't know where you're going with this but I know for a fact that it does. You forget that snooty Sandra employed me to work for them. I was given all their details. Are you going to tell me that she made the whole thing up? That there are no such people? Plus, you're forgetting that Mr Ramos paid me for my time here!'

She shot him a look of triumph at winning this argument, mixed with pity that he had chosen to come out with such a glaring lie. The combination felt good, especially after the way he had hauled her out of the café in front of everyone. Triumph and pity...she savoured the feeling for a few seconds and threw in a kindly but condescending smile for good measure.

Lucas, she noted, didn't come close to looking sheepish.

'Of course he paid you,' he said, brushing aside that detail as casually as someone brushing aside a piffling point of view that carried no weight. 'He paid you because I told him to.'

'Because you told him to...' Milly burst out laughing and, when eventually her laughter had turned to broken giggles, she carried on, very gently, 'I think you might be delusional. I know you fancy yourself as some kind of hot shot just because you happen to work for loads of rich people and you probably have them eating out of your hand...' *Especially the women.* 'But the bottom line is that you're still just a ski instructor'

Lucas kissed sweet, rueful goodbye to his very brief window of normality.

'Not quite...'

'I mean,' Milly expanded, ignoring him, 'it's a bit like me saying that I own five Michelin-starred restaurants when in fact I just happen to work behind the scenes for an average hotel in West London.'

'Worked,' Lucas swiftly reminded her and she scowled at the reminder. 'You *worked* at an average

hotel in West London. Don't forget that you're now jobless.'

'I hadn't forgotten,' Milly said through gritted teeth. 'And I still don't know where you're going with this.'

Lucas sighed and raked his fingers through his hair, then he reached for his computer, which was on the glass table next to him.

With a start of surprise he realised that for the first time in a very long time indeed work had not been the overriding thought in his head. In fact, he had a back-log of emails to work his way through, emails to which he had given precious little thought. Dark eyes lazily took in the diminutive girl in front of him sitting in a lotus position, her long hair flowing in rivulets over her shoulders. Self-restraint with a sexy member of the opposite sex had clearly had an effect on his ability to concentrate to his usual formidably high levels.

He kick-started the computer and when he had found what he had been looking for he swivelled the computer towards her.

Milly looked at him sceptically. Did anything faze this guy? Whatever the situation, he was the very picture of cool. Chewing her out in the middle of an expensive café in one of the most expensive ski resorts on the planet: *cool.* Arranging for her to stay in the ski lodge: *cool.* Telling her a string of real whoppers about the extent of his influence: *cool.*

'You're not meant to carry on sitting there,' Lucas informed her gently. 'You're meant to get close enough to the computer so that you can actually read what I've flagged up.'

Accustomed to having the world jump to his commands without asking questions, Lucas had a brief moment of wondering whether she intended stubbornly to stay put until he was forced to bring the computer to her. However, after a few seconds of jaundiced hesitation, Milly stood up and then sat on the sofa, back in her cross-legged position, so that she could read his extensive bio.

Lucas watched her. She didn't have to say anything; her face said it all: calm and superior, morphing into frowning puzzlement, then finally incredulity.

Then she did it all over again as she re-read the article, which, fawningly and in depth, traced his lineage and every single one of his achievements, from university degrees to acquisitions of companies. Much was made of his background and the limitless privileges into which he had been born.

He had been personally interviewed for this article. It had come hard on the heels of his unfortunate experience with his gold-digging almost-fiancée, and he had not been predisposed to be anything but brusque with the glamorous blonde whose job it had been to glean some scintillating 'heard it from the horse's mouth' titbits.

His coolness had not bothered her. She had practically salivated in his company and had crossed and recrossed her long legs so many times that he had asked her at one point whether she needed to use the toilet.

At any rate, the finished article had been sent to him for proofreading before it had been put online, and he had been amused to note that he had somehow achieved a god-like status, even though he knew he had been borderline rude to the woman. Money: Was there anything in the world that talked louder and more persuasively?

'I don't understand.' Milly sat back, drawing her legs up and looping her arms around them.

'Of course you do.'

'Don't tell me what I do or don't understand,' she said automatically, because there was nothing worse than an arrogant know-it-all. But he was right. She understood. 'You're not a ski instructor at all, are you?'

'Correct.'

'In other words, you lied to me.'

'I wouldn't exactly call it a lie...' Naturally he had expected surprise, incredulity even, but at the end of the day the ski instructor had been swapped for a bil-lionaire. He had taken it as a given that his new status would do its usual job and bring a smile of servile ap-preciation to her lips. None of it. She was scowling at him, eyes glinting with anger.

'Well, *I* would.' Milly was struggling to contain her anger. How dared he? How dared he play her for a com-plete fool? But then, she was just Little Miss Sunshine, wasn't she? Some comic relief for a man marooned in a ski lodge with her!

'You made false assumptions,' Lucas told her with barely concealed impatience. 'I chose not to set you straight.'

'In your world, that might be acceptable behaviour. In my world, that's called lying!' She sprang to her feet and stormed over to the window, stared out for a little while and then stormed back towards him, hands on her hips. 'I leave London to escape a creep who lied to me and what do I land up sharing space with? Another creep who lies to me!'

'That's the last time you're going to insult me by bracketing me with your loser ex!'

'Why? You seem to have a fair few things in com-mon! Why didn't you just tell me who you were?'

Because I was enjoying the novelty of being with someone refreshingly honest... Because in a world

*where wariness and suspicion are bywords, it was a
holiday not having to guard every syllable, watch every
turn of phrase, accept instant adulation without being
able really to distinguish what was genuine and what
was promoted by a healthy knowledge of how much I
was worth...*

'When you're as rich as I am, it pays to be careful.'

'In other words, I could have been just another cheap,
tacky gold-digger after your money!'

'If you want to put it like that...'

His dark eyes were cool, assessing, unflinching. She
could have hit him. How could he just *sit there* and
admit to lying to her without even batting an eyelid?
As though it was just perfectly acceptable?

Although...

The man was a billionaire. He owned a million companies. He had a hand in pretty much every pie and
he had come from money. There were no limits to his
wealth, his power, his influence, it would seem. She
could reluctantly understand that suspicion would be
his constant companion.

That thought instantly deflated her and she had to
summon up some of the old anger she had felt at the
thought that he had cheerfully lied to her.

'I feel sorry for you,' she told him scornfully and
he stiffened.

'Do I really want to hear you explain that remark?'
No one, but no one, had ever felt sorry for him or, if
anyone had, they had been at pains to conceal it. Money
engendered quite the opposite response. Money combined with good looks—which was something about
himself he accepted without any vanity whatsoever—
was even more persuasive a tool in affording him the

sort of slavish responses he got from other people. Particularly from women.

He looked at her carefully. She was as volatile and as unpredictable as a volcano on the point of eruption. It should have been a turn off and it was mildly surprising that it wasn't.

'How can you trust that anyone likes you for you?'

'My point exactly. But, before we deviate down some amateur psychobabble road, there's a reason I have brought this up.'

Milly stilled. There would be a reason, of course there would, or else he would have stayed a couple of nights and pushed on leaving her none the wiser. Certainly he would have spared himself the sort of awkward conversation he clearly wasn't relishing.

But before he got to that... She finally grasped the thought that had been niggling away at the back of her mind.

'At that café,' she said slowly, 'The owner... I wondered why he was so eager to please...why he said that I didn't have to pay the bill.'

'I'm known here.' He offered an elegant shrug. 'I don't come often but when I do I'm high-profile.'

High-profile and made of money. What had he thought of her? Babbling on and taking him for being a ski instructor? He must have thought that she was crazy. A crazy woman who chattered non-stop and had ruined his seclusion by landing on his doorstep.

'Why did you decide to come over?' she asked, feverishly pursuing her train of thought so that she could join the pieces of the puzzle together and get the complete picture.

Lucas hesitated. It was for the very reason that he had decided to descend on his ski lodge that he was now having this conversation. 'Everyone needs a break,' he informed her silkily. 'Alberto and his annoying family had pulled out and I decided that a bit of skiing would be just the thing. And, in case you're wondering, the Ramos family were over here as a favour to my mother. Alberto works for me.'

'Which was why you could engineer to have me paid for this this two-week holiday. You just had to pick the phone up and tell him and he had to obey. Is that what happens in your life, Lucas? You snap your fingers and people jump to attention and obey you?'

'In a nutshell.'

Milly wondered how she hadn't noticed before the way that he was sheathed in an invisible aura of power, the sort of power that only the super-rich had. Or maybe she *had* noticed but, in her usual trusting way, had shoved that to the back of her mind and chosen to take him at his word: Mr Ski Instructor who did a bit of *this and that* when he wasn't teaching people like the Ramos family to ski.

Maybe, just maybe, she would wake up one day and realise that people were rarely who they said they were.

'Sit down, Milly.' He waited until she was back on the sofa. Her eyes were guarded, the cheerful smile wiped off her face. He had done that. Whatever he told her, he would be just someone else who had lied to her. His mouth tightened; for once, he was finding it hard casually to dismiss someone else's emotions. Habits of lifetime, however, came to his rescue and he swept past his temporary discomfort. So he had punctured some of that bubbly sparkle. Cynicism was healthy. It prepared you for life's adversities. She would return to this very point in time and, in the years to come, she would thank him for bursting her bubble.

'I told you that I came here because I needed a break. Partially true. I'm responsible for the running of…countless companies that stretch across countless countries. I employ thousands…and I'm responsible for them, as well.'

So many revelations were piling up that she felt faint. He was a one-man employment agency. He was a guy who ruled the world, someone who dropped in now and again for a bit of skiing when he needed to unwind, someone who had the most amazing ski lodge on the planet, which he used for a few days in the year. She would stake her life on him having a house in every country, places like the ski lodge that he could use when and if it suited him.

'What do you mean when you say *partially*? You said that it was *partially true* that you came here to unwind. What other reason would you have for coming here?'

'I have been experiencing a few problems with an ex,' Lucas said heavily. Unaccustomed as he was to accounting for his actions, he was decidedly ill at ease with explaining himself to the woman sitting opposite him, but explain himself he had to.

'No, let me guess.' Milly's voice was a shade higher than normal. The whole situation felt surreal. In fact, the past few *weeks* had felt surreal. *You'd think I'd be used to dealing with surreal by now,* she thought with an edge of bitterness that was alien to her. 'The ex wasn't ready to be an ex. Did the poor woman start getting ideas about settling down with you?'

Lucas found it difficult to think of Isobel in terms of 'the poor woman'. She was anything *but* a helpless, deluded damsel with a broken heart. She was a sophisticated, hard-as-nails, six-foot model who had capitalised on the fact that, very slightly, she was acquainted with his mother. She had mistakenly figured that the connection carried weight. His parents had known her parents, both wealthy families living in Madrid, both mixing in the same social circles. The relationship had fizzled out when his father had died but she had done her utmost to resuscitate it during their six-month fling in the hope that familiarity would somehow guide him to a flashbulb moment of thinking that what they had was more than what it actually was. It hadn't but she still refused to let go.

'My relationship with Isobel was not of the enduring kind.'

'Don't you *ever* want to settle down? What was she like? Why wasn't it of the enduring kind?' Curiosity dug into her. 'Was she a gold-digger?' She pictured a kid who was too naive to comprehend all the things Lucas *did* and *didn't* do.

'I am a meal ticket for most women,' Lucas responded drily, not flinching from the absolute truth. 'Even for rich women who can manage quite happily on their trust funds. I have a lot of pull, a lot of connections. I offer a lifestyle that most women would find irresistible.'

'What sort of lifestyle is that?'

'What can I say, Milly? I have a passport to places only available to the rich and famous. It's not just about the limitless spending and the shopping sprees, it's also about the mixing and mingling with famous faces and people who appear in magazines.'

'It sounds hideous.'

'You don't mean that.'

'Being on show every minute of the day and living your life in a glass house with everybody looking in? Having to dress up for social affairs every night?

Wear war-paint and make sure you're shopping in all
the right places and mixing with all the right people,
even if they're dull and shallow and boring? I'd hate
it.'

*Which was why she had been such a breath of fresh
air—enough of a breath of fresh air to make him alter
his plans for leaving. Anonymity had brought him a
glimpse of being the sort of man who could dump his
cynicism for a minute...except cynicism was just much
too ingrained in him for him ever really to do that. And
besides, that glimpse of freedom was now gone.*

Lucas gazed at her open, honest face and wondered
whether she would be singing the same song if she were
to be introduced to that life of glamour and wealth that
she claimed she would hate. It was very easy to dismiss
the things you've never personally experienced.

'All this is by the by,' he said with a shrug. 'The fact
is that Isobel has been annoyingly persistent in thinking that we can salvage something and carry on. She's
refused to fade away and, having finally reconciled herself to the end of our relationship, she's decided that a
little healthy revenge might be called for. When I went
looking for you in the town, I was snapped.'

'Snapped?'

'Surely you can't be *that* naive, Milly. The paparazzi
are always on the lookout for candid shots of high-profile
people. In fairness, I don't know whether I was snapped
by the paparazzi or by some interested visitor who recognised me. Or maybe Alberto's wife just happened to
let slip to someone who let slip to someone else that I
was staying at the lodge with you… Whatever picture
happened to be taken of us together consolidated the
story. I would think that someone who knows Isobel

posted it to her on a social network and it went from there…'

'Sorry, but you're losing me. What story? There *is* no story. Not unless it's the story of the ski instructor who wasn't a ski instructor.'

'Are we back to that?'

'Tell me what you're talking about,' Milly said because he was right. What was there to gain from going over trodden ground? So he had lied because he was suspicious of the human race and in particular of women. She could tell him a thousand times that she found it insulting and offensive but he would just look at her blandly, shrug and imply that her point of view was inferior to his.

'Isobel has somehow managed to get hold of the fact that I'm here with you.'

'You're not here *with me*.' She flushed hotly at the unspoken implication buzzing in the air between them like a live, dangerous electric current.

'And I'm perfectly sure,' Lucas intoned in a voice that was suddenly hard and devoid of emotion, 'that she is all too aware of that. But she's a woman scorned and she's decided that a little malicious mischief is just what I deserve. She can't have me so why not make life as hellish for me as she can, to teach me the valuable lesson that, when it comes to dumping, she's the one who decides to do it?'

Milly frowned in confusion. For someone who had an exceptional grasp of the English language and how to use it to maximum benefit, he seemed to be struggling with his words. 'Okay…' She dragged out that one word while trying to grapple with whatever he was attempting to say to her.

'There's something else I should mention,' Lucas

admitted. 'Another reason I came here was to have a break from my mother. She's been ill and, ever since her extremely successful operation, she's managed to convince herself that time is no longer on her side...'

'I'm sorry. Happens with older people sometimes,' Milly murmured. 'My granny had an operation on her hip two years ago and, even though she can run up a mountain faster than a goat, she still thinks that she'll wake up one morning and she won't be able to stand. Sorry. I interrupted you. What does your mother have to do with this? Lucas, I haven't got the foggiest what you're talking about.'

'Isobel,' he said heavily, striving to stem the anger in his voice when he thought of where his ex had landed him, 'has presented my mother with whatever picture was snapped of us in town and has intimated that...' he shook his head and cursed fluently under his breath '...we are somehow involved in some kind of romantic situation.'

He flushed darkly, remembering the way his libido had gone into orbit when he had looked at her. Yes, he had toyed with the tantalising thought of taking her to his bed. Had that thought somehow manifested itself in whatever expression he had been snapped wearing? Had he been looking at her with some kind of sexual intent? Had some idiot's camera caught him off-guard with a look in his eye that had lent itself to some kind of misinterpretation?

Milly's mouth fell open. She didn't know whether to be horrified, incredulous or just downright amused. No. Not amused. His expression was grim. If she laughed, then he wouldn't be laughing along with her.

'But that's ridiculous.' *Who in their right mind would link the two of us together romantically?* 'I've been here for a couple of days. How on earth would anyone suppose that we're somehow *romantically linked*?' She tried a laugh of sorts and, as expected, he saw nothing funny in the situation. 'Besides, I'm here recovering from a broken heart. Don't forget I was due to be married less than a month ago...'

'She's implied to my mother that we may have known one another longer than a mere couple of days. She knows how I feel about involvement and permanence because I told her, and she knows that the last thing I would want is to find myself trapped in a situation where my mother thinks that I may have ditched my bachelor ways...'

'How do you feel about involvement and permanence?'

'Another time, Milly. For now, you just need to know that they don't form part of my lifestyle choices.'

Milly burst out laughing. 'I just can't picture it!' She gasped. 'I just can't imagine you sneaking around my miniscule two-bed house, comforting me after my break-up. Somehow I don't think you're the kind of guy to go unnoticed! And then what? We planned a secret rendezvous here via snooty Sandra and her band of clones? It doesn't add up. Any fool would be able to see through that in seconds!' She sobered up. 'But that was a mean trick. I guess she fell in love with you. Poor woman.'

Lucas raised his eyebrows, momentarily disconcerted. If he hadn't had proof positive that Milly wasn't interested in what he brought to the table, he would have put her down as just another gold-digger with a slightly different approach. 'I'll cut to the chase,' he said tightly. 'She's told my mother that we're slightly more than an item. My mother is now under the impression that we're going to be married. Isobel showed her whatever candid snapshot got taken and presented her case as the utter truth because would I have gone for someone so…different from what I usually go for if it weren't for the fact that we were serious about one another?'

'What do you usually go for?' She mentally answered that question for herself before she had finished asking it. The guy was drop-dead gorgeous and rolling in money as an added bonus. Guys like that only went for a certain type and that type wasn't *her*. 'No, don't answer that,' she told him quietly. 'I'm thinking you like lots of supermodel types, stunning arm-candy. I'll bet your jilted Isobel was tall and skinny and looked like a model.'

'She *was* a model.'

'So she's pulled a pretty clever trick in showing your mum a picture of dumpy little me, because why else would you be in the same *room* as me unless it was serious. Am I right?'

'That's more or less the size of it. She must have glossed over the holes in the story and ran amok with the rest because my mother's fallen for whatever she's been told hook, line and unfortunate sinker.'

'Do you know what, Lucas?' She breathed in deeply and marvelled at how complicated her life had become ever since Robbie had entered it—lying, cheating Robbie who had come along and wreaked havoc with her perfectly enjoyable, uneventful, contented life. And, not satisfied with that, fate had decided to carry on where Robbie had left off and had thrown her a blinder in the form of the man now looking at her with dark, lazy intent.

'I think I need a break from the male species. In fact, I might take a permanent break from them. Anyway, I don't know why you've told me all this. I'm sorry your mother now thinks that you've found the love of your life but you'll just have to tell her the truth.'

'There is an alternative…' He stood and flexed his arms, stretching out from having sat in one spot for too long when he had wanted to move around, walk some of his restlessness away.

'Which is what, exactly…?' Milly looked at him cautiously as he prowled through the vast open space. *His* vast open space. She still found it hard to grapple with the reality that all of this belonged to *him*. That said, she had recognised a certain something the very first time she had met him: a certain air that spoke of power; a certain arrogant self-assurance that made a nonsense of him being someone as relatively unimportant as a ski instructor. Even a drop-dead, improbably gorgeous ski instructor.

Another telling example of her stupid ability to trust even when she was staring evidence to the contrary in the face.

'You're broke, you're out of work and you'll probably return to London to find all your possessions tossed onto the pavement, awaiting your urgent collection.'

'My landlord wouldn't do that,' Milly said coldly. 'Tenants *do* have rights, you know.'

'Not as many as a landlord whose primary right is the one to have his rent paid.' He paused to stare down at her and Milly grudgingly gazed back up at him. 'Here's the deal. I employ you for a couple of weeks—three, max—to play the role of loved-up wife-to-be. We will stay with my mother in her house in the outskirts of Madrid, a beautiful city by the way, and we can break up over there. My mother will be saddened but she will recover. Normally, I wouldn't go to this much trouble but, like I said, she's been ill and she's mentally not quite there yet. I don't want to present her with a litany of low tricks and lies. She will be upset and confused, especially coming hard on the heels of wanting me to settle down. I will give her what she wants and, when she sees how impossible I am, she will understand why marriage is off the cards for me for the foreseeable future.

'And here's what you get out of this: a fat pay cheque, a five-star, all expenses paid holiday in Spain and, afterwards, I will ensure that you're set up with a damn good job in one of the three restaurants I own in London, with full use of one of my company apartments for six months until you can find alternative accommodation to rent. Whatever you were earning in your last job… Put it this way, I'll quadruple the package.'

'And in return I lie to your mother.'

'That's not how I see it.'

'Plus I lie to my grandmother as well, I suppose? Because what am I supposed to tell her when I don't return to London? Plus I lie to my friends, as well? Thanks, Lucas, but no thanks…'

CHAPTER SIX

So why was she now, a mere day and a half later, sitting in splendid luxury on a private plane heading to Salamanca on the outskirts of Madrid?

Next to her, Lucas was absorbed in a bewildering array of figures on the computer screen blinking in front of him. The 'this and that' had kept billionaires busy and hard at it.

Milly sighed. She knew why she was here; she was just too soft-natured. It was an emotional hazard that was close cousin to the 'overly trusting' side of her that had propelled her into naively believing that the billionaire with the private jet had been a ski instructor—which in turn had been the same side of her that had encouraged her to think that Robbie the cheat had been in love with her rather than mildly fond and willing to exploit.

'You're sighing. Tell me that you haven't done a U-turn on your decision.' Lucas snapped shut his computer and sprawled back in the oversized seat, which was just one of the many perks of having his own plane— no unwelcome strangers crowding his personal space and as much leg room as he needed. He was a big man.

He looked at her, his dark eyes lazily drifting over the baby-smooth, soft curves of her open, expressive

face. She had tied her long hair back but, as usual, unruly curls were refusing to be flattened into obedience.

'What would you do if I told you that I had? We're
in mid-air. Would you chuck me out of your plane? I
still can't believe that you actually *own this,* Lucas.'

'I don't employ strong-arm tactics, Milly. So no, in
answer to your question, I wouldn't chuck you out of the
plane. And I'm getting a little tired of hearing you tell
me how incredulous you find it that I happen to be rich.'

'You can't blame me. I don't meet many people who
own ski lodges and private planes.' Her voice bore the
lingering remnants of accusation.

'I suppose I should be grateful that you're no longer
lecturing me for being a lying bastard like your long-
gone ex-fiancé. Why are you sighing? If we're going
to do a passable imitation of being a loved-up couple,
heavy, troubled sighs aren't going to sell it.'

In response, Milly released another sigh as she absently looked at the stunningly beautiful face gazing at
her with just the slightest hint of impatience.

'You never told me why you're so averse to settling
down.'

'You're right. I didn't.'

'Why not? I've told you loads of stuff. The least you
could do is fill me in, or am I supposed to be the clueless girlfriend?'

Lucas raked his fingers through his hair and stared
at her in silence for a few seconds. 'I don't confide.'

'And I don't pretend to be someone I'm not.'

'Bloody stubborn,' he muttered under his breath.
'Okay, if you really want to know, I had a poor experience when I was young. Take one pretty girl, making
me so out of my normal comfort zone that I didn't think
twice about believing the clap trap she concocted, add

a phoney pregnancy threat and I give you the sort of gold-digging experience that's made me realise that, when it comes to permanence, the only kind I will ever go for is of the business arrangement variety. I'm a fast learner when it comes to mistakes and never making them again.'

'That's awful,' Milly said, appalled. 'How old were you?'

'This isn't a continuing discussion, Milly.'

'But how old?'

Lucas shook his head, exasperated. 'Nineteen.'

'So you had a bad experience when you were a teenager and you've let it ruin your adult life and all the choices you make?'

'*Ruin?* Wrong word. I prefer *affect*. Like I said, I learn from my mistakes.'

And he wasn't about to budge. She could see that in his eyes and in the grim seriousness of his expression. It chilled her to the bone.

'But what if you one day fall in love?'

'Not on the cards. And, Milly, let's put this conversation to rest now.'

'I never thought that large scale lying was on the cards for *me,* yet here I am…' She rested back and stared off at nothing in particular.

Lying was just not part of her nature and ye here she was, immersed in the biggest lie of her life, and all because she had had a vivid image of his mother, frail, vulnerable, bitterly saddened and disappointed at having to be told that she was the victim of a lying ex-girlfriend. She knew first-hand how much lies could wound. She also knew that men could be utterly blind when it came to health issues. If someone had been recently mown down by a bus and, when asked how they were, replied, 'just fine,' the average man would be insouciantly inclined to accept the answer at face value.

The average man would also be highly likely to underestimate the impact of disappointment on a sick and elderly person. Who knew how Antonia, Lucas's mother, would react if she discovered the depth of the lies told to her? Stress killed. Everyone knew that. Whereas, if she were to see for herself just how unsuited Lucas was to her, Milly, then the termination of their so-called relationship would be no big deal. And unsuitable they most certainly were, especially after what he had just told her...

And, face it, there were all those other perks that would certainly make the horror story called her present situation so much easier to bear: job secured, accommodation secured, no nasty landlord banging on her door demanding to know when his rent would be paid.

She would be able to put her grandmother's mind at ease that her life was back to normal and *it would be*.

'I guess your mother was disappointed that you weren't prepared to tie the knot with your girlfriend. I guess she doesn't know about your hang-ups.' She turned to him, wanting to hear just a little more about her competition, because now that they were en route to unchartered territory she could feel butterflies beginning to take up residence in her tummy.

'My hang-ups. You really have a way with words. You conversationally go where no other woman has gone before. My mother may want me to settle down,' he said drily, 'But even she sussed that Isobel wasn't going to be the perfect candidate for the position of stay-at-home wife.'

'Because...?'

'Because Isobel was more jet-setter than home-

maker. I think it goes with the territory of being a supermodel. Something about being treated like a goddess
when, in fact, you're no more than a pretty face.'

'Jet-setter…'

'Glitz, glamour and an unnatural love of having cam-
eras focused on her.'

'The sort of girl you tend to go out with.'

'Why the hundred and one questions, Milly?'

'Because I'm nervous,' she confessed. The way he
described his ex was a fine example of a man who attached himself to just the sort of woman he was in
no danger of wanting to commit to. Casual sex. She
shouldn't even bother to speculate on his motivations
or lack of motivations when it came to women.

'Think of the wonderful payback and your nerves
will disappear. Trust me.'

Milly scowled because, however wonderful those
paybacks were, they weren't the reason she had agreed
to engage in this little game of fiction and, the closer
the plane got to their destination, the more she wondered whether her impulse to do what had felt right at
the time really was such a clever idea.

Her impulses *had* been known to let her down.

'I didn't agree because of the…paybacks.'

Lucas's eyebrows shot up and he gave her a slow,
disbelieving smile.

'You're so suspicious,' Milly muttered.

'You're telling me that your sole reason for agreeing to pretend to be my soon-to-be-departed fiancée is
because you felt sorry for my mother, a woman you've
never met in your life?'

'Mostly. Yes.'

'Nice word, *mostly*. Open to all sorts of conflicting
interpretations.'

'Sometimes you really annoy me, Lucas.' Right now he was doing rather more than annoying her. Right now she wished that he would return to his obsessive contemplation of whatever high-powered deal he was in the middle of making, because his attention on her was making her feel all hot and bothered.

Having travelled with nothing suitable to wear for warmer temperatures, she was in a thermal T-shirt, jeans, her thick socks and trainers and the whole ensemble made her skin itch.

'I'm just trying to… Wondering how…to pretend to be someone I'm not.'

'You mean how to pretend to be someone in a relationship with me?'

'I've never done anything like this before. I'm not the sort of girl who likes fooling people. It doesn't seem kind and, whether you want to believe me or not, yes, the paybacks will certainly make my life a whole lot easier when I get back to London but mostly I'm doing this because I hate thinking that your mother's had her hopes raised only to have them dashed, and cruelly dashed at that. I honestly can't believe that anyone could tell such a horrendous lie to someone who hasn't been well, just to get revenge because you let her down.

'Has your mother *ever* been keen on *any* of your girlfriends?'

'Not that I can recall offhand…' And that had never bothered him until she began making noises about wanting him to settle down because 'who knew what lay round the corner for her?'.

He knew what she thought of the Isobels of his life, the never-ending stream of decorative supermodels who enjoyed basking in his reflective glow; who simpered, acquiesced and tailored themselves to his needs. He, personally, had no problem with any of those traits; his work life was high-powered and stressed enough without adding more stress to the tally in the form of a demanding girlfriend. His mother, always grounded, was of a different opinion.

It occurred to him that this little game of make-believe might have an unexpected benefit.

Milly was as normal and as natural as the day was long. Were it not for his inherently suspicious nature, he would truly believe that, as she had stated, she had agreed to this well-intentioned charade from the goodness of her heart. She was just the sort of wholesome girl he would never seriously consider as a life partner in a million years. No; like it or not, if and when he decided to tie the knot, it would be with someone who saw marriage through the same eyes as his. It would be with someone who didn't need his money, someone who understood the frailty of the institution and recognised, as he did, that marriage stood a far better chance of success if it was approached as a business proposition.

If his mother saw for himself just how unsuited he was for a girl like Milly—and for Milly read all women like her—not only would she accept it when they 'broke up' but she would understand that her dreams of romance and falling in love were not his. She would get it that his plans for himself lay in a different direction. It would be a salutary learning curve that would succeed where explanations had in the past failed.

'My mother is a firm believer in true love and happy-ever-after endings,' Lucas intoned with a corrosive cynicism he made no attempt to disguise. 'She married the man she fell in love with as a teenager and they stayed married and in love until the day he died. She has high hopes that I might continue the tradition and she doesn't see it happening in the arms of any of the supermodels I've ever dated.'

'There's nothing wrong with true love and happy-ever-after endings. You might have had *one* bad experience, but you can't knock the real thing because of that.'

'I'm surprised to hear you say that after what you've been through.' But he wasn't. She struck him as just the sort of hopeless romantic who nurtured secret dreams of the walk down the aisle in a big wedding dress, with a sprawling line of best-friend bridesmaids in her wake. The sort of girl who eagerly looked forward to testing her culinary skills in her very own kitchen while lots of little Millies pitter-pattered at her feet. Just the sort of girl his mother imagined for him and precisely the sort of girl he would run a mile from, because he'd had his learning curve when it came to all that nonsense about love.

'Just because I was let down—'

'Dumped by a guy who absconded with your best friend.'

Milly flushed hotly. 'There's no need to ram that down my throat.'

'A little reality goes a long way, Milly.'

'If by that you mean that it goes a long way to turning me into someone who doesn't believe in love and marriage, then I'd rather not face it.'

'Well, considering I have no time for any of that, it should be a cinch demonstrating to my mother just how incompatible we are.'

'If we're that incompatible, then I'm wondering how we ever got involved with one another in the first place,' Milly said tartly. 'I'm broken-hearted and vulnerable after a broken engagement, and you swoop into my life and decide that I'm the one for you even though I'm the last person on the planet you would get involved with? How does that make sense, Lucas?'

'Like I said, my mother is a devotee of fairy stories like that.'

'Then she doesn't know you at all, does she?'

'Do you ever accept anything without questioning it out of existence?' He shook his head and sighed with a mixture of resignation and exasperation. 'People believe what they want to believe even if evidence to the contrary is staring them in the face. My mother believes in true love without any encouragement from me, I assure you. So she won't find it odd at all that you've swept me off my feet.'

Milly blushed and looked away. 'Does she know about your experience with that girl when you were still a kid? An excusable mistake when you were too young to know better.'

'Is that your way of introducing your analysis of the experience?' He shot her a glance of brooding impatience, which she returned with unblinking disingenuousness. 'Which I'm seriously regretting telling you abou. To answer your question, no, she doesn't.' His gaze became thoughtful. 'Which brings me to one or two ground rules that should be put in place.'

'Yes?' What would it take to sweep a man like Lucas off his feet? she wondered. Someone amazing. And that person existed, even if he didn't think so. His parents had been happily married, as had hers. Her grandmother had told her numerous tales of how much in love her parents had been. Inseparable, she had said. Growing up, Milly had never tired of looking at snapshots of them together; had never tired of hearing all the small details of the childhood sweethearts who had grown up together and had never wavered in their love for one another. Maybe those tales had formed the person she was now: idealistic and eternally hopeful that she would one day find the right guy for her.

If it was inconceivable that someone like Lucas, jaded and cynical, could ever be attracted to someone like her, then it was equally inconceivable that someone like her, optimistic and romantic, could ever be attracted to someone like him.

'Ground rules…' he repeated gently, snapping her out of her reverie.

'Oh, yes, you were about to tell me.'

'Ground rule number one,' he said, frowning, because never had he ever had to work so hard at getting a woman's attention, 'is the importance of remembering that this is just a temporary charade.'

Milly looked at him, eyes wide with puzzlement. 'I know *that*.'

'By which,' Lucas continued, taking advantage of her full, concentrated attention before she could drift off into one of those doubtless cotton-candy fantasies of hers, 'I mean that you don't get ideas.'

'What on earth are you talking about?' Enlightenment dawned as he stared at her with unflinching intent. 'Oh, I get it,' she said slowly, as colour crept into her face and her heart picked up angry speed. 'You don't want me to start thinking that the game is for real. You really are the limit! Do you honestly imagine for a second that I would be stupid enough to fall for a guy like you? Especially after everything you've told me?'

'Come again?'

'You think that because you happen to be okay looking, because you happen to have a lot of money, somehow you're an irresistible catch! And you may just be for all those supermodel women who like being draped over your arm, getting their pictures taken whenever they're with you, but I meant it when I told you that I can't think of anything worse! Least of all with a guy who's said that he sees marriage as a business transaction!'

'Sure about that?' Lucas's mouth thinned, a reaction to the unfamiliar sound of criticism.

'Quite sure,' Milly informed him scathingly. 'I could never be interested in a man like you. I'm sure you have wonderful qualities…' She paused for a heartbeat while she tried to imagine what those wonderful qualities might be. Certainly sensitivity and thoughtfulness didn't feature too high.

Although, a little voice pointed out, *isn't his attitude towards his mother an indication of just those qualities, lurking there somewhere underneath the cool, hard, jaded exterior?*

'But,' she continued hurriedly, 'I go for caring, sharing fun guys.'

'Caring? Sharing? Fun? This may come as a shock, but when it comes to fun I can't think of a single woman who's ever complained.'

'I'm not talking about *sex*,' Milly said derisively, scarlet-faced, because really what on earth did she know about sex? Her life had not exactly been littered with panting suitors desperate to strip her naked and climb into bed with her. Sure, there had been interest. She had even gone out with a couple of them. But none of those brief relationships had ever stayed the course. Either she was too fussy or she just wasn't clever enough to play the games that most women knew how to play, the games that trapped men. Not that she had ever had any inclination to trap any of the guys she had dated briefly.

She went a shade pinker as she wondered how Lucas

would react if he knew that she was a virgin. The virgin and the rake, poles apart, the most unlikely pretend couple in the world!

'I'm talking about the sort of caring, giving man who shares the same belief system as I do; the sort of man who wants the same things that I want—love, friendship, a soulmate for life...'

'Sounds thrilling,' Lucas said drily. 'You're omitting passion. Or is that sidelined by the friendship, soulmate angle?' He shot her a wolfish grin that made her skin prickle, made it difficult to keep her eyes focused on his lean, dark face. 'Never mind, I get the picture, and I'm glad that we're singing from the same song sheet. That being the case, you will have no need to pretend. I imagine our conflicting personalities will be enough to demonstrate to my mother that our relationship is not destined to last longer than it takes for you to rustle up a hot meal.' He shrugged elegantly and shot her a crooked smile. 'Feel free to share all your home truths about me!'

'I most certainly will! And...one other thing.' The plane began dipping, preparing to land. 'I'm afraid I didn't come prepared for warm weather.' She thought wistfully of the innocent little ski-resort job she had mapped out as part of her recovery programme. 'I hadn't expected to find myself on a plane to Madrid.'

'Believe it or not, there are shops there. A free wardrobe is part of the package.'

'I don't feel comfortable with that.'

'Then we can agree on a repayment schedule— although you might want to settle into your new job when you get back to London before you start working out how to transfer money into my account for a handful of clothes.'

'I wonder how it is that I never spotted just how *infuriating* you could be.'

'That could certainly be one of the things you tell my mother that you dislike about me,' Lucas pointed out. 'Although who knows how she might react to the shock of hearing a woman speak her mind? You have to bear in mind that she's had a stroke.'

'You're telling me that no one ever speaks their mind when they're around you?'

'Frankly, no. Although you're more than making up for that.'

The small plane touched down smoothly, skimming over the landing strip like a little wasp before slowly grinding to a halt. Conversation was abandoned amidst the business of disembarking, after which a long, sleek car was waiting for them, complete with uniformed driver.

Cool, early spring temperatures greeted them. She was fine in what she was wearing but, stepping into the car, which was the height of luxury, she was suddenly and acutely aware of just not quite blending into her surroundings. What was appropriate gear for travelling in a luxury chauffeur-driven limo? She was sure that there would be some sort of dress code and, whatever it was, it certainly wasn't what she was wearing. His mother might disapprove of supermodel girlfriends, but supermodel girlfriends would match expensive limos; supermodel girlfriends would pull off luxury houses and private planes…

And suddenly she felt that tug of self-consciousness that had been her occasional companion growing up— the little pang of knowing that she really wasn't too sure when it came to the opposite sex, of knowing that she would never really make it into the inner sanctum of the cool set, even though she got along just fine with them. Lucas's mother might have whimsical dreams about her son finding a suitably wholesome, down-to-earth girl but she would discover fast enough that wholesome, down-to-earth girls were not fashioned for ridiculously wealthy lifestyles.

Her eyes slid across to where he was sitting, casually at ease in his expensive limo. His sense of style was so much a part of him that he could have been wearing a bin bag and he would still have looked stupendously sophisticated. Stupendously sophisticated and utterly, bone-meltingly, sinfully *sexy*.

He was right. There would be no need for her to pretend because there was no way his mother could fail to notice just how ill-suited they were as a couple. She wouldn't be deceiving anyone. She would just have to be herself. This was going to be a little adventure, nothing to get all worked up and anxious about. Life threw curve balls and she was catching one. When again would she find herself in this position—freed from all responsibility; no job, nothing waiting for her back in London, suddenly free to do exactly what she wanted to do?

She rested her head back and half-closed her eyes, and when she turned to look at him after a few seconds it was to find him staring right back at her. He had the darkest eyes imaginable and lashes most women would kill for. The perfect, beautiful symmetry of his lean face should have made him too…*pretty,* but there was a harsh, dangerous strength there that made him 100 percent alpha male.

Her heart skipped a beat. She was supposed to be romantically involved with the guy! What a joke. As though someone like him would ever look at someone like her! Even that gold-digger who hadn't been a supermodel had probably *looked* like one. But for a few heart-stopping seconds she imagined what it might feel like to be touched by him; to be seduced by that rich, dark, dangerous, velvety voice; to have him run his hands over her naked body.

She bit back a stifled gasp as moisture pooled between her legs and a heavy, tingling ache began in her breasts and coursed through her body until she felt hot and uncomfortable in her skin.

It was a physical reaction that was so unexpected and so blindingly powerful that she felt faint. Faint, giddy and slightly sick. She couldn't remember feeling anything like this when she had been with Robbie. In fact, she couldn't remember feeling anything like this *ever.* She was shockingly aware of her own body in a way she never had been before, aware that she wanted it to be *touched,* wanted the strange tickle between her legs to be alleviated.

She dragged her eyes away from his mesmerising face, mortified at the suspicion that he could see exactly what was going through her head, and even more mortified when she belatedly remembered what he had said about making sure she didn't start getting ideas.

'How long before we get, er, to your mother's house?' she asked because talking might distract her from what was going on with her body.

A little over an hour. An hour of sitting next to him in the limo, trying hard to rein in her wandering mind. An hour of pretending not to notice the muscled strength of his forearms; the taut pull of his trousers over his powerful thighs; the length of his fingers; the sexiness of his mouth; the way his voice curled around her, tantalising, tempting, as velvety smooth as the finest dark chocolate.

Every confusing sensation racing through her body

and running like quicksilver through her head crystal-lised to demonstrate, conclusively, just how inexperi-enced she was when it came to the opposite sex. And, as if that wasn't bad enough, she couldn't even rely on good old common sense to point her in the right direc-tion or else she wouldn't be sitting here, pressed against the car door to create maximum space between them, babbling like the village idiot because it was better than letting any disturbing silences settle between them.

At the end of half an hour she knew more about Ma-drid than she did about her own village where she had grown up because she had plied him with questions. By the time they were drawing into Salamanca, she could have done a doctorate on the subject.

Not only did his mother have a house in Salamanca but she also had a house in Madrid for those times when she fancied an extended shopping trip to the city, or when she visited friends and wanted somewhere to stay over.

It hadn't been used in a while because ill health had interrupted her usual routine, she had been told.

'Relax,' Lucas told her wryly. She was staring at him, mouth parted on the brink of yet another ques-tion. There seemed to be no end to them. He politely refrained from telling her that he had never known any woman to talk as much as she did. 'You're not walking into a dragon's den.'

'I didn't think I was,' Milly lied.

'Oh, yes, you did. That's why you haven't drawn breath since you started asking me to give you a ver-bal guided tour of Madrid and its surroundings. If we'd been in the car for another hour, you would probably have extended your parameters to the rest of Spain, be-cause you think that talking calms your nerves.'

'I'm not nervous. We've agreed that neither of us has to pretend to be anything other than what we are.'

'You're nervous. And you're the girl who wasn't nervous when she was plying me with questions about my past. Don't be.' He gently tilted her chin away from him, directing her to look through the front window, and her eyes widened at the mansion approaching them. She had barely noticed when the limo had pulled off the main road. 'We're here.'

Milly's mouth dropped open. The low white house with its red roof sprawled gloriously amidst a profusion of shrubs, flowers and trees. The intense blue of the sky picked up the even more intense, vibrant colours of the clambering flowers of every shape and variety, and everything melded harmoniously together into picture-postcard perfection.

Standing at the front door was a tall, striking woman leaning on a walking stick. Black hair was pulled back from an angular, handsome face.

'I have no idea why my mother can't let one of the maids get the door.' But there was affectionate indulgence in his voice and Milly had a vivid image of the boy beneath the man, the unguarded person beneath the cynical, hard-edged adult in control of an empire. He was a loving son and she had a moment of piercing happiness that she had agreed to this unexpected charade.

'She probably just can't wait to see you.'

'To see *us*...' The limo swerved smoothly to a halt and, as they emerged from the car, she felt the heavy weight of his arm sling over her shoulders. 'We are, after all, the loving couple,' he whispered into her ear and the warmth of his breath made her want to squirm. 'At least before the rot sets in...' And, to prove his point, he curved his hand under her hair to caress the nape of her neck.

And then, barely breaking stride, with such natural- ness that anyone would have been forgiven for thinking that what they had was real, he paused, dipped his head and covered her mouth lightly with his.

Just a brief meeting of tongues, enough to do dev- astating things to her body, then he was pulling away, hand still caressing her neck. The epitome of a man in love.

He couldn't have been more successful at killing her nerves because how could she be nervous about facing his mother when her thoughts were all over the place at that what that casual kiss had done to her body...?

CHAPTER SEVEN

ANTONIA ROMERO WAS an elegant, quietly spoken woman who immediately put Milly at ease. She ushered them in warmly, allowing Lucas to kiss her on the cheek and then fret at the fact that she had come to the door herself when she should be resting, when there was help in the house to do things like answer doors.

'I just couldn't wait to meet Milly…' she protested, drawing Milly into the living room, where tea and pastries were waiting for them on a low glass table while a pretty, smiling maid hovered in the background, ready to leap to service. 'And I know you must be tired after your trip but I'm dying to hear all about your romance. I knew it. I just knew that son of mine would end up finding true love with a real woman and not one of those plastic dolls he's spent his life fooling around with.'

Milly sneaked a surreptitious look at Lucas to see how he was handling his mother's criticism and he caught her eye and grinned, eyebrows raised.

'Didn't I tell you that my mother has no problem saying exactly what she thinks?' He shooed Antonia back to the sofa as she automatically rose to pour them tea and hand round the pastries. On cue, the maid leaped into action and refreshments were served before the maid vanished out of the room, shutting the door behind her.

With Antonia on the low, damask pink sofa facing her, Milly had a chance really to look at her hostess. There were fine lines of strain around her eyes and mouth and she was borderline too thin, barely filling the black, shapeless dress that hung down to her calves, yet it wasn't hard to see that she must have been a great beauty in her day. Not that she was exactly ancient now. At a guess, Milly would have put her in her mid to late sixties.

She tried to maintain the chirpy smile of a woman in love as Lucas helped himself to a few more pastries before subsiding right next to her on the sofa, a replica of the one on which Antonia was sitting, his thigh pressed against hers.

She had been leaning forward, perched on the edge of the sofa, her hand primly linked on her knees, and now he pulled her back so that she tumbled against him.

'What would you like to know?' Lucas's voice was teasing as he fondly addressed his mother. 'You have limited time for questions because you should be taking it easy.'

'I'm sitting,' Antonia retorted, smiling. 'How much easier can I take things? Please don't join the queue along with all my friends who have insisted on treating me with kid gloves ever since I got ill.'

'Why don't you explain…?' Lucas brushed aside Milly's hair and delivered a feathery kiss on the side of her cheek, just enough to send the heat spiralling through her.

Milly's eyes glazed over. If she wasn't under a microscope, she would have punched him, because he was the one who had propelled her into this awkward situation; how fair was it that she was now being dumped in the thick of it, having to concoct some vaguely realistic lie? Not very.

Antonia was watching her expectantly and Milly reluctantly stumbled into a suitable tale of sudden love and searing romance. She swept aside the minor detail of her broken engagement as just a bit of nonsense from which she had thankfully escaped because, had she not, how else would she have found herself with Lucas? Fate.

Good word. Antonia picked up the cue and reminisced over her own wonderful marriage. Fate had thrown her and her husband together from such a young age.

How could Milly resist confiding about her own parents, also childhood sweethearts? She couldn't. They had died too young but desperately in love; she felt scared at the thought of being deserted by those she loved, but she still believed in love with all her heart, whatever the risks it brought. She was thinking of Lucas and the mystery gold-digger when she said that. Belatedly, as Antonia nodded approvingly, Milly remembered that this was not supposed to be a bonding experience. She cleared her throat and wondered whether she should shove the man at her side into picking up the baton and continuing their fictional tale of love.

'Of course.' She decided against that course of action because who knew what he would say? He hadn't uttered a peep while she had been in confiding mode, although she had felt him edge a little closer to her, all the better to...*what*? Prolong his mother's incorrect assumptions? 'Wonderful though our sudden love is, I have to admit that your son can be a little...*forceful*.'

'Too forceful?' Antonia asked, and Milly ruefully inclined her head to one side, as though seriously giving the question house room, before erring on the side of tactful.

'Borderline arrogant,' she sighed, patting Lucas's thigh without looking at him. 'I guess it's something to do with having grown up in the lap of luxury. I'm afraid I grew up in the lap of, well, rubbing pennies together and trying to make ends meet...' She left Antonia to make the obvious deduction, which was that they were worlds apart and therefore incompatible in a fundamental area. The first of many, if only she knew.

Antonia seemed delighted with her admission. 'So good,' she murmured, tearing up, 'that you've finally come to your senses...' she smiled at her son and leaned forward '...and realised how much more fulfilling it is to have a real woman at your side. My dear, let me tell you about my dearest husband and myself. We rubbed many a penny together before Roberto's career began to take off! I could tell you a hundred tales of having to choose between paying the bills and buying food, especially in the beginning when we owed the bank so much money...'

'Thank you so much for helping me out there,' was the first thing Milly said when, an hour and three pastries later, they were being ushered up to their bedrooms. 'Why didn't you...why didn't you...?'

'Launch into a speech about why our fast and furious romance is destined to crash and burn within the next fortnight?'

He hadn't known about how she felt about her background. Orphaned as a kid and brought up by her grandmother, yet never looking back and blaming an unfortunate past. Still believing in the power of love even though abandonment issues should have made her wary and cynical, disinclined ever to trust anyone to get too close. Still ever-hopeful, the eternal optimist.

He had known women who had been blessed with the best life could offer and still managed to moan and complain about nothing in particular.

'Bit soon for the cracks to be showing, wouldn't you agree?'

At the top of the landing, the maid turned right and they both followed, Lucas breaking off to say something to the maid in rapid-fire Spanish that had her laughing. Their cases had been brought up whilst they had been in the sitting room.

'Your mother's really lovely,' Milly admitted. 'It's going to be a shame when she has to face up to the fact that you're so obnoxious that no one in their right mind would ever put up with you.'

Lucas looked down to see whether she was joking, but her expression was thoughtful and earnest.

'There are times when I can't actually believe that I'm hearing what you say correctly.'

Milly stopped and looked at him with a little frown. 'Do you have any idea how arrogant you were when you led me to believe that you were someone you weren't? I may only have been the chalet girl, but you just didn't see why you should be honest with me. For a start, you assumed that I was the sort of low life who would be out to see what I could get if I knew you were rich, and then you just didn't give a damn if you weren't honest. You didn't care about my feelings at all. I know you had one bad experience with a gold-digger but that's no excuse to just assume that everyone falls into the same category, guilty until proved innocent.'

'How did your feelings have anything to do with… anything at all?'

'You barely apologised for having duped me,' Milly told him flatly.

Where had that come from? Lucas, frustrated, raked his fingers through his hair and stared at her, lost for words.

'You just *assumed* that it was okay because you can do what you want to do without bothering to consider other people.'

'Is this conversation going anywhere?' he questioned in a driven voice. He glared at the maid, who seemed to be suppressing a smirk.

'I'm projecting…'

'You're *what*? I have no idea what you're talking about.'

'I'm projecting ahead to when you mother sadly discovers what a selfish, self-centred guy you've turned out to be.'

'I'm guessing she's probably wised up to those traits a while ago,' Lucas said drily, eyebrows raised. 'And, while we're on the subject of scrupulous honesty and caring about the feelings of others, have you mentioned to your grandmother what's going on in this part of the world?'

Milly flushed. 'I didn't see any point in worrying her by going into details.' It wasn't as though this was going to be a long-term situation. Two weeks—three, absolute max—he had told her when she had agreed to his plan. In those weeks, even if a dramatic break-up hadn't been staged, they should have covered the important phase of their fairy-tale romance revealing shaky foundations.

In those couple of weeks, he had privately thought, his mother would put to bed all ideas of trying to see him settled with the woman of her dreams. She would kill off notions of fairy-tale romances insofar as they pertained to him and she would resign herself to cheerful acceptance that what he wanted out of life, emotionally, was a far cry from what she thought would do him good.

She was his mother and he indulged her but, at the end of it, it was his life and he would choose its outcome whether or not it flew in the face of her ideals. This exercise in harmless fiction would be a gentle learning curve for her.

'I'm only going to be here for a short while and, when I return to London and my life's all sorted out, maybe then I'll let her in on some of the details.'

'You honestly think your life's going to be *all sorted out* when you return to London?'

'You said that…'

Lucas waved aside her predictable cry of protest. He had offered to have a formal agreement drawn up listing the conditions of this arrangement, what she would be given at the end of it, but she had airily told him that that wouldn't be necessary.

'I'm not talking about the job and the accommodation and the money, Milly. I'm talking about your blind faith in life always turning out for the best.'

'I don't have to listen to this.' She turned away and felt his hand gently stay her.

'If my mother's long overdue a little learning curve, then you should take this opportunity to put in place one of your own. Reality doesn't disappear because you decide that you'd quite like it to.' He nodded to the maid, who had tactfully moved to stare through one of the sprawling windows on the landing, ears blocked to any conversation—although Milly didn't think she spoke a word of English, so that probably was a step too far when it came to fulfilling her unspoken duties.

Milly watched, mouth open in anger, as he sauntered off, once again speaking Spanish, once again making the maid giggle. The maid might have been an old retainer well into her sixties, but it was obvious that he could still work the charm offensive on her.

Which was something he couldn't be bothered doing in *her* case.

How dared he think that he could bring his jaundiced views to bear on *her* life?

Placid by nature, she could scarcely credit the fury bubbling up inside her as her brain began functioning once again, and she tripped along behind him, barely paying attention to the magnificent surroundings.

The house was in the style of a rambling ranch. A short flight of stairs led up to the first floor, which, like the floor below, was wooden-floored, the wood gleaming from years of polish.

The corridor opened out in places into small sitting areas and curved round in other places, leading to nooks and crannies, various bedrooms and sitting rooms. It should have been disjointed and higgledy-piggledy but in fact there was an attractive coherence about the honeycomb nature of the layout, something whimsical and charming.

A lot of light poured in, thanks to large windows at regular intervals, a couple of which were fashioned of stained glass so that the bright sunlight was refracted into thousands of splintered shapes.

Through the windows, as she marched along in Lucas's wake, she could see extensive lawns and the bright turquoise of a swimming pool.

She stopped behind Lucas as the maid disappeared

into one of the bedrooms and she hovered, arms folded, still simmering.

'Good news and bad news.'

'Huh?' Snapping out of her reverie, Milly focused on his swarthy, handsome face. He leaned against the doorframe, the very picture of cool elegance.

'The good news is that it's a vast bedroom, complete with two sofas. There are even twin wardrobes. The bad news is that we're sharing it.'

The maid had vanished and Milly stared at Lucas, heat flooding her cheeks.

'You told me that there was no way your mother was going to…going to stick us in the room together! You told me that your mother was very old-fashioned, that she hadn't been brought up on a diet of sex before marriage. You *said* that she might know what you got up to but she'd always been adamant that you wouldn't get up to it under *her roof.*'

'I have a feeling that on those occasions when I showed up with a woman in tow she decided that the best way to avoid contributing to a loveless union was to locate us at opposite ends of the house.'

'Is that all you can say?' Milly hissed as her anger headed a little bit further north.

'At the moment, yes.' He pushed himself away from the doorframe and strolled into the guest suite.

Normally, he was given his usual room in the other wing of the house. He had barely noticed that they were being shown to a room in the opposite direction.

'How is this supposed to work?' Milly persisted, hands on hips as she followed him through.

'You should shut the door. The last thing we need is for wagging ears to hear us at each other's throats.'

'I thought that that was supposed to be the whole intention.'

'Not on day one. Now shut the door, Milly.'

'Bossy,' she muttered, stepping into the room with the unwillingness of someone entering a torture chamber.

How was she supposed to share a room with the man standing in front of her? How could he look so cool and collected when she was suddenly a bundle of nervous tension?

'You might want to freshen up,' Lucas said neutrally. He nodded in the direction of the *en suite* bathroom, which she saw was as big as the bedroom, which was huge.

'We can't share a room.'

'I won't be breaking that to my mother at this point in time, Milly, so you might as well settle into the idea. What's the problem anyway?'

'The problem is that I don't even *know* you...'

'It wasn't a problem when we were in Courchevel,' Lucas pointed out with infuriating logic. 'And frankly, thanks to your reckless habit of saying what you want and asking whatever questions you choose to ask, you probably know me a lot better than most.' And that was a shocking revelation. But true. A certain, intangible unease snaked through him.

'We weren't sharing a *bedroom* there. We were sharing a *mansion*.'

'But, on the upside, at least now you know that I'm not a homicidal maniac or a ski instructor on the lookout for a body to take to bed.'

'I didn't sign up for this.'

'For what, exactly?' His voice was silky smooth and those midnight-dark eyes watching her speculatively made her feel hot and tingly all over.

All those forbidden thoughts that had crowded into her head from the very first moment she had laid eyes on him surfaced with frightening ease.

Thoughts of him touching her, tasting her; crazy, stupid thoughts that were just the product of a fevered mind unbalanced by the trauma of a broken engagement.

Except, when was the last time she had thought about Robbie? How traumatised had she really been, exactly? If her heart had been broken, wouldn't she have still been cooped up somewhere, licking her wounds and thinking about a future that wasn't going to happen?

'Cling to the prospect of what you're getting out of this,' he advised her. 'And, if it puts your mind at ease, I'm happy to take the couch.' He'd contemplated the enticing prospect of taking her to bed—before she had discovered who he really was and all the advantages that came wrapped up with him. She might make a big deal of her maidenly virtue, but how long would it be before she began really looking round his mother's mansion; before she heard about all the other houses he owned, scattered across the globe like unused jewels waiting to be aired when the occasion arose?

Take one self-confessed romantic, tie it up with a broken heart and then into the mix throw one billionaire with a healthy libido and what did you come out with?

Complications. It didn't take a genius to figure that one out. And, when it came to complications of an emotional nature, well, that was something Lucas could do without.

So if that quirky *something* about her got to him…if there was something about her unruly hair and sexy little body that got his imagination firing on all cylinders…he would have to put it to rest. He was accustomed to getting exactly what he wanted with the opposite sex but, in this instance, his hands were tied and he wasn't about to untie them so that he could play with a bit of fire.

Milly eyed the couch with jaundiced eyes. Okay, so he wouldn't be sharing the bed with her—the gigantic king-size bed with its gauze canopy—but she would still be *aware* of him sleeping only a matter of metres away.

And that shouldn't be a problem. *He* certainly didn't see it as one. Maybe he had flirted slightly with her, in his few days as a ski instructor, but that was then.

'I'm not accustomed to sharing a bedroom,' she protested feebly and his face relaxed into a disbelieving, mocking half smile.

'You were engaged…' He drew that one sentence out as though it was explanation in itself that she wasn't quite telling the truth.

Milly reddened, mouth dry. 'You keep reminding me of that,' she said in a valiant attempt to change the course of the conversation because she didn't like where it was heading. 'I guess in a minute you'll start lecturing me about not facing reality and being a hopeless romantic and burying my head in the sand…'

Lucas narrowed his eyes on her. 'You didn't share a bedroom with the guy?' he asked, honing in on the truth with deadly accuracy. He watched the way she guiltily glazed over and licked her lips. He knew that he shouldn't pursue the topic because, frankly, there was no point. This wasn't a 'getting to know you' exercise, after all, although stable doors and horses sprang to mind, resuscitating that unease he had earlier felt. *They knew each other… Like it or not, weird though it seemed…*

'I don't think that's any of your business,' Milly said

haughtily. 'And I think I'll have that shower you mentioned…'

'Course it's my business,' he told her with just the
sort of slow smile that implied that shrewd mind of his
was leaping to all sorts of correct conclusions about her
relationship with Robbie. 'We're in love. Isn't that what
star-struck lovers do—share everything?'

'You…you're…' She spluttered furiously at him and
he grinned.

'You're like a little spitting cat.'

'If your mother was a fly on the wall, she'd get a
pretty good picture of how *not* star-struck lovers we
are!' She could all but get the words out. The man was
infuriating! There wasn't a human being on the planet
who could work her up so fast and so effortlessly.

'Or…' Lucas held her gaze but he was still grinning
'…she might decide that a little volatility is good when
it comes to…being in love and star- struck…'

'Well, she'd be wrong,' Milly hissed, making a bee-
line for her case and rummaging until she had located
some clothes. 'And now, if you don't mind, I'm going
to have a bath.'

Sure you don't want me to join you? The instinctive
riposte was on the tip of his tongue but then the thought
of actually doing that, of actually sliding into the warm
water with her, soaping her, feeling her curves pressed
against him, slammed into him with the force of a run-
away train and his mouth tightened.

'I have work to do,' he said abruptly. 'Take your time.
Dinner's usually served around seven-thirty. Early by
Spanish standards but my mother's schedule is no longer what it was. I'll either come and get you, take you
down to the dining room, or I'll dispatch one of the
maids to show you the way.'

Running a bath, door firmly locked, Milly figured that this was how it must feel like to be a toy at the whim of an unpredictable owner. He had managed to rile her, provoke her and then, when it felt as though she actually *needed* to have some sort of full-blown argument with him, needed to wipe that annoying, laid-back grin from his face, he changed, just like that, for no particular reason.

Boredom.

She eased herself into the bath and closed her eyes. He had suddenly become bored. He enjoyed provoking her and he knew he could. It amused him. But, like a kid with the attention span of a flea, his amusement had a very short sell-by date because, however *different* he might find her, she just didn't have what it took to hold his attention for longer than five seconds. Thank goodness this was all just a fabrication! Because if it wasn't then she would never be good enough for him, would she? Being *different* didn't count. Being a *novelty* didn't count.

She mentioned that over dinner. A fabulous dinner served by a different maid. A typically Spanish meal of paella rich with seafood with lots of salad. Just a casual little remark when there was a lull in the conversation, a little throwaway observation about her *sheer amazement* that she and Lucas had become involved, because they were just so different, because she was just the sort of girl he would find boring…

Antonia had smiled and talked about opposites attracting and then, sensing something intense in Milly's expression, had kindly listed all the ways that relationships worked when two people complemented each other by bringing different personality traits to the union.

Lucas had failed to take the bait with the opening. Was he still of the opinion that his mother should have a honeymoon period before the cracks began showing?

When Milly thought of that bedroom, waiting for them to share it, she was of the opinion that the cracks should surface sooner rather than later.

She thought so even more when, over coffee in the sitting room, yet another room new to her, he draped his arm over her shoulders, sitting next to her with the indolent casualness of a man with his woman. His low, sexy voice was warm and teasing. He absently played with her hair. When she spoke, she could feel his breath warm on her cheek as he looked at her.

Antonia was taking in everything, eyes shrewd, and if *he* didn't see that then Milly certainly did and it was the very first thing she said to him when Antonia excused herself for the night, leaving the two of them alone in the sitting room.

'You *could* have helped me out when I began listing all the reasons why we didn't make sense as a couple.' She sprang to her feet and plonked herself down on a chair far away from him although, even though there was now distance between them, she could still feel the weight of his arm around her and the warmth of his thigh pressed against hers.

'Did you *see* your mother? She thought it was *cute* that I was pointing out all our differences!'

Lucas shrugged and Milly gritted her pearly-white teeth in pure frustration.

He hadn't seen his mother this happy in a while. How long had she been secretly harbouring hopes that he would meet the woman of his dreams and bring her home? She had dropped hints in the past but she had really only begun pressing him after her illness. But had she been fretting long before then?

'The time isn't right for a two-pronged attack.'

'There's no question of an *attack*.' Why did he have to be so dramatic? she wondered. Why did he have to make her out as the bad guy in this when she was only here because of him and only gently laying the foundations for their break-up because that was what she had been primed to do?

'And,' she continued, 'I'd rather you didn't sit so close to me...'

'Sit so *close* to you?'

'I just think that your mother might find such public displays of affection a little embarrassing, that's all.'

'We're sharing a bedroom. Somehow I don't think she's going to swoon because I stroke your thigh now and again. Did she look embarrassed?'

'That's not the point.'

'The point is, I have no idea what you're talking about. I'm not going to retreat to the furthest corner of the room. That would be unnatural. Furthermore, I don't see why it's such a big deal.'

'The big deal,' Milly said with a ferocious whisper, because how could he be so *cool* when she was all over the place? 'Is that I'm still in the process of getting over something pretty big and pretty horrible and maybe I need just a little more physical space than you're giving me. Lord knows what your mother must secretly think of me.' A sudden thought occurred to her. 'What if she thinks I'm a gold-digger? After all, one minute I'm engaged to one guy and the next minute I'm going out with a billionaire.' She wrung her hands in despair at the misconception.

'What if she thinks I *targeted* you...? It makes horrible sense in a way, doesn't it? What if she imagines that I'm just one of a long line of women who want you for what you can do for them…?'

Lucas raised his eyebrows and held up one imperious hand to stop her before she could begin exploring this new theme in exhaustive depth.

'She doesn't think that,' he told her flatly. 'Nor does she think that you're somehow emotionally unstable and fickle because you're going out with me hard on the heels of a broken engagement.'

'You can't say that.'

'Oh, but I can and I have.'

'What do you mean *you have*?'

'I told my mother that this was not a case of you jumping from one man to another without pausing for breath. I've explained that I'm not a rebound love affair—which, as you can imagine, would not have sat well with her.'

'When did all this explaining take place?' Milly asked in frank bemusement.

'When you were soaking in the bath for two hours,' Lucas said drily. *She thinks you're impossibly brave. As I do…*

'And she believed you?' Milly aimed for an incredulous laugh. 'I know you could sell ice to Eskimos, Lucas, but women are very intuitive when it comes to stuff like that; when it comes to matters of *the heart*…'

'Which is why she knows it's the truth,' Lucas told her with silky assurance. 'She's met you, talked to you and she knows—like we both do, Milly—that whatever you had with your ex-fiancé wasn't love. You may be the jilted girlfriend, and that's not a great place to be, but you're not the heartbroken jilted girlfriend. So your little speech about feeling uncomfortable sitting too close to me because you're nursing a broken heart is, frankly, a load of rubbish. Maybe you're scared of being too close to me because you think I'm going to make a move on you...'

And hadn't the thought crossed his head more than once? *Good job he had iron self-discipline and was smart enough to spot danger before it spotted him.*

'Not going to happen. Or maybe,' he mused thoughtfully, 'you're scared because you think *you* might make a move on *me*...'

Milly could feel herself burning up as he shoved his version of reality down her throat. There was nothing he said that had not occurred to her before, even if only in passing.

And that included the shameful fact that she found the man physically attractive, that she had flirted with silly fantasies...

'In your dreams,' she told him tartly. But she heard the faint wobble in her voice. She wasn't accustomed to playing these sorts of games. She was straightforward; she had never found herself in this kind of situation. She was walking in unchartered territory and it was only her survivor's instinct that told her that, whatever she did, she should not show him that he was right. That maybe, just maybe, that bed held unspoken terrors for her because she could picture, far too easily, what it might be like *to have him in it next to her...*

CHAPTER EIGHT

MILLY GAZED AT her reflection in the mirror but she wasn't really focusing on the face staring back at her. She was thinking of the past week and a half.

Behind her, the king-size bed that had filled her with horror was just…a king-sized bed. Her fears had been unjustified. At least, unjustified except in the deepest, darkest corners of her mind where fantasies of Lucas still swirled around with dangerous strength, power-ful riptides lying in wait for the appropriate moment to suck her under, or so it felt.

They barely shared this private space. Antonia al-ways retired before ten, at which point Milly would head upstairs, leaving Lucas downstairs, where he would work until the early hours of the morning. She neither heard nor saw him when he finally made it to the bed-room because she was always sound asleep. The only evidence he left that he occupied the room at all was the barely discernible imprint on the sofa where he had slept, because he was always up and moving by eight in the morning.

The man hardly needed any sleep at all. She, on the other hand, had always been able to sleep for England.

The linen he used for the sofa was always shoved neatly in the wardrobe.

Twice she had woken needing the bathroom and her
heart had been pounding as she had tiptoed her way past
where he had lain sprawled and asleep, half-naked, the
thin duvet barely covering him.

That fleeting glimpse of him sadly had been yet more
fodder for her very active imagination.

If only this stupid charade had done what it should
have done and exposed his failings. At this point in
time, shouldn't he have morphed into an arrogant bore
with too much money for his own good? Shouldn't the
impact of his good looks have done her a favour by di-
minishing?

She sighed and peered a little more closely at her reflection. The hair looked wilder than usual but she had
given up trying to tame it. Was this the look she really
wanted to go for? Wild hair and a strappy dress, and
high-heeled sandals that were *so* not her thing?

She and Lucas, at his mother's urging, were going
to have a supposedly romantic dinner out tonight. She
had given Milly a stern talk on buying something pretty
for the occasion, because she had not been shopping,
and had managed to use what she had brought with her:
jeans; T-shirts; more jeans; jogging bottoms.

So, despite lots of protests, she and Antonia had
spent much of the day out. There had been no need to
venture further afield into Madrid because Salamanca
boasted designer shops for every taste. These were just
the sort of things that were undermining the 'cracks
in the relationship' that should have been happening
by now.

Every crack Milly tried to break was papered over
by Antonia, who seemed to think that her outspoken-
ness was a charming and refreshing change from all the
limpets who had cluttered her son's life before.

And in the meantime, while all this was going on, she was seeing sides to Lucas that chipped away at her defences.

He was ferociously intelligent and, whilst he was good at listening to other sides of an argument, he liked to win. Over dinner—which was usually when she saw most of him, because his days were spent working to make up for the fact that he wasn't actually in his office or on a plane going to meetings somewhere or other across the globe—they talked about everything under the sun. Antonia might generate the topic, but they would all contribute. And the topics flowed from one to another, from what was happening in the news to what had happened in the news, sometimes years previously.

He was a loving son without being patronising. He was very good at teasing his mother, and Milly's heart always constricted when she witnessed this interplay between them.

Of course, she and her grandmother were very close, as she had insisted on telling them a couple of nights ago, but it was still something to have grown up without a mother figure. Or a father figure, for that matter. She might have had a sip or two too many at this point, Milly recalled uncomfortably. She had held the floor for far too long and she might even have become a little tearful towards the end. She shuddered thinking about it.

He was also funny, witty and downright interesting. He had travelled the world. It helped when it came to recounting fascinating anecdotes about faraway places.

Her heart picked up speed as another treacherous thought crept into her head like a thief in the night: she looked forward to his company. She spent her days in the grounds, sometimes by the swimming pool reading her book, often in the company of his mother. But, when five o'clock came, she always felt a stirring in her veins, as though her body was beginning to wake up and come alive.

And that wasn't good.

In fact, it frightened her because, face it, Lucas was as distant as he had promised. Yes, when they were in each other's company he was warmth and charm itself but, the second his mother wasn't around, a shutter dropped and he became someone else. Someone cool, controlled and somehow absent.

Now, she noticed, he had stopped sitting quite so close to her on the sofa and the physical shows of affection…the little touches on her shoulder, her cheek, her arms…had dropped off.

She guessed that this was his subtle way of informing his mother that all was not quite right in the land of wonderful love and happy-ever-afters.

Had Antonia noticed? Milly didn't know. She had thought of trying to open a discussion on the subject, maybe starting with a few vague generalities before working her way up to her and Lucas and what they had, and then ending by finding out what Antonia's thoughts were. But she always chickened out because she wasn't sure she would be able to hang on to her composure if the questions became too targeted.

Right now Lucas was downstairs. He usually stopped working around six so that he could spend some time with Antonia while Milly was upstairs having a bath, changing…analysing her thoughts and coming up empty handed.

And, while Milly relaxed downstairs, usually with a glass of freshly squeezed lemonade, he took the opportunity to get cleaned up. It was a clever game of avoidance that Antonia didn't seem to notice, but Milly noticed it more and more because she was noticing *everything* more and more.

Tonight, Milly entered the sitting room to find Antonia there sipping a glass of juice, her book resting on her lap.

Like all the other rooms in the splendid house, this one was airy and light with pale walls and furnishings and adjustable wooden shutters to guard against the blistering sun during the hot summer months. And, as with all the rooms, the air was fragrant with the smell of flowers, which were cut from the garden several times a week and arranged by Antonia herself in an assortment of brightly coloured vases to be dispersed throughout the house.

'I wanted to see how the dress looked.' She beamed and beckoned Milly across and then ordered her to do a couple of turns so that she could appreciate it from every angle. 'Beautiful.'

'I don't know about that,' Milly said awkwardly. 'I'm not accustomed to wearing dresses.'

'You should. You have the perfect figure to carry them off. Not like those scrawny women my son has dated in the past. Like boys! Simpering and preening themselves and looking in every mirror they pass! *Pah!* I tell him, "Lucas, those are not real women, they are plastic dolls and you can do better than that"...' She smiled smugly and waved Milly into a chair.

'We have our differences,' Milly said weakly, determined to head off an awkward situation at the pass. 'You might think that those model types are no good for Lucas but in fact...*in fact*...they suit him far more than you might imagine. I mean...' She leaned forward and stared earnestly at the handsome woman in front of her whose head was tilted to one side, all the better to grasp what was being said because, impeccable though her English was, she still became lost in certain expressions. 'It's okay to be outspoken but, in the end, it can get on a guy's nerves.'

'Is that what happened to your last boyfriend?' Antonia asked gently. 'Was that why it all fell apart, my dear?'

Milly blushed. She had breezily and vaguely skimmed over the details of the broken engagement that had supposedly encouraged her into the arms of her one true love, Lucas. Antonia had conveniently not dwelled on the subject. Now, she was waiting for some girlish confidence.

'It fell apart,' Milly said slowly, 'Because he didn't love me and, as it turns out, I didn't love him either.' This was the first time she was actually saying aloud what she had been privately thinking. 'I was just an idiot,' she confessed. 'I'd had a crush on Robbie when I was a teenager...' She smiled, remembering the gawky, sporty kid she had been, more at home with a hockey stick than a glass of vodka, which had been the in drink at the time with all the under-age drinkers: the alcohol could be camouflaged by whatever you happened to dilute it with and parents could never tell you were actually getting a little tipsy at parties.

'Robbie was the cutest boy in the class. Floppy blond hair, gift of the gab. Plus, he would actually take time out to chat to me. It felt like love, so when he showed up in London and asked to meet up I guess I remembered what I used to feel and somehow transported it to the present day and decided that those feelings were still there, intact. He was still cute, after all. He brought back memories.'

And he had known how to manipulate her weaknesses to his own benefit but, in the end, it took two to tango. He had made inroads into her common sense because she had allowed him to.

'But what was I saying…?' She gulped back the temptation to cry just a little.

'You were saying…' Lucas's voice from behind her made her temporarily freeze '…that you got suckered in to a dud relationship with some guy who was never suited to you in the first place.'

He had been standing by the door, unnoticed by both his mother and Milly, and he couldn't quite understand just why it gave him such a kick to hear her finally admit what he had suspected all along.

She had not been occupying Heartbreak Hotel, as she had fondly and misguidedly imagined. Of course she had known that, he had seen it on her face when he had chosen to point it out to her, but it was still gratifying to hear her admit it.

Not, he hurriedly told himself, that it mattered in any way that was significant. It didn't. She might be amusing, feisty, way too open for her own good…in short, all the things he never encountered in his relationships with women…but that didn't make her available. She had been available to a simple ski instructor but to the man he was? No.

But, hell, it was getting more and more difficult by the second. He always made sure that temptation was safely out of the way by burning the midnight oil in front of his computer, although he knew that his mind was only partly on work. Too much of it, as far as he was concerned, was preoccupied with visions of her in that bed—and those visions were all the more graphic because he knew how she slept, sprawled in sexy abandon with the duvet tangled about her body.

He'd bet all his worldly possessions that that was not the way she started out. No. He imagined that she tucked herself tightly underneath those covers, *swaddled* herself in them, but somewhere along the line, when she was happily gambolling about in deep REM, her body had other ideas on how it was most comfortable. And that was not wrapped up like an Egyptian mummy.

Twice she had gone to the bathroom in the early hours of the morning, tiptoeing past the sofa in such slow motion that it had taken all he had not to burst out laughing.

Her sleepwear would be a passion-killer for most men, but the baggy T-shirt with the faded logo, reaching mid-thigh, did crazy things to his system, sent it soaring into the stratosphere. She might wear the least flattering outfits known to womankind, but her body was luscious and sexy, the jut of her full breasts promising more than a handful, the shapeliness of her legs tempting him to find out what lay between them.

He flushed darkly now as he recalled the rigid erection those thoughts had induced as he had showered.

He wondered, with some irony, whether this was what happened when the guy who could have it all was denied the one thing he found he wanted.

The sooner this charade came to an end, the better. Not least because his mother appeared to have fallen in love with the woman and that had not been on the agenda. But they were going out tonight, just the two of them, and he wouldn't mince his words.

The time for pulling the plug had come.

He was sick of waging war with his libido. He had to
return to the land of the living, his offices in London.
His mother was getting far too involved in their pretend love affair for his liking. And, anyway, who knew
whether Milly was getting a little too accustomed to the
good life? That was a consideration that had to be taken
into account. Surely. Wasn't it?

'How long have you been lurking by the door?' Milly
said accusingly and Lucas strolled into the room to take
up position by the window, perching against the broad
window sill with his arms folded.

Here comes Adonis again, Milly thought absently,
*and shouldn't I have become accustomed to this by
now?* She could see him a million times and still be
startled by his dark, stunning beauty.

'I don't *lurk*...' His features were perfectly controlled, as was the tenor of his voice, but he had to steer
firmly away from the soft swell of her breasts jutting
against the soft fabric of a flimsy, strappy dress. Hell,
she wasn't even wearing a bra! It bordered on indecent,
even though the style was modest enough.

There was something about the shimmering colours,
though...blues and creams that made the fall of her
curly red hair even more vibrant...and she was wearing
make-up. Just a bit. Just sufficient gloss on her full lips
to tease any red-blooded man to distraction.

He felt himself harden and he looked away from her
momentarily, gathering himself, before indulging in his
usual light-hearted banter with his mother. The fiercer
his desire grew, the more distance he had to try and put
between them. Those brief touches were like matches
flung onto dry tinder.

'Now, make sure you use Carlos...' his mother was
telling him as he walked towards Milly, who was ris-

ing to her feet, as graceful as a ballet dancer in some strappy little sandals that showed off newly painted toenails.

'Is this the drink-driving lecture?' Lucas slipped his arm around Milly's waist and felt her soft body against his, which was a predictable challenge to his self-control. 'Don't worry. I'll be using Carlos. If I remember correctly, he has a fondness for that little wine bar not a million miles away from the restaurant. He can enjoy himself with a plate of pasta and a big bottle of mineral water.' Her breasts were just above where his hand curved on her ribcage.

As soon as they were through the front door, he dropped his hand and moved away from her.

Talk about being obvious, Milly thought, stung because he was so clearly turned off by her. She slid into the back seat through the door that Carlos held open for her and didn't glance in Lucas's direction as he levered himself in and sat next to her.

He hadn't even commented on her dress. Her normally bubbly nature was flattened by that and she was cool as they drove towards the town, choosing to stare through the window at the scenery and replying to his attempts at conversation in stiff monosyllables.

'Are you going to tell me what's wrong?' Lucas drawled once they were out of the car and in the restaurant, which was a cosy Italian that obviously appealed to the beautiful and the wealthy.

'Nothing's wrong.' Milly reluctantly looked at him and her heart picked up pace. He was staring at her, his dark eyes lazy and unfathomable. Was he comparing her to the sort of women his mother disliked but he didn't?

'Spit it out.'

'Okay—what's wrong is that you're not making any

attempt to sort this business out. We've been here nearly two weeks.'

'I didn't think you were in any rush to get back,' Lucas said mildly.

'That's not the point. The point is that I don't like lying to your mother. I feel we're getting close to one another…'

'Then make sure you pull back, Milly. She's not a substitute mother because you lost yours.'

'That's a rotten thing to say!'

Lucas sighed and raked his fingers through his hair in frustration. 'It is and for that I apologise. In actual fact, I have been thinking the same as you. It's time to start letting my mother know that this situation between us isn't going to work. For one thing, I'm sick to death of sleeping on that sofa. I'm a big man. Far too big for a sofa. I never even did that in my teenage years.'

'You never slept rough?'

'Never. But we're getting off topic here. We will have to be a bit more proactive. I admit, I've been at fault here…' Yes, he had. He had preferred to enjoy the atmosphere in the house, his mother's delight with his latest conquest, so different from her reactions to the few women she had met over the years. Lazy. He had been lazy. 'Tomorrow, we stage an argument. It shouldn't be too difficult. We have precious little in common.' He shrugged with the usual graceful nonchalance that Milly found so seductive.

Milly drank some of the white wine that had found itself into the oversized glass in front of her. She had hardly been aware of a waiter pouring from a bottle.

'If we have so little in common,' she mocked, 'then how is it that we haven't been at each other's throats by now?'

Lucas flushed. It was a good question. 'It's called the route of least resistance. When my mother has been around, it has been all too easy to let her see what she has wanted to see, but I have a life to get on with. I can't afford to spend much more time here. Naturally, I will commute on weekends, but I need to be back in the saddle. I need to return to London. As do you. So that you can make good on the bargain you struck with me. Have you told your landlord that you will no longer be needing his flat? Or house? Or wherever it is you live?'

'House. I've already told you that.'

'My short-term memory can be occasionally short.' The house she had shared with her so-called good friend. Of course he remembered! He remembered everything, every little detail. Too much.

'And, no, I haven't told my landlord yet. I can email him in the morning but you have to give me your word that you won't renege on our agreement. I don't want to find myself without a roof over my head.'

'You did as you were asked. Naturally I will keep my end of the bargain.'

He was barely aware of ordering another bottle and, by the time they had finished eating, they were two bottles down and were making inroads into a third.

'And what do you think our staged argument should be about?' After a brief lull in hostilities, Milly picked up the thread of what they had been discussing earlier. The meal was finished, the bill paid; when she stood up, she had to focus, *really focus,* to stop herself from teetering on her unfamiliar heels.

He reached out to steady her and his hand remained there at her waist.

'You've had too much to drink,' Lucas murmured.

'Maybe we could weave *that* in. Maybe you could turn me into an alcoholic.'

'My mother would never buy it.'

'Because I'm such a *boring* girl-next-door type?'

'Where did *that* come from?' He stopped dead in his tracks and spun her to face him. Of their own volition, his fingers sifted through her hair and brushed her cheek.

Milly was transfixed by that gesture. He was staring down at her and she experienced a weird, drowning feeling. He was right. She'd drunk too much. She couldn't peel her eyes away from his handsome face.

'You should stop looking at me like that,' Lucas said huskily and Milly half-closed her eyes.

'Like what?' she breathed.

'Boring girl-next-door types don't look at men the way you're looking at me…'

Milly reached out and tentatively touched his cheek, and was blown away when she realised that that was what she had been longing to do since…*for ever*. She let her hand linger there, feeling the roughened stubble on his chin, while her heart carried on beating like a sledgehammer inside her.

'No,' Lucas said shakily. 'Come on. Carlos is waiting.'

And he meant it. However tempting she might be, he wasn't going to make love to her. No way. The prospect enticed and, yes, *frightened* him in equal measure. It was an unfamiliar feeling. It disturbed and unsteadied him. It smacked of a loss of control.

'I'm going to put you to bed as soon as we're back.' He was dismayed when she nodded and nestled against his arm. She smelled floral, clean, *young*.

'So, tell me what vices you're going to give me,' Milly encouraged, at once sleepy and yet never so wide awake. She felt alive to everything: to the scent of him; to the rough feel of the linen jacket he had flung on before leaving the house; to the way his chest rose and fell as he breathed. 'I've always thought it must be nice to have a few vices.'

Lucas wasn't doing much thinking at all. He cleared his throat, shifted, failed to budge her…knew that he didn't want to anyway, not really. The key thing was that he wasn't going to make a move on her.

'Not a cry I've often heard,' he remarked drily.

'I guess you heard what I was telling your mother about Robbie…having a crush on him. He was so cool when he was young.'

'And now less so,' Lucas reminded her shortly. 'A loser, in fact.'

'I bet you think that everyone's a loser compared to you,' Milly murmured, wriggling so that she could tilt her head and look him directly in the eye.

Her breath caught in her throat and her racing heart slowed, along with time, which seemed to stand still altogether.

Her kiss took him by surprise, reaching up on tiptoe as she did, and it was so sweetly, disarmingly innocent; the gentle, tentative probing of her cool tongue a breathless, feathery flutter against his lips..

He shuddered and stifled a groan. 'This isn't part of the deal,' he muttered unsteadily.

'I know. But remember those vices I wished I had? One of them was to just…*let go*, not take guys so *seriously*…' She traced the outline of his jaw, could sense him wanting more against his will and that filled her with a heady sense of power. When he pressed a button so that opaque glass separated them from Carlos, she smiled.

So the big break-up was going to start tomorrow. And then, in a heartbeat, she would be back in London, back to reality… But, right now, *this* was her reality and why shouldn't she grab it with both hands? If he pushed her away and stormed off in revulsion, then so be it, but deep inside she sensed that he wouldn't do that.

'You see them and you what…? Want to marry them?'

'I see them and I start wondering how they would fit in on a long-term basis.' Which was pretty badly in every case thus far, few though those cases had been. 'Sort of, "hi, how are you? What are your thoughts on big families…?"' She felt him shudder and laughed. 'I know. You're horrified. I bet you'd run a mile if a woman asked you a question like that. I mean, you gave your heart away and you got burned, right? So you're not up to giving it away again.'

'You got that right but, word to the wise, don't mention that particular bone of contention to my mother. She might not quite see my side of the story.'

'Oh, I won't mention anything that might give her the wrong idea about us,' Milly said with a hitch in her voice. She didn't want to think about going. Not right at this moment.

What she wanted…

She covered his big hand with her much smaller one and guided it to her breast, and she felt him slip a little lower in the seat.

'Hell, Milly! No. You…don't know what you're doing…' But he kept his hand there, felt the rounded fullness of her breast, and wanted to do so much more that it was a physical ache. His erection was so hard that he could barely move.

'I *do* know what I'm doing. For the first time in my

whole life, I know what I'm doing.' Her voice was insistent as she unbuttoned the top two pearl buttons of the dress, allowing him more access to her and loving, absolutely *loving,* the way he was making her feel. 'I'll be gone in a few days and I won't be seeing you again… And…you make me feel…'

'How do I make you feel, Milly?' *More than a handful.* She was well endowed; if Carlos hadn't been in the front seat, driving them slowly with an impeccable lack of interest in the goings on behind him, he would have taken her right here in the car.

'Curious,' she confessed with the honesty that was so much a part and parcel of her personality. 'You make me feel curious.'

CHAPTER NINE

THE KING-SIZE BED that had been her hiding place for nearly two weeks seemed suddenly to have expanded until now she felt as though it was consuming all the space in the room. It was the only thing she could see.

Milly's body was on fire. 'Sexually daring and adventurous' were not descriptions that could ever have been applied to her. The truth was that she had never felt particularly bothered by her lack of experience in this field. She had kissed a few guys and had been content enough to leave it right there. Now, though, her head was filled with possibilities.

'This…isn't a good idea.' Common sense half-heartedly tried to prevail but Lucas recognised it for what it was: a flimsy attempt to hold off something that felt inevitable. He had already dumped his jacket downstairs and his fingers were hooked under the polo shirt, ready to yank it over his head. He was breathing fast as he stared at her, not trusting himself to get any closer, because that flimsy attempt at common sense wouldn't stand a chance.

'Why not?' Milly asked with reckless abandon. She took a couple of steps towards him.

They hadn't switched on the light, and the bedroom was bathed in pale moonlit rays sifting through the big windows. His beautiful face was a mix of shadows and angles, his eyes glittering as he watched her nervous progress.

He felt nervous, as well. Unbelievable.

'Don't you fancy me at all?' she asked, placing the palm of her hand on his chest and feeling the steady beating of his heart underneath it.

'What sort of stupid question is that?' Lucas returned roughly. He covered her hand with his and guided it to the bulging hardness of his erection pushing against the zip of his jeans.

Milly shivered, unbelievably turned on. So turned on that she forgot to be scared that this was going to be her *first time*. With trembling fingers, she hitched down the zip and heard his sharp, indrawn breath with a jab of pure satisfaction.

She had taken a chance, had been prepared to stomach his rejection because her own shameless craving felt like something requiring satisfaction before she packed her bags and walked away. The feel of his arousal was proof that he wanted her, too, even if he didn't think it was a good idea.

With a growl of impatience, Lucas pulled off the polo shirt, revealing a bronzed, muscular body that was as exquisite and as perfect as the rest of him. Any wonder she had dumped all her reservations? Breathing shallow, she ran her fingers lightly over his torso, pausing to circle the tight, brown nipples.

'We're supposed to be lovers...' She looked up at him with a wry smile. 'Aren't we?'

'How is it that you haven't felt this pressing need to touch me before?'

'Who says I haven't?'

Lucas's smile was triumphant. Common sense flew

through the window. He began unbuttoning the tiny pearl buttons, taking his time, until the top half of the dress was gaping, allowing him to see tantalising glimpses of her soft breasts.

'You weren't wearing a bra,' he murmured huskily. 'That was the first thing I noticed when I saw you this evening.'

'I had no idea you even noticed what I was wearing, considering you didn't say anything.'

'The sight left me speechless.'

Milly smiled. 'Speechless in a good way?'

'Speechless in a way that made me want to do what I'm about to do now.' He hooked his fingers under the spaghetti straps of the dress and slowly pulled himself down until he was feasting his eyes on the proud jut of her breasts.

Milly stood absolutely still, which was the only way she could think of to restrain herself from pulling the dress back into position. She didn't want to think of all the lovely bodies he had looked at before because she was not built like one of them.

'Don't say anything.'

'Not hard. I find...' He circled one rosy nipple with his finger and felt her shudder. 'I find myself without words...'

'I'm not tall and skinny. I'm short and well-endowed... Sorry.'

Lucas looked at her in genuine amazement at her self-denigration. 'I've never heard anything so ridiculous in all my life.'

'Thank you for that.' Romantic fool she might be but she could also be as realistic as he assumed she was not, and she was realistic enough to know that what he saw was the novelty of a differently shaped body and a differently fashioned personality from those to which he was accustomed. But the moment would be lost if she embarked on that sort of conversation. It was a topic best left alone.

She walked shakily towards the bed and seconds later he joined her, tossing the condom he had sourced onto the small bedside table.

'Take off the dress,' he commanded. 'No, just let it fall open... Yes, like that. I want to see you...' He straddled her prone body and just watched, savouring the tight buds of her nipples. He removed his jeans and enjoyed the way her eyes skittered away from his pulsing erection before looking once again. 'Feel free to touch.' He barely recognised his voice.

Milly gulped and tentatively tugged down the boxers. He was impressive in his girth, his erection as big, as powerful and as striking as he was. She took it in her hand and instinct took over. At first, she kept her eyes half-closed, but then opened them and looked at the shiny head in her hand then, growing braver, she sat up and took him into her mouth.

She tasted him and felt him shudder, move and arch back. His fingers had coiled in her long hair. The salty taste of him was an aphrodisiac, sending waves of pleasure and yearning through her in equal measure.

She moaned when he pushed her back. Her underwear was wet, her own arousal soaking through the cotton, and she wriggled and kicked herself free of it, parting her legs in an attempt to cool between them.

'You're burning up for me.' Lucas slipped exploring fingers into her and her breath caught in her throat as he found her clitoris and began rubbing it, gentle, persistent strokes that made her arch her body up, transported like she had never been before in her life.

She didn't want to come. Not like this. She pulled him to her and kissed him and Lord…it was beautiful. It was a kiss meant to be lost in. His tongue against hers was gentle and demanding at the same time. She could taste the essence of the guy who wanted to move slowly and yet was desperate to sate his hunger. His steel shaft brushed against her and she opened her legs a little wider so that she could feel its hardness against the parted, delicate folds. She moaned softly into his mouth, quivering when his erection pressed against her clitoris, threatening to push her over the edge.

She broke apart and captured his face between her hands. 'There's something I should tell you.'

'Now isn't the time for sharing confidences,' Lucas breathed shakily. He pinned her arms above her head and ordered her to keep them there.

Then he lowered his head to taste her succulent nipples, circling first one then the other with his mouth, drawing them deeply in then teasing the stiffened bud with his tongue.

Milly couldn't bear it. It was beyond pleasurable. It was also a completely new experience. She wanted to tell him that she was a virgin. He deserved to know, didn't he? Or else he might expect her to…be like all his other women. She wasn't sure what that meant, exactly, but she thought that creative gymnastics might be involved.

She half-opened her mouth and a gasp of pure pleasure came out instead of the haltering admission she had been formulating.

He was licking her nipple, watching her, enjoying the hectic colour in her cheeks, enjoying the way she couldn't keep still, all her little soft moans and whimpers.

Her full breasts jiggled as she writhed under him and he was driven to capture her other nipple, suckling on it until the moans became husky and uncontrolled.

He'd never felt the need to rush his love-making. Sex was an art form and pleasure had to be given and taken in equal measure. He was a master of taking things slowly, of the languorous intimate exploration, but right now it required a great deal of self-control not to grab the condom on the bedside table, stick it on and just…*take her.* Where his skinny supermodels were all sharp angles and jutting hip bones, Milly was soft, silky smooth and sensually rounded.

He curved his hand along her side, mouth still firmly clamped on her breast, then over the gentle swell of her stomach to slip between her legs, although once there he simply smoothed her inner thigh. His knuckles brushed the soft down of her pubic hair, and he itched to delve deeper, but all in good time.

Very slowly…and trying hard to douse his raging libido by concentrating on something, anything, other than the sex bomb squirming under him…he licked a trail along her stomach, starting from underneath her heavy breasts and working all the way down to her belly button.

He tipped his tongue into the sensitive indentation and felt the whoosh of her breath as she inhaled sharply. She had pressed her legs together and he gently but firmly eased them apart in preparation of tasting her but she tugged him by his hair and he glanced up to meet her feverish eyes.

'What are you doing?' Milly whispered, yearning for his mouth to touch her in her most private part, yet horrified at this outrageous show of intimacy.

'Nothing while you're pulling my hair out.'

'It's just that…'

'Don't tell me that no one has ever tasted you… there…' Could his libido get any more out of control? he wondered.

'I…' Confession time—but her vocal cords protested at ruining the moment and what difference would it make anyway? She still wanted him, wanted *this*.

Lucas slanted a bone-melting smile at her and her fingers slackened their grip. She fell back, eyes closed, cautiously opened her legs then sucked in deeply and held her breath as his tongue began to tease her open, flicking over the stiffened nub of her clitoris. She exhaled but had to breath in quickly again because sensations were running rampant through her.

She was burning up all over and panting. No part of her could keep still under the force of the fire spreading through her body, wafting through her in waves, making her arch up against his mouth, and there he kept her by placing his hands firmly under her butt.

He brought her close, so close that she wanted to cry out, then pulled back, teasing her body in a way that had her breathless and shamefully pleading for him to enter her.

She felt rather than saw him fumble for the condom he had earlier fished out. She watched, cheeks hot, as he expertly slipped it on, never taking his eyes off her face. She felt that she should have done more—clambered over him, perhaps, enticed him with the promise of new, acrobatic positions—but she dismissed that jag of insecurity. The hunger blazing in his dark eyes left no room for her to doubt that he was as turned on as she was.

He nudged the thick head of his arousal into her, and she tensed and stifled a little yelp as he inserted more of his tremendous girth into her, plunging deep and hard. She stiffened, eyes wide and panicked, and he stopped as realisation dawned.

'Tell me you're not a virgin,' he gasped, his whole body so still that it sent a ripple of alarm racing through her.

'You said that this was no time for confiding.' Milly pulled him down to her, raising herself slightly so that she could kiss him.

'Oh, Milly of the not-red hair, I'll take my time… I'll be gentle…'

He did, teasing her with his arousal, nudging it slowly in, withdrawing it, enticing her until her little whimpers became pleading moans. It was agony. But there was no way that he was going to hurt her, no way that she would ever think back to this night as anything but utterly memorable. Why that meant so much to him was something he shoved away.

She was wet and slippery as he eased himself deeper, taking his time as he had promised, until she was crying out for him to take her and take her *now*.

With a groan, Lucas thrust deep into her, and after the first sharp shock of his entry her body settled around him, responding to his deep, fierce thrusts, and the orgasm she had come so close to having when his mouth had been exploring her built into something wild and unstoppable.

She cried out and he placed a hand gently over her mouth, lifting his hand and grinning, then kissing her and coming as his mouth was still on hers, tasting her as his big body shuddered.

Spent, he backtracked and registered what she had confessed earlier.

'You're a virgin.' He eased himself off her and

flopped onto his side then immediately propped himself on one elbow to stare at her.

And this was why he had stayed away. Not that he'd known that, but still, he'd known enough: had known that she wasn't tough like the women he dated; had known that she was one of life's romantics; had known that she was still in a vulnerable place. That she was a virgin took a stupid situation and threatened to turn it into a very messy one.

But, hell, the sex had been good.

A virgin. He'd never placed any value on that particular virtue at all but now he wanted to take her all over again, show her things she had never experienced before, teach her, make love to her with all the gentle command at his disposal.

None of it made sense but he couldn't fight the realisation. Since when had he become a he-man bore who got a chauvinistic kick out of bedding virgins? What next? Belting out a Tarzan yell and looking for a vine to swing on?

But he couldn't contain a deep sense of mystifying satisfaction.

'You should have told me.'

'I was going to. Does it matter?'

'What I don't understand is *why*?'

'I don't want to talk about this.' Milly rolled onto her back and stared up at the ceiling. This had been the most wonderful experience in her entire life. Nothing had prepared her for all the amazing sensations that had bombarded her entire body; nothing. And yet all he could take away from it was the fact that she hadn't told him that he was her first.

Lucas propped himself up, invading her space so that she was forced to look at him. 'I apologise if I wasn't up to your high standards,' she managed to choke out and his eyebrows shot up.

'What the heck's going through your head, Milly?'

'What do you think?' She drew in a deep breath and said what was on her mind. 'We've just made love, and I know that it's probably not a big deal for you, but the only thing you seem to care about is the fact that I've never done this before. Is it because you're... I know those women you dated...supermodels...'

'Don't *ever* run yourself down to me, Milly. Ever. That has nothing to do with...anything.' He sighed his frustration. Even the way she *looked* at things was different. Why the instant rush to denigrate herself? In so many areas she was the most outspoken, cheerful and upbeat woman he had ever met...and yet there was an insecurity there that was reflected in the wounded, accusing eyes looking at him.

He had a moment of disturbing tenderness that threw him for a few seconds and then he rationalised that it was because he didn't usually do this, didn't usually have cosy conversations with women after sex. But naturally Milly would want to have that conversation because this had been her first time and by nature she was confiding and talkative. Of course she wasn't going to keep quiet and uncomplaining when he rose from the bed to have a shower and check his emails.

'I expressed puzzlement that you were still a virgin because you're so damned hot, Milly.'

She allowed her hurt to dissipate a little. 'I'm not.'

'Are we going to waste time playing the "no, I'm not—oh yes, you are" game?' He brushed a lock of hair from her cheek and hardened at the thought of taking her again.

Milly was tempted to tell him that she quite liked the

idea of that game. 'I practically threw myself at you. Most men would take what was on offer even if they didn't fancy it.'

'I'm not most men and we seem to be coming back to the fishing for compliments game. I fancied you the minute I laid eyes on you at my ski lodge.'

'You did?' Now she *definitely* wanted to hear more.

'And now here we are, in bed together, and trust me—I enjoyed every second of the experience. In fact, if I didn't think you were sore, I would repeat it right now all over again...' He cupped her with his hand and her eyelids fluttered. 'Why me?'

'Sorry?' Milly dragged her addled brain into some sort of functioning order and frowned.

'You're hopelessly romantic...'

'Not *hopelessly.*'

'Romantic enough for me to wonder why you would choose your first experience to be with me, under these circumstances. I'm curious as to why you didn't sleep with the man you presumed you were going to marry but you were happy to hop in the sack with a guy you definitely won't be ending up with.'

'I haven't sat down and analysed it but...I guess, maybe, I just needed...'

'A tonic? A pick-me-up? And I happened to be the nearest suitable medication to hand? Wasn't the ex man enough to entice you into bed?'

'The ex didn't fancy me,' Milly said bluntly. 'So he didn't put much effort into trying.'

'And you didn't bother to try either.'

'I...' *I was never the sort of girl to make the first move.* Yet she had made the first move with Lucas, hadn't she? Was it because she'd had nothing to lose?

Or was it because she had never grasped the full meaning of lust until she'd met him?

'I suppose I was waiting for the big night.' In love with the thought of being in love, but she'd never fancied Robbie. Lucas had shown her that; lust and love were two separate things, miles apart. She stared at his lean, dark face for a few disorientated seconds. 'You're right. Stupidly romantic. This is real life. Maybe subconsciously that's what I wanted, to connect with real life...'

'A man could be hurt.'

'I can't picture you ever being hurt. I mean, so hurt that you wanted to cry.'

'Oh, Milly. The things you come out with. So, ironically, we're lovers for real but still on course for self-destruction...' He brushed his fingers over her nipple, which hardened in fast response. 'Shall we think about how we do that while we rediscover each other again...? Or maybe we'll have to do the thinking *after* the rediscovery has finished...because I guarantee you won't be thinking when we're making love...'

Lucas pushed himself away from his desk and restively strolled towards the bank of windows that overlooked the city. He was back in London, back in his towering office, back in the thick of it. This was his reality. The two-and-a-half weeks spent with his mother playing Romeo to Milly's Juliet had been a mirage, flimsy and insubstantial, easily blown away after a fortnight. Then, business as usual.

So what the heck had happened?

He raked fingers through his hair frustratedly and silently cursed himself for letting things get out of hand. It was a mess. They had returned to London, his mother none the wiser that their relationship, whilst it had become physical, was just a sham. Marriage was not on the cards. *Longevity* was not on the cards.

But that was nearly two months ago and now…

Entrenched. And in a place from which an exit had to be made. Accustomed as he was to making the most of a bad situation, Lucas decided that this was something from which a positive could be drawn. Perhaps it had been foolish to imagine that he could take Milly to Spain and, in the space of a mere week or two, manage to convince his very astute mother that their brief romance was drawing to its sad but inevitable close.

Wasn't it better this way? The relationship had lasted long enough for its demise to be more credible. They had got to know one another and unfortunately familiarity had bred contempt. His mother would not have witnessed the decline in their relations. It would be easy to report back that they were no longer an item. Disappointment all round, but that was life.

He prowled restlessly through his vast office. It was late. He was probably the last man standing in the office. Milly, now settled into her new apartment and her new job, was having an evening out with her new colleagues. A drink at some pub somewhere with a meal to follow.

What colleagues?

Lucas impatiently pushed away any line of pointless speculation. It was good that she was making lots of friends. So what if some of them were men? It was to be expected. She had smartened up her act when it came to her dress code. He had, she had told him more than once, given her confidence in the way she looked, in her body. She had had a ritual getting rid of most of her old clothes, which, much to his amusement, she had insisted in showing him piece by deplorable piece. He had never seen such a vast collection of shapeless items of clothing in one place in his life before. Then she had dragged him out shopping.

He gritted his teeth at the thought of some guy seeing her in some of the stuff they had bought together. The red dress with the plunging back; the tight black jeans; hell, some of the sexy underwear...

He only had himself to blame for the situation he now found himself in. He had known from the very beginning that she was vulnerable. He had known that she was the sort of romantic who got lost in house and garden magazines and gazed longingly into the windows of bridal shops. She had a strong nesting instinct and was a home-maker by nature. She had loved cooking for him and he, who had never allowed any woman the privilege of cosy home-cooked meals in his kitchens, had found himself trying out new recipes and working while she sat cross-legged next to him, watching rubbish on television.

Was it any wonder that she had fallen in love with him? Was it any wonder that she had risen to the futile challenge of trying to make him see that his teenage error of judgement was just a little something that 'true love' could overcome?

Before she had even told him, he had *known*. She wasn't good when it came to hiding things. She wore her heart on her sleeve, and he had seen it in her eyes but had chosen to ignore it because he enjoyed her company and the sex was better than brilliant.

But he wasn't going to marry her and just the thought of being the object of her love, just the memory of those hopeful, trusting, *adoring* eyes on him, filled him with a sense of claustrophobia.

Love was for fools. He had learnt that the tough way. She knew that and if she had chosen to ignore it, then, *hell*!

The long and short of it was that he had taken his eye off the ball...and now...

He made his mind up, grabbed his jacket and left the office before he had time for any weakness to seep in.

He, of course, had a key to the apartment. It *was* his, after all; why wouldn't he? On a couple of occasions, he had left work early and headed straight there, letting himself in and working until she returned.

In a short space of time, she had made inroads into the decor. The perfectly cool, bland apartment now bore just the sort of homey touches that should have warned him that she was settling into it, just as she was settling into him.

Pictures on the mantelpiece. Scraps of paper with handy recipe titbits pinned to the stainless steel American-style fridge-freezer with jokey magnets. Lots of flowers because, she told him, it had always been her grandmother's habit to fill the rooms with things from outside. Good Feng Shui, apparently. He had laughed and drily told her that he had lived quite happily without such touches in his own place. She had suggested some kind of water feature; he had firmly squashed that idea, but he suspected that its absence was only short lived.

He had to wait for over an hour and a half before he heard the turn of the key in the door and, in that hour and a half, his mind had been everywhere but on work. For once, the joys of deal making had failed in its duty to distract him.

'Where've you been?' was his opening question as

she entered the sitting room and Milly started, then smiled as her breathing returned to normal.

He had been on her mind all evening. So she had told him, just blurted it out; she hadn't been able to help herself. She had fallen in love with him and it had been just too big a deal for her to keep inside. She didn't even know when the process had begun. Maybe the seeds had been sown in Spain, when she had glimpsed sides of him that were so curiously appealing. Certainly, she now knew that her fate had been sealed by the time they had fallen into bed together that first time and she had sunk deeper and deeper the longer she had spent with him.

It was crazy, she had known that, but love was crazy, wasn't it? It wasn't something you could explain on a sheet of A4 paper, like a maths problem with a solution. If love made sense, she would never have fallen in love with Lucas. But she had. And, the minute she had told him, she had wished that she could yank the words back into her mouth and swallow them down. He had gone perfectly still, hadn't replied, and when he *had* spoken it was as though he had chosen to ignore what she had said.

And his eyes were grave now as she tentatively walked towards him.

'We need to talk.'

'Why?' Milly smiled quickly. 'You always tell me that there are far better things to do than talk.'

'But, first, where have you been?' That question hadn't been on the agenda.

'I told you, Lucas, that I was going out with some people from work.'

Lucas scowled and tried not to let his imagination run away with thoughts of who those people were. She looked bloody amazing. Just the right side of tousled, her red hair trailing down her back, her tight jeans showing off every succulent inch of her body, as did the clingy long-sleeved top. The fact that she was wearing a pair of flat sneakers did nothing to detract from the look and he angrily felt himself harden in automatic response.

He dismissively waved aside her explanation just in case she thought that a detour down that road was going to happen.

'What's going on, Lucas?' As if she didn't know. One sign of love and he was getting ready to bolt. Things were just fine as long as they were having sex. The charade was well in place then! But she had crossed a line; she had forgotten what he had told her about not getting involved and had committed the mortal sin of not only disobeying the edict, but of telling him that she had.

'I think you know. And sit down; stop hovering.'

'I'm not sorry I said what I said,' Milly imparted with just the sort of driven honesty that he felt had landed them in this mess. 'And I never said that I was asking you to love me back.' *But she was.*

'This is no longer a working proposition.' He was somehow angry and bewildered as to how it was that these seemed to be the hardest words ever to have left his mouth. He had known that it was going to end sooner or later. So why did each syllable feel like broken glass? Maybe it was because he hadn't been the one to determine the timing of the end. He had been pushed into it because unforeseen circumstances had forced his hand. That made sense. He, of all men, did not like having his hand forced.

Milly opened her mouth but nothing emerged. She stared at him, wide-eyed, not daring to speak in case she started doing something really humiliating…like pleading and begging. Because, for the life of her, she couldn't envisage life without him.

Stupid Robbie and her broken engagement had been a walk in the park in comparison. This was the real thing. This was love, and hearing him tell her that their relationship was over was like staring down the barrel of a gun and waiting for the trigger to be pulled.

Did she regret her honesty? No. Was she going to compound her horror and dismay by really pushing the boat out and bursting into tears? Absolutely not!

'I get it,' she told him quietly. 'And I agree.'

CHAPTER TEN

A WEEK AND a half later, Milly could still scarcely believe that she had shown such fortitude in the face of the groundswell of misery that had been gathering at her feet.

So she had hung on to her pride, but at what cost? He was on her mind twenty-four-seven. She thought of him when she was working, when she was relaxing, and she dreamed of him when she was asleep.

He hadn't argued with her when she had conceded defeat. He had wanted out and she hadn't fought to bar him from the exit he was desperate to take. But he had been as quick to rush through the open door as she might have expected. He had continued the conversation: had told her in a cool, detached voice that he had never been in it for the long term; that he had warned her that commitment was off limits for him; that she should have known that after everything he had told her. His voice had been thick with accusation.

She had agreed with him.

'Off the cards and especially with someone like me,' she had obliged him by pointing out. All the time, her heart had been beating so hard and so fast that her breathing was short and raspy.

'With anyone. I'm not interested in a long-term relationship and I should never have allowed myself to be swept into something with a woman who was vulnerable and in search of a life partner.'

'I may have been vulnerable but I was *not* in search of a life partner! And I may have fallen in love with you, but has it occurred to you that I'm not as ditzy as you think I am? Has it occurred to you that I *know* we're not suited?'

Of course it hadn't occurred to him.

'We're different people from different backgrounds,' she had persisted. 'And that might not make a difference, but we're also like oil and water. You're darkness to my light. I'm not suspicious and distrusting of everyone; I like giving people chances. And I know you think I'm naive and stupid because I should have learned from Robbie and what happened but maybe, just maybe, that makes me a happier person than you, Lucas! You had one crappy experience and you've let it dictate the rest of your life! How does that make sense?'

'So you're prepared to carry on as we are with no expectations?' he had mocked. 'You're fine if I tell you that I'm more than happy to take you to my bed but that's all there is to it?'

Naturally she wouldn't have been fine with that and her brief hesitation had given him all the answer he had needed.

But what if she *had* agreed? What if she had buried her feelings under the sort of hard veneer that he would have been able to deal with? What if she had taken up his proposition and shut away the side of her that had wanted more, that would always want more? Would that have been a better decision than the one she had made? She wouldn't have spent the past week and a half thinking about him whilst staring at the walls of his apartment and thinking that she would have to move out sooner rather than later.

She almost, but didn't quite, regretted that she hadn't thrown his stupid job and his stupid free apartment right back in his face but common sense had thankfully kicked in because she would have been in an even worse position than she was now. She would have been hurting emotionally, and positively haemorrhaging financially, because a cursory glimpse at the ads for jobs in the catering industry had told her that there were no jobs to speak of. She would have been on the first train back to her grandmother, and there would have been no jobs there either, so she would have ended up doing something and nothing just to make ends meet.

It had left a sour taste in her mouth because the last thing she had wanted to do was to accept the terms and conditions of the proposal that had so roundly backfired in her face. But sometimes pride just had to take a back seat, and she was very glad that it had, because she loved her job and loved living in the heart of London, such a far cry from her former digs.

Her friends had all been mightily impressed as well, although she had omitted to tell them the details of how she had landed up where she had.

She had simply said that she had been lucky enough to have found herself in the company of a guy who had felt sorry enough for her to have lent her a helping hand. It was bad luck to have found herself at the ski chalet without the job she had anticipated, but it had been extremely good luck to have found herself there in the company of the guy who actually owned the ski chalet, along with a whole load of other stuff; a guy who had heard her unfortunate story and had been kind enough to lend a helping hand.

Ha. She had nearly choked when she had expanded on his *kindness*. She had turned him into a benevolent, avuncular, father-figure type, which couldn't have been further from the truth!

If they had been a little curious as to why she had suddenly decided to become the stay-at-home type who no longer needed to talk incessantly about her misfortunes, they had not said anything, and she knew they figured that she was just experiencing the aftershocks of what had happened with Robbie.

In time, she would confess all, but right now she needed time out from…*everyone*.

She had just showered and climbed into a pair of baggy joggers and an even baggier T-shirt—because she had lost the desire to wear tight and sexy clothes now that she was back to being on her own—when she heard the ring of the doorbell, and she froze, because there could be only one person who would ring that doorbell, having got past Eddy, the porter who manned the desk downstairs.

Lucas.

He had a key to the apartment, which made sense bearing in mind it belonged to him, but he always used the doorbell, only letting himself in if he knew that she wasn't going to be in.

Her mouth went dry and she gulped in deep breaths because the thought of seeing him again filled her with pleasure and trepidation at the same time.

In the length of time it took her to traverse the wooden floor from sitting room to door, she had dissected, dismissed and re-dissected a hundred possible reasons for this unexpected visit.

In the starring role on her wish list was the tiny ray of hope that he had miraculously decided that they were

suited after all, that he had made a terrible mistake. Or
even, she was ashamed to concede, that he had missed
her and would she climb back into bed with him? She
would say no, she was pretty sure of that, but it would
do her a power of good just to think that he, in some
small way, missed her as much as she was desperately
missing him.

Her heart was preparing to soar and she had to school
her features into just the right level of indifference as
she pulled open the door.

'My dear!'

'Antonia…' Milly forced a smile but she was taken
aback to find his mother on the doorstep. She hadn't
spoken to Antonia since the split, and she felt guilty
now about that, because they had developed a strong
bond in the short time they had been in each other's
company. 'I…eh…have been meaning to get in touch
with you…'

'You look a little peaky, my dear.'

'Please, come inside. I… What brings you to London? I didn't think that you would be okay to travel
overseas…just yet. Can I offer you something? Tea or
coffee?'

'I thought I might surprise my son with a visit,' Antonia confided. 'And a cup of coffee would be lovely,
my dear. Decaf, if you have it. Caffeine any time after
six in the evening ruins my sleeping patterns.'

'That reminds me: well, I guess you've come… I
would have called…' *To further compound your disappointment by filling in all the gaps Lucas might have
left in the saga of why we had broken up? Added to the
story of personality clashes, simmering rows and different hopes and dreams?*

'It's even nicer seeing you face to face, Milly, my

dear. I've missed having you there at the house. It felt rather empty and quiet after you and Lucas left. Of course, I was in tremendous spirits, but nevertheless… How quickly we become accustomed to having pleasant company around us.'

Milly could feel her face getting redder and redder and her body hotter and hotter.

'Well, you look amazing,' she said truthfully, *even though the tremendous spirits may have taken a recent battering.*

'I feel it. I guess I'm just buoyed up by Lucas's turnaround.'

'His turnaround…?'

'Finally coming to his senses and seeing the value of settling down.'

For a confusing few seconds, Milly was appalled at the question that had instantly sprung into her head: *Who* was he planning to settle down with? How fast could one man move when it came to women?

'So—and I know I'm being an interfering old witch here—but I came over so that I could sit you both down together and find out when I can start looking forward to the big day…'

'*The big day,* Lucas…and I'm quoting here. So *what* in heck's name is going on?'

Milly had finally managed to get hold of Lucas, who was personally protected from hassle with anyone he might not wish to talk to by an army of people in charge of security checks. She actually had his direct line but, the second she had been redirected, she had had to engage in the usual barrage of questions from his guard dogs.

She was in a filthy temper by the time she actually

heard his dark drawl at the other end of the line, which was possibly why her stomach didn't instantly go into nervous knots.

For the first time since he had walked out, Lucas felt alive at the sound of her voice and that, in itself, was bloody infuriating.

'I have no idea what you're going on about, Milly. You can't commence a conversation in mid-sentence and expect me to instantly be clued up.'

'You *know* what I'm talking about! Guess who I just had a visit from?'

'Can't think. No time for guessing games.'

'Your *mother*!'

Lucas sat up and digested this piece of information. 'My mother...' he said slowly.

'Strangely,' Milly all but shrieked down the end of the line, 'she seems to be under the impression that we're still an item!'

'Where are you?'

'Where do you think I am, Lucas?'

'How would I know?' he answered with silky smoothness. 'It's after seven on a Friday evening and you're a single woman...'

'I'm at home.' How could he think that she would physically be able to go clubbing when she was in love with him? Or was he just judging her the way he judged himself? He would have no problem doing that. If he possessed a heart instead of a lump of cold where a heart should be...

'I'm on my way.'

Milly fought the temptation to get a little more dolled up than she was. Maybe swop the baggy jogging bottoms, which she knew he loathed, for something a little more attractive. He could take her as he found her, she decided. He could explain why his mother was still in the dark and then he could be on his way.

She was as cool as a cucumber until the doorbell went half an hour later and there he was. All dark, tall and broodingly, sinfully gorgeous. Just the right side of dishevelled with the sleeves of his white shirt rolled to the elbows and his jacket slung over one shoulder. A sight for sore eyes and she just wanted to stand there and stare.

'So...' She pulled open the door and stepped away from him, not trusting herself. 'Mind explaining...?'

Lucas couldn't peel his eyes away from her. She was wearing just the sort of outfit he had always teased that she needed to wean herself away from. It hid every delectable curve, and yet she was still so enticing, still so damned *sexy*.

He'd missed her. It was as simple as that. He hadn't been able to focus, had lost interest in deals that should have netted all of his undivided attention, could not even be bothered to rifle through his little black book for other women. And he had told his mother nothing because...

'I need a drink. Something stronger than a cup of tea.'

'You *need a drink*? This isn't a social call, Lucas.' Milly finally looked at him and her treacherous eyes skittered away. She clasped her arms around her body, hugging herself.

'No. It's not.' He headed straight for the kitchen, directly to the cupboard where he knew she kept a practically full bottle of whisky, and he poured himself a hefty glass, keenly aware that she had padded in behind him. He imagined her arms were still folded and her full mouth would be pursed in a moue of frustration.

She loved him. She *had* loved him. Did she still?

'I intended to tell her...'

'But somehow you didn't manage to get round to it? Even though you speak to her every other day? That titbit just managed to *get lost* amidst the chit chat?'

'No.'

'Okay...' She looked at him hesitantly, picking up vibes which, for once, he wasn't bothering to hide. He had sat down at the kitchen table and was nursing his drink, not looking at her—again, a little weird, because it smacked of the sort of indecision not associated with him. She felt in need of a stiff drink as well but instead made do with a glass of juice from the fridge before sitting opposite him at the chrome-and-glass table.

'I could have told her but...I needed time.'

'Time for what?'

'Time to come to terms with the fact that we were really no longer an item.' He looked at her with serious intent and swallowed a mouthful of the whisky, not taking his eyes from her flushed face. 'I thought...when you told me that you loved me...'

'I don't want to go there.'

'We don't have a choice.'

'We do!' she cried. 'I said what I said and there's no point going over it!'

'I've never believed in love.'

'I told you—I get that.'

'You don't. You don't because, as you said, I let one crappy experience dictate my future where you, my optimistic Milly, would never have allowed that to happen. So, no, you didn't understand. Not really.'

He shot her a crooked, hesitant smile.

'Do you know that you were the first person I ever told about Betina and my youthful error of judgement?

And I knew that every time you raised the subject, which was often, you were trying to come to terms with the way I thought, because it was so unlike the way *you* would think. I should have been enraged at having that one confidence thrown back in my face time and again. I wasn't.'

He looked at his glass, circled the rim with his finger.

'We're all creatures of habit to some extent. My habit lay in the way I thought, the way I conditioned myself to think. For me, marriage would be about something that made sense because love made no sense. My head told me that you made no sense. You were just so damned young, you wore your heart on your sleeve, you were looking for the same happy-ever-after ending my mother believed in—the same happy ever ending I had no time for. I had built my box and I had no intention of stepping out of it, even though I knew you wanted me to. Am I losing you?'

He shot her the ghost of a fleeting smile that made her world tilt on its axis.

'I'm following you and you're right—I didn't understand, not really. Plus I was, well, I've never been that secure about my looks and I was...'

'Jealous?'

'No. Yes. Maybe.'

'Just maybe? Because I've been eaten up with jealousy thinking about all those men you might have been seeing behind my back in the last week or two.'

Milly's heart soared. She wondered whether she was hearing correctly. She half-leaned forward just in case she missed something and that devastating smile broadened as he read her mind.

'You can't let go, and I'm sorry about that, but...but you don't have to explain.'

'I do, my Milly, because I find that I let go a long time ago. I never realised it because I was just waiting in a holding bay for the right woman to come along and mess with my heart.'

The silence stretched between them. When she finally extended her hand along the table and he linked his fingers through hers, she experienced a rush of so many emotions, all vying for prominence, that she felt faint.

'I ran scared when you told me how you felt. I didn't know how to deal with it, Milly. And yet, I couldn't bring myself to tell my mother that it was over between us. I had the strangest feeling that if I said it out loud, if I vocalised it, then I would find myself in a place of no return. I couldn't face the thought of losing you but I didn't know how to make it right between us. My head was still waging war with my heart. The fact is, I love you. I was falling in love and I didn't even recognise the symptoms because I was so stubbornly and arrogantly convinced that I was immune.'

He absently played with her fingers in a way that was thrillingly intimate. 'You came into my life and you woke me up, Milly of the not-red hair, and my life is nothing without you in it.'

'And I love you,' Milly said with wrenching earnestness. 'I never loved Robbie, but you knew that, didn't you? When I think of what my life could have been if I hadn't found out the truth…' She shivered. 'I didn't want to fall in love with you either,' she admitted. 'I know you think I'm a hopeless romantic…'

'You are and I thank God for that.'

'But I still knew that you weren't a good bet and I was still fighting my own silly demons; still thought that you were just, well, that you'd never look at someone like me. Even though…' she dimpled at him '…you cured me of that.'

'Would you have felt that if I had continued being a harmless ski instructor?'

'You're never harmless and why, out of interest, didn't you tell me your true identity from the start?'

'It was liberating. You had landed there, like someone from a different planet, no airs, no graces and no knowledge of just how wealthy I was. You fascinated me from the very first moment I met you. And now, here we are. You are the love of my life, Milly, and I can't imagine life without you in it.'

'Okay.'

Lucas laughed. 'Is that all you have to say? When you're usually a woman of so many words?'

Milly grinned. 'I'm full of surprises.'

'And I want to be the one to find them all out, every day, for the rest of my life. Will you marry me? I'm asking that on behalf of both me and my mother…'

Milly laughed and rose, moving to sit on his lap so that she could feel his arms around her, holding her close, never letting her go.

'In that case, since you've brought your mother into the equation, what can a girl do but accept?'

* * * * *

MILLS & BOON®

MODERN™

POWER, PASSION AND IRRESISTIBLE TEMPTATION

A sneak peek at next month's titles...

In stores from 20th March 2015:

- **The Billionaire's Bridal Bargain** – Lynne Graham
- **Carrying the Greek's Heir** – Sharon Kendrick
- **His Diamond of Convenience** – Maisey Yates
- **The Italian's Deal for I Do** – Jennifer Hayward

In stores from 3rd April 2015:

- **At the Brazilian's Command** – Susan Stephens
- **The Sheikh's Princess Bride** – Annie West
- **Olivero's Outrageous Proposal** – Kate Walker
- **The Hotel Magnate's Demand** – Jennifer Rae

Available at WHSmith, Tesco, Asda, Eason, Amazon and Apple

Just can't wait?
Buy our books online a month before they hit the shops!
visit www.millsandboon.co.uk

These books are also available in eBook format!